WHEN THE SNOW FALLS

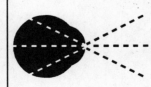

This Large Print Book carries the
Seal of Approval of N.A.V.H.

WHEN THE SNOW FALLS

FERN MICHAELS
NANCY BUSH
ROSANNA CHIOFALO
LIN STEPP

WHEELER PUBLISHING
A part of Gale, Cengage Learning

 GALE
CENGAGE Learning·

Farmington Hills, Mich • San Francisco • New York • Waterville, Maine
Meriden, Conn • Mason, Ohio • Chicago

GALE
CENGAGE Learning®

LIBRARY OF CONGRESS CATALOGING-IN-PUBLICATION DATA

When the Snow Falls / by Fern Michaels, Nancy Bush, Rosanna Chiofalo, and Lin Stepp.
  pages cm. — (Wheeler Publishing Large Print Hardcover)
  ISBN 978-1-4104-7327-1 (hardcover) — ISBN 1-4104-7327-9 (hardcover)
  1. Love stories, American. 2. Christmas stories, American. 3. Large type books. I. Michaels, Fern. II. Bush, Nancy, 1953- III. Chiofalo, Rosanna. IV. Stepp, Lin.
PS648.L6W4787 2014
813'.08508—dc23   2014031617

Published in 2014 by arrangement with Zebra Books, an imprint of Kensington Publishing Corp.

Printed in the United States of America
1 2 3 4 5 6 7 18 17 16 15 14

CONTENTS

■ ■ ■ ■

CANDY CANES AND CUPID

FERN MICHAELS

■ ■ ■ ■

CHAPTER 1

Monday, December 1, 2014

Hannah Ray glanced at the calendar. December already, a month and a holiday she dreaded every year. Christmas. If asked why, and she had been on numerous occasions, she would pause for the briefest of moments, as though she were truly contemplating the question, and then she would give her standard reply: "You know, I'm not really sure." Friends and colleagues would then look at her as though she were out of her mind, but it was simply the truth.

Growing up in Florida, she'd never really been bitten by the holiday bug. While she honored the religious aspects of the sacred holiday, she personally thought all the hoopla was nothing more than just one more reason for giant corporations to increase their already more-than-insanely-adequate bottom lines with even more in the way of profits, and for their CEOs to line their very deep pockets with even more money. Hannah smiled when she realized that she sounded exactly like her father, who, it just so happened, used to be one of those CEOs of a giant company. But Hannah had always assured him that he had a heart.

When he'd keeled over from a heart attack five years ago, she was shocked. Her father had always been meticulous about his diet. Red meat no more than once a week. Fish only three times, and the other days were vegetarian. An avid runner who ranked high in his class when he was nearing seventy, he'd looked at least ten years younger than most men his age. His sudden death derailed her for a while, but she knew he would want her to continue to pursue her career. After passing the bar, Hannah decided she didn't want to be confined to a courtroom. So she applied for her Florida private investigator's license, which she received without a hitch, opened an office in Naples, and one year later was so busy she had hired three full-time agents, two retired police officers as part-timers, and Camden, her best friend and personal assistant, who played a large role in running the office. Hannah didn't know what she would do without Camden's excellent organizational skills as she herself wasn't the most organized in a "paper" kind of way. Her ability to keep details clear in her head was her major talent. While Camden could locate a Post-it in a pile of a thousand, Hannah could tell you what was written on the Post-it and in what color ink.

Less than a month short of thirty-four, Hannah was pretty set in her ways, and again, she had her father to thank for that as well. Her mother had died of breast cancer when Hannah was six, leaving her father to raise her alone. With no family of his own to guide him through the waters of single parenthood, Frederick Ray did the best he could. Hannah had missed her mother after her death, but with the passage of time, and the fading memory of a six-year-old child, she was soon conversing at dinner with her father about all sorts of very adult financial and legal matters. They would discuss the law as it pertained to Ray Enterprises, a conglomerate of manufacturers that produced items ranging from high-end perfumes to plastics. When he died, her father left everything he owned to her, which enabled her to choose what she wanted to do in her professional life. While she was a voting member of the boards of directors of the various companies controlled by Ray Enterprises, she was fortunate that Albert, who had been her father's right-hand man, continued to perform in that same capacity for her, relieving her of the burden of day-to-day involvement in the affairs of those companies. Not only was he the one who acted on her behalf at board meetings, but he was like an uncle to her, and she trusted him implicitly.

Of course, Camden came in a close second. They were the same age, shared many of the same interests, and when it was time to close shop, neither she nor Camden had any trouble removing her professional hat for a night out on the town, or often a quiet meal prepared in Hannah's ultramodern kitchen. Both had taken an avid interest in cooking when they had started packing on a few extra pounds last year. Once a week, if their schedules permitted, they would take turns making dinner. Of course, dinner always included a bottle or two of wine. Comfortable with each other, they would chat about fashion, makeup, anything except work; then, as with most single females, they would discuss their current dating situations. Sadly, more often than not, neither one was having much success in that area. Not because they worked too much, and not because there wasn't quite a fine selection of available men in southwest Florida, but because both women were extremely finicky about men.

As a result, Hannah and Camden were planning to spend the upcoming holiday together, doing absolutely nothing except lounging on the beach and catching up on their favorite authors' new books. Both agreed this was the best possible decision, given that neither had close family or any reason to do anything else.

Most of her high-profile cases were coming to an end, and she hadn't planned to take on any more until after the New Year. She'd given all her employees a two-and-a-half-week paid vacation beginning December 18 and ending Monday, January 5, 2015. They were ecstatic and couldn't stop talking about her generosity. She liked her team and thought of them as friends first, then coworkers. She was not a "me boss, you employee" employer.

Her father had often told her that in business one accomplished so much more by being kind and generous to one's employees rather than bossy, demanding, and condescending. To this day, Ray Enterprises, along with H.R. Investigations, had some of the happiest employees around. And Ray Enterprises was among the top five businesses on

Fortune Magazine's list of the best companies to work for.

Two weeks of bliss, she thought, as she pulled up her schedule for the upcoming week. Two weeks of sun, sand, and surf, and, if she was lucky, she could delve into those books she had recently received from Amazon.

Clearing her mind, Hannah scrolled through her iPad mini. The firm had three consultations scheduled that afternoon. One was with an insurance company that suspected an injured employee collecting workman's compensation was doing so illegally. That would be a breeze to solve. She would have Ed, her number-one part-timer, do the consultation and go out on a surveillance mission, his specialty.

Next was a young woman who suspected that her husband was cheating on her. Hannah detested this part of her work and tried to distance herself from it as much as possible, but sadly, the need for it was a reality in life, and someone had to do it. Marlene would meet with the woman, as she was the expert at anything requiring a telephoto lens and being incognito, plus she was extremely nosy, always an added bonus in the private-investigation business.

The last consultation for the day she

would take care of personally since the client had requested that she do so.

Last year, Hannah had been hired to keep tabs on an abusive husband when an ignorant judge had released him on his own recognizance after he had been charged with beating his wife to a pulp. Because the man happened to be from a wealthy family, several members of whom were well-known attorneys, the judge assured his wife's attorney that she would have nothing to fear from her husband and certainly not his family, even going so far as to imply that she had brought the beating on herself.

Hannah immediately contacted Grace Landry out in Colorado, told her the woman's story, and personally put Leanne on a plane to Denver. Once the abused spouse was at Hope House, Grace's shelter for battered families, Hannah breathed a sigh of relief. She'd stayed in contact with Leanne and was saddened when she learned that the woman had recently returned to Fort Myers to make an attempt to reunite with her abusive husband. And it was because of this that she had decided to pull in a few favors at Health Park Hospital. Two days ago, Leanne had been admitted to the hospital with a broken nose and a cracked pelvis. Hannah planned to confront Leanne's husband, Bruce Wells, and make a special trip to visit Leanne. This wasn't her usual modus operandi, but she was passionate about those who suffered abuse at the hands of people who were supposed to love them the most and anyone who bullied others. You might say that it was her Achilles' heel.

Stuffing her iPad in her briefcase, she grabbed her purse and raced out the door, locking it behind her, only to remember the cell phone she'd left in the master bath when she'd been blow-drying her hair. As soon as she inserted her key in the lock, she heard its familiar xylophone ringtone. "Darn," she muttered as she raced through the condo to the master suite.

She hit the green ANSWER button. "Hello?" she said, a bit winded.

"Hannah?" came a male voice.

"Yes, this is Hannah Ray. How can I help you?" She dropped her briefcase on the floor and plopped down on her vanity stool, staring at the face in the mirror. Straight blond hair, brown eyes. A regular face, she thought, nothing remarkable.

"It's Max Jorgenson."

It took a couple of seconds for Hannah to call up the image that went with the voice, but when she did, she was all smiles. Max

16

Jorgenson. The Olympic gold-medal skier. Grace Landry's husband.

She grinned. "And to what do I owe this honor?" she asked in a teasing tone. She'd been a bit impressed when she'd met Max through Grace.

She could hear him clearing his throat. "I'm not sure you would call this an honor. It's more of a favor."

A favor? From her? Hannah hadn't a clue what Max Jorgenson wanted from her, but if he'd bothered making the phone call personally, then it must be something very urgent and important.

"Anything, Max. Just say the word."

He chuckled. "Don't say that just yet. Hear me out."

"Hey, anything for you and Grace. She really helped me out last year, and as it just so happens, I might need her services again. Same client. A sad situation, but go on. You called me. What gives?"

"I need you to come to Colorado. Mid-December if possible," Max said.

Hannah visualized all her plans for sun, sand, and surf swirling right down the drain.

In a voice she hoped didn't relay just how much she did not want to travel out West, she said, "Of course, Max. Just give me the time and place, and I will be there."

17

"I knew I could count on you," Max said, then gave her the details before thanking her again and clicking off.

"No sunning. No reading. No relaxing on the beach. There goes my Christmas vacation."

CHAPTER 2

"You know I wouldn't ask you if it wasn't important," Max said. "It's not like you to have holiday plans. I know you, old man, remember? We go back a long way."

Liam McConnell shook his head, then spoke into the phone. "Don't remind me how long, okay? I'm not getting any younger, and trust me, it shows," Liam said in a deep voice that still held traces of an Irish accent even though he'd been living in the United States since he was a young boy. "So, go on, tell me, what's so damned important? I'm all ears."

For the next fifteen minutes, Max updated Liam on the situation at Telluride. He knew for a fact that Liam McConnell was the best in the business when it came to information security. He had a bachelor's in Criminal Justice, a Harvard law degree, and had worked with the Federal Bureau of Investigation for two years before going out on his own. He was one of only a few experts on electronic-information security. Max knew that Liam could pick and choose when and where to work, but he was also sure that Liam wouldn't turn him down. He was offering his best cabin at the resort as long as he wanted and, of course, he would pay him whatever his usual fee was. Then he had an added surprise, but he wasn't going to mention that just yet. Something Grace had cooked up, and he'd agreed wholeheartedly, though that wasn't the main reason for his wanting Liam's help in finding the culprits who were trying to destroy his business.

"And you think one of your employees is hacking into your systems?" Liam asked.

"More than one," Max said.

"You do realize I am at my beach house on Sanibel Island and planned to spend December fishing and relaxing?"

"No, I didn't. If you can't do this, I understand. I just wanted the best. And you *are* the best," Max added with a lilt in his voice.

"Ah, you do know how to get to a man's heart. All right. I am yours. For two weeks. If I haven't located the source, then I'll have had a free ski vacation, and you, my friend, will be shit out of luck."

They talked more, laughed about old

times, then Liam wrote down the date when he would need to fly to Colorado. After they finished their call, he had a strong suspicion his old ski buddy had something more than a job waiting for him.

Liam shook his head and reached for his iPad. Plans were made to be changed. While he disliked the idea of spending Christmas at a ski resort where hundreds of people would be filled with holiday cheer, he supposed it could be worse. In all honesty, he'd truly been looking forward to spending a few weeks at his home on Sanibel Island, but Max was a good friend. Liam counted his few close friends as priceless. If forgoing a bit of fishing meant helping his friend out, he consoled himself with the thought that he could fish any time. With that in mind, he called Pierce, his pilot, and made arrangements to have his Learjet available for a trip to Colorado.

Liam wasn't much for holidays. Any of them. Too much money spent on silly things, in his not-so-humble opinion. He remembered a woman he'd been dating last year. She'd spent a small fortune on a fountain pen for him. He'd wanted to take it back to the store where she'd purchased it and insist she use the money for something meaningful, like a charitable organization. He had more expensive fountain pens than he could count. And to be honest, he liked BIC pens much better. The woman — he couldn't recall her name — had been deleted from his list of female contacts. The list was getting slimmer and slimmer. The women who knew him knew that he was fairly well-off. Indeed, that seemed to be the major attraction he held for them. Unfortunately, for him it was an instant turnoff.

Whatever happened to women with respect? Brains? Goals other than marrying a rich man to take care of them, to provide them with meaningless baubles and fancy cars? He was sure he'd remain a bachelor because there didn't seem to be that one special woman who couldn't get past his wealth. Or, if there was, he hadn't met her yet.

CHAPTER 3

December 17, 2014

Hannah was in a foul mood when her plane finally touched down at Denver International Airport. The flight had been turbulent, the man seated next to her had snored throughout the flight, and she had not been one bit happy at having to leave Leanne and her domestic situation behind. Camden had promised to keep a watch over her, but she knew that they could only do so much. Leanne had to realize that there was nothing she could do that would salvage her marriage; she had to want to make the necessary changes in her life herself. Sadly, Hannah feared that she might not be able to force herself to make those changes before it was too late.

As soon as Hannah exited the plane, she found the ladies' room, repaired her makeup, and began her search for the area where Max had a limo waiting. She liked the thought of riding through the Colorado mountains in the back of a limo. Though she disliked the cold, she had to admit that the snowcapped mountains were breathtaking.

The drive would give her a couple of hours to rest and prepare herself for the work ahead. She hoped to find Max's hackers, do what was needed, and still have time to enjoy her planned staycation at the beach. She did not like snow. She did not like to be cold. And more than anything, the thought of being at an upscale ski resort during their busiest time of year made her wish for the comfort and quiet of her beachfront condo.

"Suck it up, girl. It ain't happening, Hannah," she muttered to herself as she made her way through the crowds. She wound her way through the travelers, some loaded with tons of luggage, others with sets of skis, snowboards, and all the heavy-duty gear required to freeze in luxury. She did not understand why people would willingly place themselves in freezing temperatures and actually call it fun. But again, she was a Florida girl through and through. After a tram ride and a trip up an escalator, she spied the exit, where her limo waited. Just as Max had said.

"You must be Miss Ray?" a handsome young man with caramel-colored skin dressed in a navy blue uniform asked as he saw her approach the limousine.

She wanted to correct him. It was *Ms. Ray,* but there was no use starting out on the wrong foot when she already had one strike — the presence of cold air and gobs of snow rather than warm sunshine and a sandy beach — against her. She'd let it pass. After all, it was true. She was a *Miss. Ms.* just sounded better to her.

"I'll take that," the limo driver said, reaching for her carry-on and opening the door for her. "Miss," he said, indicating that she should get inside.

"Yes, of course." She slid across the plush seat and inhaled the unmistakable scent of real leather. A rich man's scent, she thought as she tucked her pocketbook and briefcase on the floor next to her boot-clad feet.

Cut the attitude, Hannah. This is what it is. Work for a friend. Get over it. Do your job, then go home and enjoy the rest of your time off!

"Mr. Jorgenson said you wouldn't mind?" the driver said again.

"What? I'm sorry," she said. "Must be jet lag."

"I have another passenger to pick up. Mr.

25

Jorgenson said you wouldn't mind sharing the limo. He has more than one client to pick up today. It's the busy season, you know?"

Hannah wanted to say, "No shit," but kept it to herself. And who was this other passenger? Another ski bum taking advantage of Max's good nature? She decided to ask. "So who are we picking up?" She tried to sound cheerful, as though she were truly grateful to have a companion for the ride.

The young man slid into the driver's seat, then hit the button that opened the window that separated the driver from the passengers. "He's a business associate, miss."

"Of course," she replied. What had she expected other than a ski bum? Max Jorgenson was a big-time resort owner, a former Olympic gold-medal winner. It only made sense that he would have associates visiting him year-round. And if they got in a few days on the slopes, all the better. If you liked that sort of thing, which she didn't.

"We just have to drive to the general aviation side of the airport; it won't take long," the driver informed her as he pulled out into a long line of traffic preparing to exit the airport.

"That's fine. I'm in no hurry at all," she lied in the sweetest voice. She was starting not to like herself very much. *Maybe I should refer to myself as Ms. Scrooge.* She smiled at the unbidden thought.

"Thanks, because we're going to be in some heavy traffic. Tomorrow evening is the beginning of Hanukkah, so we've got plenty of travelers who want to be settled in at the resort before the holiday begins at sunset. Mr. Jorgenson says this is going to be a record-breaking year."

"That's wonderful," she replied, trying hard to keep the sarcasm out of her voice. *For him.*

"I know. I'm just thrilled to be a part of it all. My kid sister, she's twelve, hopes to make it to the Olympics one day, so I'm hoping I can make a connection for her." He stopped speaking, as though he'd revealed too much. "I mean, I don't know Mr. Jorgenson well enough to ask him if he'd coach my sister or anything like that, it's just that she's very talented and needs all the breaks she can get."

Hannah wanted to add that she could almost guarantee the breaks, but they might not be the kind he was hoping for. She didn't, though. "Have you talked to Max about your sister?" she asked, trying to show some form of sincere interest.

"No! I wouldn't dream of it. At least not

yet. I . . . well, I plan to play it by ear."

"Well, if you'd like, I can put in a good word for you. I'm sure Max would be more than willing to coach your sister, especially if she's as talented as you say. If not, I'm quite sure he could put you in contact with another coach." She didn't know that at all, but the poor kid seemed so excited when he talked about his sister that Hannah suddenly felt sorry for him. Trying to make it in a tough world. It was hard these days. Even more so if you didn't have the luxury of wealth and family to support you. She had no clue if that was the case now, but it was probably close enough. The kid wouldn't be driving a limo just for the fun of it. At least she didn't think so.

"You'd do that for me? I'm practically a stranger."

True, but she could tell he was decent. In her profession, the ability to size people up was absolutely necessary. And this young guy was legit. And she would make sure his sister got the training she needed, even if it meant paying for it herself. Anonymously, of course.

"Just write your name and number down, and don't forget to give it to me."

He reached inside his shirt pocket and whipped out a shiny gold business card.

28

"This has all of Tasha's info, and mine. I'm kind of like her agent since our mom died two years ago. She used to drive her to practice every day, but I can do that now with this job. And by the way, I'm Terrence."

"It's nice to meet you, Terrence. I'm Hannah Ray." She was sorry she'd been the slightest bit snotty. This kid was trying to make something of his and his sister's lives. She'd help him and his sister. She made a mental promise to herself to arrange for Max or someone else to coach the Olympic hopeful.

Hannah might do lots of crazy things, but one thing she *never* did was break a promise. Even one she had made only to herself.

CHAPTER 4

"I'm not sure how long I'll be remaining here," Liam told Pierce. "You can stay if you want, or not. Up to you."

"Then I'd just as soon go home. I hate this cold weather, and you'll need someone to keep an eye on your place, right?" Pierce teased, knowing full well that he had the use of the beach house on Sanibel Island while Liam was out of town.

"Of course, and I trust you to make sure that my boat, the *Ferretti 690,* catches a few fish while she's out and about."

Liam's *Ferretti 690* was a *yacht,* but Pierce wasn't going to remind him, just in case he decided to dry-dock her while he was away.

"I think I can manage. Just give me at least a three-to-four-hour heads-up when you're ready for your return flight. I'll need to file a flight plan and prepare the Learjet."

Learjets and *Ferretti 690s.* One might be excused if one thought that Liam McConnell had been born with a silver spoon in his mouth, but that was not the case at all. Hard work and a few wise investments in his younger years had assured him that his financial future was secure. Not to mention that his security fees were right up there with the likes of Gavin de Becker, a world-renowned security specialist.

"I'll make sure to do that. Now, where is this limousine that's picking me up?" The two men waited on the tarmac next to the plane. Pierce wore the traditional dark slacks and crisp white shirt with gold wings on the sleeves of a pilot. Liam was dressed in faded jeans and a white Columbia Sportswear fishing shirt. Worn-out Sperrys, minus socks, completed his outfit. He casually held a denim jacket across his shoulder. It was cold but dry, and the sun was out. He knew the temperatures could change at the drop of a hat, but he was comfortable and didn't want to suffocate on the drive to Telluride. People out West seemed to crank the heaters in their cars up to full blast at the drop of a snowflake. It always made him a bit sick, but he'd keep that tidbit of information to himself. All the more reason to like Florida. Though the temperature and the humidity were horrendous in the summer, air-conditioning was everywhere. In fact, most places kept the air-conditioning cranked up all the way in the summer months. Liam would take that over the cold any day of the week.

He slapped Pierce on the back. "Have a safe flight home. You need me, you know where to find me."

"Will do, my friend." Pierce spied the approaching limo and motioned for it to pull up alongside the jet so he could transfer Liam's suitcase from the underbelly of the aircraft. The limo's trunk popped open, Pierce tossed the small piece of luggage inside, then shook hands with Liam. "Later."

Liam waved, then directed his attention to the limousine driver. "Mr. McConnell? I'm Terrence. Mr. Jorgenson sent me."

"Hey, I appreciate the lift. Nice to meet you." Liam shook Terrence's hand.

"Just so you know, I have another passenger. She's a business associate of Mr. Jorgenson's. She's nice." He opened the door, then closed it quickly before the cold air could slip inside.

Liam slid into the seat and saw the attractive blonde seated across from him.

Max Jorgenson, you sly devil. Let the games begin.

CHAPTER 5

Ever the gentleman, Liam introduced himself using only his given name. He was a bit on the paranoid side when it came to women these days.

"Nice meeting you, Liam. I'm Hannah Ray," she replied in a professional voice, emphasizing *Ray*.

A subtle dig of sorts. He liked that.

He scrutinized her as she sat across from him. Shapely legs covered in black tights and black suede boots indicated she had taste. She wore a burgundy trench coat that covered the upper half of her body. Honey-blond hair and eyes the color of a good whiskey with tiny green flecks dotted around her pupils. His vision certainly hadn't been affected by aging. Not that forty was old. Hadn't someone recently told him forty was the new thirty?

After a few awkward seconds, he acknowledged her introduction by holding his hand out to her. "It's my pleasure."

She reached across the expanse that separated them and took his hand in hers, almost yanking it back when she felt a jolt of desire so sudden that it frightened her. Taking a deep breath, she quickly shook his hand, then pulled away. "Nice." And was he ever, she thought, as she raked her gaze over him. He had to be well over six feet tall because his long, denim-clad legs almost touched hers. Jet-black hair sprinkled with gray at the temples, and clear blue eyes; this man was a bona fide hunk. What the heck? She hadn't reacted to a member of the male persuasion like this since . . . ever!

A couple of more seconds of silence, then they both began talking at once.

"— So what brings you here?" Hannah asked.

"— I take it this isn't a vacation for you?" Liam said.

"Let's start over. Ladies first," Liam said, his wide grin revealing strikingly white teeth against a tanned face.

Hannah decided he was a ski bum. She saw that he went sockless, and this confirmed it even more. *Who lives in Colorado and went without socks in the winter?* But she told herself not to judge. He was very handsome, and he appeared to be very self-

34

assured. Maybe he was arrogant and condescending like Richard Marchand, an asshole pharmacist she had once dated. No, she thought to herself, there just couldn't be another man like dear old Richard. Realizing that he was waiting for her to start their conversation again, she smiled. "Sorry, I was wool-gathering. Long flight, and it's cold here."

He laughed. "Colorado is usually cold this time of year, no doubt about it."

"Excuse me," Terrence said, as they exited the airport. "Would either of you like something to eat before we hit I-70? I have drinks but no food, and it's a long drive: about six hours, and that's in good weather, without a lot of traffic."

"Six hours! Please tell me you're joking?" Hannah said, not caring that she sounded like a whiny brat. She had just spent almost four and a half hours on a plane, and now she had a six-hour limo ride? And apparently that was if she was lucky!

Liam removed his phone from his shirt pocket and punched in a number. "Pierce, you still at the airport? Good. Don't leave. I'm coming back. I'll explain when I get there."

"Maybe I should call Mr. Jorgenson," Terrence said as they waited at a traffic light.

35

"He'll be upset if I arrive without his guests."

"I'm calling him now," Liam said, and scrolled through his phone until he located Max's cell number.

"Max, I'm in Denver and just realized I'm still six hours away. Pierce is still at the airport with the Learjet. Can you arrange for someone to be there in say" — he looked at his watch — "two hours tops? Good. I'll tell him. Later," he said, then clicked off.

He turned in the seat so that he was facing the front of the limo. "Terrence, Max says you can have the night off. Said for you to spend the evening having fun and to stay at the Hilton in Denver tonight. Wants you to take your time driving back tomorrow. He also said he would make sure Tasha knows you're okay."

"Well, if that's what Mr. Jorgenson wants, then his wish is totally my command." Terrence grinned. "Yours too, Mr. McConnell, Miss Ray. I hope to see you both at all the Christmas festivities. They're going to light up the mountain this year. It's gonna be a sight to behold."

Hannah knew that she must've heard Terrence correctly; she wasn't hard of hearing. Yes, she'd heard all about the holiday events, but what she'd really heard and took in was the name. *McConnell. Liam McConnell.*

Anyone and everyone in the private sector of the law-enforcement business knew of his reputation. He was the best in electronic-security assessments. Meaning hackers could not hide from this man. And if they did, he would find them. His success rate was 100 percent.

"If you'll get us back to the general aviation side ASAP, I'll be forever in your debt," Liam said to Terrence.

Terrence made an illegal U-turn, then headed back to the airport. "Right away, Mr. McConnell."

"Do you mind filling me in on the change of plans?" Hannah singsonged. "Or did you forget there is someone else to consider?" Maybe he *was* an asshole like Richard Marchand.

"I apologize. I don't see any reason to ride in this limo for six-plus hours when I have a perfectly good Learjet with an awesome pilot who, as luck would have it, hasn't left the airport yet. I think Pierce can get us to Telluride in a little over an hour." He paused, then continued, "If you'd rather not fly with me, I'll understand. I am a total stranger."

Hannah smirked. "If Max knows you, then

37

I'm sure you're not some psycho serial killer I need to fear." She wanted to tell him she knew exactly who he was, but no way was she going to give him that satisfaction. And to think she'd felt a tiny bit of desire when he'd done nothing more than touch her hand. She needed to get a life beyond work. And maybe a little bit of romance somewhere in between.

"You do inspire confidence, Miss Ray."

"Thank you," she said, her words laced with sarcasm.

Fifteen minutes later, Terrence had arrived at the airport and pulled inside the gates that led to the private hangar area, then drove down the tarmac, where Pierce was doing his preflight check. He waved as they parked the limousine by the sleek aircraft.

Terrence hit the trunk button, but before he could race around to the back of the limo, Liam had already removed both pieces of luggage from the trunk. Hannah climbed out of the limo, stretched, and walked to where Liam stood and took her luggage by its handle. "Thanks, but I can carry this." She didn't want him thinking she was a weak, wimpy woman who needed a man to do what some considered "men's work." She was *not* one of those types at all. Independent to the core, it was something she'd learned from being raised by a single father.

"I can see that," Liam said, his words edgy, a bit sharp.

Hannah focused her eyes on his. "Look, I think we've started off on the wrong foot. I don't want to be here, and I don't know about you, but I am about to freeze to death just standing here, and I am hungry. Can we start over?" Hannah felt deflated, like she'd stepped out of her body, almost as though she were having some kind of metaphysical experience. It wasn't like her to give in so easily. *But,* she thought, *really, what am I actually giving in to?*

Liam grinned. "Must be the high altitude. It sometimes has a strange effect on people, right, Pierce?" Liam called out, as the pilot finished his preflight check. "Remember how badly it affected the president during the debates back in 2012?" He laughed and shook his head.

"Whatever you say, Liam. Though just so you know, Telluride Regional Airport is one of the highest commercial airports in North America at more than nine thousand feet above sea level. It sits atop Deep Creek Mesa, and the view of the San Juan Mountains is totally awesome."

He adjusted his aviator glasses and continued. "You might want to load up on water while you're out here. Supposed to help with altitude sickness. If that kind of thing bothers you."

It hadn't before, but he wasn't sure about their passenger. "Ms. Ray? Have you ever had any trouble with high altitudes?" Liam asked.

She shook her head no. "Though this is only my second trip out West. Last time I was here, I didn't ski, so if you're asking me about those altitudes up there" — she directed her eyes toward the snowcapped mountains — "I wouldn't know, since I've never been up on one of them. For better or worse, I am definitely not a lover of cold weather. I am Florida born and bred. Long live the beach."

She wanted to stomp her boots, anything to get out of the freezing, stark cold. And she was starving. "Didn't someone mention something about food awhile ago? I could use a bite to eat."

"I just placed an order with the airport's catering crew," Pierce told her. "They'll have a little bit of everything on the plane." He looked up when he saw a van heading their way. "They're here now," he said, motioning toward the catering truck.

"Great. Just what I want, more airplane

food," Hannah muttered.

"This isn't the same stuff the commercial airlines serve," Pierce informed her. "Private flying does offer a few amenities that the big commercial guys don't. Good food is just one of the perks, right, Liam?"

Hannah didn't want to burst the pilot's bubble. She'd flown in more Gulfstreams and Learjets in her time than she cared to remember. She wasn't a big fan of flying any way you looked at it. It was just another form of transportation as far as she was concerned. "Then let's get on board," she said, then asked before she forgot, "Does the plane have a ladies' room?"

"It does, and it's quite modern, too. The commode even flushes in midair," Pierce said, then they all burst out laughing.

Hannah smiled. "That's good enough for me."

"About time, I'd say," Liam added. "I wasn't sure if I wanted to spend another hour in your company!" He laughed hard, then winked at her. Hannah wanted to come up with a snappy comeback but couldn't think of anything appropriate, so she gave him her sexiest smile and winked back. "Are you sure?" she couldn't help adding. Teasing him, that's what she was doing! And, by gosh, she liked it!

"Okay, you two, enough. I say let's get this bird in the air so we can all sit back and enjoy all these goodies," Pierce suggested, and nodded to the food the two caterers were carrying onboard.

Hannah and Liam said their good-byes to Terrence. She saw Liam tuck a bit of cash in the young boy's hand and gave him a quick wave before turning toward the aircraft.

Liam brought his luggage up the short flight of steps. Hannah followed behind, dragging her carry-on inside with her. It wasn't like there wasn't enough room for a half dozen more passengers, complete with their luggage. "You have a preference where you'd like to sit?" Hannah asked Liam, while he tucked his luggage beneath a seat.

"Not at all. Sit wherever you're comfortable. This is going to be a quick flight; we'll be lucky if we have time to eat all that food Pierce ordered."

"Speaking of food, I'm ravenous. You mind if I dig into those boxes?" Hannah asked.

"Be my guest," Liam said. "It's probably a good idea to get our food. And then we can buckle up for the rest of the journey."

Inside the cabin, at the rear of the plane, was a wet bar on the left and a restroom to the right. Liam stood very close to Hannah as she tried to maneuver around in the small space so she wouldn't be practically rubbing up against him. Next to a stack of paper plates, she spied a Styrofoam container with several different types of deli meats. Another had cheeses of all sorts, and there was a variety of breads. She made fast work of slapping a few slices of turkey on some whole wheat bread, added some lettuce and a squeeze of whole-grain mustard. There were pasta salads, potato salads, and bean salads. She took a scoop of each before backing out of the cramped quarters.

"What would you like to drink?" Liam asked, stooping to peer inside a small refrigerator. "We've got soda, beer, and somewhere in here we should have bottled water." He pulled out a few cans of soda, then grabbed two bottles of water. "Water work for you?"

Hannah had just taken her first bite when Liam spoke to her. She nodded and held out her hand. Chewing and swallowing her food faster than normal, she felt a chunk of lettuce go down the wrong pipe. She started coughing and gasping, trying to force the lodged piece of lettuce either up or out. Liam dropped his sandwich onto his seat, lowered himself, and came up behind her, wrapping his arms around her sternum. Before she could understand what he was doing, the lettuce flew out of her mouth, landing smack dab in the middle of Pierce's perfectly pressed white shirt the moment he entered the cabin.

The three were quiet for a few seconds, looking from one to the other, then all three began to laugh so hard they had tears in their eyes. Hannah was embarrassed, but not so badly that she couldn't laugh at herself. When they calmed down enough to talk, Hannah was the first to speak. She opened the bottle of water, took a sip, then said, "I do believe you just saved my life, Mr. McConnell."

"I think I am going to have to agree with you this time," he said.

"What is that freaky thing that happens to the person who saves the life of another?" Pierce asked while dabbing at his shirt with a wet napkin. "I heard it somewhere as a kid; if you save someone's life, then they owe you a lifelong debt. The person who does the saving has to take responsibility for that person's life. Supposed to do anything to help you whenever you're in need, something like that."

Hannah almost choked again. "I think some kid made that up. Really, who would do something like that in this day and age?"

"Save a life or take the debt?" Liam asked.

Hannah had the grace to blush. "Thank you for saving my life, though in all honesty, I think the lettuce was about to leave on its own, but one can't say for sure. So thank you again, Liam." She liked the sound of his name on her lips. "Your debt for chivalry is paid in full."

"Hey, now wait a minute, don't I even get the chance to ask for what kind of . . . payoff I'd like?" He grinned as he scooped the sandwich from his seat.

About the time Hannah was ready to answer, Pierce pulled in the hydraulic steps and closed the aircraft's door. "You two better be buckled in and ready to roll. It's time to get this bird in the sky." He lowered himself into the cockpit. "And I mean it, too. Remember, as the pilot, I am in charge, and you *will* obey my orders."

CHAPTER 6

"I hope he's not threatening us," Hannah said, adjusting her seat belt.

"Nah, he just loves to fly, says the skies are his mistress. He reminds me I'm not a pilot as often as humanly possible."

They were taxiing down the runway. Liam lowered his head to his chest, mumbled something under his breath, then looked across the small aisle. "I hate takeoffs. I'd never be able to fly my own plane even if I wanted to, which I don't. That's what Pierce is for."

"So he works exclusively for you?" Hannah asked.

"Meaning is he at my beck and call twenty-four/seven? No, not at all. He flies for Flex Jet. Several companies purchase an aircraft together and share the cost of owning it. Makes it easier for those who can't afford to have a multimillion-dollar aircraft just sitting there. So, when he's not on vacation, Pierce has to be available for them. He's staying at my house while I'm out here and will return for me when I'm ready to go home. I guess you could say we're both on vacation. Mine just happens to be a working vacation."

Hannah raised her brow in question. "Did Max Jorgenson call you around the first of the month?"

"Yes, and trust me, I am going to make him pay. Big-time." He managed to smooth out the sandwich he had dropped on his seat when he'd helped Hannah as she was choking. He took a bite, chewing and grinning at the same time. A piece of bread clung to his lower lip, and Hannah found herself wanting to reach across the small space between them to brush it away. She had to mentally command herself to refrain from doing so. Though she wondered how he would react if she did. The thought made her smile.

"What's so funny?" he asked. He wiped the crumb from his lip.

If only he knew, she thought. "Max sent for me then, too. I wonder why the two-week wait?" Suddenly Hannah wasn't so sure Max actually had a hacker. That's what he'd said, wasn't it? And given Liam's reputation, surely he wouldn't have called him all the way to Colorado just to . . . *fix the two of us up?*

No, no, no! I'm being ridiculous. We're here to work, then return to our lives and enjoy the rest of the holiday season. Max would not go to such great lengths. She mentally removed the images of her and Liam together from her mind.

"You're not eating?"

She looked at the sandwich sitting on the napkin covering her lap. "I guess almost choking to death has taken away my appetite."

"At least have some of the potato salad; it's really good," Liam insisted as he scooped a bite between his lips.

She found her plate and fork and proceeded to eat every bite. "What can I say? I guess I was hungry, choking or not."

Pierce announced they'd reached their flying altitude, and Liam seemed more relaxed. His large frame appeared to sink into the plush seat. Hannah didn't know what to make of her reaction and scrutiny of this man. This wasn't her normal reaction at all.

"So Max sent for you, too. I understand he's experiencing a bit of in-house snooping," Liam explained. "Both electronically and the old-fashioned way. Files — the paper kind — have gone missing, some

48

cash. I hope between the two of us, we can find the culprit. Not a good time for a thief, Christmas and all."

Hannah nodded. "That's when they crawl out of the cracks. At least in my experience." She paused. "Do you know me?" she couldn't help but ask. Hannah always believed in cutting through the flesh and going straight for the bone.

"I know *of* you. You've got quite a reputation."

"Thank you. I could say the same for you, but I'm sure you already know that," she added with a smirk.

"I've worked all over the world. It's only logical that one's success in this field is acknowledged," Liam said without a trace of arrogance.

That's true, Hannah thought.

"Do you find it odd that we both have law degrees, yet we're doing . . . undercover work?" Hannah asked. They did have a few things in common, she admitted to herself. Was this really the reason Max had sent for them? A holiday romance? No, Max wouldn't take advantage of that. Or would he? She had to admit, she didn't know him well enough to make the assumption.

Liam chuckled and ran a hand over his stubbled chin. "No, not at all. I studied criminal justice first, then got my law degree. I wasn't sure where I wanted to go, then the electronic field exploded, and it turned out that I was pretty good at it. Did a couple of years working with the FBI's Cyber Crime Unit, then decided I'd rather work alone and, as they say, the rest is history."

"Impressive," Hannah replied.

"Your résumé isn't too shabby, either," he observed.

My résumé? Has he actually checked into my background?

Hannah didn't respond.

"You've got a very good reputation, Ms. Ray. Both you and your firm. Surely you know your name is recognizable? I'm impressed," he added.

"Thank you. Yes, we're pretty well-known, at least in Florida. We don't do too much out of state, or out of the country, for that matter. I like to stay close to home."

"That's one of the reasons I decided to leave the Cyber Crime Unit. Too much travel."

"I wouldn't think there would be a need to travel as much since most of the work is electronic, via the World Wide Web."

Liam cleared his throat. "Let's just say certain clients want you on their turf. The days when I had to take such clients are gone," Liam added.

"Then why are you traveling now? Did Max threaten you or something?" Hannah asked, though she was grinning when she asked the question.

He laughed, too. Hannah found she liked the sound, deep and throaty. *Darn, this needs to stop. Now.* She was not on her way to a ski resort to find a date, she reminded herself. She was supposed to catch a thief.

"You know Max. He didn't actually threaten me. He simply said he needed me, and here I am. We go back a long way. I'd do just about anything for him, and he knows it."

"I've only met him once, through his wife, Grace. She protected a client of mine, and sadly, that same client is in need of her services again. Whether or not she will use them is another matter entirely. Unfortunately, there isn't much one can do in cases like that. I only hope she comes to her senses and makes a decision to end her very bad marriage to an abusive jerk. Her husband is turning out to be a very dangerous man." Hannah stopped. What was she doing? Client discretion was a priority. She knew better, but in her own defense, she hadn't named any names.

"Grace is a good egg, no doubt about it. I really admire her. Plus, they've got that cute little girl now. Max adores being a husband and father; I'm so happy he's finally found his bliss."

"I suppose so," she commented lamely.

Liam reached for her paper plate, and his, then tossed them in a small plastic bag he'd removed from the pocket of the seat in front of him.

"Thanks."

"We're coming down; I can feel it. So I take it you haven't found your bliss?" Liam asked, as though he were asking her what her favorite flavor of ice cream was. Or was she just reading more into his comments and questions because she'd assumed Max had plans for the pair other than catching a thief? Most likely the latter.

Hannah peered out her window. The snow-covered mountains were breathtaking. Tall pines of all shapes and sizes looked like miniature Christmas trees placed strategically down the side of the mountain. "It's beautiful out there. Minus the cold," she said, hoping to avoid answering his question.

"Certainly different from what we're used to," he responded. "Though Florida has a beauty all its own. Especially Sanibel Island.

I love it when I get to spend time there."

She smiled. "Sanibel is awesome; I love it there, too. I almost purchased a condo there, but since my offices are in Naples, I decided it would be best to stay closer to home. I love Naples, too, but it's growing too fast for my tastes."

"You realize we're practically neighbors?" Liam said. His blue eyes twinkled like sapphires.

Heat crept up her neck, settling on her face. She turned away so he couldn't see her. She was freaking blushing! Thirty-three, about to turn thirty-four, on Christmas Eve no less, something she made sure no one knew, and here she was blushing like a highschool girl with her first crush.

"Did I say something to offend you?" Liam asked sincerely.

Taking a deep breath, and hoping her flush wasn't as bad as it felt, she answered, "No, not at all. I was just . . . calculating the distance."

"By land or water?" he asked teasingly.

"Land, actually."

"It's roughly forty miles by land and around twenty-five through the Gulf."

She laughed. "Good to know."

Pierce chose that moment to come over the intercom system. "Folks, it's time to fold up your tray tables and make sure you're buckled in 'cause we're about to touch down. And Liam, I mean it. Wear the damned seat belt."

Hannah's eyes traveled to Liam's waist. "You're not buckled in! Shame on you."

"In all the excitement, I forgot."

"Right," Hannah kidded. "Seems like Pierce knows your habits quite well."

He nodded in the affirmative. "I'm hoping to get to know yours a lot better, too."

Hannah didn't know what to say, so she said nothing. Five minutes later, they were on the ground. Thank goodness, she thought, because if she'd had to come up with an answer, she wasn't sure what she would've said.

CHAPTER 7

Hannah said good-bye to Pierce and thanked him for saving her from a long drive. "I can't imagine why Max didn't have me fly directly to Telluride, so thanks again." She shook his hand and made her way inside the small airport. Actually, she was very suspicious of the entire setup, but she'd give Max the benefit of the doubt for now.

Liam stayed behind, apparently taking care of any last-minute plans he and Pierce had. She'd overheard them talking about Pierce's planned fishing trip, and it brought tears to her eyes. Even though her father had been a business tycoon, he never lost his love of fishing. Hannah had accompanied him on many trips, and she, too, enjoyed the sport, though she refused to keep her catch, always tossing the poor creatures back into the water. Her father respected this, and he, too, would toss whatever he caught back into its home waters. She did know he didn't practice this when it was just he and his buddies. And that was okay with her. She wasn't that unreasonable when it came to nature. She knew the fish she enjoyed so much at The Captain's Table, her favorite waterfront restaurant in Naples, didn't magically appear out of a manufacturer's deep freeze.

"Ms. Ray?" a young woman behind the counter asked.

"Yes?"

"Mr. Jorgenson has a car waiting for you and Mr. McConnell. He said to tell you he was sorry he couldn't be here personally to drive you to Maximum Glide but gave directions to where each of you is staying."

Hannah saw the green-and-white plastic name tag on the woman's beige blouse. "Thank you, Mandy. I'm sure we can manage without him."

The woman looked to be in her early twenties. Black hair cut in a sleek bob, creamy skin untouched by the sun or time, she smiled, revealing a mouthful of silver braces. "He said you could, and I'm supposed to give you this." She handed Hannah a large gift box. Wrapped in shiny silver-and-gold paper with three giant bows — a red, a green, and a gold one stacked atop one another. Good grief! Was she supposed to bring a gift? She'd been such a Scrooge when it came to Christmas, she had to admit she was not up on all the latest holiday etiquette. She took the package from Mandy. "Thank you," was all she could manage to say. The box was extremely heavy, and Hannah wondered what was inside.

"Mr. Jorgenson told me that you were not to open the box until you were settled in your condo. He was very adamant about that. He even told me I'd get in all sorts of trouble if I didn't insist on emphasizing the importance of this. I hope it's okay with you?"

Poor Mandy. The young woman looked as though she was about to cry. "I promise." Hannah placed her hand in the air, with her thumb and pinkie down so that her remaining three fingers were in the correct position as she proceeded to recite the Girl Scout Law. " '*I will do my best to be* honest and fair, friendly and helpful, considerate and caring, courageous and strong, and responsible for what I say and do, *and to* respect myself and others, respect authority, use resources wisely, make the world a better place and, be a sister to every Girl Scout,' and I promise not to shake or peep in Max's box."

Mandy shrieked, "Oh my gosh! How did you know?"

Hannah nodded at the picture on the countertop. Mandy was a Girl Scout leader.

Mandy removed a tissue from the box on her desk. "I forget that's here sometimes. How cool is this?"

"Then you trust I won't open the box?" Hannah asked with a grin.

"Absolutely. From one Scout to another, I trust you wholeheartedly."

A clapping sound from the airport entrance caused both Hannah and Mandy to turn around.

"Very well said, Ms. Ray. You never mentioned you were a Girl Scout," Liam said as he strolled toward them.

"Well, it isn't exactly something that comes up in everyday conversation. Mandy has been given strict orders from Max to give me this" — she nodded at the shiny wrapped present on top of the counter — "and if I open it before I'm settled in at the condo, then not only am I in deep trouble, but she could be as well. When I saw this picture" — she indicated the silver-framed photo — "I knew that one Scout would trust another, especially if I recited the Girl Scout Law."

"I like that. A true Girl Scout."

"Mr. McConnell?" Mandy asked inquiringly.

"That would be me," he said.

"This one is for you." She reached beneath the counter and pulled out another box, only this one was larger. "Mr. Jorgenson asked that I give this to you. Same deal. You can't open it until you are all settled in at the cabin. You've got the hottest address at Maximum Glide; you know that, right? Are you two famous or something? Mr. Jorgenson has rolled out the red carpet for both of you," Mandy said, then continued, "Not that you have to be famous or anything to have the red-carpet treatment. We get a lot of famous people here. Tom Cruise, for one. But we all recognized him."

"Ah, I hate to disappoint you, but we're here to work for Mr. Jorgenson. So, no, we are not famous in the sense that you think," Liam answered for both of them.

"I'm sorry. I didn't mean to be rude, I'm just a bit on the nosy side. At least that's what everyone tells me."

Hannah spoke up. "Nosy is not a bad thing. If you ever get tired of freezing and want a change of scenery, look me up." She reached inside her purse and gave Mandy one of her business cards.

"Oh, cool! You're a private eye! And in

Florida. Wait until I tell Jason, my boyfriend. He will truly be impressed. He's always after me for being so nosy. Are you for real? About looking you up and all?" Mandy asked, her eyes as wide as the moon.

"Sure, we can always use an extra set of eyes. Of course, there is training and certification required, but in my business, nosiness is considered an added bonus."

Hannah and Liam laughed together. "Yes, it is in mine, too."

"Don't tell me, you're a private eye, too," Mandy said in such an excited tone, Hannah thought the young woman was about to lose her voice entirely.

"Sort of. Now, if we could get that car Max promised, I am ready to call it a day. What with the time difference and all, I think it's nearing my bedtime." Liam winked at Hannah as he said this.

"Yes, mine, too," she added, then felt like kicking herself. Did he think she was implying something more than sleep? Surely not. He was an adult, the same as she. He acted like one, and she was acting like Mandy, a young woman starstruck by anything out of the ordinary.

"I'm sorry. I talk too much, too. Jason tells me that all the time."

Hannah silently agreed with the mysterious Jason, but she'd keep that to herself. Mandy was just young and excited.

"Here are the keys. Mr. McConnell is supposed to drive; again, this is from Mr. Jorgenson, not me," Mandy added. "I have to follow the rules."

Mandy came from behind the counter with a small bellman's rack. She placed their packages from Max on it, then Liam took his and Hannah's suitcases and placed them beside the packages. He reached for his wallet and took out a hundred-dollar bill. He placed it in Mandy's hand. "Take Jason out to dinner on me," he said, leaving the girl speechless.

"But . . . I'm not," Mandy said, then stopped. "Okay, I will do that. Tonight. Thank you so much, Mr. McConnell. And Ms. Ray. I'm going to tell Jason what you said about nosy being a good thing, too. Now, follow me," she said, and proceeded to pull the cart through a set of automatic doors. A blast of air sent shivers through Hannah. She tightened the belt on her coat and stuffed her hands in her coat pockets before stepping out into the blistering cold. It was much colder in Telluride than it had been in Denver.

"Aren't you cold?" Hannah asked as she followed behind Mandy and Liam.

"Freezing," he shouted.

The wind was picking up, making it hard to hear and be heard. Hannah wanted sunshine and hot sand between her toes right now. She did not like being cold. Not one little bit.

Mandy led them to a bright yellow Hummer with the engine running. "This is for you to use as long as you're here," she said.

Did Mandy think they were a couple? Surely not! Had Max implied that when he'd arranged for only one vehicle?

Liam opened the passenger door. "Go on, get inside. You're freezing." For once, Hannah agreed and let him take control of loading their luggage and those mystery packages.

A minute later, he was in the driver's seat. Only she saw that he now wore the denim jacket he'd been carrying. He made a few adjustments to the seat and the mirrors, then put the vehicle into DRIVE.

"Stop!" Hannah shouted, then lowered her voice to a normal volume. "Sorry. Your seat belt. You forgot to fasten your seat belt."

He looked down. "Habit. I hate the things." He put the Hummer in PARK, then fastened his seat belt.

"Yes, but they're a lifesaver."

"You're right. Now let's get this clunker

on the road," Liam said, turning to her. He gave her the sexiest smile, and her heart flip-flopped.

She was in deep trouble for sure.

"So it says here," he glanced at the sheet of paper he'd found on the dash, "that I'm to drop you off first at Forest Hills. That's the name of the condos where you'll be staying," he explained.

She wanted to say "duh" but kept it to herself. She'd already acted like a jerk more times than she cared to remember. As soon as she was settled in, she was going to call Camden and tell her about this . . . setup, if that's what it was. She was becoming more suspicious by the minute.

Liam was a good driver, even on the slick and winding road that led to Maximum Glide. There were piles of snow on both sides of the road, and Hannah was reminded of Florida and how easy it was to jump in her car and drive anywhere without worrying about icy roads and bad weather. Yes, they had hurricanes, and yes, it rained a lot in the summer months, but rarely was she in a situation where she couldn't just jump in her little red Thunderbird and go. Now, Liam was driving very slowly, never taking his eyes off the road. She didn't want to distract him, so she glanced out the window at the scenery.

The small town was decorated with strings of bright, colorful lights. Pines of all kinds were draped with giant red bows. Even the traffic lights were decorated. Giant plastic Santas in sleighs with reindeer appeared as though they were about to take flight from the rooftop of a restaurant named Snow Bunnies. Hannah couldn't help but grin as she saw yet another business decorated in shiny red and green lights that blinked "Merry Christmas!" Telluride was definitely caught up in the spirit of the season.

"Well, what do you know? Max's directions are right on the money. Looks like we've arrived at your destination, Ms. Ray."

Forest Hills.

"I'm to see you to the front desk and nothing more, as per Max's instructions," Liam said as he pulled the yellow Hummer up to the guest-entrance parking area. "No questions asked."

Hannah opened the passenger door. "And I suppose this is as per Max's instructions, too?"

"You got it," Liam replied.

CHAPTER 8

Liam found the turnoff to Gracie's Way without any trouble. The directions were quite clear, but frankly, he wasn't so sure he wanted to be this high on the mountain, even if this cabin was Maximum Glide's top vacation rental.

The inside lights were on just as Max said they would be, plus the entire outside of the cabin had been decorated with thousands of colorful lights. Giant pine wreaths with red ribbons tied around them were in every window.

Liam hit the garage control Max had left in the car and pulled the Hummer inside. He shut off the engine, then clicked the key fob to open the Hummer's hatch. He grabbed his luggage and the ridiculously large package and entered the cabin through the door leading to the kitchen.

He was pretty impressed when he stepped inside. The kitchen was enormous, with a giant range, two ovens, and more counter space than anyone could ever use. Liam set about exploring his new temporary digs. A Sub-Zero refrigerator was stocked with enough food for an army. Liam took out a can of Coke and guzzled it as he scoped out the kitchen. A table and chairs made of real logs seated twelve. Red and green rugs were scattered over the honey-colored wood floors. A great room off the kitchen boasted a giant fireplace across an entire wall. A fire had been started, and the smell of pine and something sweet filled the giant room. "Max doesn't do anything by halves," he said to himself as he wandered through the rooms. He followed the staircase that led upstairs to two bedrooms plus a loft. He located the master suite at the end of the hall.

Centered in the room was a giant king-size bed made of the same honey-colored logs as the walls. The bathroom had a huge, glassed-in shower. A giant Jacuzzi tub stood smack-dab in the center of the bathroom. "Good old Max," he said. Heated towels and plush bath sheets were strategically placed, and pleasantly scented soaps were on the long, dark green marble countertop. Two mirrors, their frames made out of branches, made him laugh out loud. "Talk about bringing the outdoors inside. Leave it to Max. He's really into this."

Satisfied that he'd be living more than comfortably for the next couple of weeks, Liam went to the kitchen to retrieve his luggage. He was about to take advantage of that Jacuzzi.

A bellman escorted Hannah to her condo. He insisted, telling her she was listed as a top-priority client by the owner, and duty required that he obey his instructions. More Max, she wanted to say, but didn't want to get the guy into any unnecessary trouble. He unlocked the door for her, then stepped aside, allowing her to enter first.

When she saw the view, it almost took her breath away. "Oh, wow," she said. "This is glorious."

"It's pure heaven, isn't it?" the bellman concurred.

For a few seconds, she'd forgotten she wasn't by herself in the room. "It is," she said, then handed him a twenty-dollar bill. She hoped that was enough. Her social skills were a bit rusty.

"Thank you, ma'am. If there is anything you need, my name is William. Here is my number." He handed her a card. What was this? Her personal escort/bellman?

"Thanks, but I think I have everything I

need, at least for now."

"Shall I draw a bath for you before dinner?" he asked.

Hannah felt like an eighteenth-century heroine in a romance novel. What the heck. "I would like that very much, thank you, William." She'd play along with this. It wasn't like she had a man — or anyone else, for that matter — to draw her a bath at home. Well, come to think of it, she took showers at home, so there really wasn't any need.

"Indeed, ma'am. How shall I select the temperature?" He stood ramrod stiff next to the wall-to-wall windows that allowed a full view of the majestic mountainside. It truly was breathtaking. Of course, she could say this now because it was warm inside, and a fire was burning in the real-wood fireplace. The scent of something sweet lingered in the air. This was not a bad scene for snow and cold. As long as she stayed inside, she'd be fine. All she had to do was find Max's thief, aka hacker, then she could go home. For now, she'd make the best of it.

"Very hot, William," she said. "I'll just take a look around while you tend to my bath." She laughed. If Camden heard her now, she'd crack up. If her employees heard her now, they would bust a gut.

"Yes, ma'am," he said before heading down a long hallway to what she assumed was the bathroom.

The entire wall of the living area was glass, which was the big wow factor. Across from the window was a floor-to-ceiling rock fireplace. Plush sofas in soft beiges faced one another. Several tables were scattered throughout with books and magazines. Brightly colored pillows were placed invitingly throughout the area, just begging for one to curl up with a good book or simply enjoy the view of the mountains. She found the kitchen to be just as perfect, with a small dining-room table for six, stainless-steel appliances, and a black-bear theme throughout: bear canisters, salt-and-pepper shakers, a paper-towel holder, plus place mats and matching curtains. Hannah liked the idea of the bears as long as they were just a decoration. Anything more . . . well, she wasn't sure how she'd react if she were to encounter a real live bear.

The condo, at least as much as she'd seen so far, was eminently, completely suitable for her. As soon as William left, she planned to soak in the tub and call Camden. She wanted to check on Leanne, and to tell her about Liam McConnell.

William chose that moment to appear. "If

you need anything else, please call the number on the card and I will see to your every need."

"Thanks, William, I'm good for now," Hannah said, hoping he was finished. She wanted that bath and a strong cup of coffee. She wondered if she asked William for a cup of coffee, exactly how many seconds it would be before a steaming mug was in her hand. That was something she didn't care to find out at the moment. Or any time soon, for that matter. No use getting spoiled rotten when she would be leaving sooner rather than later.

"Then I'll be waiting for you at eight o'clock promptly."

She must have had a strange look come over her face because William looked quite shocked at whatever her expression was. "Mr. Jorgenson has arranged for you to join him for dinner tonight at Eagles Nest."

And here we go again, she thought. *More Max.* "I wasn't told, but if it's on the agenda, then I'll be ready at eight." And not a moment sooner, she wanted to add. It was just after five. That gave her three hours to relax in the tub, talk to Camden, and prepare a list of questions for Mr. Max Jorgenson. And make herself presentable, just in case Liam was invited to this dinner, too.

Something told her that he would most certainly be there as well.

"Then I'll see you at eight o'clock," William said before nodding and quietly leaving the room.

She wanted to run behind him and lock the door, not because she felt unsafe but because she feared he would return and offer some other service.

"This is the life," she said out loud. "No, it's not. I have the perfect life in Naples; close to perfect, anyway. I come and go as I please, I have a very successful business, I love my work, I love my friends. And if I wanted to live like this, I could. I certainly have much more than enough to support this sort of lifestyle.

"Yes, Hannah, you are talking to yourself. Now go make the coffee."

She rummaged through the cupboards, finding them fully stocked. "Did I expect anything less?" she asked herself as she found a bag of Elevation Coffee. "Never heard of it," she said, then read the label: *Join the mile-high club.*

"Okay, let's see if this merits joining the mile-high club."

Hannah made fast work of preparing the coffee. While she waited for it to brew, she found her cell phone in her bag and turned it on. She had a few voice mails, but nothing urgent. She punched in Camden's cellphone number. Her friend answered on the first ring.

"I was starting to worry. You said you'd call when you landed in Denver and, according to my schedule, you're about three hours and four minutes behind. What gives?"

Camden was the most organized person on the planet. Hannah loved those skills in their professional relationship, but as her friend, she wasn't so sure she cared for them. But she had promised to call. She'd been sidetracked. Big-time.

"I'm in a condo in Telluride. I have a manservant, and Liam McConnell flew me here in his private jet," Hannah explained as she made her way back to the kitchen. She found a dark green mug with black bears on it and filled it to the brim. She took a sip. Good stuff. She might consider joining the mile-high club, at the least the one that served such good coffee.

"Slow down and start from the beginning. I thought you had a long ride ahead of you. Explain," Camden said.

For the next twenty minutes, Hannah told her about meeting Liam, and how Max seemed to have arranged everything so the two of them would be thrown together. "I'm having dinner with Max tonight at eight o'clock. William plans to escort me to dinner."

"And you're wondering if Liam McConnell received the same invitation?"

"I'm pretty sure he did. I would guess we're going to discuss whatever it is that Max brought us here for."

"Makes sense," Camden said, but she didn't sound 100 percent convinced.

"Is there something you're not telling me?" Hannah asked. "Because if you're up to no good, I will find out."

"Good grief, Hannah! What would I be up to? I have no clue what's going on, at least no more than you do. From what you've said, it sounds like you're attracted to Liam, and maybe you're trying to read more into the situation than what's really there. It has been awhile since you were in a relationship."

"Coming from Miss Hot Lips herself, please!"

"For your information, and not that's it any of your business, but I just so happen to have a date tomorrow night with someone," Camden singsonged.

"Someone? That could be a bird in your case," Hannah teased. Camden truly didn't

73

get the meaning of the word *date,* at least not in the sense that she was using it now. She used the word as it suited her needs.

"Well, it's not. Remember Art Greenfield?"

Hannah tried to recall the name. "No, I don't remember him. Should I?"

"Remember the guy who was caught stealing catalytic converters from the Lincoln dealership in Cape Coral last year?"

Hannah almost dropped her mug of coffee. "You're going out with a thief? Please tell me I heard you wrong."

"Not him. Art was his assigned counsel. He defended the guy," Camden explained.

Hannah gave a sigh of relief. "That's good news. So, how did this come about?"

"I was at the grocery store earlier, he was buying lox or something, and we started talking. He invited me over to his family's house tomorrow evening to celebrate the first night of Hanukkah. It starts at sundown."

Camden would make sure to bone up on any and all Jewish traditions before her date, of that Hannah was certain. Which was good. Camden needed a little bit of romance in her life, too. They both did. They worked too hard and too much. And neither was getting any younger. They'd discussed having families, and both wanted children and all the traditional things that went along with raising them. Camden was also an only child.

"Good. I'm happy. I wouldn't want you spending the holiday alone."

"Oh, stop it! You don't give a hoot about holidays. Never have. Unless Liam has suddenly changed your mind," Camden retorted.

"No, he has not. And I've never said I didn't like the holidays, I just think it's silly to . . . it's okay when you're a kid."

"Sure, whatever you say, Ms. Scrooge," Camden teased.

Odd, since Hannah had referred to herself as Ms. Scrooge just a few hours ago. "Listen, I need to ask about Leanne, then I have to go. Did you see her at the hospital today? Was that brute of a husband skulking around?"

"Leanne is okay. She's still in a lot of pain, and no, that bastard was nowhere to be found. I think I've finally convinced her to take out an order of protection against him, but she's really afraid of him and his family. I feel so bad for her."

"Keep trying to convince her, Camden. Do whatever it takes. Get ugly if you have to. It just might save her life."

"I can do ugly. I'll stop by first thing in the morning to check on her."

"Thanks. Keep me posted."

"I will. And let me know how dinner goes with Liam tonight," Camden added, then said good-bye before Hannah could respond.

She poured another mug of coffee and headed for the master suite.

A giant tub was filled with steamy, scented water. An array of bath products had been placed in a basket next to the tub. "Perfect," she said before stripping down and sliding into the warm water.

"Decadent, if I do say so myself. Colorado might be cold, but right now I'm loving it," Hannah said as she succumbed to the amenities.

CHAPTER 9

The ride up the mountain to Eagles Nest was quite unique to the area, Hannah learned. She and William traveled in an enclosed snow coach, which he explained to her was an MPV, a multiple-passenger-vehicle type of sleigh with skis. They were pulled by a small, tractorlike contraption, and Hannah was delighted when she learned that the snow coach had heat. What she didn't know, and William had neglected to tell her, was that Eagles Nest was one of the highest fine-dining restaurants in North America, at almost twelve thousand feet. She'd never been so high on a mountain in her life and wasn't sure if she was a wee bit frightened or just a little bit excited at the thought that she *might* see Liam at dinner.

Inside, she was greeted by a young man dressed in an elegant black suit, though he wore a Stetson on his head, which kind of ruined the image for her. But she remembered what part of the country she was in and knew this was accepted as normal. She tried not to laugh.

The restaurant itself was beautifully decorated for the holiday. Several giant spruce trees were placed throughout the rooms, all decorated with bright-colored lights and western ornaments that blended perfectly with the western decor. Hand-hewn beams and what appeared to be furniture made from wine barrels gave the place a rustic ambience. Eagles Nest was inviting, to say the least. Several wood-burning fireplaces throughout made it comfortably warm, and the stone floors and exposed wood beams added to the frontier flavor. Sheepskin throws were tossed casually over the backs of sofas and chairs. Hannah found herself wanting to curl up and get comfy, but maybe another time. Tonight's dinner was all about business. She'd dressed with that and warmth in mind.

She wore her black tights and boots with a dark green wool skirt and matching sweater. Her burgundy coat, along with a matching scarf and gloves, completed her ensemble. She'd need a warmer coat if she lived here, but this would do since she only planned on running in and out of the cold; she certainly had no plans to frolic in the snow. Though she had to admit, it might be fun. It was the cold she didn't like. If only you could have snow without the cold.

The dressed-up cowboy, as she thought of him, led her to a small room that overlooked the mountain. A table for six was set, yet there was no sign of Max or anyone else. The cowboy must've seen her look of surprise. "They're outside at the wine bar. Would you care to join them?"

An outdoor wine bar? In these temperatures? Of course she wanted to join them.

"No thank you; I'll stay inside if that's all right," she said politely.

"Of course. What may I bring you to drink?" the cowboy asked.

Hannah had a brief flash of dipping beer from a trough and offering her horse the first sip but tried to erase the image from her mind as quickly as it came. Maybe she *was* suffering from a bit of altitude sickness. It wasn't like her to have such bizarre thoughts. She did have a quick wit, but this wasn't witty. This was nuts!

"Your drink, ma'am?" Cowboy repeated.

"I'll have a glass of white wine," she said, and gave him her sweetest smile. "Is that proper here?" she asked, exaggerating her Southern accent a bit.

Cowboy smiled. "It's mighty proper,

ma'am. Now, if you will excuse me."

He'd gotten her joke or dig or whatever one wanted to call it.

Hannah sat down at the table, not caring if it was rude. She was tired, and hungry, and really thought this dinner might be a quick bite, business discussed, then she could call it a night. Max Jorgenson was going to get a piece of her mind. She'd no more had the thought when the man himself walked through the doors that led to the outdoor wine bar.

"Hannah, I'm sorry I wasn't here to greet you. A couple of ski bums caught me and I couldn't get away."

She stood up and offered her hand. This was a business dinner, not a social gathering. "That's perfectly fine. It gave me a few minutes to admire the view."

"Please, sit down." Max pointed to the chair she'd just vacated. "I know you're tired, and with the time difference, I apologize, but I wanted to give you the heads-up as soon as you arrived."

Max sat in the chair across from her. Apparently, it was just going to be the two of them for dinner. Her heart sunk a bit when she realized the large table must be part of this semiprivate room. He wore dark slacks, a turtleneck, and a ski jacket with his name sewn on the breast pocket. She had to remind herself he was a world-famous Olympian. Of course people would want to pull him aside and talk to him about his gold medals. Which reminded her of a promise she'd made.

"I know this isn't the right time, but is it ever the right time?" she asked but didn't wait for him to answer. "Today, the young man in the limo, Terrence. He was so kind, and sweet. He mentioned he'd lost his mother, though I do not recall if he mentioned how recently. He has a younger sister, Tasha."

"Of course I know Terrence and Tasha. He works for the limo service at the resort. Though I was unaware that his mother had passed away."

"Apparently, Tasha has high hopes for the Winter Olympics," Hannah explained. "Terrence wants to find a good coach for her. He said she was extremely talented. Though I know absolutely nothing about the sport, I am a good judge of character. If Terrence says his sister has talent, I am inclined to believe that she does."

The cowboy brought her wine and placed it on a napkin in front of her. She took a sip, then continued with her story. "He's working here in hopes . . . he didn't say this, but I believe he's hoping you'll see Tasha ski and possibly coach her. If not, is there someone you would recommend? I'll take care of the costs personally." Hannah took a deep breath, then another sip of wine.

"You remind me of Grace," Max said. "A soft heart."

"I'll take that as a compliment," Hannah replied.

"As it was meant."

"Thanks," she said. "Do you have someone in mind? I would love to be able to help those two kids, especially this time of year." She couldn't believe she had just said that.

Especially this time of year. Whatever happened to Ms. Scrooge?

Camden might be onto something with this holiday stuff. Maybe Hannah was getting a bit soft in her old age. Of course she wasn't *that* old, but still.

"I will personally invite Terrence and Tasha to the party we're having Sunday evening. I'm lighting up a couple of the trails. Ella's all excited this year. She's at that age where everything is fascinating to her."

"I can only imagine," Hannah said for lack of a better response. She knew that Ella was around three or four, and that was about it. "I really am serious, Max. If Tasha shows signs of talent, I want to . . . sponsor her, or whatever they do these days. In addition to all the stock Dad left me, I've got millions in the bank just sitting there earning a paltry bit of interest. I'd much rather see some of that money used to help Tasha's career if she's anywhere near as good as Terrence says."

"I will take care of your request, I promise. If Tasha really wants to ski, I'll train her myself. Ella's not interested yet. Patrick's stepdaughters, Amanda and Ashley, love to ski, but I don't think they're interested in a career. I need something else to do besides run this crazy resort. Speaking of that, I want to give you some of the details, but Liam is late. Seems he got stuck in the Hummer, and I had to send Patrick to pick him up. That's why I'm running behind. I should have told you. If you want to call it a night, I'll certainly understand. I know Liam would, too."

"No," she practically shouted. She lowered her voice. She didn't want Max to see how excited she'd gotten at the mention of Liam's name. "This is important. We need to get started as soon as possible. I'm not here to play," she added.

"I take it you didn't open the box Mandy gave you?"

The box! She'd forgotten all about it when she'd arrived at the condo. After having her coffee and talking to Camden, she'd taken a long bath, then had to rush to make sure she was ready promptly at eight o'clock. She hadn't wanted to keep William waiting outside her door.

"No. I'm sorry I didn't get around to it. I was a bit rushed," she explained.

"No worries. You can open it later."

The cowboy returned to the table just in time to greet Liam and another man. When she saw him, her entire being filled with happiness. "Ms. Ray, Max, sorry I'm late. I couldn't get that damned Hummer to move."

"Patrick is the resident Hummer expert. I'm sure he can take care of whatever it needs," Max said.

"Now that we're here, let me introduce Patrick to you, Hannah."

She stood and held out her hand, "Nice to meet you."

"Likewise," he said, then they all sat down. Liam sat next to her, while Max and Patrick sat across from them. Perfect arrangement, she thought excitedly.

"Patrick is the one who discovered the money missing from The Snow Zone. That's our biggest ski shop. Stephanie, his wife, is the manager, but since they've had little Shannon, she hasn't wanted to work too much, and I can't say that I blame her. Candy Lee, her assistant, has taken over Stephanie's position until she goes back to college after the New Year. She's worked for me since she was in high school. I trust her implicitly, so we can rule her out."

Liam wore a dark gray sweater over a chambray shirt. She saw that he still wore the jeans he'd had on earlier, but he'd added socks and boots. And she'd seen him remove a heavy-duty black parka when he came inside. He wasn't really dressed for this kind of weather, either. She liked that about him, too. He wasn't a wuss. She'd dated a few of those and had vowed never to do so again.

"And where do I come in? You said you're being hacked. How do you know this, and what's being messed with?" Liam asked.

"All of the bank accounts associated with The Snow Zone. Every other day there is a wireless transfer. And apparently, the bank believes it to be legitimate. I've contacted the fraud unit, so they're aware of what I suspect, but at this point they're telling me there isn't anything they can do since the transfers appear legit," Patrick explained. "Max, Grace, Stephanie, and I are the only ones with access to the bank accounts. And I know for a fact that we're not ripping Max off."

Did Hannah detect a trace of defensiveness in Patrick's attitude, or was he simply at a complete loss, just as Max appeared to be? She watched him as Liam continued with his questions.

"Of course you're not, don't even go there," Max said, shaking his head.

"When did the first transfer take place?" Liam asked. He pulled out the iPad he'd tucked inside the back of his jeans. His fingers moved across the touch screen so fast, Hannah could see why he was so skilled. He didn't waste a second. "And how much was taken?"

"Exactly one month ago today," Patrick said.

"And it was twenty-five thousand dollars," Max said.

"Whew! That's a pretty hefty sum," Liam said, as his finger continued to fly across the touch screen.

"What about new employees? Do you perform background checks? Anyone you've hired who might have a bit of computer knowledge they forgot to mention on their job application?" Hannah asked. Though she'd left her laptop in the condo, she did have a small pad and pen in her purse. She removed it and started taking notes. When she saw Liam smile, she said, "I'm a pen-and-paper kind of girl." As soon as she said it, she wished she could take it back. She wasn't a girl at all. She was a grown woman and didn't want to come off as some sappy, lovestruck kid. But he didn't know that, so she felt she was safe for now.

Lovestruck?

She would definitely have to think about that word, but not now. Later. When she had time to truly contemplate what was going on in her head. It had to be altitude-related, didn't it?

"We hire dozens of people. Almost daily. Most of them are seasonal, here to work and ski for free. It's the skiers' way. They come from all over the world. We do a basic background check, drug testing, but that's it. People come and go so often, I sometimes wonder why I even bother," Patrick said.

"Because you're the general manager and it's part of your job. And you're damned good at it, so don't start blaming yourself," Max insisted. "This could happen to any business, especially one the size of this one."

"How much do you take in daily? Just at The Snow Zone," Hannah asked.

Patrick looked at Max. "You really want

me to give her the figures?"

"Of course I do. We can trust Hannah and Liam, and it's not like I'm cheating the IRS, for crying out loud!" Max seemed a bit ticked that Patrick wouldn't want to give them the financial figures.

Patrick removed a pen from his pocket, scribbled something on his cocktail napkin, then slid it across the table for both Hannah and Liam to see.

"Okay, so we are talking big, big bucks. Whoever is doing this knows that, compared to this" — Hannah tapped her index finger on the cocktail napkin — "twenty-five thousand dollars is pocket change. To the resort. To them, most likely, it's a small fortune."

"So what can we do to catch whoever is doing this?" Max asked.

Liam spoke first. "I'll need to get into your system, which should be pretty simple since we're not talking about an entire floor of servers or anything like it. It shouldn't be hard to track. I'll want to set up in The Snow Zone, if possible, since that's where the shop's main computer is located. If not, I can access it by other means."

"I can work as extra holiday help," Hannah said. "The sad part is, I know absolutely nothing about ski equipment, or skiing, for that matter."

"We could send you in as a live model," Liam suggested. "You've certainly got the looks and build for it. You could wear a new ski suit every day, entice the customers to purchase whatever you're wearing."

Hannah was glad the lighting in the room was dim because she could feel the heat rising to her face. A model? And he thought she had the looks *and* the body for such a job? She didn't know whether to laugh or call him a sexist for eyeing her up. Though she'd certainly had her eyes on him.

"Hannah?" Max asked, "would you be willing to do that? I agree with Liam. It's actually a fantastic marketing idea. If sales increase, I'll make sure to do this again. So, what do you say?"

"That's fine, but I have one favor to ask." She knew she was about to come off as silly, but what the hell, she was about to become a model, and she was a blonde. "If anyone, and I mean anyone, lays a hand on me, I want your permission to knock the shit out of him."

All three men looked at her as though she'd lost her mind, then they all started laughing. Softly at first, then it got a bit louder, and a bit louder still. So loud, in fact, that Cowboy returned to the table with another man whom Hannah guessed to be the manager.

"I take it that means yes," Hannah said, then stood up, letting them know she was truly ready to leave.

They all nodded and watched her as she stormed out of the room.

Liam was the first to get up and follow her. "Hannah," he called out when he saw her enter the ladies' room. "Wait."

She stood at the sink and splashed her face with cold water. The door creaked open slowly. She didn't look to see who it was because she was too pissed to care. She tossed another handful of cold water on her face. What the hell had she gotten herself into? Was she supposed to prance around in some stupid ski costume and let the customers cop a feel just because they could?

"Hannah?" Liam came up behind her, and she practically jumped out of her skin.

"This is the ladies' room, you idiot! Get out!"

"Calm down, Hannah. You've mistaken the guys' reaction. Trust me, I know what I'm talking about."

She grabbed several paper towels and rubbed them against her face. "Then fill me in. I have never felt so degraded in my life! I am a professional, a freaking attorney, not some, some . . . hot-looking chick who needs perverts pawing all over her."

"And we all agree with you. You're not that kind of woman; I mean, you're hot, but not in that way." He stopped, as though trying to piece together what he really wanted to say, and it wasn't coming out right. "Look, no one meant to offend you. And I certainly didn't mean to imply anything . . . bimbo-ish." He raised his eyes to meet hers. "God knows you're anything but that, Hannah. Trust me, you're . . ." He couldn't say what he really wanted to say. Not now. Way, way too soon to be having the kind of thoughts he was having.

"I'm what? Go on, I can take it."

"Okay, but remember this is coming from me as a man, and not a professional. You are gorgeous, Hannah Ray, you're built better than most models, and, yes, I looked, and, no, I am not sorry."

Well, she didn't have a snappy comeback for any of that, so she said what came naturally. "Thank you. I think," she said. "I'd better get back to the table. I am so hungry I could eat a bear."

"Me, too," Liam said, and opened the door for her. He stood beside the door. "Ladies first."

CHAPTER 10

Hannah wanted to open the box, but she was too tired. As soon as William escorted her back to the condo, all she could think about was sleep. Tomorrow. The box would keep another few hours. She was on Florida time still, and even though there was only a two-hour time difference, she felt it in seconds. She tossed her wool skirt and sweater on the floor, grabbed a pair of Miss Piggy pajamas from the luggage she'd yet to unpack, then found the closest bedroom and practically fell on top of the bed. After pulling the heavy covers over her, it was only minutes before she drifted off into a deep, heavy sleep.

The xylophone tone of her cell phone woke her. She opened her eyes and tried to familiarize herself with her surroundings. Then she remembered she was in Colorado, and why she was here. And then she remembered last night.

Her cell phone continued to ring in that annoying tone. "Okay, okay," she muttered as she threw the covers aside. Her cell phone was lying on the bathroom counter, where she'd left it last night. She slid her finger across the phone to answer the call. "Hello," she said in a dry voice.

"I take it you just woke up," Liam said in his sexy, slightly accented voice.

"You'd be right. What do you want?" she asked, none too kindly.

"Did you forget we start our new jobs today?"

Dang! She'd overslept. "Uh, no. I just overslept. Tell me what the plans are." She needed William right now. She'd bet anything he could make a mean pot of coffee. She saw his card and was tempted to pick it up and call, but since she was already on the phone, it would make no sense whatsoever to have Liam hold on while she called William over to make her coffee. Instead, she went to the kitchen and proceeded to prepare a pot for herself. As soon as she hit the BREW button, she wandered into the great room, saw that the fire was still slightly ablaze, tossed a log on top of the red embers, then plopped on the sofa to admire the view. She was still waiting for Liam to tell her the plans when she heard a knock

93

on the door. "I'll call you back," she said, then hit the END button and tossed the phone on the chair.

Another knock. "Be right there," she said, wondering if anyone had any patience this morning. Or manners.

She yanked the door open without bothering to look through the peephole.

"Good morning to you," came Liam McConnell's cheerful voice.

She instantly became wide-awake. She instantly looked down at her Miss Piggy pajamas. "Oh shit. Come on in."

He roared with laughter. "There is nothing pretentious about you, is there?" he asked as he followed her into the kitchen.

"If there was, it's gone now," she muttered as she filled two mugs with coffee. "Sit. And don't speak until I finish my coffee."

He did as instructed, but he didn't let her command distract him from gazing at her. His blue eyes were the color of the sky at night, his smile as white and clear as a perfect pearl. Hannah quickly finished her coffee and got up to pour herself a second cup. "You want more?" she asked.

"No, I'm fine. I had a pot of coffee at the restaurant this morning."

"What time is it, anyway?" she asked.

"Ten after twelve," he said, looking at his watch.

"What? I never sleep this late!" Embarrassed, Hannah tried to come up with a possible reason why she'd slept so long. It had to be the altitude. "Do I look sick to you?" she asked him.

"No. Do you feel bad?"

Did she? She wasn't sure. "I don't know."

"Why don't you take a hot shower? I'll whip up something to eat and then we can get down to business."

She nodded. "Sure, I'll be just a few minutes." She warmed her coffee and took it with her. She glanced at the clock on the opposite side of the table. Unless it was wrong . . . no, Liam had said it was after twelve. She ran back into the great room to get her cell phone. She knew the time automatically changed when she entered a different time zone. She found it lying in the chair she'd vacated earlier. She looked at the clear white numbers. It was ten after seven. Seven in the morning.

"Liam McConnell, you ass!" she shouted before heading back to her room. She was going to give him a piece of her mind as soon as she showered and dressed. Noon, my ass, she thought as she turned on the water and took a scalding-hot shower.

Ten minutes later, she returned to the kitchen, where Liam had made himself at home. Not that she cared. The smell of frying bacon and toast made her realize just how hungry she was. She'd ordered a bowl of soup for dinner last night, and it hadn't been enough, but at the time she hadn't wanted to linger at Eagles Nest any longer than she had to. She'd been too tired to think straight. Now, she was clearheaded and starving.

"So you can cook, too," she said as she poured herself a third cup of coffee.

"I can do many things," he assured her, keeping his back to her.

"And I can only imagine what they are," she tossed back.

He filled a plate with a dollop of scrambled eggs and two slices of thick bacon and gave it to her.

"Toast and jam are on the table. And you don't have to imagine anything if you'd rather not."

"Thanks, but imagination is good. Seriously, though, you didn't have to do this. But then again, you didn't have to call me and wake me up this early. So maybe you did have to do this. If I remember correctly, The Snow Zone doesn't open until nine."

"And you were going to sleep until what,

eight thirty?"

"You're here, I'm awake, it doesn't matter now. So" — she forked up a bit of egg — "how are we going to work this today?"

"Max wanted you to wear the ski suit that's in the box you probably still haven't opened. Said it's the spiffiest — his words not mine — ski suit on the market. You'll be representing the manufacturer. Max will give you a new suit each day, and you'll just walk around. Kind of like the casino girls do out in Vegas."

He laughed and held up his hand. "I'm teasing. Seriously, I would ask Candy Lee. Max said she knows what the customers want, so let's wait until we're there before we get all bent out of shape."

"I'm not 'all bent out of shape,' Liam, trust me. I just don't like being lied to, that's all."

"I'm sorry. I don't require much sleep. I assume the rest of the world doesn't either. I promise not to wake you again."

Hannah nodded and chewed her food. "Apology accepted. What about you? Are you going to be able to work at The Snow Zone or not?"

"Max wants me to set up in his office. I can connect from there. This isn't a complicated system, so there shouldn't be a problem."

As ticked as she was that he'd awakened her and seen her at her worst, she felt a tiny bit sad at the thought that they weren't going to be working together. In the same building. Lovestruck, isn't that what she'd thought last night before she'd responded to the guys' reaction to her when she'd asked if it was okay if she kicked butt if she were touched in a way she wasn't comfortable with? Yes, it was, and she was not going to go there. Not now.

"Good. I'll want to take a look at the applications for the past three months to start."

"Done. Though they're electronic. You've a computer with you?"

"Yes." She went to the bedroom and grabbed her laptop and cord, bringing both to the kitchen table. "I guess this will work as an office," she said, indicating the kitchen with a bob of her head. She booted up her laptop, then hit a few keys. "Send me the applications to this address." She turned the computer around so he could read the e-mail address. He touched the iPad screen a few times, then Hannah heard the familiar ring letting her know she had mail. She opened the files and started reading through them. Nothing stood out, nothing unusual, but she knew that finding something unusual was the exception, not the rule. It was the things that didn't stand out that were often overlooked.

"I sent you the ones I haven't looked at, just so we're not doing double the work," Liam explained as he continued to read the applicants' information.

Hannah finished her toast, rinsed her plate, and placed it in the dishwasher. "You want more coffee? I can make another pot," she said, just to be nice. He *had* made her breakfast.

"No, I'm good."

Hannah quickly cleaned up the breakfast dishes, then headed back to her room, where she'd left the box. Knowing what was inside kind of ruined the excitement for her. She and her father rarely exchanged gifts at Christmas, so the only time she really had had presents as a child was on her birthday, and since that was on Christmas Eve, they were always wrapped in Christmas wrap. She didn't know why, but as a child, it had always made her sad to have her gifts wrapped that way. It was as though her birthday was just too close to the holidays to bother with anything extra. Maybe this was behind her reason for not bothering with the holidays? Her father had tried to be both a mother and a father to her, but there were some things a child needed. Specially wrapped birthday gifts were one of those things. If she ever had children, she would make such a big deal over their birthdays that they would remember them forever as being the best days of their lives.

Crap! She was going off track again. It had to be this altitude. She was going to down about ten gallons of water. Isn't that what Pierce had told her to do? Without another thought, she removed the bows and carefully unwrapped the pretty paper.

She removed a shiny red jacket with matching ski pants from the box. "Nice." A matching hat, gloves, and scarf followed. A pair of red UGGs. "Nice again," she said out loud. How did Max know that red was her favorite color, or was it just a co-incidence? No matter, she liked what she saw. She read the size, and it was also cor-rect. Grace must've taken a good guess. Women were talented at that sort of thing. There were no tags to remove, and she wasn't sure what she should put on first, then she saw the handwritten list.

The red-hot chilis and the matching top. The red wool ski socks, the ski pants, the red-and-gray shirt, then the jacket. The handwriting looked to be that of a young girl. She'd bet this came from Candy Lee, the young college student who was managing the ski shop while Stephanie was away on an indeterminate maternity leave.

She needed to look the part, so she went into the bathroom, braided her long hair in a French braid, then proceeded to apply her makeup as though she truly were a fashion model. She had good skin, so she added a bit of tinted moisturizer. She needed to look like an outdoorsy type. She was, but in a beachy way. She applied bronzer, then a dusting of rose-tinted blush across her cheeks. Using black liquid eyeliner, she lined both eyes, flicking the edge up to give her a bit of a cat's-eye look. Two coats of mascara and a swipe of Dr Pepper–flavored lip balm. She checked her reflection in the mirror. Not bad for thirty-three, she thought. The beginnings of crow's-feet were starting to form around her eyes. She'd have to be much more diligent with the sunscreen. She was a Floridian, and Floridians used sunscreen as if it were hand lotion. She certainly did, and so had her father, which was probably one of the reasons he had aged so well. She grabbed her purse and her ski jacket. She felt a swirl of excitement as she headed back to the kitchen.

Hannah couldn't wait to see Liam's reaction when he saw her.

She found him still seated at the kitchen table. When he realized she was standing there, he looked away from his iPad.

He simply stared at her. There were no words needed. Hannah could tell he thought she was hot. Very hot.

She gave him a sexy grin, then twirled around. "So, think I'll pass as a model?"

"I'd hire you in a heartbeat," he said, then stood. "Let's get this show on the road."

CHAPTER 11

They rode to The Snow Zone together in the yellow Hummer. "I take it this thing isn't going to leave us stranded," she quipped as they wound over the winding road that led to the main area of Maximum Glide and The Snow Zone.

"There wasn't anything wrong with it last night. Patrick said it didn't move because I left the emergency brake on."

Hannah laughed. "That's a good thing, then."

"Well, I felt pretty stupid."

"You're not stupid, just in an unfamiliar car. I always mess something up when I'm in a rental. Give me my little red Thunderbird any day."

"You look like you'd own a red car," Liam said.

"Red's my favorite color. Isn't it odd that these ski clothes just so happen to be red? Don't you find that the least little bit strange?" She needed to know if someone had checked up on her. Maybe Max had contacted Camden, or maybe Grace had. For some silly reason, it mattered to her that whoever put this outfit together knew it would be perfect for her. Had it come from anyone else other than Max, she would have thought the coincidence a bit on the creepy side.

"Wait until you see the skiers on the slopes," Liam said as they pulled into The Snow Zone's parking lot. There was only a smattering of trucks and SUVs so early. The slopes didn't open until nine, so Hannah had a good half hour for Candy Lee to train her on what to do and what not to do. They'd agreed last night that when the shop was empty, Hannah would use the time to continue reading over the applications. Liam had sent her forty-seven, and she'd gone through three of them already. At this rate, she'd be reading them every spare minute she had. She wanted to find out who was stealing from Max and why. She did not like thieves and enjoyed catching them when she had the opportunity.

Liam parked the Hummer next to a black one. "Patrick's here." Liam pointed to the Hummer. "Max says he's the king of Hummers."

"Good to know," Hannah replied.

"Yep, it is."

"As you said, let's get this show on the road. We've got a thief to catch."

"Hannah, wait a minute," Liam said. "I know we're here as professionals, and there isn't time to . . . play around, but if we have an extra hour or so, would you ski with me? I haven't skied in years, and I can't imagine enjoying it with anyone else but you."

She hated cold weather. Hadn't she made that clear? She *was not* cold now. The ski clothes kept her extremely warm. She did not know how to ski, but right now, she was willing to learn. "You know what, Liam McConnell? I detest cold weather and snow, but I'm so warm right now, I am going to have to take you up on your offer. Just to see if this ski stuff really does keep me warm all day." She was grinning from ear to ear when she spoke, so she was sure Liam knew that she was fine with skiing. "But you need to know: I have no clue how to ski."

"Listen, I was taught by the best. I'll show you a couple of moves. If you don't catch on, we'll have a hot toddy. Sound reasonable enough to you?"

She wanted to tell him it was the best offer she'd had in years but didn't want to come off as hard up and desperate. She was just picky, that's all.

"It sounds like a plan. Now, let's go introduce ourselves to Candy Lee."

They were greeted at the main entrance by Patrick. They still had half an hour before the shop opened to the public. "That suit looks great on you," Patrick said as soon as he saw her.

"I like it. And red is my favorite color," Hannah said. She was so excited, she just couldn't keep it out of her voice. She probably sounded like a teenager, but she was happier than she'd been in a very, *very* long time. And it had something to do with Liam, of that she was sure. Not lust. Well, yes, lust, just not full-fledged, knock-you-down, drag-you-to-bed lust. She didn't know him *that* well, and she had never been a bed hopper.

Inside the shop, they were greeted by the pleasant scent of pine mixed with cinnamon and chocolate. Christmas music was playing in the background. A giant spruce was centered in the middle of the store. Hannah walked over to the tree and touched a delicate glass ornament in the shape of a mitten. And it was red, too. She laughed. "This tree is beautiful."

"I decorated it myself. I do it every year. Or at least every year since I've worked here. You must be Hannah, the fashion model. That suit fits you like a glove. You'll have the guys crawling over you like spit on snow."

"Candy! For crying out loud, do you always have to be so gross?" Patrick asked.

Hannah and Liam laughed.

"It's okay, Candy. In my business, I've heard much worse," Hannah informed her.

"And you'll hear more today, trust me. The ski bums cuss like sailors and the snow bunnies eat it up. Disgusting, don't you think?"

Again, Hannah laughed. "I promise I won't be offended and yes, it is disgusting. Now, why don't you tell me a bit about this ski suit I have on, just in case one of the bums or bunnies asks."

"Okay, listen up. This particular jacket you're wearing is one of the latest styles. Made for a woman, girl, whatever, the cut is slim. Some girls really want to show off their figures when they're skiing or snow-boarding. The jacket is lightweight; the insulation is synthetic. It has a great warmth-to-weight ratio, meaning it'll keep you nice and toasty without all the bulk. You'll appreciate this when you have to pee, too. Easy to get into and out of. The pants, I meant. They have thigh vents that help to release excess heat." Candy Lee stopped and smiled at Patrick.

He rolled his eyes. "Knock it off, Candy."

"That's what it says on the label, trust me. I have it memorized. Basically, all you need to do is shake your booty a bit, smile, and leave all the details to me."

Hannah let out a deep sigh. "It's been awhile since I've flirted, but I'll do my best. Now, is there someplace I can set up my laptop so I can do a little brain work when I'm not shaking my booty?" Hannah asked.

"In the office; I cleaned the desk for you. It was covered with empty donut boxes and *People* magazines. I can't imagine what Stephanie would say if she saw how messy her office was." Patrick narrowed his gaze at Candy Lee.

"I've been too busy to clean up. By the way, some man keeps calling here for Stephanie. He's rude, too. I told him she was away on maternity leave, but he keeps calling anyway."

Patrick, Liam, and Hannah instantly became alert.

"Why didn't you tell me this?" Patrick asked.

"Men call here for Stephanie all the time, Patrick, you should know that by now. Just because she married you doesn't mean other men don't find her attractive. I'm still trying to figure out what she saw in you."

"Enough, Candy, and I mean it. This isn't the time or the place. You know we've had some serious theft going on here. If Max hadn't vouched for your character and honesty, Hannah and Liam would probably be running a background check on you right now."

Candy's mouth dropped open like a treasure chest. "Do *you* think *I* have something to do with all this theft, Patrick? Because if you do, I am quitting right this very second. You really are an asshole, you know that!"

"Candy, wait!" Patrick called out, but she was already heading for the back of the store.

"I shouldn't have said that. Candy Lee is one of the best employees we have. Excuse me while I go to apologize."

"Don't bother, I heard you," Candy Lee called out from the back of the store. "I'm telling Max, too, just so you know," she said as she made her way back to the front of the store.

"Seriously, Candy Lee, tell me about this man you said was calling Stephanie."

"Yes, you should. It might be something, or not," Hannah said as kindly as possible. The young girl's feelings had been hurt. She felt bad for her and would try to make it up to her later. Patrick was a bit of an asshole, but she knew he was good at his job. His relationship with Candy Lee was rough, but one could tell that they really did like each other. At least that was Hannah's current assessment of the situation.

Liam whipped out his ever-present iPad. "Can you remember how long ago this particular man began calling?"

Candy Lee took a deep breath, then slowly let it out. It was a calming technique Hannah recognized.

"About a month ago. I remember because he called like three times in one day. He was rude, but then I got rude back, and he started acting all ass-kissy with me. I tried to explain to him that I didn't know when Stephanie was coming back to work. She'd just had a son, I told him. She wants to spend as much time with her baby and the girls as possible. He hung up on me that time."

"I'll get the phone records, though I doubt it will do any good," Hannah said. "Unless you can be as specific as possible with dates and times."

"He usually calls in the morning, that much I know. Right after we open. I think he's probably some perv who saw Stephanie in the shop and is getting his kicks by calling all the time."

"Okay, it's time to open up. Candy Lee, you make sure to show Hannah the ropes. If anyone, and I mean anyone, lays a finger on her while she's prancing around, she has Max's and my permission to knock the shit out of him." Patrick grinned at Candy Lee, and she grinned back.

"Can I add a punch, too?" she asked eagerly.

"If you have to. What I need from you more than anything is to monitor the phone. If this guy calls, I want you to write down the exact time he called, and look at the caller ID. Shit, why didn't I think of that?" Patrick asked.

"I already did. It comes up as a private number," Candy informed them.

"Then I'll need you to record the exact time. Try to remember exactly what he says. Get a feel for him; ask him a question. Come on to him if you have to, or say something to piss the guy off. His tongue might loosen a bit," Patrick indicated.

"He's right, Candy," Hannah said. "Try to get friendly with him, see what he says. Now, I'm going to set up in the back office. Patrick, you want to show me around?"

Hannah hated walking out of the room

without telling Liam 'bye, or see you later, but the doors opened, and a crowd of skiers piled in.

And they were all wearing red ski suits.

CHAPTER 12

Hannah managed to get through twelve of the applications in between strutting her stuff and acting like an airhead. Candy Lee sold six of the ski suits at fifteen hundred bucks a pop. No wonder Max's sales receipts were off the charts. Maybe she should invest in a ski resort herself. It was almost four o'clock by the time Candy Lee told her the doors were locked. "That guy didn't call today. I wish he would. I want to help catch him. I wish I'd paid more attention."

"That's okay; you didn't know. I sent my associate a printout of the phone bills for the past three months. She'll find something. She's good." Max had e-mailed her copies of all the bills and she'd sent them to Camden, explaining about the modeling job that kept her out on the floor. Camden said she wanted overtime pay. Hannah agreed, and remembered to ask her to call as soon as she returned from her Hanukkah date with Art.

Hannah had hoped Liam would stop by, but he hadn't. They were here to work, and she had to remember that. If time permitted, maybe she'd invite him for a drink tonight. In her condo. She'd invite him for a working dinner. She would cook. She loved to cook. While she made dinner, he could go through the files.

No! No! No!

She had to forget about spending time with Liam, at least until they finished this job. She was ashamed at her own thoughts.

"That dude is out back in the yellow Hummer waiting for you," Candy Lee said. "He's been there for about thirty minutes."

"Let me get my laptop," she said, hurrying to the back office and grabbing her purse and computer.

She was about to leave through the back door when Candy Lee stopped her. "Wait! You need tomorrow's ski suit. I've spent quite some time looking you over today. I think we need to put you in something tighter, not so warm. So, this is what I want you to wear tomorrow." She handed her two large shopping bags. "Don't worry, I've got all the right sizes. You'll like this outfit, too. It's partially red. Now, go on so I can lock up."

Hannah gave the girl a hug. She really liked Candy Lee in spite of the tough exterior she showed the world. "I'll see you tomorrow at nine o'clock sharp," Hannah said before hurrying out the door.

Liam waited in the Hummer. Hannah knocked on the window before opening the passenger-side door. "Didn't mean to startle you. Candy Lee said you'd been out here for a while. You should've come inside. The kid makes a mean hot chocolate." She put the bags on the backseat, then fastened her seat belt. She looked at Liam. He wasn't wearing his seat belt.

"Buckle up," she said as he backed out of the parking place.

"Yes, ma'am. Bad habit, I know."

"So, did you work on the system? Any chance you found the thief who's stealing Max's money?"

"I have a couple of hits, but nothing is one hundred percent yet. All the hits were at one of the five or six local Internet cafés. That doesn't make it easy, but it's not so difficult that I won't catch them. They were all in the late afternoon, so whoever is doing this is probably a local. Goes to one of the cafés when he knows most of the locals are either working or on the slopes. There is no obvious pattern as to which of the cafés they go to on a given day. With only fifteen transfers so far, it could take months before an outsider could find the pattern. And it could be a function of the traffic at the cafés.

"It's not much, but it's something. I called Max. Told him what I'd found. I also told him about the calls Candy Lee's been getting. His antennae went up immediately. Did you get anything back on the phone records?"

"I haven't checked my e-mail yet. If there was something significant, Camden would've called. So I guess that means no." And her heart leapt with joy. She'd get to work another day at The Snow Zone, prancing and probing. Never in a million years had she ever had even the slightest thought that she would enjoy spending time at a ski resort, much less modeling for an appreciative audience. Never say never, her dad had always said. And damned if he wasn't right.

"So we spend the rest of the night going over more of the applications," Hannah said.

"Actually, Max gave me the night off," Liam said.

"Lucky you," Hannah replied sullenly, like a pouting child.

"And lucky you, too, if you accept my invitation."

"Okay, where and what time?" Hannah

said a bit too quickly.

Liam chuckled. "Anxious for a night out on the town? Even though it's supposed to drop way below zero tonight?"

"I'll wear this jacket. I kid you not, I haven't been cold at all today. Whatever this stuff is made of really does work."

"I can guarantee that if it didn't, there wouldn't be as many skiers out in this crazy weather."

"I believe you."

"A friend of Max's wife is directing a Christmas play tonight at the local high school. He asked us to join him. Said to tell you Grace and Ella would be there, and Stephanie and her girls, plus a few others he wanted you and me to meet. Are you game?"

She'd never been to a Christmas play in her life. Of course she was game. She'd spend the night out in the cold if Liam McConnell were beside her.

"Sure, it'll be a fun way to kill some time. When should I be ready?"

"The play starts at seven, so say, six thirty?"

"Six thirty it is," Hannah said.

Thirty minutes later, she was soaking in the tub and singing at the top of her lungs.

" 'Jolly old Saint Nicholas, lean your ear this way . . .' "

Chapter 13

The school gymnasium was packed as it was opening night for *A Christmas Carol.* The play was being directed by Angelica Shepard, a former Broadway star who'd recently married Dr. Parker North, a trauma doctor from Denver. This information was included in the program they received as they made their way to the front row, where Max had reserved two seats for them. They'd made a few wrong turns trying to find Telluride High, which had cost them precious time. They'd planned to meet Max's other guests before the start of the show, and they still would, but not until afterward.

Hannah wore a pair of slim-fitting black wool slacks with her black boots. She wore the purple, red, and black ski top Candy Lee had given her for tomorrow and its matching jacket, hat, scarf, and gloves. Her legs were a bit cold, but her upper body was warm and toasty, just as Candy Lee had explained.

They settled into their seats. The crowded gymnasium was completely silent except for the sound of a baby with the hiccups. A few soft laughs could be heard, then all went silent as the deep maroon curtains were opened.

Hannah watched in fascination as the young actors and actresses performed the story of Ebenezer Scrooge. The stage was set to resemble an old house in need of repair. The young student in the starring role performed as though Charles Dickens's tale of Scrooge had been written for him exclusively. When Scrooge was later visited by the ghost of his former business partner, Jacob Marley, the audience oohed and ahhed. A couple of small children cried and were taken out of the gymnasium.

Hannah couldn't take her eyes away from the stage. She was so caught up in the action, she didn't realize that Liam had taken her hand in his until he gave her a squeeze when the Ghost of Christmas Present took Scrooge to visit the impoverished Bob Cratchit, where he was introduced to a very ill Tiny Tim, who might die because Scrooge was too cheap to pay Bob Cratchit a decent wage. In Act Two, when the Ghost of Christmas Yet to Come frightens Scrooge with visions of his own death, and former associates will only attend his funeral if lunch is served, Hannah gave Liam a return squeeze. In the final scene, when Scrooge was transformed on Christmas morning, with love and joy filling his heart, Hannah's eyes filled with tears. This was her during Christmas, minus all the mean stuff.

The audience gave the kids a standing ovation, and the clapping lasted so long that Hannah's hands were beginning to sting. She'd never been so touched by something so simple. Though she knew the story, she'd never really connected its true meaning to herself, but this was so her. She'd even referred to herself as Ms. Scrooge. No more. She wiped the free-flowing tears from her face and sat down when the director, Angelica, came out onto the stage. She thanked her students, the parents, the volunteers, and the art department at the local community college. And once again, there was a standing ovation.

When all the excitement had simmered down a bit, Max said he wanted to introduce Hannah and Liam to the guests they were supposed to have met before the play.

"They're serving cookies and punch in the cafeteria. Let's meet up there; we'll be able to hear better."

Liam and Hannah followed Max through the crowded gymnasium down a long hall that was decorated with Christmas trees cut from green construction paper. Bells and angels and snowflakes had been placed neatly on bulletin boards. Hannah couldn't get enough of the cheery scene. How had she missed this as a child? It wasn't as though she'd had a bad childhood. Her father had been wonderful, but sadly, he hadn't bothered to share the joy one should share with a child and their loved ones during this festive time of year. Like the fictitious character created by Charles Dickens, Hannah had experienced a life-changing moment, only hers wasn't nearly as dramatic as the story of Scrooge. But it was far more of an eye-opener. She would not let another minute pass without being forever thankful to Angelica Shepard and the students at Telluride High. As a matter of fact, she had all those millions at home just sitting in the bank. She would find something charitable that she could be a part of, maybe something to help children from abusive homes. Yes! That was it. She would talk to Grace later and see what she thought of the idea.

Cheered by her newly discovered love for Christmas and the joy it brought to so many, Hannah couldn't wait to call Camden and tell her about her experience.

In the cafeteria, Max had gathered a large group of people, and one by one, he introduced Hannah and Liam.

"This is Stephanie, Patrick's wife. And this" — Max fluffed the blond curls on the head of a little baby boy — "is Shannon Patrick Edward O'Brien, future Olympian."

"You don't know that," said a young girl with dark brown hair and large brown eyes. She appeared to be around ten or so.

"Amanda, mind your manners," Stephanie said. "This is my daughter, Amanda. And this" — Stephanie motioned for another girl, who had been talking with a group of kids her age and was the spitting image of Amanda to come over — "is Ashley, who is thirteen."

Both girls shook hands with Hannah and Liam.

Next they were introduced to Ella, Max and Grace's daughter. "I'm three," she said, and held up three pudgy fingers.

"It's nice to meet you, Ella. I am three, too, but twice," Hannah explained to the little girl with dark hair and green eyes just like her mother's.

The little girl didn't have a clue what Hannah was referring to, but since everyone else laughed, she laughed right along with them.

"This is Bryce, Grace's brother, and his beautiful wife, Melanie."

More handshaking and nice-to-meet-yous. Hannah knew she wouldn't remember everyone's name, but at least when Max spoke of them, she would be able to recall their faces. Faces she always remembered; names . . . well, not so much. That was Camden's job.

Patrick kept looking around, then spied a couple, raced across the room, and practically dragged them across the cafeteria. "This is my sister Claire and her fiancé, Quinn Connor. They're attorneys, too. Quinn is from Ireland."

Liam stepped forward to shake his hand. "Nice to meet ya," he said with an overly exaggerated Irish accent.

"And ya, too," Quinn said in a genuine Irish accent. "We'll have to talk shop another time."

"Nice meeting you both," Hannah said. There were so many people, she was a bit overwhelmed by it all. In a good way.

"Okay, I think you've met most of the clan. We're all going to Eagles Nest for a late dinner, minus the kiddies, of course, if you want to join us. We'll take the gondola up, though. No snow coach this time." Max searched the group, stopping when his eyes found Grace. They were a handsome couple, Hannah thought. Though she didn't think Max could hold a candle to Liam, but now wasn't the time or place for those kinds of thoughts.

"Do you want to go?" Liam asked her.

"I'm game if you are," Hannah said excitedly. "I am hungry, come to think of it. I don't think I've eaten since breakfast."

"Then I'll take that as a yes." To Max, he said, "We'll meet up in say" — Liam looked at his watch — "half an hour?"

"Perfect. Grace's mother, Juanita, is in town tonight, so she'll handle the kiddies. She's got some help, I think." Max looked at Grace.

"Yes, her *beau,* as she calls him, is hanging around tonight," Grace said. "Mom is a widow, but I think that might change soon."

"How nice," Hannah said. "I guess we'll see you at dinner."

Finally, they were able to make their escape. When they were inside the Hummer, Hannah leaned back against the headrest. "I think this has been the best evening of my life. And to think what I've missed all these years. I am going to make up for it, I promise."

"What have you missed?" Liam asked as

he carefully maneuvered through the parking lot.

"Christmas. I've missed Christmas."

On the drive to the gondola, Hannah gave him the condensed version of her life and her distaste for the holidays.

"I've never been big on celebrations, but I never had anyone to celebrate with. But now I think that's changed for me as well."

Hannah said nothing. She let the silence of the night envelop her and wrap her in the best gift of all.

The future and all its possibilities.

CHAPTER 14

The next day, nothing happened at The Snow Zone. No calls, no weirdos wanting to poke her. And when Camden called, there was no news on the phone records. She'd stayed out too late last night and enjoyed every single moment, but today she was truly tuckered out. And to think she'd agreed to ski with Liam after they'd finished up for the day.

Max met up with them long enough to tell them the slopes were theirs for as long as they wanted and insisted on keeping two of the bunny-hill lifts open just for them.

"This is employee time, too. Don't forget, these people live to ski. Tasha and Terrence are skiing, too. Don't say anything to either of them. I want to watch her first. If I see she's got a bit of talent, I'll pop up on the slopes. I need to loosen the old bones anyway. Haven't had time to ski."

Hannah and Candy Lee went to the rental

shop, where she was fitted with ski boots, beginner skis, and poles. "Oh. My. Gosh. My feet feel like they weigh a ton," Hannah said as she slowly walked out of the rental shop.

"You'll feel as light as a feather once you start gliding through the snow. We have four inches of fresh powder. It'll be perfect for you. Have fun." Candy Lee waved and headed for her car. She had a date tonight, and she had told Hannah that while she could ski anytime she wanted, she didn't always have a date. Hannah told her that she completely understood.

Liam waited for her at the bottom of the bunny hill. She carried her skis over her shoulder as she'd been instructed. She dropped them on the snow-covered ground next to Liam's. "I'm a bit nervous. Are you?"

"A little, but you're with me. I won't let anything happen to you." He looked in her eyes, and Hannah knew what was going to happen next.

His lips were warm when they touched hers. He tasted like peppermint and chocolate. She kissed him back, softly, her lips gently touching his. The slight kiss sent butterflies to her stomach, and she was sure they were dancing. Liam raised his mouth from hers and gazed into her eyes. "This is okay?" he asked.

She didn't bother to answer with words. She stood on her tiptoes in the uncomfortable ski boots and pressed her mouth against his. Waves of desire burned in the center of her, unlike any she'd ever experienced. Liam took that as a sign and deepened the kiss. He parted her lips with his tongue, and she allowed him free rein over her lips, her tongue, her teeth. He continued to explore her mouth until the sound of a snowmobile blasting past them brought them back to earth.

They broke away from one another, and each felt a bit shy, different, as though their first kiss had changed the status of their relationship. And it had, for both of them.

Terrence and Tasha came flying through the snow once again, stopping this time when they saw that the couple was no longer in a lip-lock.

"I knew you two were a couple; don't ask me how, but I did," Terrence said as soon as he removed his helmet. "This is Tasha."

"I've heard a lot of good things about you. Your brother told me about your dream of becoming an Olympic skier. I think it's fantastic."

"Thanks," Tasha said shyly. She was petite

but muscular. Her honey-colored skin was flushed from the cold, but Hannah knew the girl could have cared less. She saw two sets of skis hooked on the back of the snowmobile. "I'd love to see you ski a bit before I give it a try. Maybe I can learn something from you," Hannah said, then looked at Liam and winked. He knew what she was up to. He gave her a slight nod.

Tasha put her skis on first, then her helmet and gloves, along with a pair of goggles. "You're not supposed to go on the mountain without goggles unless it's sunny. Right, Terrence?" She looked to her brother for approval.

"Right, but Miss Ray and Mr. McConnell are guests of Mr. Jorgenson. I think he'll let them get by without them just this once."

At the mention of Max's name, Tasha's eyes lit up like a Christmas tree. "He's the best, you know. Ever."

"So I hear. Go ahead, show us your stuff. We'll be waiting here."

Tasha didn't need to be told twice. She and Terrence took the lift up to the top of the mountain. Somewhere out there, Max would watch her, and she'd either get her hopes and dreams crushed, or — and for some reason, Hannah was almost sure this would be the case — Max might've found another gold-medal winner.

Twenty minutes later, Tasha came flying down to the bottom of the mountain like a speed demon, but graceful as ever. Terrence was several hundred feet behind her, but both Hannah and Liam saw Max in the distance as he slowed down, waiting for Terrence to join his sister at the bottom of the run.

When they'd taken off their helmets and poled their way over to where Hannah and Liam waited, Max zoomed down the rest of the run, then stopped beside them, sending snow flying through the air.

"Max Jorgenson!" Tasha shouted. "I. Can't. Believe. This."

Terrence appeared to be truly shocked. Neither was expecting to see Max. Hannah was thrilled to be here to share in the moment. She knew just by the look on Max's face that he'd seen something special in Tasha, just as Terrence had said.

"How would you like to have me as your new coach?" Max asked the young girl.

There were no words. Just happy tears and hugs.

All those present knew that they would never forget this moment: the birth of a new Olympic-class skier.

CHAPTER 15

Hannah and Liam had spent the better part of the next day locating the culprit who'd hacked into The Snow Zone's computer system. The result had come as a shock to everyone, except for Stephanie.

Glenn Marshall, her abusive ex-husband, who'd recently gotten out of prison early for good behavior, had been behind the entire plot. While serving time in the state penitentiary in Cañon City, Colorado, he'd become best buds with his cellmate, a young guy who happened to be serving the tail end of a five-year sentence for credit-card fraud and identity theft. He was smart and computer savvy, and Glenn saw him as a way to grab some heavy-duty cash, as well as to spy on his ex-wife and daughters.

Philip, the computer expert, had been out of prison for three months before Glenn was released and had used the time to case the joint, so to speak. With what he had learned, they'd plotted to steal as much money as they could from The Snow Zone. The next part of their plan was to travel to Mexico, where they would open a strip club with the money they had stolen.

When her ex was identified as one of the perpetrators, Stephanie was shocked, humiliated, and mortified. Grace and Max knew this was in no way her fault, and, to be on the safe side until things settled down, both insisted that she and Patrick take the girls to Hawaii for the rest of the year. Not wanting to put his family in harm's way, Patrick agreed immediately and was now training Terrence to act as his temporary replacement. Max would be there, too, but this also provided an opportunity to help out Terrence and Tasha. They were good kids with a bright future ahead of them. They needed a break, and it seemed that this year Santa was in a very giving mood.

Tonight was the big ski party, when the main trails would be lit up just like a real Christmas tree, and Tasha would get to show her stuff to the locals and the media. Max had dropped a few hints, and before he knew it, the lighting party had become the big event of the Christmas season at Maximum Glide.

The biggest surprise of all: Hannah absolutely loved to ski! She'd picked it up instantly that first evening on the slopes, and in a matter of two days was skiing the blue runs like an old pro. She and Liam were both having the time of their lives. She hated to go home, but she knew that while this was a special time for both her and Liam, their relationship would deepen when they returned to Florida. Her heart felt light, and she knew that was because she was falling madly in love with Liam McConnell.

And he felt the same way; he'd hinted as much when he'd kissed her a second time.

Lovestruck? Yes! Snow? Yes!

Cold? Absolutely!

EPILOGUE

The ski runs were as bright as the stars as several hundred people waited to see the girl who was being touted as the next Lindsey Vonn.

Tasha Alexander was sixteen years old and after tonight, her life would change forever.

The announcer called for Tasha to take her mark at the top of the mountain. Crowds were gathered at the base of the mountain, all hoping to catch a glimpse of the new Olympic hopeful. Though she had obviously missed the February 2014 Winter Olympics in Sochi, the sixteen-year-old Tasha would be ready for the Winter Olympics in PyeongChang, South Korea, come 2018.

All watched in silence as the petite girl wearing a hot-pink ski suit flew down the mountain, weaved in and out of the flags without touching a single one, and came to a perfect stop at the end of the run, where the crowd cheered her on, beginning to chant, "Tasha, Tasha, Tasha."

She bowed and waved her hot-pink helmet in the cold night air.

"You know that we're watching history tonight," Hannah said as she and Liam stood with Max and Grace in a special stand set up for the media.

"I know. And we're going to share our own history, too. You okay with that?" Liam whispered in her ear, sending goose bumps down her spine.

"I'm very definitely okay with it."

"Then let's go home to Florida tonight. Pierce can be here in a matter of hours."

Hannah didn't want to ruin the moment, but right now she didn't want to return to Florida. And she had to tell him why.

"I don't think I've ever told this to anyone, but I'm going to tell you. On Christmas Eve, I'll turn thirty-four. I have never had a birthday present that wasn't wrapped in Christmas paper. I would love to have a real, bona fide birthday party at Eagles Nest. Does that sound childish or what?"

"Wow! I had no clue. You should have told me."

"Well, it isn't something a grown woman goes around telling. It's silly, but I remember when I was little, I always felt slighted,

136

cheated in a way. Dad was great, but never once did he bother to wrap any of my birthday gifts in anything except Christmas paper. I always felt like my birthdays were too much trouble since they were on Christmas Eve."

"Well, Ms. Ray, I will make you a promise. From now on, you are going to have the biggest and the best birthday party money and I can plan and buy. But right now, how would you feel about taking a midnight stroll through the snow?"

"I never thought I'd hear myself say this, but I would love to." Hannah stopped. "I forgot something. I need to make a phone call. I know this is bad timing, but I promised Camden I would call and check on Leanne and Art."

"Okay. I'll just step aside and give you some privacy," Liam said, then turned to walk away.

"No! I want you beside me. In case I get too cold. You'll have to wrap me in your arms to keep me warm."

"Now there's an idea for some birthday-party wrap. Me and you," Liam said. He kissed her, then pulled her next to him.

"Now make that phone call and be quick about it. I can't wait to take that walk and smooch in the snow."

Hannah laughed loudly. This was almost too good to be true. But it is what it is, and she was going with it. All of her reservations about the holidays and men were going to be a thing of the past, just like the Ghost of Christmas Past in *A Christmas Carol.*

She dialed Camden's number. Camden answered on the first ring.

"You're late; you realize that, don't you?"

"Yes, I do, but I have a good excuse. Now, first of all, tell me about Leanne."

"She's still in the hospital, but I convinced her to get an order of protection. She's agreed, and I've taken care of all the paperwork. All I'm waiting for is Judge Sturgis to sign the papers. The cowardly hubby has skipped town, but that was to be expected. With all that family money behind him, I'm sure they'll keep him hidden for a very long time. Leanne said she wants to return to Hope House when she gets out of the hospital. I told her we would make all the necessary arrangements. You think your friend Grace will let her go back?"

"Of course she will. I'll call her tomorrow and explain the situation. Grace will help her, I'm sure. Now, we haven't talked about your date with Art. How was it? Is he a keeper? Did you like his family? Do they like you?"

"Good grief, Hannah, you sound exactly like my mother! I swear, if I didn't know better, I'd think she had been reincarnated and come back as you. I mean that in a funny way, so don't say anything. Art. Okay. Art is absolutely the nicest guy I've met in a very long time. His mom and dad are two adorable little Jewish people with white hair and sparkly blue eyes. They sort of reminded me of a miniature Mr. and Mrs. Claus, but I didn't want to tell them that, them being Jewish and all. Seriously, they're adorable. I can't wait for you to meet them. You should taste her potato latkes. They're to die for. So, now that you've caught that lousy thief, when are you coming home? I just bought Stephen King's latest book for our beach staycation. I hate lying out alone."

"I'm not sure when I'll be home. I know for a fact that I'll be staying here long enough to celebrate my birthday."

"Okay, there is something you're not telling me. Spit it out."

"What makes you think that?" Hannah asked, her voice radiating the joy that suffused her entire being.

"Come on, Hannah. How long have we known each other?"

"I can't remember. Long enough."

"Well, if you really want to know, it's been

seven years, three months, and two days. That is how long we've known one another. Long enough for me to know you're keeping something from me. Now spit it out."

Hannah took a deep breath, wrapped her free arm around Liam's waist, and whispered into the phone, "I think I've met the man of my dreams."

She looked up at Liam. He whispered in her ear, "And I know I've met the woman of *my* dreams."

"I can't hear you, speak a little louder," Camden said.

"I am only going to say this once more, then I am going to hang up because I have been invited for a midnight stroll through the snow with *the man of my dreams*!"

"You're kidding me, right?"

"No, Camden. I have never been this serious in my life. One more time. Liam McConnell, the security dude I told you about, the one with the Learjet. He is the man of my dreams, and I am going to hang up now so I can go on that stroll. Good night, Camden."

" 'Night, Hannah. And hey, congratulations."

Hannah pushed the END button on her phone, then turned to the man of her dreams.

"Are you ready to take that stroll now? I think I've got everything that needs to be under control controlled."

"Let's go, Hannah Ray. I've waited for this moment for a lifetime," Liam said, his voice filled with love.

"Ditto, Liam. Ditto."

Together, hand in hand, they strolled down the snowy path, knowing that this was just the beginning.

■ ■ ■ ■

WHITE HOT CHRISTMAS

NANCY BUSH

■ ■ ■ ■

CHAPTER 1

Christmas . . .

It was less than a week away and I wasn't ready for it.

About a month ago, my boss and mentor, Dwayne Durbin, had called me and said he was moving his investigation business from his cabana on Lakewood Bay to an office on B Street in the city proper. I was initially resistant. I mean, first of all, it was almost Christmas. Second, I like Dwayne's cabana. At one time, he'd tossed out the idea that we could use his attic as an office, and I should have said, "Great idea," and just gone with it, but instead I'd complained about its steeply gabled roof, seeing myself smacking my head into the rafters time and again, so that idea tanked. Last, I was afraid that his relocation meant he was jettisoning me, his almost partner, though I'd been wrong about that.

But back to Christmas . . . It was coming

at us with the speed of a freight train. Though I'm not a holiday traditionalist with the need to throw up scads of decorations and plan parties and dinners and family get-togethers and buy copious amounts of presents for all and sundry, the upcoming holiday and the weather report of rain, freezing rain, and then snow, diminished any interest I might have had in helping Dwayne move. He had to offer me my own office before I perked up, a small one across the short hall from the bathroom, while he took the main space. Then, finally, he'd tossed out the pièce de résistance: The new offices shared a common wall with a wine bar that had just opened.

I can throw away my reservations and scruples pretty fast with the right incentive. Wine . . . right next door? I was in. Dwayne seemed to want to stick with me, though I'd barely cut my teeth as a private investigator, so if he's game, I was, too.

Now I sat down at my desk, which I'd set up to face the door. I happily swiveled my chair with one foot. This was all right. I'd added a skinny credenza on the back wall, which sat beneath a high, narrow window. The window faced the front of the building, and I could see outside each time I walked in the door, though from the outside you couldn't see much more than my office ceiling. Above the credenza was a four-prong electrical outlet for the charging of myriad electronic devices. Dwayne had asked for it to be moved from its original place down by the floor, as he had for the outlet in the main office, too. It was almost too good. We'd been working out of his living room since our partnership began, and this was like, *real.* My cell phone was currently charging away on the credenza, and I'd propped my new laptop on my desk.

I touched a key on the laptop. I have a love/hate relationship with it: I love that it's new, I hate pretty much everything else about it. There's a steep learning curve, apparently, one I'm dragging myself up inch by inch. Computers try my limited patience. There's only one answer they'll accept or they just damn well won't work. If you don't know that answer, you're toast. I'm sure there's a computer voice out there somewhere laughing her ass off whenever I'm screaming in frustration. I've never resorted to actually hurling a laptop across the room or attacking it in some way, but, as they say, there's always a first time. I still don't own a tablet for the very reason that they're light enough to really launch. I'm too cheap to buy one, anyway.

Outside my window, I heard a group of kids strolling along singing "Jingle Bells" at the top of their lungs. Their voices weren't all that bad, but the song made my mind wander to the holidays ahead. I'm not sure what I think about Christmas as a whole. I like some of it, but all the folderol can sometimes give me the heebie-jeebies. Actually, too much of anything can do that to me. I have a very limited tolerance. When I'm getting close to the edge, like after being overloaded with Christmas commercialism and forced gaiety, it's like closing in on an electric fence. You can sense it the millisecond before you stumble into it, but by then it's too late and you're suddenly screaming with pain.

Luckily, thus far I'd managed to keep from running into the electric fence this holiday season. My mother, who lives in Southern California, has made plans with friends this year, so I've been spared a trip south, and my brother, who'd recently broken up with his fiancée and is currently circling my friend, Cynthia, told me he has no interest in getting together for the holidays unless he brings Cynthia. Since I'm still not sure how I feel about them being together, I've steered clear of any commitments. Booth had been engaged to Sharona before their breakup and I still picture them together. This thing with Cynthia appears to be a rebound, and I just see problems ahead.

I shut down my laptop and looked fondly at the brass nameplate sitting on my desk, which read JANE KELLY, INVESTIGATOR. It was an office-warming gift from Dwayne. I'm struggling not to make too much of that. Yes, I suffer from a simmering desire to jump into a hot and wild affair with Dwayne, but I tell myself daily to leave him alone. We're friends. We've been friends awhile. Yes, we've shared a kiss or two, and yes, I have a tendency to run those memories around my brain like a needle on a broken record, but I know better. Deep down, I know better. If I let his slow-talkin', slow-walkin' cowboy style and his blue eyes, dry wit and humor get to me, it will kill our working relationship. Besides, there are a lot of men out there I could date, right? About any of them would be a better choice than Dwayne. And Dwayne has backed away from me as well, so maybe we both know it's better to keep things as they are and not take them any further. At least that's what I keep telling myself . . . every minute of every day.

I have no idea what Dwayne's doing for

Christmas, and I'm not going to care because whatever his plans may be, it's best if I'm not invited. Too much mistletoe around. Too many chances to wake up in the morning after a whole lot of mistakes. My plan is to stay home this season and celebrate Christmas and New Year's solely with my newly adopted pug, The Binkster.

Romantically speaking, if self-preservation is the name of the game, put me in, coach, I'm ready to play.

I went to the door and peered into the main room toward Dwayne's desk, which netted me a backside view of Dwayne bending over a file drawer. I took a moment too long eyeing those jeans-clad legs, lean hips and butt, so I ducked back into my office and gave myself another stern talking-to.

Staying out of sight, I called, "How's the wireless setup coming?"

"Coming."

"Gonna be done soon?"

"Mmm . . . yeah . . ." he murmured distractedly.

I peeked out again and down the short hall that led to the back door. It opens onto an alley, the parking lot and the rear entrance to the wine bar. I'd been about to suggest Dwayne and I close up shop and imbibe — another bad idea, but apparently

I was listening to the devil on my shoulder, not the angel — but it was clear Dwayne was still engrossed in getting us up and running and it would be a while longer. Deciding I was being unreasonably chicken, I stepped out of my office again in time to see Dwayne run his hand down his right thigh in an absentminded gesture that was becoming habit. He was still recovering from the broken leg he'd received at the end of the summer, the result of one of the hazards of our job. Certain people just really don't like it when we probe into their lives and reveal secrets they'd rather not have exposed, and one such person ran Dwayne down in a vehicle, pinning him against a tree and breaking his leg in the process.

But he's better now. Lots better. In fact, most of the time, you'd never even know he'd been injured by the way he moves around now.

He'd been leaning over the back of his desk, but, as if feeling my eyes on him, he glanced back at me, his hair falling in his eyes. "The modem's a lemon."

"How can you tell?"

"It's not working."

Not exactly what I was looking for. "Hmmm . . . I'm impressed you already know it's the equipment. I would've blamed it on myself." I walked toward him and saw a cellophane-wrapped packet of mistletoe atop his desk. "What's this?"

He was ripping wires out of the back of his laptop, which was also sitting on his desk. Glancing at the packet I now held in my hands, he said, "Mistletoe."

"I got that. Where did it come from?"

"A tree, probably. We used to shoot it out of oak trees back home."

"Shoot it, with a rifle?"

"Yup. Some of it was pretty high up."

Knowing he was being deliberately obtuse, I decided to be ornery myself. "You know mistletoe's a parasite. Lives off a host."

"Uh-huh."

"Enough of this stuff can kill a tree. Sucks the life right out of it."

"Never known it to kill a tree."

"Can happen," I warned. "You gotta look out for parasites." When he didn't respond, I asked again, "So, was this a gift or something?"

"I bought it so that we could stick it over the door and see what happens between us."

My mouth dropped open, but then I saw his amused sideways glance and pulled back. Though Dwayne and I have had our romantic moments, I've managed to keep from going to bed with him thus far. We've

152

been skirting this issue in recent months, acting like we both have amnesia about the kisses . . . a few of them pretty deep kisses. Tacitly, we've both decided to keep our relationship platonic. That's why I was surprised he was even teasing about it. It rattled me more than I cared to admit, but I would rather die that let him know, so I said, "Let's get right on that."

He grinned at me, and I had to look away or risk blowing everything. "When I went to buy some coffee, they were handing them out at John's Market. I'm not trying to kiss you again."

"I didn't think you were."

"Unless you want me to kiss you."

"Nope. Uh-uh. That is not who we are." I cleared my throat. "I'm ready to get my drink on, so I'm heading to the wine bar."

"Should I join you?"

He'd straightened and was waiting for my response. Of course I wanted him to come, but I knew it was dangerous. We'd just opened an office together, and it was better to keep things at the friendship level. And anyway, I didn't want to admit that I had a thing for him. A small thing, but nevertheless a *thing.* What his feelings are for me is harder to ascertain. If I really push things, Dwayne will capitulate. After all, there was that time when he pressed me against the wall. . . . But he doesn't seem all that eager to go down that road again, either. We both know it would be a bad idea.

But then, I've never professed to be someone who's afraid of bad ideas.

With an effort, I pulled back from the precipice. "Nah, go ahead and finish whatever you're doing."

I went back to my office in search of my ski jacket, which I plucked from the back of my chair, and my wallet, which I zipped into the right jacket pocket. It was cold outside and destined to get colder. I'd never gotten the hang of using a purse very well, but I've given up entirely during working hours; too many times I've been forced to break and run, and I can't have a purse flopping alongside me when that happens.

It was looking like a solo trip to the wine bar. While drinking alone might not be the ideal social plan, it was better than not drinking at all. Before I left, I unzipped my pocket and took out my wallet, examining its contents. A trip to the ATM looked imminent. I'm notoriously cheap and had half hoped I could rely on Dwayne to buy me a glass of cheer, but that was not going to happen, and maybe it was just as well. I was definitely feeling kind of unsettled where

Dwayne was concerned.

Donning my coat, I debated whether to head out to my Volvo wagon and drive the ten blocks to the ATM or hoof it and keep my parking spot. The back lot wasn't large, and I could see we were all going to be highly competitive over the spots. I'd just decided to walk and was heading out the back when I heard the front door open and Dwayne say, "Good afternoon," in his Texas drawl. Most times, you can't hear the Texas, as he's been an Oregonian since he was a teenager, maybe before, but he sure as hell can pull it out when it suits him. I pictured him thrusting out a hand and giving the newcomer his slow smile, while they took in his somewhat unkempt, longish blond hair and sexy, cowboy thing. I felt a little flutter of jealousy that royally pissed me off at myself. I've pretty much blown every romantic relationship I've ever had, and I'm not going to do it with Dwayne.

But it was a male voice that answered Dwayne, not a female one, and then I was bowled over when I heard him ask, "Is Jane Kelly here?"

My first thought was to feel vastly important. First my own office, and now someone coming to the agency to ask for *me*? Well, la-di-da. Dwayne's been telling me and telling me that I have all the makings of a good private investigator, but I've been very leery about believing in what I perceive to be his bullshit. I'm afraid I won't live up to the hype, and though Dwayne's the biggest reason I'm in this job, let's be honest: This line of work's dangerous. Sure, I like to pry — basic Nosiness R Us — but getting myself killed or maimed or taken hostage or God knows whatever other terrible thing might happen when you poke snakes, which is what we do, does occasionally give me pause.

I turned around and retraced my steps to give the newcomer a good hard look. He gazed back at me, and I got the sense that I knew him, but I didn't know from where. He was about my age, somewhere in his early thirties, with trimmed brown hair and a lean build. He wore a green golf shirt teamed with a pair of khakis, the attire that's just a level or two under business casual. I half expected him to ask me directions to Lake Chinook Country Club until I noticed the anxiousness around his eyes.

"Jane!" he said in relief, then rushed over and grabbed me in a bear hug. I slid my eyes toward Dwayne, who gave me the who's-that? look, but I spread my hands and shook my head.

"Well, hi," I responded.

"You don't remember me?" He pulled back in disbelief, and I got a good close look at him.

Recognition slowly surfaced. "Uh . . . James . . . ?"

For an answer, he hugged me again, even tighter. "Long time no see. My God, it feels like a lifetime ago."

James Wexford. His full name came back to me. He and I had been classmates at Braxton High in Los Angeles. We weren't great friends, didn't even run in the same circles, so I was a little surprised by his enthusiasm. I'd left LA years earlier, moved to Oregon and had pretty much dropped thoughts of Jane Kelly, The Early Years, from my mind, and James just wasn't a big part of my memory bank anyway. However, his high-school girlfriend had made a big impression on me. Darcy Collier, I recalled with a sort of mental ugh. A real pain in the ass. Precocious and smart, Darcy had been both a brownnoser and a cause joiner, enough to make me run for the hills. She'd also always wanted to be my bestest friend for reasons still unknown, and, following my usual pattern when people alarm me, I did my damnedest to steer clear of her. My recollection of her is mostly her bubbling over with loud eagerness and me sidling away whenever I happened to be anywhere in her vicinity.

"You remember Darcy," James said now, as he released me.

Uh-oh. Taking a step back, I tried to sound casual. "You dated in high school, right?"

"Did you know we got married?"

"No, I sure didn't."

"We moved to Portland a few years back, probably about the same time you did, from what I understand." He looked around and asked, "Is there somewhere we can sit down?"

Dwayne, who'd been watching our exchange with interest, gestured toward his desk. "Help yourself. Jane's got another chair in her office. I gotta head out anyway."

"You're leaving?" I asked him sharply. "You're . . . you're finished setting up?" He was being way too magnanimous. I didn't want him running out on me and he knew it.

"Got a few things to pick up," he said.

"What about the wine bar?" I was seriously trying to hint that I didn't want him to leave, but he just furrowed his brow.

"Why don't you take James . . . uh, I didn't catch your last name."

"Wexford," James said. He stuck out his

158

hand toward Dwayne, who grasped it and shook it.

"I'll be back," Dwayne said, dropping a smile on me before heading for the door. I was pretty sure his sudden need to leave had been manufactured, ostensibly to give me some time with my old friend, but in truth, he's pretty good at knowing when I'm feeling insecure and does nothing to help me, which pisses me off no end.

"Wine bar?" James asked.

"Follow me," I said, leading him down the hall to the back door.

Five minutes later, we were seated at one of the small booths lining one wall of Wine About It. We'd eschewed the bistro tables scattered around the room for something more private. A man and a woman sat at the bar, which was a huge slab of blondish wood with whorls and knotholes that had been smoothed and lacquered to a high gloss. They each had a glass of red wine and a flagon between them and had their heads close together.

James settled himself across from me and folded his arms on the wood top, a piece of prefab with none of the bar's character, though smooth and lacquered as well. My mind's eye was still watching Dwayne leave through our office's glass door, climb into his truck, which was parked out front, and drive away.

"Darcy's in trouble and she needs your help," James said.

The waitress brought us a menu with their wine and appetizers. I glanced down at the list of almonds, olives, a chèvre disk with lavender and fennel served with honey and nuts, various wheat crackers and bread sticks, and wanted them all. Holding myself back, I asked for a glass of cabernet, the cheapest on the menu though at a price that still caused my heart to palpitate, especially since I wasn't sure how much cash I had and didn't want to add to my credit card debt. But then James stepped in and ordered for me, in that proprietary way real wine connoisseurs — or at least the ones who think they are — are wont to do. I would have objected, but he finished with, "I'm buying," so I kept my mouth shut apart from saying thank you and just waited. What the hell, a free drink is a free drink, and free is a very good price.

In the name of fairness, I said, "Before we go any further, you should know Dwayne's the man in charge of Dwayne Durbin Investigations."

"But you work there."

"I work for him," I agreed. "But he's the man. Truly. I know you and I are acquaintances —"

"Friends," he corrected.

"— but you'd be better served by Dwayne."

"Well, he's not here now, is he?" He lifted his glass and waited for me to do the same. We clinked rims and then tasted the wine. So, okay, I'm not a wine connoisseur by any stretch of the imagination, but . . . it was pretty damn good. I wanted to leave it on my tongue awhile, and I think I might have lost track of the moment because I missed something and caught up only when I heard him say, ". . . didn't hang around. Besides, I want you. You, me and Darcy . . . we all come from the same place. We're compadres, y'know? You gotta hang onto that stuff. Friendship. *Roots.* That's what it's all about."

I never think of Los Angeles as a town where one has deep roots. Everybody there seems to be from somewhere else, but okay, my family and his and Darcy's had been there long enough for us to graduate high school. However, no matter what James was trying to sell me, I knew I didn't come from the same place as James and Darcy, not in terms of social equality, at any rate. Both of them were from wealthy SoCal families, whereas my brother and I had been raised by a single mother after dear old Dad ran off with his secretary and started a new brood with her. Let me add that I have no contact with either my father or those half siblings, which works for me and, apparently, for them, too.

But the point is, by no means were Darcy, James and I from the same place socially or economically, though my mother always made sure Booth and I had everything we needed and has done all right for herself over the years. My common ground with Darcy and James began and ended at Braxton High. Go, Tigers.

"We need to hire you," James was going on. "Just tell me what your rates are; we can pay. Darcy and I are very comfortable."

"Well, that's great," I answered, for lack of anything better to say. I didn't know what Darcy's problem was, but the last thing I wanted to do was reunite with either one of my old classmates. Was I being crabby and unreasonable? No . . . I have too strong a recollection of Darcy swooping in on me and trying to intimidate my other friends, as if I were some prize to be claimed. She'd wanted me for her own, and she was a bull about going after what she wanted. Now don't get me wrong, I like myself quite a bit. But that doesn't mean I'm not wary of others who find me irresistible for no good reason that I can see.

"Let me tell you what happened," James said, inhaling a deep breath as if he were getting ready to launch into the yarn of the century.

I interrupted before he could start. "How did you know how to find me?"

He blinked, as if he couldn't believe the question. "Social media."

"I'm not on social media," I stated firmly. I have resisted Tweeting and Facebooking and Instagramming or whatever, and frankly, I'm kind of proud of myself in that regard, although I'm not completely out of today's electronic world. I have taken a selfie or two.

"Somebody knew about you and put it on their page," James continued. "Darcy saw it. She has lots of friends, so when she got arrested, she asked me to find you, and somebody knew you were with Durbin Investigations. I called the number and the voice mail said you'd just recently moved to this address."

He'd clearly called Dwayne's cell, which he uses for his business as well. "Arrested?"

"Darcy's been accused of kidnapping."

Whatever I'd been expecting, that sure wasn't it. "Kidnapping," I repeated in disbelief. Then, "Oh," as I considered she might be one of those people seeking to steal their own child back from an ex.

"It's not like that," he said, reading whatever was on my face. "She's done nothing wrong. She was helping a woman, and things just kind of got out of hand."

Darcy helping someone and it got out of hand . . . I braced myself, feeling that this could be one of those stories that once told would be impossible to unhear. I could already picture myself throwing my hands over my ears and loudly crying, "La, la, la, la, la!"

"You know how Darcy is," James said on a heartfelt sigh. "Always looking out for people."

I could feel my lips pinch in as if I'd sucked on a lemon and made a show of clearing my throat so I could move my mouth around. Darcy was the kid who always waved her hand to be called on in class, and she'd volunteered at every charity event, soup kitchen, and dog rescue, and this was in high school, when the rest of us were only interested in who was doing what to whom and who had the most expensive shoes. Not that I played well in that group,

164

either, as I had a tendency to read books and play video games and generally wait for high school to end. I've always kind of known Darcy's interest in me ran in the she-needs-to-be-rescued vein, which I strenuously objected to, though she paid me no mind. Luckily, she'd fastened onto boys somewhere in there, eventually settling on James, and therefore finally leaving me alone.

"You know the Vista Bridge," he said.

"The suicide site?"

He pointed at me like *bingo*. "Darcy's with the Think Twice suicide prevention group. They're one of the groups that patrol the bridge to stop people from making a fatal mistake. We're all waiting for the city to do something about the problem. A lot of people could be saved if there were just some barriers erected."

"Uh . . . I thought barriers *had* been erected." The iconic Vista Bridge had been around since the early nineteen hundreds and was a beautiful Portland landmark that spanned one of the busiest city highways. It was also a favorite spot for determined suicide jumpers, and as yet, no one has come up with the answer to solving the problem because the bridge is listed on the National Register of Historic Places and would need to be fitted with architecturally appropriate barriers at a multimillion-dollar cost that's currently not in the city's budget. If you polled me on the issue, I would be reluctant to add permanent screening/walls to the bridge. I mean, people who want to end their lives by jumping off a bridge will probably just go to some other bridge, won't they? And Portland's a city of bridges, of which Vista is just one.

But then, I spend most of my energy trying to save my own skin, so I'm clearly no judge.

"There are temporary barriers," James enlightened me, "but you can get around 'em if you really want to, and some of these poor unfortunates really want to."

"So, what happened with Darcy?"

"This woman. This . . ."

"Poor unfortunate?" I suggested, when he seemed to be struggling for the right words.

"Bitch," he said, surprising me by his vehemence. "She climbed up on the barricade and was working her way around it to jump when Darcy stopped her. Darcy risked her life to do it. She took her home and really poured her soul into saving the woman. Her name's Karen Aldridge, and Darcy talked to her for hours and calmed her down. It took all night, but Darcy felt

Karen had really turned a corner. But now Karen's claiming that Darcy kidnapped her. Held her against her will! My God, the police came and escorted Darcy to the station!"

"Wow," I said, for lack of a better response.

"You said it," James agreed. "It was a real mess. Luckily, the DA is at least halfway reasonable. He suspects it's a trumped-up charge, so they're not planning to prosecute, thank God. I mean, Karen could have left any time that night but chose to stay with Darcy. Yes, the gates were locked, but it wasn't as if Karen was chained to a chair or anything. If she'd really wanted to leave, Darcy would have let her out."

"Okay . . ." I said. I wasn't exactly sure how I could help.

"Darcy's such a good person. It's just been devastating. She's been meaning to get in touch with you, but now it's imperative. She needs a good friend on her side. She can tell you more about the lawsuit."

"The lawsuit?"

"That awful woman is suing Darcy. Well, suing us. For *millions*. Can you believe it?"

"Well . . . huh. Sounds like she's found something to live for," I pointed out. James did not appreciate me finding anything a

167

wee bit humorous in their plight and pulled back from me. If he were a turtle, he would have retreated into his shell.

"It's not a laughing matter."

"Sounds like you need a good lawyer, not a private detective," I pointed out.

"Oh, we have that, too, but Darcy really wants to talk to you."

"I . . ." I looked around the wine bar, trying to think of a way to ease out of the whole thing. A good friend of Darcy's I was not, and I sensed another tar baby if I got involved at all. I could well picture Darcy plying her special brand of advice and concern on a hapless, would-be suicide, and I could see this person — Karen Aldridge, in this case — running out of Darcy's house in a panic, hanging onto the bars of the gate and screaming for help. Maybe this wasn't exactly the picture of what transpired, but it was close enough in my book. For sure I'm no expert on the mind of someone contemplating suicide, but it had to be damaging to be with Darcy.

I could also see how a crafty lawyer might find a way to make a few bucks off the wealthy Wexfords through the use of an unstable client. Not saying that was the case here, but come on. Moneyed people have been sued for far less.

James's cell phone emitted a quick beep that sounded like a text had come through. He glanced at the screen. "It's Darcy. She wants to know if you're coming today."

"Coming where?" I shook my head. "I've got a dog at home waiting for me. Maybe . . ." I was going to say tomorrow, but my tongue wasn't forming the word.

"To the house. She needs to see you today. I was sent to bring you back. My car's just out front."

"James, I can't. I really do have other obligations."

"Well, go home first, and then I'll pick you up there."

"No . . . no . . ."

"Jane, we pay well."

I stared at him, painfully aware of how much my bank account could use a boost. "I can drive my own car," I said slowly.

"Then you'll do it? You'll come by tonight? Good. I'll tell Merina there'll be three of us for dinner."

"Merina?"

"Our cook. Darcy's a fabulous chef, but Merina helps out, and since this terrible debacle, she's taken over."

I stared at him. I was torn between running for my life and the thought of sitting down to a complete dinner. James hadn't shown a flicker of interest in Wine About It's appetizers, while my saliva glands had gone into overdrive. Now, at the mere mention of a meal, I swallowed hard for fear that I might drool. I asked, "What time?"

CHAPTER 2

James and I said good-bye at the office's back door and he circled the building to look for his car, which was parked outside the front of the building. I unlocked the door and walked back down the short hall to the main room, where I found Dwayne slamming down a heavy box full of files onto the credenza, lining it up with another box. There were several more on the floor.

"You're back," I observed.

"Just picked up some old case files from the house," he said.

"Where are you going to put them?" I had a faint buzz on from the wine and was waiting for it to clear before I headed home. It was about four o'clock, so I had some time before my seven p.m. dinner with James and Darcy.

"Don't know yet. I'm going to scan 'em onto the computer and then figure it out."

"Wow," I said, surprised. Dwayne's in love

with hard copy and has made a point of making me write down all my notes.

"I'm keeping files from the last few years right here," he said, kicking a cowboy-booted foot in the direction of his credenza, "but I want 'em on computer, too."

"You're getting so high-tech, I can hardly stand it."

He snorted at that.

I noticed the mistletoe was no longer in sight and asked him about it. He said he was giving it to Darlene, his sometime cleaning lady, which I found sort of disappointing. I helped him organize files and even learned how to scan them, but at a little after five I decided I'd better go. I'd told Dwayne about the case, such as it was, but he just nodded and distractedly said to keep him informed. He'd just wrapped up a couple of minor jobs that I wasn't involved in and now was apparently free and easy for the holidays, but he hadn't asked what I was doing, and I hadn't offered up any information, so we were just . . . getting the office together and that was it.

I stopped by an ATM on the way home, and my balance reminded me why I'd taken the Wexford job. My cell rang as I was nearing the turnoff to my cottage, and I recognized the ringtone I'd chosen for my mother. I had to wait until I was in my driveway before I could answer or risk getting a ticket. The cottage I rent is on a flag lot, so the driveway's on the long side before I reach my front door. I have a new, almost landlord who has a tendency to drop in unexpectedly, so I did a quick survey but didn't see his car or any signs that anyone else was there. The back of the house is on one of Lake Chinook's canals, so it's possible someone could come by boat.

"Hey," I greeted Mom as I pulled in front of my cottage.

"Merry Christmas, almost. I was thinking about what I'd like for Christmas from you, so I thought I'd give you a call and let you know what it is, talk it over with you."

I pulled the phone from my ear and squinted at it. My mother, who invests in real estate and has managed to do very well for herself businesswise and therefore is too busy to lay any kind of holiday guilt trip on me, wanted a gift? She just doesn't play those kinds of games, and we've always gotten on famously because of it. This, however, sounded bad already. I put the phone back to my ear. "I'm not flying your way for the holidays. I actually have a case of my own."

"With a retainer and everything? Good

for you," Mom said enthusiastically.

No . . . no retainer, though the promise of money was there. I wasn't sure what kind of case it was yet, but I'd wanted to toss that out to forgo any kind of pressure she might exert. Not that she's known for coercion, but anything can happen. "I'm meeting with the client tonight."

"Oh, okay. Actually, it's something else. Do you remember me mentioning my friend Roberta Lambden? The one who lives in Portland."

"I know you have a friend here," I said carefully.

"Well, she's in need of a little help. She and her husband, the rat bastard — he's always been a rat bastard, don't get me started — recently split up. He's basically kicked her out of the house. I don't know what he did to have such total control of their assets, but he's got her over a barrel. She needs a place to stay for a few days, maybe till Christmas. I told her —"

"No."

"— that I would talk to you —"

"No."

"— to see if you had room. It would just be for a few days."

"Mom, I have one bedroom. You know how small the house is."

174

"But you have a couch, right?"

"Mom . . . no. I have a dog, and a busy life." Even though I was protesting, I could hear in my voice that I was weakening. "I'd like to help your friend, I really would, but I don't think it's going to work."

"She doesn't have much money. I could wire her some . . . maybe she could stay in a low-end hotel," Mom mused.

"No, don't do that." The thought of my mother shelling out hundreds of dollars for a friend I could easily house was anathema. I was torn between selfishness and selflessness.

"It would mean a lot to me," Mom said.

"Okay, give me her number and I'll call her."

"Don't worry. I already gave her yours, so I'll just let her know that she can call you any time."

Any time. Hmmm . . . "Okay."

"Thanks, Jane," Mom said, heartfelt. "You've given both Roberta and me the best Christmas present ever."

We talked for a while longer, and I tried to convince myself I'd done the right thing. I may struggle with the commercialism of the holidays, but really, isn't this what Christmas is all about? Sharing, giving . . . making my mother and her friend happy?

Sure, I was going to have a complete stranger living with me, but what the hell? I'd be helping someone in need. There's a reason marriages break up at this time of year, and people are depressed, and yeah, suicidal, with all of the stress that runs parallel to all the fun and good cheer.

When I entered the house, my pug, The Binkster, jumped down from the couch where she'd been sleeping and circled my legs a few times, wagging her curly tail enthusiastically. Luckily, she's not much of a barker, although she's had her moments of alerting and protecting me. I've only had her a few months, and I resisted her as much or more than I'd just resisted taking in my mother's friend, but hey, adopting a dog had worked out, so maybe this would, too. I don't know what I'd do if The Binks wasn't part of my life. I never really understood the attachment you can have with an animal until I became The Binkster's owner. It's like scary; I'd kill for my dog.

I played kissy face with her, which means I lean over and she gives me a quick tongue lick on my lips, which I thought was gross before I had a dog and now look forward to. She's very stingy with her kisses. Not really into PDA, I guess. But she curls up against me every chance she gets and we watch a lot of television together.

"I can't stay," I told her as I walked into the kitchen and pulled out her bag of low-cal kibble. She has a healthy appetite and I have to watch everything that goes into her mouth like a hawk. The first time I took her to the vet, I got scolded because she was gaining weight that she didn't need. Since then, I've learned to exhibit tough love when it comes to the food intake, so I poured a paltry fistful of kibble into her bowl and then watched her scarf them down.

"Best fifteen seconds of the day," I said aloud as I refreshed her water bowl, but she was too busy to acknowledge my wit.

I patted her head on the way out. The Binkster ran into a moving car a few months ago, an accident that nearly stopped my heart. Luckily, she wasn't hurt as badly as I'd first imagined, and she's made a full recovery, though the fur's still growing back on one of her legs. Before the accident, I was already obsessed with her, but now I've moved into crazy dog person territory. I've found this is acceptable behavior for dog owners, so I don't stress about it.

The Wexfords' house was an imposing Tudor behind a wrought-iron gate and a circular drive. I had to ring a bell to be admitted, and as the gates swung inward, I thought of suicidal Karen Aldridge being brought here by Darcy and "talked to" all night. Man, I don't know. I think I might have found a way to scale the walls, depressed state or no. A little bit of Darcy goes a loooonnnnggg way.

I wondered if she'd offered food to Karen Aldridge during her stay.

"Chamomile tea," Darcy said, when I posed the question to her fifteen minutes later. She'd been waiting on the other side of the door, apparently, because it flew open after the first rap of my knuckles. She whisked me inside, and I was afraid she was going to link her arm through mine so we could stroll along, but she restrained herself.

"She was just shaking like a leaf," Darcy was going on. "She didn't want to die, but she didn't realize it at first. When I gave her the tea, the cup rattled so much, she sloshed it on the carpet. See?" She pointed out a small brown stain on a thick carpet that covered the expanse of the large sitting room Darcy had shown me into.

"We sat right here," she said almost wistfully, pointing to two wingback chairs that were angled to face each other and covered in a wild pattern featuring peacocks. She also had a peacock-tail antique brass screen in front of the fireplace, which was merrily throwing off gas heat. It was cold enough that I wanted to warm my hands by it, but Darcy had practically grabbed me by the shoulders and steered me to where I now stood. A ten-foot-high, lavishly decorated Christmas tree was situated in front of the windows, so that anyone coming to their house would see it first.

Darcy hadn't changed much in the twelve years since I'd last seen her. She was still slim and attractive, with short, frosted blond hair and artfully made-up blue eyes. She wore a wool, cranberry-colored dress and brown leather boots and was as earnest as ever. There was not an ounce of humor in her smile, which was strained and fell completely off her lips as soon as she had me captured inside the Wexford enclave. I had asked her where James was, and she'd said, "Upstairs," and that's all I got out of her for the moment. I'd chanced a look at my watch to see what time it was: straight up seven. I sure hoped they ate on time. They'd gotten me here with the promise of dinner and I prayed we would eat first, but no such luck.

"I talked to her for a long time," Darcy said, motioning me to one of the peacock chairs. I sat down gingerly. There was a museum-like, don't-touch quality to the room. I'd bet if anyone had spilled tea on her rug besides Karen Aldridge, the person she'd been so desperately intent on saving, Darcy would have had that stain immediately cleaned and the bill sent to the perpetrator *tout de suite.*

"How long?" I asked.

Darcy appeared to be lost in her remembrance of her time alone with Karen. "What?"

"You said you talked to her a long time. How long was she here?"

"Oh, I don't know." She waved a hand. "Ten hours . . . twelve, maybe."

"You kept her here for twelve hours?"

"It went by in a blink." She seemed to come back to herself. "It's so good to see you, Jane. So good." She'd said the same thing when she'd met me at the door and had squeezed me tight enough to force air from my lungs in a choking gasp. "I can't believe you're a private detective. No, scratch that: I totally believe it. You're just the type to go out and do something incredible."

"I don't know how incredible it is."

"It's *totally* incredible. If only more people would follow their dreams. I always have, and I have a terrific life with James because of it. We've forged our love, all these years. You know, when you have so much love inside you, it's just fantastic to meet a soul mate who feels just the same."

I have this theory that people who bandy words like soul mate around are covering up some deficiency. Prudently, I kept that to myself. "So, the twelve hours went by in a blink, and then what happened? Did you drive her home? How did she leave?"

"James took her. She was crying by then. Her defenses had broken down and she'd really gotten in touch with her core. She told me how grateful she was that I'd saved her."

"She told you that?"

"Well, not in so many words, but yes. Her body language. She hugged me so tight when she was leaving . . . she just didn't want to let go. I had tears in my eyes, too."

And lo and behold, her eyes filled with tears anew. She shook her head and looked away, pressing her knuckles to her lips.

"James said she's suing you," I said.

"That's right," James said, striding into the room at that moment. He'd changed into a long-sleeved shirt and jacket. No tie, thank God, as I hadn't even considered this dinner might be formal-ish. Luckily, I'd changed into my good jeans and tucked them into boots, and I'd purposely put on a red, V-necked sweater in a nod to the season. One of my better outfits, even if I was still a lot more underdressed than either of them, but then, it's kind of my MO, so I wasn't going to feel bad about it.

"The lawsuit's complete bunk," James said. "Karen knew Darcy was trying to help her. She was grateful, until that lawyer got a hold of her."

"James is a lawyer, too," Darcy put in, smiling adoringly up at her husband. He put a comforting hand on her shoulder.

"I don't see how I can help you," I started, and Darcy's head whipped around.

"Oh, but you can. You need to talk to her," she declared. "She's been all turned around. If someone doesn't step in, she could be right back up there on that bridge!"

"We want you to meet with Karen," James added. "Talk to her. She's getting some bad legal advice, but she's not going to listen to either me or Darcy." There was the soft tinkling of a bell, and James said, "Dinner's served."

I waited as James helped Darcy to her feet, then followed them down a walnut-wainscoted hallway to a room with an elegant chandelier above a long, dark, polished table with no less than five red poinsettia plants artfully arranged along its center. Three place settings sat at the far end. James seated Darcy, then me, then took a place at the head of the table.

It felt a little like playacting, and I was definitely starting to feel underdressed despite my intentions not to, but with this intro, I figured the food had to be pretty spectacular.

Those hopes were dashed when a middle-aged woman carrying a soup tureen waddled in as if her feet hurt. She waddled back out without saying a word, and I waited as James thanked her, then opened the tureen and began ladling up a thick green liquid into Darcy's bowl. He then held out his hand for mine.

I handed it over carefully, wondering what that soup was. Note to self: ask what's on the menu before saying yes to a dinner invitation.

James saw my look and said, "It's kale soup. Darcy and I are trying to eat healthier."

"Ahh . . ."

Darcy said, "It's just such a food fest around the holidays. We're trying to keep things in line." She shook her head dolefully. "Y'know, I kept her from jumping, and we really got along. Why is everybody so *mad* now? What else was I supposed to do?"

"Who else is mad?" I asked, spooning up some of the green glop. Thankfully, it tasted a helluva lot better than it looked.

"We asked Andrew Jagger to represent Darcy," James said, pouring me another glass of red wine from a crystal decanter. I reached for my wineglass, also crystal. I was glad it was heavy and dense rather than some delicate, spindly wisp that I might snap in half without thinking.

"He works with James. Or, James works with him," Darcy said, sipping at her glass of wine. "That's why we moved to Portland; James is a partner at Connington, Long and Barrow."

I made appropriate noises and we settled in to eat. The bad news was that that was apparently the extent of the meal. I learned that Merina, the sometime cook, could prepare about four recipes that Darcy had perfected and then had her make for them. Darcy's own much-vaunted skills in the kitchen seemed to have fallen into disuse, if they'd ever truly existed. I know it's a little unfair, the way I continually judge her, but those high-school years are burned into my brain.

I escaped an hour later with the promise

to meet with Karen Aldridge. I tried, once again, to point out that they should probably just rely on their lawyer, who seemed to be a good friend, but Darcy wouldn't hear of it. She walked me to the door and out to my car, hanging onto my arm and keeping me from getting in, even though a very cold rain was pelting down.

"I'm so glad to see you again," she said, giving my captured arm a squeeze. "When James was offered this great job in Portland, I thought, 'Jane Kelly's there, so let's go.' My money's in investments and this house, so it was an easy move. I planned to look you up. At least this terrible injustice has given us a chance to renew our friendship."

"Uh . . . yeah. . . ."

"When are you going to contact Karen?"

She'd given me Karen's address and place of work, which she'd apparently inveigled from her during the chamomile tea marathon, so there was no reason to wait. "I'll go tomorrow." I was anxious for her to let go of me. Darcy nodded and I mumbled thanks for the meal, and that I'd be in touch. She hung onto my arm for a moment longer, then finally let me go.

I exhaled as I got behind the wheel. Sheesh. Being with Darcy was exhausting. *That* hadn't changed over the years. Switching on the radio, I heard "It's the Most Wonderful Time of the Year" as hailstones the size of The Binkster's kibble pounded on the roof of my car in rapid-fire, silver streaks.

I was woken from a dream about termite-like bugs eating the walls of my house by my ringing cell phone. It was the default tone, I realized, as I chased away the remnants of the dream, fully aware that it was part of the worry I had about my almost-new landlord, Chuck Narwood. He was someone I knew from the Coffee Nook, my regular morning hangout, and he was loud and full of excess bonhomie, with all the warmth of a boa constrictor. My current landlord was in the process of selling the cottage to Chuck, who'd swooped it up with glee. He just loooovvved the idea of being my landlord, and though the deal is still in escrow, I now live in a permanent state of low-grade anxiety, believing I should move just to get away from Chuck but believing more that leaving the canal and . . . well, my home, will only make things worse.

As my hand scrabbled for the phone, I heard The Binkster inhale a long doggy snort, as if I'd ruined her beauty sleep. She was curled up next to me. I try to get her to sleep in her little furry bed, and she does during the day, but she's certain that if I'm in the bed, she should be, too, and well, fine. It's not like anyone else is sharing it with me these days.

"Hello?" I answered.

"Jane? This is Roberta Lambden. Carole told me I could call you. You're an angel, an absolute angel to let me stay." Her voice clogged, and she couldn't go on for a moment. "I . . . don't know what I'd do without my friends."

"Uh, hi . . . did Mom tell you I only have a couch in the living room?"

"Yes, dear. It'll be fine . . . just fine. . . ." She started struggling again, and I spent the next ten minutes soothing her and giving her directions, and even telling her where I kept a spare key.

She said she would be by later in the day with her personal items, and when we hung up, I flopped back down on the bed and stared up at the ceiling.

Christmas . . .

The way things were shaping up, this was going to be one of the worst on record for me. Were Roberta and I going to be spending it as a lonely couple? I made a note to myself to pin Dwayne down on his plans. Then I made a second note, reminding

187

myself to forget the first one.

The Binkster and I went outside to the deck through wisping snowflakes that melted before they hit the ground. We headed down the steps from the deck to the sloped yard, where she nosed around for the right spot to squat. This always takes longer than I expect as she's very particular about where she drops her fanny. She can access the backyard through her dog door, but the job gets done faster if I tag along.

My thoughts were on the task at hand — wrangling a meeting with Karen Aldridge — and I hadn't come up with a solution by the time The Binks was jumping up the back stairs to the deck and slipping through the flap of her dog door so she could quickly get to her feed bowl. She was impatiently waiting for me as I entered, twirling around in tight circles, as I dumped some more kibble into her bowl. I was mentally kicking myself for not signing Darcy and James to a contract. I had this idea about offering Karen a free lunch if she would just meet with me, something I always fall for, but I didn't feel like forking over for a meal unless I was going to be reimbursed by Darcy and James.

So thinking, I put a call into Darcy, who didn't pick up. Maybe it was too early for her. I thought about leaving a message, but the world's gone text mad and no one seems to listen to personal voice mails unless they have to. I cut off the ringing phone and texted her:

Forgot to have you sign contract. Will bring by this morning.

Most mornings I run the two and a half miles to the Coffee Nook for my usual black coffee, but the weather looked like it could turn into out-and-out snow or sleet at any moment, so I took the Volvo instead. As soon as I walked into the place, I knew I'd made a mistake. Chuck was there, big as life, and as soon as he saw me, he called, "Jane! I gotta stop by today and check out the winterizing. S'posed to get damn cold. Don't want to burst any pipes."

"Don't want to burst any pipes," I repeated reluctantly. My current landlord had never been nearly so conscientious, and I was already kind of missing the neglect. I could maybe drain a pipe myself, but I knew from experience there was no stopping Chuck once he got started, and explaining to him that he wasn't really my landlord yet was a technicality he would dismiss as if he were swatting a fly.

Plucking a paper cup from a stack, I filled

it up with regular coffee from a thermal carafe. Seeing that Chuck was going to be there awhile, I made some excuse to leave earlier than usual and hightailed it out of there. I drove down to the new office and parked in the back lot, letting myself inside with my key.

Dwayne was already there, scanning away. "You're early," he said.

"Back at 'cha. What's so all-fired interesting about document scanning?"

"Just want the work done."

I get the feeling Dwayne's itching for a big case. He didn't like being sidelined a while, and he's not the kind who does well with inactivity. I brought him up to date on my evening with the Wexfords, finishing with, "I'm going to try to meet with Karen Aldridge today."

"How're you gonna do that?"

"I don't know. You want in?" I didn't really expect him to say yes, but when he seemed to be mulling the idea over, I sweetened the pot with, "I was thinking about inviting her to lunch."

"On whose dime?"

"Mine . . . once I get the Wexfords to sign a contract with expenses."

"I'll join you," he said, which blew my

190

mind, until I remembered how bored he was.

While I was waiting for Darcy to call me back, I helped Dwayne with the scanning. It was pretty easy work, and it gave me a chance to glance over old files that went back before I came on board.

"What are you looking at?" Dwayne asked, coming up behind me and peering over my shoulder.

I let the paper feed into the copier and said, "Nothing."

"That was a case I did for a friend," he said, moving away.

He'd clearly seen the file that had interested me. His tone was dismissive, but I'd caught a glimpse of the handwritten note he'd saved and tucked inside, in a woman's hand, saying her husband had learned of her phone calls to Dwayne. There was just something intimate about it that had caught my attention, and I couldn't completely let it lie. "Who's Lisette?"

"She was a client."

"Sounds . . . like maybe more than a client, from the tone. . . ."

He didn't look up from the paper in his hands. "Not my finest hour."

Now I was definitely blown away. "You got involved with a client?" I hate to say it, but I felt jealousy slide through my veins.

"Mmm."

"What does that mean?" I asked.

"What do you think it means?"

"Dwayne . . ." I held up my hands in surrender.

"We dated. It was a mistake."

"You dated while she was married?" I could hear the scorn around the edges of my voice. I'm not normally so judgmental, but Dwayne knows how to make me crazy.

"Before. She was my girlfriend for a while, then she married somebody else, then she called me when she suspected he was having an affair."

"Oh." That was better . . . minutely. "Was he having an affair?"

"Nope."

"Nope?"

"He was having two."

"Two affairs? At the same time?" To Dwayne's nod, I declared, "Good God, what a lot of work."

"That's how he got caught. Mixed up his two honeys, and one tattled on him."

"Honeys?"

"Is mistresses better?" he asked me.

"Not much. I can't decide whether I'm offended or entertained."

"Anything else you want to know about

Lisette?"

"You don't need to tell me anything."

He gave a short chuckle that was more like a snort. I narrowed my eyes at his back when he turned back to his box of files. It bugs me that Dwayne thinks he has my number, and maybe he does, but that doesn't mean it's not irritating.

About that time, the front door opened, and James and Darcy walked in.

"Yoo-hoo!" Darcy greeted, waving a hand. "Thought I'd come to see you at your office to fill out the contract." Her eyes drifted over to Dwayne, who was smiling at her but hadn't left his box of files. She came to attention and zeroed in on him like a laser before sauntering over to him. I felt my teeth go on edge.

She's happily married. She's not interested in Dwayne, and he would never be interested in her.

James asked me, "You have a boilerplate contract?"

"Well, sort of. Let me get it ready." Reluctantly, I left them to go into my office and flip open my laptop. I sent a copy of the contract with Durbin Investigations' going rates to the printer, and then headed back into the main office as quickly as I could. By this time, Darcy had sidled right up to

Dwayne and was cooing everything she said to him. I looked at James, but he was reaching for the contract that Dwayne had grabbed from the wireless printer and either didn't notice or didn't care.

I tried to ignore Darcy's gooey interest in Dwayne as James wrote a check for the retainer and handed it to me. I, in turn, handed it to Dwayne, who shot me a quick smile that made me feel proud. Our first cash inflow at the new office. If Darcy hadn't been so annoying, I would have basked in the good feelings of the moment, but I had to keep them in check as it took another ten minutes before I managed to shoo Darcy out the door. James lingered to ask Dwayne a few questions, which made me wonder if he was already regretting passing him over for me. Well, I had sung Dwayne's praises, so if that was the way it came down, so be it. I wasn't in love with either Darcy or James, but they'd come because of me and that's what mattered.

Luckily, all precipitation had ceased for the time being, though the clouds were low and gray as I walked Darcy to her car, a white BMW. "So, Dwayne," Darcy said to me, as she stopped next to the vehicle. "He is hot." She waved a hand in front of her mouth and whistled.

"You think so?"

"White hot," she confirmed. "You know what I'm talking about."

"I just don't look at him that way," I lied. "He's my boss, my coworker . . . my friend."

"Oh, please." She peered at me closely. "You want to do him, I can tell."

"I'm going to call Karen Aldridge and see if she'll meet with me," I said. I was desperate to change the subject and was doing my utmost not to let her know.

Darcy was not to be diverted, however. "I bet James is asking Dwayne about you right now. About whether you and he might be interested in taking things to a new level."

"We just work together. Dwayne'll tell you the same." Actually, I was starting to sweat. Good God, all I needed was for these *people* to interfere. Didn't I have enough problems where Dwayne was concerned?

"James saw how drawn I was to Dwayne. He's sensitive that way. I'm sure he's attracted to you, too."

"Who? What do you mean? I don't know what you mean," I stuttered, aware that I was starting to babble but unable to stop myself.

James strode through the office door at that moment and headed our way. Darcy watched him approach, a funny smile on her lips. "Oh, you know. . . . I was thinking about a little foursome fun with all of us."

All of us? I think it took a full five seconds to pass before I truly believed the message she was sending. By that time, James had sidled up next to her and was looking at me, also with a weird smile. I saw this out of my peripheral vision because I couldn't meet his eyes. My own were fixed on Darcy.

"I don't follow," I said.

"Oh, don't get panicky. I just meant some role-playing, but you would end up with Dwayne, of course, and I would be with my husband." She gave James a quick, loving squeeze.

"I honestly don't know what to say to that," I said.

Heaving a sigh, James said, "Darcy, you've scared her to death."

No shit, Sherlock. My legs were backing me away from them, but I ran right up against Dwayne's truck. I pressed myself against it as if I could morph into the paint if I just tried hard enough.

"Jane doesn't scare," Darcy disagreed, but then she took a good hard look at me and I heard her say, "Hmmm."

I had this mental image of Darcy rubbing herself all over Dwayne as a means to whetting her sexual appetite. Contrary to what they believed, I wasn't scared, but the needle on my ick meter had zoomed to the red zone.

"Christmas Eve would be a good time —" Darcy began.

"Nope," I cut her off.

"Well, if your holidays are full, then —"

"Not then, either," I said.

"I haven't given you a date yet," Darcy pointed out coolly.

"Give it up, Darcy," James said on a sigh.

"You didn't . . . say anything to Dwayne, did you?" I burst out in horror.

"I just talked to him about the lawsuit," James assured me.

"Maybe we should ask him," Darcy suggested, glancing back at the office door.

"No!" James and I shouted at the same time, though his voice wasn't quite as loud as mine. "I've got to get on the job," I said, pulling myself away from the truck and circumventing its grille as I hurried back to the office. I tried to be cool, but I was running and screaming in my head like a little girl. As soon as I was safe inside, I shut the door behind me, turned the lock, then skedaddled toward my office.

My behavior caused Dwayne to shoot me a curious look. "What?"

"I'm just going to . . . uh . . . put in a call

to Karen Aldridge." I moved to my office.

"Why are you walking sideways?"

"No reason." Inside my office, I threw myself into my chair and then tried to marshal my scattered thoughts. Part of me was truly annoyed at myself. So, they liked things a little kinkier than I did. Big deal. The world was vast and, as they say, it takes all kinds.

I was honestly more worried they would bring up the idea to Dwayne, who suddenly appeared in the aperture of my office door. "How are you going to invite her to lunch?" he asked. "She won't want to see you, since you're friends with the Wexfords."

"Not friends. I'm not friends with the Wexfords."

"I'm just saying, you might want to try some other tactic than just offering up free food to this woman. I know that's your go-to, but it's not necessarily hers, especially since she's suing them."

"And suicidal," I said. "Y'know, I don't really know if I'm the right person to handle this job."

"Something happened," he said, a line drawing between his brows.

"No. I think you're right . . . I'll just come up with a different plan."

"Like what?"

"Geez, Dwayne, I don't know. I haven't managed to think of something in the last three seconds."

He gave me that you're-hiding-something-from-me look, but he disappeared back into the main office. When I'd finally cooled off enough to think clearly again, I decided it would be best to do a little reconnaissance on the woman first. I wanted this job over and done with *tout de suite.* I could congratulate myself all I wanted on bringing in some business, but the Wexfords had gone from being merely annoying to downright repugnant.

"I'll take a rain check on the lunch idea," I called to Dwayne as I headed down the hallway to my car.

"Did they say something to you?" he called back to me.

"No. No. Everything's copacetic. I'll see you later."

And I racewalked the last few yards to the rear alley and my car.

CHAPTER 3

Karen Aldridge worked at a coffee shop in Northeast Portland, in one of the newly gentrified neighborhoods that offered great restaurants, bars, upper-end condos, Whole Foods stores and bicycle shops. It was on the east side of the Willamette, the river that divides Portland in half. I was traveling across the Marquam Bridge when it began to snow in earnest. Now, I like the idea of a white Christmas as much as the next person, but in my mind the snow's coming down in beautiful, drifting flakes outside my window on Christmas morning, not days earlier in the midst of midday traffic.

I made it to the shop, Joe's Jo, the name spelled out in blue neon script inside the front window. I had to drive around awhile to find somewhere to park as the place was popular. I finally snagged a spot just ahead of a woman in a silver Honda and received a stiff middle finger, a snarl of lips and teeth and a blurred vision of short, dyed black hair as she drove by in a spurt of snow and fury.

"Merry effin' Christmas to you, too," I muttered, locking my doors and hurrying through the swiftly falling flakes to the opposite curb. Luckily, the snow was a mere film on the roads so far, as I was not equipped with snow tires, studs, chains or four-wheel drive.

I entered and was met by a musical jingle-jingle as Joe's Jo had one of those little bells over its front entry. Garlands of fake holly were wrapped around every conceivable sill and counter edge, and there were red, gold and green ribbons braided through the handles of the mugs on a nearby tray. Several tables were taken, and two women were standing and talking in line in front of me, the gist of their conversation being how much they had to do before Christmas came. I moved in behind them, and a girl wearing a red-and-white-striped Santa hat and green-and-white-striped elf shoes offered up a tray of samples: itty-bitty squares of some kind of layered chocolate bar. I took one and popped it into my mouth — freakin' wonderful — and was seriously planning to snatch another, but she was too quick for me as she slipped around to greet another customer.

"What are those?" I asked the woman at the cash register. She was in her fifties and the name embroidered in white thread on her green apron read TRINA. So far, I didn't see any other employee who could possibly fit Karen's thirty-ish age range.

"Covet Bars. Aren't they good?" She pointed in the general direction of a glass case, and when I saw them in their full form, about the size of a graham cracker, and their ridiculous price, I understood the name. Covet I would. Purchase I would not.

"I'll have a small cup of regular coffee," I said.

"Room for cream?"

"No, thanks."

I was just beginning to think I'd struck out when the door jangled open again and the newest customer burst in. I immediately turned away as the short, dyed black hair was a giveaway to my bird-flipping parking spot foe. I could feel my back stiffen as I waited for her to get in line behind me. Instead, she walked past me to the short hallway that led to the bathrooms and beyond. As I took my coffee and eyed the elf with the samples, hoping for another swipe, she returned to my line of vision, tying a green apron around her back.

I didn't even have to look. Sometimes you just know. But I gave the embroidered name on her apron a glance anyway: KAREN.

Well, okay. It wasn't the first time I'd gotten off on the wrong foot with someone. I collected my coffee and took a seat at one of the empty, two-person tables. Sipping my drink, I watched her surreptitiously. Maybe she didn't know I was the one who'd taken her spot. As if she suddenly felt the weight of my stare, she flicked me a look, but it was mostly of disinterest. I relaxed a little and took her in. She was in her mid- to late-twenties and wore a lot of eye makeup to achieve that sullen, goth, runway model look. I had to remind myself that she'd recently been suicidal because her attitude seemed more angry than depressed. But then, I was running off my own limited knowledge of the issue, so what did I know? Nothing Darcy or James had said had prepared me for Karen the person. I'd felt sorry for her, but I could now sense my empathy slipping away. I told myself I wasn't being fair, but when I looked at her cold, set face, all I could see was someone in a really bad mood.

But then, she'd been forced to spend all those hours with Darcy, and who knew what that could do to a person's psyche.

It was about twelve thirty, but the coffee crowd was still going strong and maybe did all day long. I suspected Karen had just gotten back from a lunch break when she and I tangled over the parking spot. I was debating about how to approach her, thinking maybe a phone call would be the way to go, when she suddenly was standing right next to my table. I had to crane my neck to look her in the eye.

"You took my parking spot," she stated flatly.

So much for thinking she hadn't known who I was. "Uh . . ."

"Are you gonna be long? Because I'm in a tow-away zone, and if you're leaving, I'll take your spot when you go."

"Don't you have to . . . be behind the counter or something?" I asked, stalling.

"Are you staying or leaving?" she demanded.

Every once in a while someone really pisses me off and I go into confrontation mode without even thinking about it. After receiving her jutting middle finger and now her snotty attitude, I was ready to go to the mat. "I'll give you the parking spot right now, but I want something in return," I told her, rising from my seat.

She reared back in alarm. "What?" she

asked, blinking.

"I want to talk to you about Darcy Wexford. What time do you get off?"

"F-four . . ." she stammered, clearly knocked off her game.

"I'll be back at four," I told her. I thought about stuffing a bill in the little breast pocket of her apron because I liked the image, but it was way too personal, and anyway, I didn't want to waste a dollar on her.

I drove home with an eye on the weather. Snow had ceased for the moment, and traffic was moving fine. I had about two hours to kill in between traveling time, so I stopped by the office. I planned to check in on The Binks before I returned to Joe's Jo. I was starting to feel a little sheepish and downright mean about the way I'd reacted to Karen. I sure as hell wasn't helping her mental health.

When I walked in, Dwayne was seated at his desk, and his Glock lay on its newly cleaned surface. I'm not much of a gun person, but I can see that I might have to change my thinking as the various and sundry baddies I run into don't share my same feelings. I said, as an opening salvo, "Where can we go shoot some mistletoe out of trees?"

Dwayne looked up at me in surprise, then considered. "I've got a friend about two hours from here who's got a shotgun and a big farm with some oak trees. I could ask him."

"Good."

"Maybe I should have hung on to the bag I had."

"I want to shoot my own," I said.

"Thought you didn't like guns."

"Look at me, I'm evolving."

Dwayne tried to assess my mood, then shrugged. "All right. I'll give him a call."

An hour later, I left Dwayne on the phone, still trying to reach his buddy. I told him I'd see him the next day, then headed home. My mind was full of thoughts of Darcy, James and Karen Aldridge. As I turned into my drive, I was definitely wishing I'd stayed out of their messy affair, no matter what they paid me. Well, okay, no, I wanted what they were paying me, but it just was such a —

"Oh, holy God," I muttered, screeching to a stop before I hit the white van currently backed up to my house. For a moment, I thought my current landlord had finally come through on his promise to unload the previous owner's junk out of my garage so I could park there. Immediately, I knew that was too good to be true, as I witnessed a middle-aged woman and a guy in a plaid shirt and jeans wrestling a Christmas tree out of the back of his van.

"What — what — whose is that?" I asked, as soon as I was out of my vehicle and hurriedly following them to the front door.

The woman threw her arms around me as if I were her long lost daughter. I'd been moving forward pretty fast, and when she suddenly bear-hugged me, I skidded to a stop that nearly toppled us both over. "Roberta?" I guessed.

"Oh, you're such a doll, such a doll! Jane, I've been wanting to meet you. Your mother is so wonderful. You're such a lucky girl."

I couldn't see her face because she was squeezing me so tightly. Over her shoulder, I watched a man in a red plaid flannel shirt heft the tree to my front door, plop it onto the tiny porch and stare back at us with a long-suffering look.

"You brought a Christmas tree?" And here I'd pictured an overnight bag with makeup, toiletries, a pair of pajamas and an outfit or two.

"I'd already ordered it. That's how quick this has been. It's already paid for, but I couldn't let him have it when . . ." Her voice had risen into the tight, squeaky range.

I patted her on the back and tried to ease myself away. "Well, I didn't have a tree, so it's all good."

"Really?" She dabbed at her eyes with a tissue she must carry all the time. Those eyes were big and brown and filled with woe. She was about four inches shorter than I was, with ash-blond hair cut in a no-nonsense straight style that just reached her chin. She was trim and wore gray pants and a loose pink shirt. A little angel pin made of carved green glass was affixed to her upper left shoulder.

She began babbling away some more about how absolutely great Mom and I were, how distressing her life had abruptly become and how she loved the holidays, but this year was going to be really tough. The deliveryman looked at me askance, and I opened the door and led them both inside. Well, that's what I thought, until I realized Roberta had already used the extra key and there was a trail of stacked boxes snaking across my living-room floor. I have a tiny fireplace that I don't often use, so after our silent helper put the tree in a stand that Roberta had brought along as well, we positioned the tree in front of it. It looked as if Roberta had shuttled all her belongings to my house, but when I commented on the amount she was bringing in, she assured me she had a whole storeroom full as well.

"I just couldn't leave anything with him. These are my things and she can't have them!"

"She?"

"Oh, your mother didn't tell you? Gary has a *girlfriend.*" The way she imbued the word with abhorrence and disgust put it in the four-letter-word range. "She just found him, zeroed in and took him over, and he's such a dolt he can't see her for what she is."

"Parasite?"

She harrumphed. "I was thinking more of the c word."

I wasn't going to touch that one with a ten-foot pole, but luckily she informed me quickly enough, "Cheap. And crass, too. Mouth like a truck driver."

"Ahhh . . ."

A week, Mom had said. *Just through Christmas.*

The Binkster had been overseeing the deliveryman putting up the tree, but she'd since retired to her little doggy bed and had now placed her chin on its edge, her eyes following me closely. I suspected she was worrying about what would be happening next, and I felt her pain.

After the deliveryman left, I tried to apologize about the bedroom situation, but Roberta waved me away. She'd heard it all already and didn't care. She was just darn grateful she had a place, other than a motel, to immediately land.

"I have to get going," I said, glancing at my watch.

"Oh, sure. Please. Do what you need to do. The doggie and I will be just fine." She went over and patted The Binks's head a couple of times. "Won't we, boy? Come on up on Berta's lap." She started dragging The Binks out of the bed, and The Binkster frantically rolled her eyes my way.

"You know, we've got a bit of a flea problem," I lied. "That's one of my errands. Get some flea medicine. Advantage, or First something . . ."

Roberta immediately eased herself away from the dog but leaned into her face. "Oh, poor guy," she said.

"Gal . . . girl . . . The Binkster's a female."

"Really?"

This has proven to be the running gag of my life. Everyone, but everyone, assumes The Binkster's a male because she sports a face like the old-time actor Ernest Borgnine. "I'll be back," I said, and I was gone.

Dwayne called me as I was meandering around Lake Chinook, eating up time. The snow had stopped for the interim, so I'd parked outside of Foster's on the Lake, my favorite eating establishment when I feel flush. The proprietor, Jeff Foster, thinks I'm a total cheapskate and resents that I try to mooch free drinks and food off his staff. He's as much of a skinflint as I am, but he only works in the evenings, so I was left alone to ply my skills on Manny, one of my favorite bartenders. He was only up for comping me a diet cola, which was fine, as I wanted to be on my toes when I interviewed Karen Aldridge, and besides, the wine bar was still calling me if I wanted to get my drink on.

"Hey," I answered my cell.

"Tomorrow at ten," he said. "We'll have to leave by about eight."

Mistletoe hunting with Mr. White Hot. "I'll meet you at your house."

"Where are you now?" he asked.

"On my way back to see Karen Aldridge at her place of employment. You were right. No need to ask her to lunch."

There was a hesitation on his end. This

was very un-Dwayne-like, so I asked, "What?"

"Your friend Darcy called me."

Speaking of white hot, there was the jolt of pure fear. "Oh, yeah?" I asked cautiously.

"She was talking around something, but she wouldn't get to what it was. She said I should ask you."

All the crass, cheap, truck driver swear words Roberta had complained about ran across my mind. I didn't utter one of them, luckily, but I sure wanted to. "I don't know," was all I managed to mumble, and I clicked off as quickly as I could.

Darcy was someone to avoid. I'd known it, I knew it, and now I'd been reminded again. Good. God.

I was feeling a lot more sympathetic toward Karen when I reentered Joe's Jo. For inexplicable reasons, I'd found a parking spot a lot more easily my second time in the area. About the same amount of people were milling around the shop, though the elf with the Covet Bars and middle-aged Trina weren't in evidence. Karen was the only one behind the counter.

"It's four," she said to me, like an accusation.

"Yeah, I know. That's why I'm here."

"Well, I really get off at five. I just said

four because . . ." She shrugged.

Because I'd pissed her off and she'd tried to lie to me but had done a terrible job of it. I was glad she hadn't gone the other way and said six because then she would have been gone and I would have made the trip for nothing. "I'll wait," I said, taking my same seat.

The hour passed slowly. My mind alternated between Darcy getting naked and draping herself around Dwayne and Roberta hauling The Binkster out of her bed and feeding her grapes and chicken bones and everything else harmful to dogs. It was a mental horror show, and the slowly revolving minutes made the torture go on and on.

Maybe I shoulda had a drink after all, and I'm not talking coffee.

Finally, a young guy whistling "Jingle Bells" strutted in and went for one of the green aprons and Karen was released. She walked up to my table and plunked herself down. She'd had some time to think, so before I could say anything, she jumped in with, "I don't know who you are or what you want, but I don't have anything to say to you. I told that woman and her husband that they could talk to my attorney!"

"Darcy asked me to —"

"I don't give a shit."

"You've threatened to keep the police involved if the Wexfords don't meet your demands," I said. "Even though the DA doesn't really think there's a case."

"She kidnapped me! Of course there's a case." Her eyes were practically bugging out in fury. I wanted to tell her to try to keep her voice down because people were starting to stare but sorta knew already that it would be wasted breath. "She took me there and kept me against my will!"

"The thought is, you didn't have to get in the car with her."

"Have you met her? Do you know how *crazy* she is?"

"I know Darcy," I said doggedly, aware that I was treading on shifting sand. "She's a little bullheaded sometimes, but she tries to help people." It was difficult getting that last part out because of my own feelings about Darcy.

"I'm suing their asses," Karen said firmly. "They've got all that money. They want me to live, well, fine. They can pay off my student loan, and they can buy me a house as nice as theirs."

"That's one way to look at it, I suppose."

"I don't really want to send her to jail, but I was feeling so low and she made everything a million times worse. Those people on the bridge? They're not supposed to touch you. They can talk and talk and talk, be my guest, but don't *touch* me."

She inadvertently reminded me about the group Darcy had joined, Think Twice. It wasn't the main group that patrolled the bridge. That honor went to Friends of the Vista Bridge. I didn't know a heck of a lot about Think Twice, but it didn't sound specific to the Vista Bridge, or maybe any bridge.

"Look, I don't want to talk anymore," she said abruptly. "I've got a lawsuit going and nothing you can say can talk me out of it."

"Okay."

"Okay?" she repeated suspiciously.

"I'll let Darcy know that you're un-swayed."

"That's it?" she asked, perversely annoyed that I'd given up so easily, apparently. In point of fact, she'd pushed some of my buttons in a way I had yet to analyze. My overall hit was that she just didn't seem like someone who would attempt suicide, and though there was ample evidence to the contrary, once the thought was in my mind, it burrowed in deeply.

I left a few moments later, but I waited in my car. It took another forty-five minutes before Karen decided to leave, and by then it had been full dark for nearly an hour.

I followed her home. I knew where she lived. Darcy, in all those hours, had managed to extract a lot of information from her, but I felt like following her anyway. It seemed like there was more to the story, and I wasn't going to get it unless I dogged her. When she didn't head to her apartment, my antennae lifted. My curiosity increased when, after a trip to a convenience store for chips, salsa and red-and-green Peanut M&M's — enough of my kind of food to make my stomach groan — she drove back across the river to the west side.

Where's she going? I wondered and then realized she was headed in the general direction of the Vista Bridge. My palms grew sweaty as I considered she might be thinking about a second attempt, so I was relieved when she parked across the street from a nearby apartment complex. A few minutes later, she walked through a thin layer of sloppy, wet snow, up a set of outside steps and to a door at the end of the row on the second level. She rapped on the door, and when it opened, I caught a glimpse of a skateboarder type in a watch cap and baggy clothes before the door closed behind them. A boyfriend? A friend? What did he think about her suicide attempt? I wondered.

CHAPTER 4

As I was in the area, I drove to the Vista Bridge. Snowflakes were flirting with gravity as I reached the iconic structure and I drove over it slowly, noticing both the temporary chain-link fencing that Karen had tried to climb over and the two people standing stoically in the cold, a man and a woman who stood on opposite ends of the two-lane structure. I crossed the bridge, then pulled to a narrow spot on the side of the road, the only place around that had room for me to squeeze in even temporarily. It was near the woman, and she stared at me with laserlike intensity as I approached.

"I'm not going to jump," I assured her, though her expression didn't change. "I'm investigating a suicide attempt from about a month ago."

"Oh." She relaxed a bit and nodded. "The girl that's suing that . . . woman."

Something about her tone led me to

believe she wanted to say "suing that crazy woman" but thought it might be inappropriate, considering her job was supposedly counseling people from making an emotionally charged decision that could end their lives.

"Darcy Wexford," I supplied.

She pressed her lips together, as if to hermetically seal them as she bounced a little on her toes to keep warm.

"I just met with Karen, the woman she . . . took to her home," I prodded.

"I'm not with Think Twice, but their rules can't be that much different than any other groups', and we're not supposed to do anything like that."

"Darcy just acted impulsively."

"Stupidly, more like it. Sorry. She gave all of us such a black eye, no matter what group we're with, and now there's a question if we should even be allowed to patrol." She sniffed in disgust.

"Is there anyone from Think Twice patrolling now?" I looked hopefully at the man on the opposite end of the bridge.

"No, but you could ask Paul about them. He knows a few, I think." She inclined her head toward him.

While we were talking, a steady stream of traffic had been moving across the bridge as it was rush hour. The structure didn't feel wide enough for me to walk along it and deal with the traffic, too. I wanted to have a heart-to-heart with Paul, so I headed back to my car. It took an interminable amount of time before I could get the Volvo turned around and headed back across the bridge. There was nowhere to pull over on his end at all, so I drove around the neighborhood for a while before finally pulling into a no-parking zone near some houses that must have spectacular views of Portland's downtown. I knew I was risking a ticket, but I needed to be thorough. Sometimes I can hear Dwayne in my head, asking me if I've followed every lead, pulled every thread, tried my bestest. Since I'm a bit of a slacker by nature, I get highly defensive. I can recognize my flaws, all right, but it's another story when they're pointed out to me.

Paul watched me approach over a thick gray scarf that was wrapped around his neck and covered his nose and mouth.

"Hi," I said, then explained I was looking into the attempted suicide and alleged kidnapping of Karen Aldridge. "The lady over there said you might know other people with Think Twice," I said, hooking a thumb toward the woman I'd just spoken with.

"You mean besides Darcy Wexford?

Maybe her husband, although he doesn't patrol Vista. Think Twice starts and begins with Darcy, a made-up group for the benefit of Ms. Wexford. It's all for show."

Although this coincided with many of my feelings about Darcy, perversely, I felt compelled to defend her. "She did stop Karen from killing herself," I pointed out.

"She'll try again."

He sounded so grimly confident, I let that one go.

"She has a boyfriend who lives near here," I said, apropos of nothing, but it was on my mind.

"Karen Aldridge? No."

"She does," I insisted. "I just saw her go into his house."

"Sure it wasn't her brother? I heard she told Ms. Wexford that he was a black belt or something, and if she didn't let her go, she was going to have her brother take care of things."

"Meaning?"

"What do you think? Word is, he's one mean son of a bitch."

"Word from . . . ?"

He shrugged. "Check with Darcy Wexford if you want more. That's all I've got."

I wondered where the brother fit into Karen's life. I thought of my own brother, who was with the Portland PD and trying to work up to detective. Booth and I are close, even though we don't talk to each other on a regular basis. If he believed I'd attempted suicide, he would be by my side night and day until he assured himself I was fine. I wouldn't be able to get rid of him.

But then, he's not a mean son of a bitch.

By the time I got home, I was half starved, and I was wondering if I should pick myself up something to eat when I remembered that I had a houseguest. Well . . . damn. Was I supposed to worry about feeding Roberta, too? It seemed rude to just ignore her.

When I parked the Volvo and climbed out, I was greeted by Christmas music throbbing from inside my home. Oh, no, I thought, worried about The Binkster. If it was this loud outside . . .

I opened the front door and beheld a Christmas tree festooned with tinsel, strings of what looked like real cranberries and lit *candles* on the boughs.

". . . beginning to look a lot like . . ."

"Holy God," I breathed in fear.

". . . Christmas, ev—"

Seeing me, Roberta turned down the iPod she had set up in its docking station, then returned to where she'd been standing: in the center of the room, staring at the tree.

She turned to me with moist eyes. "It is beautiful, isn't it?"

"I — yes — but I — the candles —"

And that's when The Binks toddled toward me with a little jingle, jingle, jingle. Around each of her paws was a red-and-white circle with a bell on it. She walked just far enough into my line of sight for me to get a good look at her, but she wouldn't take one more step. Her expression was half tortured, half pissed off.

"This is how they did it in yonder years," Roberta said, touching one of the candleholders that was strapped onto a tree limb.

"They didn't live that long, either," I pointed out, hurrying to my dog to remove the instruments of torture from her legs.

"She doesn't have fleas," Roberta informed me with a sniff. When she saw I was removing the bells, she asked, hurt, "You don't like Jingle Paws? I saw them in the store and just had to have them. I knew they'd look so cute on your little doggie."

"I don't think they're really working for her," I said tautly, holding back my annoyance with an effort. I was going to have to have a long talk with Mom as soon as I could get away from Roberta.

I was trying to figure out how to leave politely to forage for food, but it turned out

Roberta had made something in my tiny kitchen. Sandwiches. Really good ones, out of chicken breasts she'd sautéed and then diced up and mixed with mustard and herbs and put between slices of nutty wheat bread with butter lettuce, onions, tomatoes and I don't even know what else. They were sitting on a plate on the kitchen table, even decorated with little sprigs of parsley. My annoyance melted. I could have eaten three, but I held back after wolfing down one as I stood looking out the back window at a mixture of rain and snow stippling the surface of the canal. Instead of kicking her out as I'd intended, I asked Roberta to blow out the candles on the tree, which was dry enough to already be dropping needles on the ground.

Roberta reluctantly obeyed as she regaled me with tales of how Christmas had been celebrated in "yonder years." I have to admit, after listening to her, I kind of thought it was lucky we had as many forebears as we did. Fire was a definite hazard before electricity. There's just no escaping that fact. Give me a cool-to-the-touch string of colored LED lights any day. Candles? On the tree? Really?

Before bed, I filled a pitcher of water and replenished the tree stand's receptacle. Then

I climbed into bed, and The Binkster hurried after me, propping herself against the side, standing on her hind legs and digging at my arm with a Jingle Paws-less front foot. I hauled her into bed with me and she snorted around and circled a few times before settling down, pressing her back against mine and heaving a sigh of relief.

"You and me both, Binky," I told her, then went to sleep dreaming about Dwayne in a white, unbuttoned shirt and not a whole lot else.

I woke slowly the next morning, feeling as if a heavy, gray weight were pressing down on me, the residue of some unresolved problem. The Binkster had wriggled her way under the covers down to the foot of the bed and my toes encountered her as I turned over, dragging the pillow over my head as if that could keep me from waking and having to face whatever problem hadn't quite surfaced yet.

Darcy . . .

Oh, yeah. Her.

I flung off the pillow and threw back the covers. The Binkster dragged herself from under the covers to see if it was breakfast time. I knew I had enough of her low-cal kibble left for a few more meals but was pretty sure my own meager collection of limp carrots, condiments and packets of Taco Bell hot sauce, the contents of my refrigerator, wouldn't sustain me. My memory still lingered on the sandwich from the night before, and I wondered if there were any left.

It was then I smelled the scent of cinnamon and something frying. French toast? Both The Binkster and I turned our noses in that direction. I was out of bed and yanking on my jeans, and The Binkster was whining and pacing the top quilt as we both realized that Roberta was cooking.

I picked up The Binks. Her feet were already moving as I put her on the floor, and if my bedroom door had been open, she would have shot through with the reserve energy of a wind-up toy. I opened the door and she scrambled through ahead of me. We had to circumvent the Christmas tree on our way to the kitchen, and once there, I gazed upon Roberta shoving a spatula under a slice of toast that had been sprinkled liberally with cinnamon. Her other hand held one of my plates, and she slid the slice onto it and pointed at the table, where a newly opened bottle of maple syrup stood.

"Your syrup didn't look that fresh," she

apologized, "so, when I went to the store yesterday, I got a new bottle."

"You went to the store?" I opened up the refrigerator in a daze. It was stuffed to the gills with all kinds of produce and dairy items, and she'd even purchased a rotisserie chicken. I hadn't thought to look the night before, even though she'd made me a sandwich. Guess I'm just too used to having nothing to eat.

I ate my French toast with more decorum than I had the sandwich and fed The Binkster a few teensy bites along with her morning bowl of dog food. I thanked Roberta profusely and warned her again about feeding the dog. She beamed with pleasure and swore she wouldn't let The Binks overeat. I could tell she was on board about the dog's diet now, which was a relief, and I was too happy, dazed and confused about having someone feed me to hear the warning in her words when she said, "I'm just going to unpack a few more Christmas decorations."

"Okay," I mumbled, heading for the shower. The bulk of Roberta's belongings were in storage, so how bad could it be?

Half an hour later, I was dressed in clean jeans, a shirt and a Columbia Sportswear jacket that was warm enough for the weather and had the advantage of being water-repellant. I'd put on a pair of boots in place of my usual sneakers because I was meeting Dwayne at his place at ten for a trip to his friend's farm.

My mind was on Darcy, and James, and Karen Aldridge and her boyfriend or brother. I felt there were big pieces of information missing from everyone's account of what had transpired on the Vista Bridge. Darcy and James wanted the world to believe they were champions of the poor, infirm, underprivileged and misguided when they clearly had their own agendas. I mean, the whole role-playing with switched partners thing that included Dwayne made my toes curl and bespoke of some inner Darcy that she let come out to play only when more basic desires overrode her desperate need to keep up the do-gooder image. James appeared to just be enjoying the ride, though who knew?

And then Karen . . . Though I wanted to feel more empathetic toward her, let's face it, so far the woman had come off as hard, grasping, angry and unlikable. To date, I'd never heard one thing about Karen's family. If the guy I'd seen her with was her badass brother, why hadn't Darcy mentioned him? Did the Wexfords even know about him?

I determined that I needed to find out

more about Karen. Darcy and James were paying me, happily, so far, and though I didn't really like them and I wasn't into their lifestyle, I believed that Darcy's heart, as far as Karen Aldridge was concerned, was in the right place. Sure, she wanted to be the savior and preen in the publicity her good deed would engender her, but . . . well, she was into saving lives, and at least there was something positive in that.

I pulled up to Dwayne's cabana just as he was coming through the front door. My mind instantly went back to my dream as I watched him stride down the walk. Though he was careful with his right leg, the break in his stride was barely discernible. Like me, he wore jeans and boots, but there was no white shirt from my dreams. His was denim and his jacket was black Gore-Tex.

"Hey," he greeted me as I climbed from the Volvo and headed toward the passenger side of his truck.

"What are we shooting with?" I asked.

"Gil's got a shotgun." He gave me a sidelong look as we both climbed into the pickup's cab. "You're gonna have a sore shoulder if you really intend to do this. It's got quite a kick."

"Of course I intend to do this. What do you think? This was my idea."

"I'm just sayin' . . ."

"I know it'll pack a punch, okay?" He shrugged, which I found annoying, but I kept my feelings to myself with an effort. I wanted to shoot that shotgun, and if it knocked me on my butt, so be it.

We drove about two hours to Gil's place, which was southeast of Lake Chinook and toward the Cascade Mountains. Turned out Gil Headley was something of a mountain man, with a thick head of hair and a thicker beard, wearing overalls and a gray jacket over broad shoulders. As we pulled down his long, rutted lane, bouncing hard enough through puddles for me to wonder about the truck's suspension rods, he came out with a couple of hound dogs who looked up at him with wagging tails, then at us with less welcoming enthusiasm. Gil cradled a shotgun in his right arm.

The rain and snow had diminished some as Dwayne pulled the truck to a stop and we both got out. Gil and Dwayne shook hands, and Dwayne introduced me as his partner. Gil wasn't much of a smiler. When he shifted the gun to his left arm and then offered his hand, I shook it, as solemn as him. I figured any man holding a shotgun deserves great respect.

I slid a look toward Dwayne as Gil led us

around the back of the house and through the gate of a field. No question, Dwayne had interesting friends.

The oak tree stood by itself at the far end of the field, top heavy with huge balls of mistletoe. Gil gave a quick demonstration of how to use the gun, then placed it in my hands. It was heavy and awkward, and I started having misgivings immediately. To say I'm a chicken is an understatement. I value my own hide, and my desire to shoot something had faded . . . like by a lot.

"Want me to fire it?" Dwayne asked, and there was something indulgent about his tone that brought back my annoyance ten-fold.

"I'm ready," I snapped and saw Dwayne hide a smile. Sometimes I wonder what the hell I see in him.

I lifted the gun to my shoulder and aimed for a big chunk of mistletoe attached to a high limb. The wind shook rain from the limbs and blew it in my eyes. I steadied the gun, aimed and fired.

The kickback damn near knocked me off my feet. My head buzzed a little from the loudness of the report.

But damn if I didn't blast that mistletoe apart. It rained down in fluttery little pieces.

"All right!" I yelled as Gil took the gun

from me. I can't tell you how jubilant I felt. What is it about destroying things that helps tame aggression? Nothing I like better than smashing a can beneath my heel before I put it in recycling.

Gil took aim at a couple more of the thick balls of mistletoe, blasting them out. "You know it's a parasite," he said.

"Yes, sir." I picked up a few little sprigs of the stuff and shoved them in my pocket. "Souvenirs," I told Dwayne, who fired the shotgun a few times as well, though most of the mistletoe was already gone.

I was in a better frame of mind on the drive back, I brought Dwayne up to date on my meeting with Karen Aldridge and my surveillance of her afterward. I also related seeing her being admitted by a skater dude type to his apartment, and that the man patrolling the bridge, Paul, thought that he might be her brother. I finished with, "It just seems strange that there's been no mention of him. Not by either Darcy or James. Karen was with Darcy for twelve hours or so. You'd think she would have mentioned her brother in all that time, but all I've heard about is the lawsuit and that she's suing Darcy for kidnapping."

"Was she seeing a therapist?"

I gave him a look. "I don't know that either."

"Ask Darcy. Karen musta told her something."

"You'd think. . . . Even if Karen has one, no therapist's going to talk to me."

"I wonder what sent her to the bridge. Has she tried this before?"

"Again, Darcy never said."

"Talk to her again," he advised.

"Yeah," I said without enthusiasm.

When I was back in my Volvo, I drove to the office and sat down at my desk, where I'd left my laptop. Normally I take it home with me, but I'd forgotten it and now, with Roberta taking over half my space, I was glad it was here. I did some Internet research on suicide bridges in general and Vista Bridge in particular, and sure enough, it appeared suicide victims chose certain methods and didn't generally change tactics if they tried multiple times. Someone was quoted saying that despite deterrent structures built on bridges, and the efforts of groups like Friends of the Vista Bridge and Think Twice, the overall suicide rate had not appeared to diminish. Jumpers dissuaded from one bridge tended to find another.

I thought about Darcy, doing her bit to

save lives. *I really should like her better.*

As if she knew she was in my thoughts, my cell phone buzzed, and I saw that she was on the other end of the line. I thought about not answering. Craven, I know, and counterproductive, but I just didn't want to talk to her.

The phone stopped ringing while I was making up my mind. *If she calls back, I'll answer,* I told myself, but when the phone began merrily chiming away again and I saw it was her, I had to force myself to pick up. "Hey, Darcy," I said.

"Did you talk to Karen?" she asked eagerly.

"Yes, we met at the coffee shop where she works."

"Did she say anything?"

"I didn't convince her to stop the lawsuit, if that's what you mean."

"Where are you now? The office?"

"No, I'm —"

"Oh, there's your car! I just drove up. Shame on you, trying to avoid me." She laughed. "Come on, Jane. Sorry I scared you about Dwayne. Did he talk to you about the plan?"

I was still getting over the fact that she was right outside and I probably didn't have time to run out the back to the wine bar when her last words arrested me. "What plan?"

"Maybe he hasn't had a chance to yet. We talked about things last night over a glass of wine at that great wine bar next to your building. Have you been there? The wine selection is fantastic, and the hors d'oeuvres are really a cut above. Not that I tried anything but the olives and almonds, though those salmon and toast bits really looked scrumptious. When —"

"What plan?" I demanded again. My heart was pounding. She and Dwayne had gone to the wine bar together? "James and I went to Wine About It the day he asked me to meet with you."

"Oh? He did say something about wine, or food, or something."

"Dwayne never mentioned any plan," I said testily, trying to keep her on track.

"Well, he's kind of cagey, too. Just like you. I swear, you both are trying to make me work way too hard. Life should be easier, you know?"

"Is that why you throw yourself into causes? To make your life easier?"

"You sound mad, Jane."

"Not mad . . . just concerned about what you said to Dwayne." And why hadn't Dwayne mentioned this to me today, huh?

He'd acted like Darcy had beaten around the bush. I hated thinking there were secrets buzzing that I knew nothing of, especially when I was in some way a part of them.

"Oh, you know. . . ."

Was she deliberately trying to be aggravating? "Why don't you tell me?"

"Okay, I may have mentioned that you and I had talked about getting our juices flowing with a partner swap."

"God. Please. I hope you're joking."

"I don't know what the big deal is, Jane," she said in a huff. "Can't reasonable adults discuss natural sexual desires? We weren't made to be monogamous, you know. Even in the apes, the young males are vying for the females behind the alpha males' backs. Everybody's looking at everybody else. There's no mating for life."

"Swans mate for life," I pointed out. "And there's no mating going on, period, if you're talking about Dwayne and me in the same sentence."

"We're not swans," she said stubbornly.

"We're not apes, either. And we're not a couple, Dwayne and me. And furthermore, we're not interested."

"Maybe you should talk to Dwayne about that."

"Don't do this, Darcy. There's nothing

going on between Dwayne and me. How many times do I have to say it before you'll actually open your ears and hear me?"

The front door rattled, and I congratulated myself on not unlocking it.

"Jane, I'm here," she said into the phone, giving the door a frustrated shake.

"Go have a glass of wine," I suggested.

"Oh, hey . . ." I heard her say, followed by Dwayne's drawl. It was sexy enough for me to want to dig my fingernails into my desktop and scratch through its faux wood surface. If only my fingernails were long enough . . . well, and strong enough.

He opened the door for her, and Darcy clicked off the phone, but not before I heard her voice ratchet upward into a breathless, little-girl range that sent me shooting into the outer room.

What I beheld made me slide to a stop. Darcy, instead of wearing another put-together outfit, had opted for jeans, a black, ribbed turtleneck sweater, and a pair of black ankle boots, a hell of a lot more stylish than anything I possessed but looking like it came out of my closet all the same. She'd pulled her short blond hair into a ponytail of sorts, and I swear to God, I had one of those gulping moments of awareness that sends your heart lurching painfully and your palms sweating. She was trying to *be me.*

For Dwayne?

Maybe . . . maybe not . . . I tried to ignore the rushing in my ears. Darcy had been the same in high school, always emulating someone, like she never had an identity of her own. It was spooky and odd, and it reminded me yet again that I didn't like her.

"I've been trying to tell Jane about our earlier conversation," she was saying, spreading a palm my way and sighing as if I were such a difficult child. "She hasn't let me tell her everything."

I swivelled my gaze to Dwayne. In the glare I sent him all kinds of accusations, the one in the forefront being *you went with her to the wine bar and you never told me?*

Dwayne ignored me, though I was sending mental lasers of fury directly into his thick skull. "Do you know if Karen had a therapist?" he asked Darcy.

She lifted a dismissive shoulder, like who cares? "Dwayne, tell her what we talked about. She's dying to know."

"Darcy seems to think we're a couple," Dwayne elucidated.

"I don't know what to say to that," I sputtered. I just wanted out of the conversation. "Does Karen have a brother who lives by the Vista Bridge?"

"Maybe she does." Darcy was not to be deterred. "What I said was, *if* you were a couple, and *if* you wanted to go out together, James and I would love to double with you."

Double date? I narrowed my eyes at her. That's all she said to Dwayne?

"It's just hard to meet great couples at our age," she went on. "James and I have a lot of business friends, but catching up with someone from school like Jane is priceless. And Dwayne, as I said earlier, you feel like an old friend, too, and you know I mean that as a compliment."

Though Darcy turned innocent eyes my way, I knew the strings attached, even if she hadn't clued Dwayne in on them yet.

My gaze on Darcy, I said to Dwayne, "I'm sure you told her we're just business partners."

"I did," Dwayne said.

Darcy rolled her eyes at us as if we were just being too, too coy. "Okay, business partners. We can start with that. I want you both to come to Christmas Eve dinner. Please don't tell me you have plans with family because —"

"I have plans with family," I said.

"— we'd love to have you share a meal

with us. More than soup," she added for my benefit. "It wouldn't be Merina cooking. I know this fantastic chef who owes me a favor and has been promising a Christmas goose since last year. How does that sound?"

Dwayne said, maddeningly, "I don't have any real plans."

"Jane?" she prodded.

I shook my head, though food is always a big lure.

"Well, if Jane can't come, maybe you can," she said to Dwayne, smiling prettily.

"Okay, I'll go," I said before Dwayne could answer. I didn't want to go to her viper's nest, but the truth was, I had no plans and I really didn't want Dwayne going without me. She wasn't being completely straight with him about her intentions, a problem I planned to rectify as soon as she was gone.

Which turned out to be nearly two hours later as she hung around and hung around and hung around. It took me bringing up the lawsuit again, and asking her for details about what Karen said during their twelve-plus-hour stint together, and Dwayne saying he had to meet a client and leaving, before she finally looked at the time on her cell phone and made a sound of dismay. "So much to do!" she cried.

"So, Karen never said anything about a previous suicide attempt," I reiterated as she was leaving. "You didn't touch on that at all?"

"I told you, she said she was depressed about her life. That's all."

"No specifics."

"Jane," she said, exasperated, "why don't you ask her? No. And she didn't mention a brother or a boyfriend or a therapist. She's alone in the world. It's tragic. I still really feel for her, you know. If it weren't for James, I don't know how I would have survived in this world. And the holidays just exacerbate the loneliness."

She was edging to the door and I was following after her, intent on locking it behind her, when she suddenly turned and grabbed my forearm. "I think you're making more of the role-playing than I meant. If you're not into it, James and I are okay with that. We just want to get together with you two."

I said nothing. I wasn't sure I could trust her.

"I just want us all to be good friends. I think Dwayne would like that, too. He certainly only has eyes for you."

"Well, that's not true."

"You know why he agreed to the Christmas Eve dinner? Because he knows you're alone this holiday season and doesn't know how to be with you without scaring you away, so I set the whole thing up for you."

"You're deluded."

"I'm playing Santa and giving you what you want for Christmas, whether you know it or not."

"You're playing Cupid," I shot back.

"You said you'd come Friday," she reminded me.

"I . . . I don't know what I'm doing. Just go away."

"Promise me you'll come."

I had my hand at the small of her back, gently pushing. "I'll talk to Dwayne."

"You want him, Jane. I can tell your resistance is an act. I have a gift for reading people, knowing what they need."

I almost told her that she hadn't seemed to get Karen Aldridge even after hours of plying her with tea and conversation. "I'll call you."

"You'll see me Friday evening. Six o'clock. Dress festively."

"This is about as festive as I'm ever going to get," I pointed out. Another step or two and she'd be out the door.

She stopped and glanced down at her own outfit. "It is comfortable, but it's our work armor. It's not for special events."

Our work armor? Good. God. "Don't take this the wrong way, but you've got to get a life."

"You haven't changed a bit since high school," she said, turning back to me with a smile. She still had one foot in the doorway, by purpose or design, I couldn't tell. I clung to the knob in the hopes she would leave before I had to push her out the door by force. "You always kind of wanted to be a rebel, but you're just so sane. We've always been sisters at heart."

"I'm not sure I feel the same way."

"You want to tell me I'm crazy. It's all over your face. But you know what I'm talking about. And I just know you're going to settle this problem with Karen. Thanks, Jane. I mean it."

Then she finally left.

I shut the door, locked it and backed away. Honestly, I didn't know if she was as wacko as I believed, or if there was some sage truth in her words that I couldn't see because I was "just so sane."

Either way, I was done for the day. I thought about texting Dwayne and complaining about him not telling me about fraternizing with Darcy at the wine bar, but instead I headed home to The Binkster and possibly a decent meal provided by my new houseguest.

CHAPTER 5

The following morning, I ran the two and a half miles to the Coffee Nook. My shoulder did ache a little from the gun's backfire, but I ignored it as I went in search of coffee, conversation and a bagel, as Roberta had apparently given up cooking in favor of decorating. When I'd shown up the night before, out of sorts after dealing with Darcy's loopiness and Dwayne's apparent defection, it was to find more plastic boxes stacked around my living room, leaving a mere goat trail between the front door and the kitchen. The candles on the tree were lit again, but at least the holiday music wasn't blasting.

"What is this?" I asked Roberta, who was busily positioning garlands of fake holly and fir boughs around every door and window. There were more candles as well, trios of them nestled in rings of plastic greenery on every flat surface. A deflated blowup of a team of reindeer, Santa and a sleigh was draped atop the boxes against the wall that backed up to the garage.

"Jane, do you have a hair dryer? I just can't blow Santa on my own."

This sounded faintly dirty, but I left it, sensing she wouldn't appreciate my take on it. "Uh, yeah, but Roberta . . ."

"Oh, I'm almost done, dear. I was going to make dinner, but I went back to the house, just to make sure I hadn't forgotten anything, and Gary was there and it was terrible." With that, she dissolved into tears, and I'd had to help her into my bedroom because there was no space left to sit in the living room.

It took another hour of me finding her tissues and listening to the horror that was her ex before she felt well enough to return to the living room and finish today's decorating. I moved the boxes off the couch so she'd have a place to sleep, and in the end we retired to the kitchen, where she put together BLTs.

This morning, however, she was still asleep and didn't awaken even while I fed The Binkster and took her outside to relieve herself. I took the dog back to my bedroom and changed into my jogging gear, then headed out, locking the front door behind

245

me with my key.

It was dark as pitch, so I had a softly flashing red light strapped around my leg and reflective stripes down both legs and on my stocking cap and gloves. I try to run during daylight hours, but I needed to get the hell out and go today. Luckily, it wasn't raining, snowing, sleeting or precipitating in any way. My breath came out in visible puffs and my lungs burned from the cold, but it felt great.

By the time I arrived at the Coffee Nook, it was full of customers. I was disappointed to see that my friend, Billy Leonard, whose take on life runs along similar lines as my own, wasn't perched on one of the stools. I seated myself on one next to a guy reading the newspaper, someone I didn't know. I have to admit I feel very territorial about my place at the Nook, and when others deign to encroach, I grow tense and competitive. Still, it is a public place, and occasionally a newbie is going to wander in and disrupt the status quo.

Chuck's truck pulled into the lot just after I'd ordered my bagel. I inwardly sighed. Running into my soon-to-be landlord again was almost too much. This just couldn't become a daily event. I watched him slam out of his car and stomp toward the front door. I thought about cancelling my order, but Julie, the Nook's proprietress, had just pulled the piping hot bagel from the toaster oven and onto a plate. She added a foil-wrapped pat of butter and a wee bucket of cream cheese and slid the meal toward me.

"Jane!" Chuck boomed as he came in, throwing his arms wide.

If he thought I was going to hug him, he had another think coming. I grabbed a bagel half and shoved it into my mouth plain, then silently signaled to Chuck that I couldn't talk right now.

"I checked the pipes. Everything's A-OK, but who's the old lady living at your place?"

The decibel level of his question was in the ear-splitting range. I shook my head to confirm that, well, there was a bagel in my mouth and I couldn't speak. The old lady part was a low blow, especially since Chuck is a good fifteen to twenty years older than I am, and Roberta was likely closer to his age than mine.

Julie asked, "How's the deal going?"

She was looking at me sympathetically, but I saw the question was for Chuck. He grumbled, "Got all kinds of problems. You know how much a goddamn appraisal is? Why can't banks just use what's on a property tax statement, huh? And under-

writers are pieces of crap. Keep demanding
something more every time you get them
the last thing they asked for. A bunch of
scaredy-ass box checkers with no business
sense whatsoever. Makes you wonder what
the world's coming to when these are the
people we have to suck up to just to get a
goddamned deal to go through."

I followed enough of that to feel a spark
of hope that maybe, just maybe, the whole
thing would fall apart. Ogilvy, my current
landlord, was no peach, but I clearly hadn't
given him enough credit.

"You headin' out?" Chuck asked, concerned, as I walked into the faint light of
morning.

"Ummm," I said. I was bummed that I
hadn't had time to add either butter or
cream cheese to my bagel, but I had one-
half in my mouth and another in my hand,
and leaving Chuck felt like the best idea
yet.

"I'll drive ya," he said. "Wanna talk to you
about a few things."

I yanked the bagel out of my mouth, ready
to disabuse him of that idea straightaway,
when the skies opened up and sent an icy
shower of half rain/half sleet pouring down
in a thick sheet.

"Okay," I said.

■ ■ ■ ■

That afternoon, I watched the weather from my bedroom window because you couldn't see out any of the ones in the living room. Roberta had gotten the blow-up reindeer, Santa and sleigh operational, but they were being pelted so hard that they quickly sank into a pool of red, white and brown plastic that had Roberta gazing out at them sadly.

Chuck had been thrilled to have me to himself for the two and a half miles back to my cottage. This was, apparently, the month I was destined to pick up friends I didn't want, and I listened in silence as he blathered on about what great friends we were and how he was going to be the best landlord ever, while I slowly worked my way through my dry bagel. The only time I perked up was when he magnanimously said he was going to allow me to use the garage as soon as all of Ogilvy's stuff was out of it. Ogilvy had held a garage sale a few weeks back, but there were still remnants around. I'd always wanted to use the garage for my car, but that hadn't been my agreement with Ogilvy. Maybe there was one teensy good thing about having a switch of landlords. Maybe . . .

"Tomorrow's Christmas Eve," Roberta said in a lonely voice.

She made my heart flip uncomfortably. I didn't want to go to Darcy's house for dinner, but I sure as hell didn't want Dwayne going without me.

"Today's Christmas Eve eve," Roberta went on. "It's when Gary and I always celebrated. We never could do Christmas Eve or Christmas Day, as there were always his sisters and brother or his mom, when she was alive, and of course his dad, long ago. We made a pact to always celebrate on the twenty-third . . . today. Guess that won't be happening."

I mumbled something sympathetic. Personally, the idea of adding another special day to the season made me feel tired. The buildup to Christmas was way too long as it was, and Roberta and her husband appeared to have found a new way to drag it out even further.

"Guess I'm free Christmas and Christmas Eve this year. Do you want to do something together?" she asked.

"Maybe," I said. If I could get out of Darcy's dinner and convince Dwayne to do the same. "I have some plans I've got to check on."

"Never mind. I'm okay."

She clearly was not. "Let me see if I can move things around."

"Okay," she said in a small voice. "I think I'll go see Gary tonight . . . our special night. He tried to take everything from me, so maybe I'll show up on his doorstep, just to remind him of that fact."

That sounded like a really bad idea. "You sure?"

"He can't just sashay off with *her* and not expect any kind of reaction from me. This is my night, tonight. I'm not just gonna sit back and take it. I'm done with that."

"All right," I said dubiously.

Christmas Eve I was up early. I looked out my window at the dark sky and was pleased to see no precipitation so far. I peeked in on Roberta, but she was dead asleep on the couch. She'd gotten in really, really late, and I was dying to know how it had gone with the rat bastard, but it appeared I was going to have to wait.

I put on my running gear and rotated my shoulder a bit. Much better. Instead of my usual trip to the Coffee Nook, I ran around my neighborhood. As I passed a new home that had been erected recently where an old cabin had stood, a huge black dog with enormous jaws came racing out, howling at the top of his lungs. My heart jumped to my throat and I ran like I'd never run before, but luckily the beast seemed to know the limits of its yard because it didn't run me down and tackle me.

My panicked sprint caught up to me, however, and I pulled up lame at the end of the road. I bent over and sucked air into my lungs, my heart pounding furiously inside my chest, all this because I didn't want to run into Chuck again. What the hell. I was really going to have to grow some balls or, barring that — I didn't think it was going to happen, anatomically speaking — I was going to have to come to terms with my new living arrangement . . . or move.

I stopped in at a Starbucks that's closer to my house than the Nook, though it felt blasphemous. I just didn't want to go home right away, as I almost didn't want the day to really get going. Was I falling into the bah-humbug routine? Probably. I'd also picked up a limp from my all-out race, which irked me at myself. It was with a physical effort that I finished my latte — a bad idea, I know, since I'm mildly lactose intolerant, but the coffee's a little stronger than I like at Starbucks. Then, I squared my shoulders and headed back home in a limping walk.

I was confronted with an octet of singing elves as I walked in. They stood in two rows, their red-and-green-felt torsos snapping back and forth to the sound of ". . . up on the rooftop reindeers pause, out jumps good old Santa Claus . . ." Their faces were molded plastic with frozen grins and staring eyes. ". . . ho, ho, ho, who wouldn't go? . . ."

"Oh my God," I breathed.

Apparently, Roberta had levered herself off the couch. I could hear the bathroom sink running.

". . . who wouldn't go-oh! Up on the rooftop, quick, quick, quick . . ."

"Roberta!" I yelled. The Binkster toddled out of the bedroom, stopped in the doorway and gazed from me to the gyrating elves, whose little peaked hats stood straight up and ended in shiny gold balls, then back at me, her brown eyes long-suffering.

". . . through the chimney with good St. Nick!"

I stumbled forward and grabbed up the first elf, searching for a switch to turn it *off, off, OFF*! Finally finding it, I grabbed the next one, and the next, and the next, until all eight of them were frozen and silent, though their scary faces all gazed at me with evil smiles.

I gave myself a shake all over. Though I'm

not one of those people who find clowns really scary, I'd cracked open the door to that particular paranoia and found it really creepy inside.

As I was putting the elves back in the large open box beside them, which looked to be what they'd arrived in, Roberta came out of the bathroom, dressed for the day in a long black skirt, boots and a red quilted jacket that buttoned up the front with red-and-white buttons that looked like peppermints. "What are you doing?" she demanded.

I put the last elf inside and tried to put the lid back on. It didn't fit right, and as I struggled, one of the elves started singing again, but muted, like he'd been gagged.

"They've gotta go," I said. "All of this has gotta go." I swept my arm around the room.

"But it's not Christmas yet," she protested.

"As good as."

"You want me to go, too?"

A tinny little voice sang, ". . . through the chimney with lots of toys, all for the little ones' Christmas joys. . . ."

"I want to commit elf-icide, if there is such a thing."

She looked hurt, but she simply nodded her head. "So, no dinner tonight?"

"No dinner."

"Okay. I'll start packing up."

She walked away from me and toward the kitchen. I felt like a heel, but I didn't try to stop her.

I went to take a shower, then changed into my jeans and a V-necked, long-sleeved black T-shirt. No ribbed turtleneck this time. It wasn't much, but it helped a little in erasing the mental image I had of Darcy in one of my outfits. If she kept that up and insisted on being my friend, I might have to change my wardrobe entirely, maybe to navy blue or dark gray instead of black. I thought about adding a red scarf, but since I didn't own one, I came out in my usual colors. By that time, Roberta had hauled several boxes out to her car and was just coming through the front door again. She said, "They're predicting snow late tonight. Looks like we're going to have a white Christmas."

I couldn't do it. I couldn't kick her out. "I want you to stay," I told her. "I'm sorry. I'm basically a miserable person and have a low tolerance for fun, but don't take it personally."

She smiled slightly.

"Just no elves, okay?"

"I have a place to go."

"Stay," I insisted, certain that was a lie.

Roberta hemmed and hawed awhile, but

it was all for show. In the end, she agreed, and we were both relieved. All except The Binkster, whose liquid brown eyes followed me around in silent reproach.

I limped through the house, trying really hard to be a better host. I even went so far as to commiserate with her about what a true rat bastard her soon-to-be ex had to be because he'd kicked her out right before the holidays. Roberta didn't seem all that comfortable with me trashing him, though, so I gave up and returned to work on the Karen Aldridge case.

I was heading to the office when I made a detour, deciding instead to drive directly to the apartment I'd seen Karen enter two days earlier. I had to circle around a few times before I found a parking spot that gave me a view of the building's front door. I could also see Karen's silver Honda once again parked across the street. Squinching down in the seat, I settled in to wait.

And wait I did. Damn near half a day. I had to leave my car, as I wasn't going to lose my spot, and walk to a McDonald's that was half a mile away to use the restroom, then hurry back. I had this terrible feeling that something would happen the minute I left, but when I returned everything looked so the same that I allowed myself to believe I hadn't missed anything. Karen's car was still parked where it had been since I'd started my surveillance, so I crossed my fingers and took up my vigil again.

About one thirty, Karen and the guy she'd met at the door suddenly appeared, walking down the front steps together. Karen went straight to her car, but the dude in the watch cap and baggy pants sauntered around the corner. I was momentarily unsure what to do: Wait for Karen to pass and then drive around to see where he went? Get out of the Volvo and head toward the apartment building, hoping Karen wouldn't recognize me as I tried to catch up with the dude on foot? Pull out from the curb and cover my face as I drove past her?

In the end, I just sat paralyzed, my eyes barely above the steering wheel, waiting for Karen to drive off. She took an inordinate amount of time, but then suddenly, a gray Altima whizzed past with a *beep-beep* meant for Karen, and I saw that my dude buddy was heading into town. I caught the license plate and committed it to memory by saying it aloud about a hundred times in a singsong voice. Karen *toot-tooted* back to him and then slipped out and drove behind him. I eased out of my parking spot, did a three-point turn and joined the procession. Karen peeled off a few blocks later, but my dude friend just kept heading north. I figured Karen was going to work, so I followed the guy instead.

He took the ramp onto Sunset Highway west and drove to a Home Depot. I turned into the lot a few seconds later and saw him park near the exit doors. I nosed the Volvo into a spot a few rows over that allowed me to pull through for a quick getaway, in case he decided to turn and burn.

Inside the store, I was greeted cheerily by a middle-aged man wearing an orange-and-white apron who wanted to know if he could help me. I almost asked him where the dude in the watch cap, oversized gray jacket and baggy pants went, but figured that really wasn't what he meant.

I found my quarry just inside the door to the outdoor section, looking over a row of picked-over poinsettias. I had a pang of remorse for coming down so hard on Roberta about the elves.

As the guy was standing there, another similarly dressed dude joined him, and they started slapping hands and hooting their delight at this unexpected meet-and-greet. I kept a sideways eye on them as I examined the meager selection of outdoor furniture.

Not exactly the most popular Christmas purchase, although the prices had been slashed, slashed, slashed. It occurred to me that I could maybe pick something up for my back deck on the cheap, but I couldn't in good conscience part with money for an item I might not be able to use, should I need to escape Chuck and move. Sad thought.

The guy talk turned to cars; my dude was very proud of his Altima. Said his sister had gotten it for him. "Man, she's good," he crowed. "You remember Brad, that guy she dated for a while."

"Died in a car accident, right?"

"Yeah, him. Real depressed type. Always talking about suicide."

I felt myself react and had to turn away lest I inadvertently caught their attention. I bent down to look at a price tag, but my eyes were practically blind as my ears strained to hear every syllable.

"Didn't you say he left her some dough?" the new guy asked.

"He left her the car. That's how I got my ride, man. She gave it to me. I'm gonna trade it in for a Corvette, though."

"No shit?"

"As soon as this next deal comes down."

What deal? I silently questioned.

"What deal?" the friend asked.

"Can't talk about it," he said. "But man, we're gonna be rich!"

I heard them moving away, so I turned back. My dude had a poinsettia cradled in one arm, and the two of them were walking toward checkout. I moved in the general direction and walked out of the store about fifteen seconds after they did.

They fist-bumped their good-byes and then headed to their respective vehicles. I followed my guy back to the apartment complex and watched him reenter with his poinsettia.

Well, huh. So, Karen was working some kind of scam. I thought about it hard for several moments, then headed back to Joe's Jo. As ever, it took awhile to find a spot, but I managed one about two blocks over. I glanced up and saw the gray clouds were high, with no sign of snow yet.

Karen was inside, behind the cash register, ringing up a coffee drink while Trina held a cup beneath the foam spigot. The familiar *fsssst* of the espresso machine filled the air.

I sauntered to the register and said to Karen, "How's the macchiatto? What's the name of it?"

She glared at me and said with an effort, "Black Mamba Macchiatto."

"Ah, yeah. I see it. Black mamba's a snake."

"You gonna order something?"

Her voice dripped with venom. Very black mamba-ish. "I'll take a black coffee," I said, keeping my gaze on the chalkboard with the range of their coffee selection behind her. "I don't see Fake Suicide for Money Mocha in there anywhere," I added conversationally. Sometimes I surprise myself with what comes out of my mouth.

She went white. It sort of took me aback. Half the time I try these things and prepare myself for the furious denial that often comes as a result; I've been threatened with bodily harm by a number of colorful low-lifes who've taken offense at my tactics. So, I'd expected fury and sputtering denials and I don't know what else, but she just went dead.

"My coffee?" I prodded when it looked as if she had turned to ice.

She whipped around without a word, grabbed a paper cup and filled it with regular coffee. I plunked down the coinage and waited for her to recover, but she wouldn't meet my eyes. Another customer had come up behind me while she was getting the coffee, so I took my cup and moved out of the way. I sipped at the drink for

261

several moments while she finished with the man, who also just wanted black coffee, but she never looked up.

Huh.

"I'll see you later, Karen," I said when I headed out the door. Still no look up. I'd totally spooked her, so whatever the truth was about her attempt at suicide, I was pretty sure I was on the right track.

CHAPTER 6

On the way back to Lake Chinook, I plugged in my earbud so I could talk on my cell while I drove. I called Dwayne and, after a couple of snide remarks about his neglecting to tell me about the wine bar trip with Darcy, I told him about Karen's reaction.

"You tweaked her, huh," Dwayne said, sounding amused.

"I haven't been in the best mood. She might have received the brunt of it."

"You hit a nerve. What do you want to do next?"

"I guess I'll tell Darcy tonight."

"Yeah, about that. I don't think I'm going to make it to dinner."

I counted to three, really slowly, then said, "I was only going because you were."

"I figured. From the sound of things, she's got some offbeat idea about you and me."

"You mean role-playing with our different partners? Yeah, that's a little offbeat."

"Me Santa, you Rudolph," he said, and I could tell he was fighting laughter.

"She's not kidding," I warned him.

"Oh, I think she's putting us both on."

"Don't count on it," I said darkly. "And if I'm going to dinner, you're going with me. I'll pick you up."

I hung up before he could argue further. So, sue me. I didn't want to be with Darcy and James, but I did want to be with Dwayne. The Christmas goose sounded good, too, but there was going to be no role-playing.

"Me Santa, you Rudolph," I muttered.

I didn't go directly home, even though if I was going to get dressed for dinner — which made me wonder what in God's name that was going to be — I would have to get a move on. Instead, I went to a flower shop and fought through a bunch of last-minute shoppers to purchase an amaryllis for Roberta, sort of a peace offering and a Christmas gift. I walked out the door, stopped, had a talk with myself, then turned around and bought another for Darcy. A small part of me was actually still thinking of bagging out on the invitation. Some last-minute, near-death illness that took out both me and Dwayne. I knew I wouldn't do it, but I love to entertain these fantasies about myself.

I really wanted to get Dwayne a gift of some kind, but we had never exchanged gifts in the years we'd known each other and it would be weird to start now. I wasn't looking for a relationship with him anyway. I wasn't. Still, I wish I'd forked over the cash for a Covet Bar or two. That would have been an okay gift that Dwayne would have appreciated without thinking it was too weird.

By the time I got home, it was nearly five and I was planning another shower and mentally inventorying my closet. A deeply hidden part of myself I didn't want to acknowledge was looking forward to the evening because it was basically a date with Dwayne.

I pulled up in front of my house to find a familiar truck already parked in front of my garage: Chuck's. Groaning inside, I climbed out of my car just as he began backing up. His face was a storm cloud.

"Merry Christmas," I said.

"You'll be happy to know the bank turned me down," he bit out. "I'm not your landlord. The deal's kaput."

"Who says I'm happy?" I asked, determined to hide my sudden glee.

"Had to pick up a few things I put in the

garage." He reversed with a little spurt of his tires. My heart swelled with *schadenfreude.* I shouldn't feel so good at Chuck's expense. That wasn't the Christmas spirit, but my heart filled with joy and I could've broken into song. Sure, someone else was bound to buy the place in his stead as I didn't possess the funds to purchase it myself, but I was willing to take my chances. Better the devil you don't know, than the asshole you do.

I was actually thinking of freeing the elves as I headed for the front door. My old landlord had emptied out his belongings from the garage and Chuck had put some tools inside even though the deal hadn't been closed. There was a stack of wood inside, too, that I could probably help myself to. I've always wanted to use the garage for my vehicle, so I thought I could maybe build myself a fire on Christmas Day *and* possibly tuck the Volvo under an actual roof.

Best Christmas present ever.

It began to snow as I walked inside the house, and I was glad that Roberta had left the porch light on. I stopped a moment to enjoy the sight, watching the large flakes lazily drift downward, though they were starting to pile up faster and faster.

I stepped in to the scents of roast beef and cinnamon from the kitchen, and the vanilla wafting off the candles on the Christmas tree. There was a small stack of wood on the hearth and I realized Roberta had been able to get into the garage when Chuck opened the door. My soaring heart took a nosedive. She'd set up the Christmas Eve dinner/evening that I'd never said no to. "Roberta?" I called, heading for the kitchen, just as a splash of headlights lit up the outside of the house.

She wasn't anywhere to be found. She hadn't taken off and left those candles flickering dangerously away, had she? And where was The Binkster?

"Binks?" I called anxiously, heading back to the front door. "Roberta?" Her car was outside, so she was around. But who was this newcomer?

I stepped back onto the porch and saw a silver Honda pull up where Chuck's truck had been. Karen Aldridge's car.

I froze. This wasn't good.

"Hey," I said when she climbed out of her car. "How'd you know where I live?"

"Same way you found Bruno and me," she snapped out. "I followed you."

"Bruno's . . . your brother?" I asked, try-ing to be all conversation-like, pretending

267

that this wasn't really dangerous, especially considering the forceful way she was coming at me. I had a moment when I almost ran inside and slammed the door in her face. I've done enough process serving to have learned the move from the people who attempt to escape me.

"I didn't like you threatening me."

"I wasn't trying to threaten you," I lied, hoping my voice didn't give away my pounding heart.

"You think you're so smart. You don't know anything. And that bitch of a friend of yours has got way too much money. Oh, yeah, I always knew who Darcy Wexford was. I set it up on the bridge so she'd 'save' me."

I mistrusted this sudden confession. It didn't go with the image I'd constructed for her. "Why are you telling me this?"

But Karen just rolled on, "She tried counseling my boyfriend and he thought she was a complete wacko. She is. But she's a rich wacko."

"Your boyfriend . . . Brad? Who died in a traffic accident?"

"You know about him?" She shook her head furiously. "Some people just have bad luck, y'know? Brad was depressed and wanted to jump off the Vista Bridge, but he couldn't get near the edge 'cause Darcy was there. She talked him out of it. And then, three months later, Brad is with his friend and there's a pileup and Brad dies. It's just not fair!"

"No, it's not," I agreed.

She was shaking with rage and emotion. All of her bored attitude had disappeared. "I told him I was gonna make us a lot of money. He didn't care, but I did. And Darcy went for it. Dragged me off the fence and took me to her place, plied me with that god-awful tea and just talked and talked *forever.* It was gonna work. She would have paid me, but then you . . ."

"I don't think she would've. She's very fond of her money. I . . ."

She pulled a gun from her purse. A Glock, I realized. I lifted my hands in front of my chest, palms out, and backed up, saying, "Wait, wait . . ."

She followed me into the house. "I'm suicidal," she said. "You tried to stop me and were accidentally shot in the process."

"No one will believe that," I burbled. "Suicide victims choose one method and stick with it."

"You were harassing me," she went on. "People have seen you at my work. I've told everyone how depressed I am, and that you wouldn't leave me alone."

I backed up some more, my mind racing. I've been in tight spots before, but past experience wasn't helping me now. This woman was going to *shoot* me unless I did something fast.

Karen's gun hand was shaking. I wanted to run. Flee. Get the hell out. I half turned, planning to escape, and my shoulder hit the Christmas tree. Two candles fell over in lines of flame and the tree toppled sideways. Karen inhaled a sharp breath and I switched direction, away from the tree and into her. *Slam.* The Glock flew across the room and the tree smashed into the floor with a loud *bam.*

Karen's hands were in my hair, ripping hard, and she was screaming. It *hurt.* I tried to yank away from her. I'd flung myself at her to knock her down, but now she clung to me like a burr. Lurching to my feet, I dragged her toward the open front door.

Behind me, there was smoke and fire. Damn it. *Damn it!*

I scrambled and twisted and wrenched and she lost her grip. Staggering to my feet, I ran outside and suddenly was on the snowy ground as she launched herself into me. I rolled over and looked into her eyes. Her teeth were bared and she looked insane with rage. I smacked my fist at her but couldn't get a good angle. She grabbed my head and tried to slam it into the ground. I twisted hard and threw her to one side. Fueled by momentum and my own rising fury, I jumped on her and tried to pin her to the ground. She was wild with anger, spitting and cursing, and her body whipped around so hard I couldn't get a good hold. A distant part of myself couldn't believe this was happening.

You tweaked her . . .

You got that right, Dwayne.

She slipped my grip, got one foot beneath her. I clamped a hand on her shin and yanked. She stumbled and fell and swore, and then we were rolling in the snow. It was cold and slippery and I cursed the fact that I couldn't grab her like I wanted.

Vaguely, I was aware of someone's approach. Out of the corner of my eye, I saw Roberta, her arms laden with kindling, coming from the garage with The Binkster at her heels.

"Get back!" I screamed.

Karen started shrieking when she realized we had witnesses. "She's trying to *kill me!*"

I was outraged. I wanted to kick and punch and bite, but she wriggled from my grasp, rolling to her knees. I lunged for her

271

coat at the same moment I saw Roberta rush forward. "Stop!" I yelled as Roberta dropped a cascade of kindling onto Karen's head and she went still.

Gasping, I struggled to my feet. Karen was groaning but half-unconscious. Zip ties, I thought. I'd kept them in my car ever since I'd learned they were a great handcuffing method.

I staggered to the Volvo and grabbed the zip ties I kept in a side pocket. And that's when I saw the spreading flames. The inside of my little house was shimmering with orange and red as the Christmas tree went up in flames.

"No . . ."

My cell phone was in my pocket and I grabbed it and punched in 9-1-1. I reported the fire and my address, then bent to Karen and tied her hands in front of her. Her eyes were open, but all the fight had gone out of her. The Binkster had toddled over and was snuffling her face. She pulled back, as if in disgust, and I scooped her into my arms.

"Thank you," I said to Roberta as I heard the sound of approaching sirens.

"You were right about the candles," she said woefully. "I'm so sorry. I was making us dinner. I wanted to say how much I appreciated everything before I left. Gary and

I are giving it another try."

"You are?" We stepped back, out of the way, as the fire trucks turned into my long drive.

"I went to see him last night, and . . . well, Christmas Eve eve is still our special time."

So, that's why she'd come in so late, I realized. "Good," I said, pleased for her.

I couldn't stand seeing my cottage in flames. I wanted to smash my way inside to save something, but my dog was safe and my laptop was still at the office, so I still had everything that really mattered to me.

I gave The Binks an extra hug and she licked my face in commiseration.

EPILOGUE

The fire department got the flames under control fairly quickly, though my home was a dripping mess of water in the end. Apart from some smoke damage, the bedroom and kitchen were saved. The living room, though, was a complete disaster, and my furniture, such as it was, was ruined. The firemen cut holes in the roof for ventilation, and the snow kept coming down and melting as it reached the heat, adding to the moisture. It was just as well Roberta and Gary had reconciled because nobody was going to be sleeping on my couch ever again.

It was also lucky for Chuck, I supposed, that he wasn't the owner of the home. Hopefully skinflint Ogilvy had insurance.

I'd called Dwayne, and he arrived about the same time as the police and the EMTs, who hauled Karen away in an ambulance. Her Glock was recovered, and its chamber was found to be empty of ammunition. It kind of pissed me off. If I'd known that, my house might not be ruined, but then, Karen hadn't been polite enough to point out that she was faking.

There were a lot of questions from the police. I knew one of the Lake Chinook officers and he helped facilitate my being allowed to leave. I wasn't exactly sure where that was going to be until Dwayne said, "I'll take you to my place," in one of the tenderest tones he'd ever used in my hearing. It made me feel a little weak in the knees, and I had to tell myself that it was probably just an aftereffect of the wrestling match I'd engaged in with Karen, but I didn't believe it.

I was still holding The Binkster as Dwayne put a supportive arm around me and we walked toward his truck. My brain focused on that contact as if there was nothing else in the world to think about. We'd almost made it when another vehicle came bouncing up my rutted drive, a thin layer of snow on its roof and melting off the hood. Darcy's white BMW.

"Oh, no," I murmured, as I set The Binkster in the passenger seat of Dwayne's truck.

"I called her on the way over," Dwayne admitted. "Darcy'd been trying to get hold of you and finally called me."

"Jane!" Darcy cried, racing from the car toward me. I shrank back as a matter of course, and Dwayne tucked me in closer. "My God, are you okay?"

"Karen Aldridge did this?" James asked in disbelief, staring at the blackened roof and smoke still curling upward.

"Oh, it's my fault!" Darcy pressed her mittened hands to her cheeks. "It's all my fault."

"She was trying to scam you," I said. I'd already told Dwayne a bit of what had occurred, but now I related the entire tale to Darcy and James. I was shivering before I finished, and Dwayne had to cut me off and steer me toward the passenger seat of his truck.

"We'll figure it out tomorrow," he said.

"What about the house?" Darcy asked, staring at my smoking cottage.

"Hopefully my landlord has insurance."

"Maybe we can buy it for you," Darcy declared instantly, and James seconded, "Absolutely," as if it were a done deal.

Did they see the horror on my face? Probably not, because I ducked my head as I climbed into the truck. I didn't even have the energy to protest.

"Looks like no dinner tonight," Darcy said, sounding disappointed. "Maybe we should reschedule for New Year's?"

I found the energy to pick up The Binks and take my seat. Then Dwayne slammed the door on the driver's side and we were on the way to his house. I thrust my hands into the pockets of my coat to get them warm and discovered the little bits of mistletoe from our trip to Gil's farm, which felt like a million years ago.

I walked into the house on my own power, though I was definitely feeling shaky, and put The Binks on the floor. A bottle of red wine with a bow sat on Dwayne's breakfast bar.

"Sit down before you fall down and I'll get you a drink," he said, grabbing the bottle.

"Isn't it a gift?"

"To you and me, to christen our new office and for Christmas. Bought it from Wine About It. What's that?"

My gaze followed the direction of his and I realized he was looking at the mistletoe sprig crushed in my hand. "A parasite. I got a lot of those lately."

Dwayne set the bottle back down, then came to me and eased the mistletoe from my nerveless fingers. He held it over our heads and my eyes met his.

"What? You're not . . ."

For an answer, Dwayne leaned down and kissed me. It was a nice kiss. A pleasant one. When he pulled back, there was a moment of reckoning in which neither of us said anything. My heart was jumping around in my chest as if it didn't know where to go.

And then a car pulled up outside and a couple of doors slammed. There was a pounding at the door and, muttering under his breath, Dwayne reluctantly opened it.

Darcy and James burst in with armloads of presents. "We had them at the house. We were going to give them to you tomorrow, since tonight was such a mess, but then we thought, no, let's celebrate! Oh, Jane, you must be totally tired. We'll only stay a little while. We can do something tomorrow. It'll be a white Christmas. Maybe we could go to Timberline Lodge and drink mountain drinks."

"Or take a sleigh ride," James said.

"Or have a snowball fight!" She glanced from Dwayne to me. "What do you say?"

"Oh, goody?" I suggested.

Darcy plowed on. "I put a call into my real-estate agent and told him I wanted to buy your house. We'll get that started, too."

I looked at Dwayne and he looked at me. *Parasites,* I thought, but I was beginning to

278

have a new appreciation for them. They
might even be okay.

Dear Reader,

She's baaaaaccckkk!

One of my most asked-about characters, P.I. Jane Kelly, has finally returned in *White Hot Christmas*. Where has she been? Perched on a shelf in my mind, just waiting to get back on the page. In real time, it's been a number of years, but in Jane's world, it's only been a few weeks.

Jane first burst on the scene in *Candy Apple Red,* as the reluctant apprentice to her boss, Dwayne Durbin, whom she's been friends with for years. She fights a kind of should I or shouldn't I battle inside herself over whether she and Dwayne should take their relationship to the next level. She knows it's a bad idea. They work together, for crying out loud, but then, Jane's never really listened to her own advice. This same question follows her through the second and third books in the trilogy, *Electric Blue* and

280

Ultra Violet, and it crops up again in *White Hot Christmas.* While she struggles to keep herself from making that big mistake, she also deals with her family, her adopted pug, The Binkster, and the general lowlifes who populate her working world. All three books are available as eBooks, if you're interested in learning more!

What have I been doing while Jane was waiting to reappear? I've been concentrating on creating romantic suspense thrillers, some with my sister, Lisa Jackson, and some on my own. My latest solo effort, *I'll Find You,* now available, centers around Callie Cantrell, who's suffered the tragic loss of her son in a car accident and is struggling to find herself again. The healing starts when she befriends a little boy on the island of Martinique. Tucker seems to be a wharf rat at first, but Callie soon realizes he has a mysterious past of his own. Without meaning to, Callie becomes embroiled in the dirty dealings, dark secrets and hidden agendas of the members of the wealthy Laughlin family, a situation that could prove deadly to both Callie and Tucker.

Before the year ends, I'll have one more book out: *Wicked Ways.* It's one of the stories I'm cowriting with Lisa Jackson, and it's the fourth book in the Colony series, which features the women of Siren Song, who possess mysterious psychological "gifts." Siren Song is the name of the lodge along the Oregon coast where many of the Colony women reside, but in *Wicked Ways,* we take a trip to sunny Southern California to find a missing member who doesn't know of her connection to the others. Elizabeth Gaines Ellis is living a normal suburban lifestyle south of Los Angeles but has noticed that when she wishes for something, sometimes it actually comes true. The problem is, she's made the mistake of wishing someone dead . . . her cheating husband . . . and it looks like her wish has been granted. . . .

Hope you enjoy *White Hot Christmas* and have lots of time for happy holiday reading!

Nancy Bush

Seven Days of Christmas

Rosanna Chiofalo

PROLOGUE

Newport, Rhode Island

Christmas has always coincided with some major milestone in my life. Perhaps it's because I was born on Christmas Eve. There was a raging blizzard the day I was born and so my parents thought it would be fitting to name me Bianca, which means white in Italian.

My parents took me and my brothers to Disney World for the first time when I was seven. It was my first real vacation. We spent Christmas and the week leading up to New Year's Eve in Orlando. As a child who lived in Newport, Rhode Island, I had been accustomed to the cold and often snowy Christmases New England is known for. So being in mild, sunny Florida felt odd at first. But that was all forgotten when I entered Disney's magical world and met my favorite princesses. I'm still trying to decide which one I like more — Snow White or Sleeping

Beauty. My mom says it should be Snow White because my name is Bianca and I have chocolate-brown hair just like her.

Then there was my first kiss from Frank O'Mara on the morning of Christmas behind our church, right after Mass. I was only fourteen and couldn't have asked for a better gift than to have Frank finally notice me. Little did I know then that he had noticed — and kissed — almost all the girls in our high school. Still. It's one of my most fond Christmas memories. What girl doesn't remember her first kiss?

My maternal grandmother, or Nonna, as my brothers and I called her, died the day after Christmas when I was eighteen. She had lived with my family for the past eight years, since my grandfather died of a heart attack. I was devastated and didn't want to return to college after the holidays. Of course, my parents made me go back, telling me Nonna would want me to continue on the path God had laid out for me. That did sound like something Nonna would say. She was very religious and often found a way to insert God and her favorite saints into whatever lesson she was imparting to my brothers and me. Nonna's favorite saint was Saint Rita, which also happens to be my mother's name. My favorite saint was

Saint Elizabeth of Hungary. My grandmother was thrilled I had chosen this saint because of her own Austro-Bavarian roots. Nonna and Nonno were both from Bolzano, in the South Tyrol region of Italy, where the Italian Alps meet the Austrian Alps. Although they were Italian, they were of Austro-Bavarian heritage and also spoke German.

But I had chosen Saint Elizabeth as my favorite because she had been a princess. She was a princess of the kingdom of Hungary in the thirteenth century. Like most little girls, I was obsessed with princesses. So maybe that's why I wasn't surprised when I met Mark Vitale and our romance seemed to take on a fairy-tale quality of its own.

I met Mark last year on Christmas Eve. My brothers, Antonio and Luciano — or Tony and Lucky — brought Mark home for our special Feast of the Seven Fishes. Mark is Tony and Lucky's boss and the owner of the architectural firm where they work. Although Tony and Lucky aren't twins and were born two years apart — Tony is thirty, while Lucky is twenty-eight — they have many of the same interests, one being architecture. They went to Parsons The New School for Design in New York City and became architects.

At first, I thought it was odd that they were bringing their boss home for our holiday dinner. But Mom explained to me that Mark was very easygoing and is Tony and Lucky's friend in addition to their boss. Call me uptight, but I'm a firm believer in the old adage, "Don't mix business with pleasure." But Tony and Lucky are grown men. They can ruin their careers if they want. It's none of their little sister's business.

I was helping Mom cook the seven fish that we would be having for dinner: *baccalà* (or codfish, as it's more commonly known in English), crab legs, clams, mussels, scallops, fresh sardines, and octopus when Tony and Lucky arrived with Mark in tow.

"Bianca, can you please go out to ask Mark if he'd like something to drink? I don't know what's taking your father so long at that liquor store. You'd think he was shopping for the entire week's worth of groceries." Mom shook her head as she lowered a ladle full of clams into a huge pot of boiling fish stock. Although she lived for the holidays, she always got stressed beyond stressed preparing for them.

"Give Daddy a break, Mom. It *is* Christmas Eve. The liquor store must be busy."

"True, but I also know how your father loves to linger and examine every wine and liquor bottle to make sure he's getting only the best. He's probably having some extended conversation about grapes and wine making with the store clerks."

"He'll be home soon. Don't worry." I patted Mom on the back before pulling my apron over my head.

As I made my way to the living room, I could hear Tony and Lucky telling Mark some of their more obnoxious jokes. I rolled my eyes as I imagined this night resembling more of a frat-boy party rather than a family holiday celebration.

I stepped into the living room. Mark's back was facing me. He was quite tall, maybe six foot one, with curly, dark brown hair. I was surprised to see he was wearing jeans, although they were a dark wash and looked very expensive. A midnight-blue silk shirt complemented the jeans perfectly. He was telling Tony and Lucky about an intern he'd hired who had been making mistake upon mistake. I waited until he was done with his story before interrupting.

"Excuse me?"

Mark turned around. His eyes narrowed slightly as he took me in. I was at a loss for words. I hadn't expected Mark to be so good-looking. He raised his eyebrow as if to ask me *yes*? but when he saw I was having a hard time gathering my thoughts, he quickly came to my rescue.

"Where are my manners? You must be Bianca. Tony and Lucky are always raving about you." Mark stepped forward and shook my hand.

I smiled and glanced at my brothers, who seemed amused at my awkward moment. Trying to save face, I said, "It's a pleasure to meet you, Mark. As for my brothers, they're the ones lacking in manners." I turned my attention to Tony and Lucky. "How long were you going to wait to introduce me to Mark?"

"You have a mouth, Bianca. What's gotten into you tonight?" Lucky winked at me.

I ignored him and asked Mark, "Would you like something to drink? We have Merlot, or I could make you a cocktail. I'm not sure which liquor my father has in his bar. He's actually at the liquor store right now, so you'll have more of a choice when he gets back. He should be home soon if you'd rather wait."

"A glass of Merlot would be great. Thank you. Oh! I almost forgot, Bianca. I brought dessert. You should probably put it in the fridge." Mark walked over to the coffee table and picked up a box from Gianni's Dolci — Newport's best bakery — and handed it to me. Our fingers brushed lightly as he made the transfer.

"Thank you. You didn't have to bring anything."

"It's my pleasure." Mark smiled.

While he had smiled at me earlier, something about this smile seemed different. Warmth spread from the pit of my belly all the way up to my face. I returned his smile, doing my best to keep my expression as disinterested and cool as possible, before turning around and walking over to the liquor cabinet. Though I heard them resume their conversation, I got the sense Mark was glancing in my direction. I turned my body to the side as I poured his Merlot into a wineglass and snuck a glance. Sure enough, he was doing his best to appear as if he were paying attention to what Tony and Lucky were saying, but he looked my way twice. He didn't notice I was looking at him as well — probably because he was staring at my legs.

Men used to tell me often that my legs were my best asset. I silently thanked myself for choosing a navy-blue pencil skirt, which sat a good three inches above my knees. And my embroidered black silk stockings showed off my toned calves, thanks to my regular workouts. Keeping in spirit with the Yuletide, I wore patent leather stiletto pumps in candy red to go with a sleeveless, sequined top in the same shade. My short-cropped hair sported a small comb with faux rubies. I knew without a doubt that I looked good, and from the appreciative expression in Mark's eyes as he stared at me, he thought so too.

While I made my way back to Mark with his wine, it was now his turn to act nonchalantly, pretending he didn't notice I was approaching him.

"Here's your Merlot, Mark." I said his name in a hushed whisper and met his gaze. He paused, holding my gaze for a moment longer before taking his glass.

"Tony, Lucky, can I get you something to drink?" I asked my brothers.

"Nah. We'll wait for Dad to bring home the hard stuff."

"Aren't you going to have a glass of wine, Bianca?"

"I should get back into the kitchen and help my mother."

But just as I said that, Mom appeared, hurrying over to Mark and smoothing down her hair, which seemed to have frizzed from the steam of cooking the clams.

"Hello, Mark. I'm Rita. Dinner will be out shortly, or I should say once my husband gets home." Mom then turned to me. "It's okay, Bianca. I don't need you anymore in the kitchen."

"I'm home!" Dad's voice boomed from the foyer.

"Well, it's about time! Please excuse me, Mark."

Soon Mom's voice reached us as she mercilessly interrogated Dad, asking why it had taken him so long at the liquor store.

Mark's gaze met mine, and we erupted into laughter.

"Every Christmas Eve, it's the same story. Dad goes out to the liquor store or the bakery and takes forever to come back. And Mom gives him grief as soon as he returns." I shook my head.

"My parents weren't much different." Mark wiped tears from his eyes as he tried to control his laughter.

"Weren't? Did they pass away?"

"Yes, a year apart from each other. My mother had congestive heart failure, and my father found out he had lung cancer six months after she died. It's probably for the best he didn't live much longer after she passed away. He was so depressed without her." Mark took a sip of wine. His expression grew somber.

"I'm sorry."

"Thank you. That's why your brothers took pity on me and invited me to your family gathering tonight. I don't have any family in Newport. Both of my sisters live in California. They invited me, of course, but I didn't feel like making the trip this year. Besides, I'm very busy right now. I might even be working when I get home tonight."

"On Christmas Eve? Don't be a Scrooge!" I forgot myself and playfully swatted his arm. My heart froze once I realized what I'd done. But Mark was too busy laughing to have even noticed.

"There's no way you're going home at a decent time tonight, Mark!" Tony came up behind me. He held a glass of vodka. I glanced over my shoulder and saw my father was stocking his bar with the liquor he'd bought.

"Yeah, that's why we invited him, Bianca. Don't believe his story of us taking pity on him because his family is out of state. We knew he'd be working all night if we didn't rescue him. Besides, we managed to pique his curiosity about our Feast of the Seven Fishes." Lucky joined us with his own glass of vodka. I suddenly realized he and Tony had been eavesdropping on our whole conversation.

"Your sister's right about you guys. Where are your manners? How about bringing her a drink? What will you have, Bianca? Let me do the honors."

"Thank you, but that's not necessary. You're our guest, after all."

"Ah! One thing you'll soon learn about me is never to disagree." Mark jumped ahead of me, beating me to the bar. He introduced himself to Dad, who proudly showed him what treasures he'd found at the liquor store.

"Bianca, I forgot to ask you what your poison of choice will be." Mark looked up from the bar.

"She likes martinis," Daddy answered for me.

"Just give me a glass of Riesling, Mark. Don't go to the trouble of making a martini."

"I used to be a bartender. I can whip up a martini for you in no time, and I guarantee it will be the best you've ever had!"

"That's true. He makes some killer drinks," Lucky vouched for Mark.

A few moments later Mark returned with my martini in hand. "Voilà!"

"Thank you." I took a sip and waited a few extra seconds, enjoying the anxious look on Mark's face. Finally, I nodded my head and said, "Quite impressive."

"Thank you." Mark's face lit up as if he were a schoolboy who had just been awarded a prize.

"Dinner's ready!" As Mom bolted from the kitchen, she made her way to the dining room, carrying two large platters of seafood.

"Excuse me, Mark." I hurried over to Ma and relieved her of one of the platters of fish. I then went into the kitchen to bring out the rest of the food.

When I returned, I saw everyone had already taken their places at the dining room table, and the only empty seat was the one next to Mark's. Swallowing hard, I placed the rest of the platters I was holding down on the table. Mark stood up and held out my chair for me. I immediately blushed, especially because my entire family was now staring at us.

I whispered a thank-you to Mark but refused to look in his direction.

"I'd like you all to join me in praying the Our Father." Mom bowed her head and began praying.

Grateful to have an excuse to close my eyes and not be forced to look at Mark, I bowed my head and prayed the words to the Our Father. I felt Tony take my left hand

and raise it up into the air. Then, a moment later, Mark took my other hand and lifted it up as well in prayer. We didn't usually hold hands to pray. What had gotten into my family? I opened my eyes and saw everyone's hands were joined with one another's. I glanced at Mark and almost jumped out of my skin when I saw his eyes were also open and he was staring right at me. He flashed that devilish grin of his again. I didn't return his smile, bowing my head once more as I closed my eyes and just focused on the Our Father. And then Mark squeezed my hand. And just when I wondered if I had imagined it, he squeezed it lightly again.

When we finished praying, Mom said, "I'd just like to add one more prayer. Thank you, Lord, for letting us be together for another Christmas, and please let us remember what the *true* meaning of this season is. Amen." Mom looked pleased with herself.

"Amen!" we responded.

Mom and Dad began passing the platters of seafood around the table.

"Rita, this all looks amazing!"

"Thank you, Mark. Be sure to try the octopus salad. That's my specialty."

"It's really *my* specialty," my father said. "I taught her how to make it. Actually,

Mark, this custom is more of a southern Italian tradition. My parents were from Naples. Rita's parents were from up north, in the Italian Alps. They're more known for stews and meat dishes."

"It's *our* specialty now because we're a family, Anthony." My mother's voice sounded a bit stern, but I could tell she was holding back because of our guest.

"So, Tony, you must've been named after your father?" Mark asked.

"Yup!" Tony held up his wineglass in salute to Dad, who likewise raised his own.

"And you, Bianca? Who were you named after? A grandmother? I know it's an Italian custom to often name your children after grandparents and parents. That's what my parents did with my sisters and me." Mark was expertly cracking his crab legs. Though crab legs were my favorite seafood, I wasn't going to risk making the mess I usually did when I ate them. I was even being extra careful extricating my clams from their shells.

"It was snowing when I was born. My parents thought it would be beautiful to name me Bianca for the white snow."

"It wasn't just snowing. We had a blizzard that crippled the city of Newport. Everything was brought to a halt. And she's leaving out the most important part, Mark. It was Christmas Eve," Dad added. I knew *that* was coming.

"Really? So tonight is also your birthday?" Mark leaned his face into my line of vision so that I had no choice but to look back at him. The moment I did, his eyes darkened slightly, and he gave me the most penetrating stare. My stomach felt slightly queasy as I remembered how tightly he had squeezed my hand earlier. I felt a little light-headed. The alcohol I had consumed was probably getting to me. Who was I kidding? It was Mark who had gotten to me.

"Yes. I was shortchanged, I guess you could say, being born so close to Christmas." I took an extra long sip of my wine.

"Nonsense! We never shortchanged you, Bianca! We also made a big deal about your birthday on Christmas Eve when you were growing up. We even celebrated the day after Christmas to make it feel more special for you." Mom sounded hurt by my comment.

"I'm sorry, Mom. I was just making a joke."

"Well, I brought dessert, but had I known it was your birthday, I would've done something to mark the occasion."

"How sweet, Mark!" Mom drooled.

I decided to remain quiet.

"So, Mark, you were saying that your parents named you and your siblings after other family members. I noticed your last name is Italian. Where in Italy is your family from?" Dad asked Mark.

"My parents were born here, but my grandparents came from Varese."

"I don't think I've ever heard of it."

"It's up north, not too far from Milan."

Dad smiled. "North, south. Doesn't matter. We're all Italians."

Mom scowled. "Really? Why is it, then, that you're always saying southern Italians are the best?"

Dad blushed. "You know what I mean, Rita. Calm down. We're all from Italy. No difference."

"Hmph." Mom threw her head to the side.

I knew this wouldn't be the end of the discussion, and she'd scold Dad later for his slight against her after our guest left. I turned to Mark. "No wonder you're not familiar with the Feast of the Seven Fishes. It's more commonly practiced in southern Italy."

"That must be why. It's a nice custom. Thank you again for having me, Mr. and Mrs. Simone."

"It's our pleasure, Mark," Mom said as she stood up and started clearing the dishes.

After dinner, we gathered in the living room and Dad brought out the folding table. Tony and Lucky came up from the basement, lugging folding chairs. Playing cards on Christmas Eve was a family tradition. Usually, we played gin rummy and war because those were the only card games my mother knew. This year, Mom only played one game of gin rummy and then excused herself to go make coffee and get dessert ready. I got up to help her, but she whispered, "Keep Mark company." She winked at me.

I wanted to say he had plenty of company with my father and brothers around, but then I noticed Mark was listening to us.

I returned to the table. Once again, Mark held out my chair. Of course, it was the one next to his.

He leaned over and said softly into my ear, "Bet I can beat you at gin rummy."

"Bet you can't," I smirked.

It wasn't long before my father and brothers were out of the game, leaving just Mark and me to battle it out. Though it looked like I was going to beat him, in the end he won.

"Guess you were right. You're a good card player, in addition to being a good bartender." I began collecting the cards and putting them back in their box. Dad, Tony, and Lucky were at the bar, making themselves martinis.

"Thank you. You're a gracious loser." Mark cleared his throat.

"Very funny." I shook my head but was smiling, letting him know we were good.

"You know, Bianca, I meant what I said earlier, that had I known it was your birthday, I would've marked the occasion."

"That's sweet, Mark, but we've only just met. I wouldn't expect you to buy a gift for me."

"Well, I know you must have plans with your family tomorrow since it's Christmas, but is there any way you can spare a couple of hours? I'd like to give you a birthday experience you'll never forget."

"Hmmm . . . an experience I'll never forget, huh? You sure like to make big promises." I did my best to keep a poker face, but on the inside I couldn't help feeling flattered — and a bit intrigued as well.

"I do like to make big promises, and I always deliver. So? Think your family will let me steal you for a few hours?"

"I thought you said a couple of hours."

"Couple, few. You're a grown girl. I'm sure they won't worry if you're gone an extra hour or more. Besides, I can tell your mother loves me." Mark flashed his kilowatt smile, which I was finding more and more irresistible, so of course I accepted his date.

And that was how it all began. Mark picked me up from my parents' after our Christmas Day dinner. Beforehand, I had to listen to my brothers' comments about Mark having the hots for me, and how we had stared at each other all night long on Christmas Eve. My mother and father were thrilled that he was taking me out.

Mark showed up with a huge bouquet of white roses. *"Bianche rose per la bella Bianca."* White roses for the beautiful Bianca.

And then he whisked me off in a limo and took me to the Kingscote, a historic mansion in Newport. I was shocked to discover we would have the entire place to ourselves — well, except for the personal chef, waiter, and live jazz band. When I asked Mark how he'd swung this, he told me that every year he donated generously to the Preservation Society of Newport County. He had also done a favor for the chairman of the society, who happened to be a good friend. So it was now his friend's turn to return Mark's favor.

After eating a five-star gourmet meal, we spent the rest of the night dancing to the sultry notes the jazz quartet played. Mark held me close as we danced. And when he brought me back home and kissed me before I stepped out of the limo, I knew in that moment I was madly in love with Mark Vitale.

So after meeting the love of my life on Christmas Eve, I was able to add that to my list of memorable milestones. But I think what topped all the events — even the night we spent at the Kingscote — was a year later, when Mark surprised me with two tickets to spend Christmas in the Austrian Alps. Ever since I saw *The Sound of Music,* I'd always longed to go to Austria. The movie added even more allure to the idyllic stories Nonna had recounted of her own childhood in the Alps. I had told Mark this when I made him watch the digitally remastered version of *The Sound of Music.* Being the man Mark was, he not only remembered but made certain my dream would come true.

And as I would discover in Austria, that trip would be unforgettable — not just for Mark's amazing surprises but also because I was never again the same woman.

CHAPTER 1

Innsbruck, Austria

The Austrian Alps towered high above me, making me feel like a tiny doll in a storefront Christmas display. Though the day had started out quite mild, a strong gust of wind suddenly blew, shaking the snow from the branches of the fir and pine trees that zigzagged all the way up to the mountain's summit. I had dressed warmly in my new ski outfit, but a chill managed to race down my spine. Being here felt so surreal.

On our first day in Austria, Mark and I ran through the maze of trees. I imagined myself to be a tiny ice skater on a Christmas card depicting a perfect winter wonderland. Ducking behind a baby pine tree, I spotted Mark. His back was turned toward me and he looked from east to west, wondering where I had disappeared. Taking my opportunity, I threw the huge snowball in my hand and hit Mark dead center in his back.

He whipped around, just in time for me to scramble out of his line of vision. But he saw the flash of movement and came running in my direction. I took off before he could reach me. As I dodged the snowballs Mark flung at me, I couldn't help laughing. I hadn't felt this free and giddy since I was a little girl.

The energy I'd expended finally caught up to me and I decided to surrender. But that didn't stop Mark from continuing to hurl snowballs, although he wasn't throwing them as hard now.

"You play dirty, Mark Vitale." My racing pulse began to slow down as I breathed in the fresh mountain air.

"What? You think because you're beautiful I'll give you a break?" Mark dropped the last snowball he was holding and clapped his hands together, rubbing the snow from his gloves.

"And here I thought you were chivalrous. Hmmm!" I pouted, crossing my arms in front of my chest and looking off in the distance. Mark took me by surprise and tackled me. With all the snow blanketing the ground, I fell softly, but I was still startled from being caught off guard.

"Get up!" I giggled, trying to push Mark away, but it was no use.

"Never!" Mark's face edged in closer to mine, and our eyes met. He kissed me. His lips felt cool against mine, but I continued kissing him back.

"Enough playing for today. Let's make our way to the lodge and get some hot chocolate to warm us up."

He helped me up and dusted the snow off my jacket and pants.

"Now that's the Mark I fell in love with — not the ruthless predator who pummeled me with snowballs."

"Come on! You loved it!" Mark smiled, wrapping his arm around my shoulders as we trudged downhill.

"Even though it's just our first day here in Innsbruck, I'm having a great time, Mark."

"It's only going to get better," Mark said, looking at me with a tender expression. Then he plopped a fistful of snow in my hair before running away.

I chased him, throwing as many snowballs as I could form. But none of them hit their target. He disappeared behind a row of trees to my left. Before I could find him, he showed up again behind me and said, "Catch me if you can," and darted off as fast as a gazelle. I laughed as I raced after him.

Once we became exhausted from chasing

each other, we headed over to the lodge, which had been built in the traditional chalet style. Though it was still my first day in Innsbruck, so far everything about Austria was turning out to be exactly the way I'd always expected it to be and more. I could almost hear the von Trapp family from *The Sound of Music* singing. The chill I'd felt earlier had finally left me, and I noticed the wind had died down too. I never tired of staring at the Alps.

"Do you mind getting my hot chocolate for me, Mark? I want to enjoy the scenery a little longer before heading inside."

"Sure. I'll be right back."

About an hour later, after we'd had our hot chocolates and had gone back into the lodge to warm up, Mark said, "My next surprise for you should be arriving soon. Let's head back outside."

Before I could ask what my surprise was, I heard what sounded like a ringing in the distance. I followed Mark's gaze and saw a horse-drawn carriage decked out in bells making its way toward us.

The carriage driver halted the horses a few feet away and tipped his hat to me.

"Good evening, miss."

"Good evening."

"This is for us?" I asked Mark incredulously.

"Yes. I thought it would be fun riding in a horse-drawn carriage, complete with bells, through Innsbruck. It'll be just like those Christmas TV commercials." Mark grinned.

"You're too much!" I laughed.

"So you approve of your latest Christmas gift?"

"You don't need to get me any more gifts! This trip is more than enough of a gift!"

Mark shrugged his shoulders. "What can I say? I love surprising you. Are you ready?"

He held out his arm for me, and I linked mine through his. Helping me step up into the carriage, I noticed how beautiful the sky looked now that it was twilight. The carriage driver draped a heavy blanket over our laps. Mark scooted closer to me as we huddled together to stay warm.

The carriage took off at a steady clip. I leaned my head against Mark's shoulder as I stared at the gorgeous winter landscape before me. It was quite dark, except for the few lights from the various ski lodges that were strewn both at the base and in the mountaintops. When we approached the village, more lights from shops and restaurants greeted us.

Half an hour later, as the carriage was

making its way back to the lodge, we passed the village church, which looked even more beautiful at night and was aglow not only from the lights that hung in front of its façade but also from those that shone through the stained-glass windows.

As we got closer, I saw a choir of boys singing on the front lawn of the church. The notes from "O Little Town of Bethlehem" reached us.

"How charming!" I looked at Mark. He leaned over and placed a kiss on my cheek.

"They're practicing for the big night — Christmas Eve. They go around caroling earlier in the evening. Then they sing for the Vigil Mass at midnight."

"I keep forgetting that you've been here before."

"Why the sad face suddenly?" Mark lifted my chin so that our eyes met.

"It's silly. Never mind."

"Nothing you say can be silly. Out with it!"

I exhaled deeply and shook my head. "It's really stupid. I just wish this were your first time here too. That way we'd be experiencing it all for the first time together."

"That's sweet. Why would you think it was silly?"

"Because I know you've had a life before

me. I feel childish even having that thought."

"I can understand how you feel, Bianca. Ever since I met you at your parents' house last year, I've wanted to experience everything with you. That's probably why I brought you here, in addition to knowing you've always wanted to visit the Alps. When I came here on a business trip and fell in love with Innsbruck, I couldn't help feeling sad that I was here for work. I wished I had someone special with me. Yes, I wanted to make your dream of coming to the Alps a reality, but I also wanted to reexperience it with you. And we are doing things for the first time. I didn't take a carriage ride when I was here, and there's this . . ." Mark's voice trailed off.

"There's this what?"

"I can't say. I almost slipped. It's another surprise."

"*Another* surprise?"

"Yes, and don't give me a lecture again on how this trip was enough of a gift and blah, blah, blah. Let's relax and enjoy the last few minutes of this ride."

I laughed before planting a kiss on Mark's lips. He returned the kiss and tried to pull away, but I didn't let him.

When I finally broke the kiss, I whispered, "I love you, Mark."

"I love you too, Bianca."

That night, I remember wishing I could prolong that moment forever.

Chapter 2

The next afternoon, I was in our hotel room, taking a much-needed nap after we returned from skiing. A couple of hours later, I was awakened by a sweet fragrance. Opening my eyes, I saw white everywhere, which confused me because I remembered our hotel room was painted in hues of brick red and cream. Sitting up, my eyes finally focused on all the white I was seeing. There were bouquets upon bouquets of white roses, which had become my signature flower ever since Mark had given them to me on our first date.

"Mark! You didn't!" I turned, looking for him in bed, but he wasn't there.

"Mark! Are you in the bathroom?"

More silence greeted me. Mark never took naps and didn't even sleep much at night. I was always amazed at how he functioned on so little sleep. He often went walking when he felt restless. Sometimes he even took walks at the crack of dawn when he couldn't sleep. He was probably out walking now.

Getting out of bed, I went over to one of the vases of roses and inhaled deeply their fragrance. I smiled. He must've snuck out while I was napping to buy all these flowers. I couldn't believe I hadn't heard him placing them all around the room. Then again, I was a heavy sleeper, unlike him. Even after a year of dating, he was still so thoughtful and romantic. My thoughts soon drifted to how Mark had made love to me all night long. The sound of our hotel room door opening shook me out of my thoughts as Mark came in.

"Good afternoon, beautiful!" Mark acted as if everything were normal, like our entire room wasn't covered in roses.

I decided to play along and merely said, "Good afternoon," without looking at him, as I picked up my brush and went into the bathroom to brush my hair. It only took Mark a couple of minutes to come over to me. He wrapped his arms around my waist and began trailing kisses down the side of my neck.

I whispered, "Thank you for the gorgeous roses. You know, one bouquet would have been enough."

Mark stopped kissing my neck and looked

at my image in the medicine cabinet mirror. "What fun would that have been? And it wouldn't have been a surprise."

"Receiving flowers unexpectedly is always a surprise!" I tapped the handle of my brush gently on the tip of his nose, scolding him.

He took the brush from my hand and brushed my hair. Even though my hair was short and I could style it with my fingers if I wanted to, I still liked running a brush through it. The way Mark caressed the brush through my scalp was very sensual. I closed my eyes, enjoying the feeling, not even noticing that our conversation had stopped. When I finally opened my eyes, Mark was staring at my expression in the mirror. I could tell he wanted me, and I wanted him. Turning around, I wrapped my arms around his neck and kissed him, never releasing his lips even after he lifted me off the floor and carried me to bed, where we made love.

Mark fell asleep with his head on my chest. I thought back to the way he had looked at me earlier, while I brushed my hair. I was amazed by how he could still stare at me as if he were seeing me for the first time. His face had held the same expression as the night we met at my parents' on Christmas Eve. And in that moment, I realized that he had fallen in love with me at first sight.

CHAPTER 3

"Every bone in my body aches!" I whined as I lay outstretched on the bed.

"You're just not used to skiing. But come on! All the fun we had was worth the aches." Mark sat at the foot of our bed and began massaging my sore calves.

"Yes, it was fun, but I think I'm enjoying this even more." I smiled and closed my eyes, relaxing. Suddenly, I felt Mark's lips on mine.

"Don't get too comfortable, Bianca. We're going out soon," he said after kissing me.

"Again?"

"We still haven't had lunch, and it's almost two o'clock."

"Let's just order room service. We can light the fire and have a cozy afternoon in the warmth of our hotel." My eyes pleaded with Mark.

"Usually, I can't resist when you beg me, but not today, *Signorina* Simone. I have another surprise for you."

"I guess you've planned a surprise for me every day of our week here." I said this as a statement rather than a question because I knew what his answer would be. Mark merely smiled mischievously.

"I'm going to take a quick shower and let you rest a bit before it's your turn to get ready, but you'll have to hurry. I want to be out of here within the hour."

"Yes, sir!" I saluted Mark. He shook his head before stepping into the bathroom. I giggled.

Shortly over an hour later, Mark was driving our rental car up the winding roads of a mountain. Soon, I saw signs leading to the Hungerburg Funicular. When we had first arrived in Innsbruck, I had overheard a group of tourists in our hotel lobby saying they were headed there. I had no idea what it was, other than a tourist attraction. Usually, I liked to research the city I was traveling to, but I hadn't had time to read up on Innsbruck before we left for our trip. My job as a vet tech at a veterinarian's office in Newport left me so exhausted by the end of the workday that all I wanted to do was veg out on the couch with a glass of wine and watch TV. I loved my job and someday hoped to open a no-kill adoption shelter. My parents were looking after Frenchie, my French bulldog, and Sheila, my Australian shepherd, while I was away.

After seeing more signs leading to Hungerburg Funicular, I was convinced this was Mark's next surprise for me.

"Have you heard anything about the Hungerburg Funicular?" Mark asked after we parked our rental car.

"I know it's a tourist attraction, but that's about it."

"It's probably one of the most popular attractions in Innsbruck. It's a railway that travels up the mountain's incline with the assistance of a cable. Not only are the views astounding from the summit but the funicular itself is an engineering feat."

"Sounds cool."

"You have no idea how cool. I can't wait!" Mark rubbed his hands together in excitement.

We purchased our tickets for the funicular right as the next scheduled railway arrived, making it just in time to board before departure.

"The view is already gorgeous from this height." I shaded the sun from my eyes and took in the expanse of the panorama before me.

"This view is nothing. Wait until we get to Seegrube. There are four stations along the funicular's route. We're getting off at Hungerburg station, where we'll take the Nordkette cable car to Seegrube. That's where the views are at their most breathtaking."

With the funicular's lightning-fast speed, it didn't take long to reach Hungerburg station.

"Wow!"

"Incredible, right?"

I nodded my head.

"The Hungerburg Funicular is beyond brilliant. A London architect by the name of Zaha Hadid designed it, along with the funicular's four stations and the bridge that goes over the river Inn. The Hungerburg station itself is considered a modern architectural wonder. We'll come back to the station later. There are shops and restaurants. Also, we'll stick around until it starts to get dark. You have to see the way the architecture and the funicular light up at night."

"This is a wonderful surprise. Thank you!" I hugged Mark.

He rubbed my back and kissed my forehead before saying, "There's more to the surprise."

It wasn't long before it was time to step off the funicular and wait on line to board the Nordkette cable car. In a few moments, we were on the cable car, climbing ever higher. Usually, I wasn't afraid of heights, so I dared to glance down at the wide expanse and drop below us. I felt a brief flash of fear wash over me. Returning my gaze to the view in front of me, I took a deep breath. The Alps looked so close that I could almost imagine what it must feel like to be a falcon soaring to such heights.

Our cable car arrived in Seegrube. In addition to being able to see remarkable views of the town, we were surrounded by 360-degree vistas of mountain chains. Mark and I walked slowly, savoring the Alps' pristine landscape. I loved how the snow-covered peaks contrasted against the sky, making it appear an even deeper shade of blue.

"When I was in St. Thomas and saw the sky and water, I finally understood what people meant when they talked about Caribbean blue. I had never seen such intense hues of blue. But the blue of the Alpine sky is just as unforgettable."

"I know exactly what you mean, Bianca." Mark brushed my cheek with the back of his hand. "So, what do you say we grab a bite to eat?"

"Up here?"

"Yes, it's a town."

"I keep forgetting that people live up in the mountains, like Heidi!" I laughed.

"Well, where I'm taking you for lunch —" Mark stopped in midsentence and glanced at his watch. "Well, it's four o'clock now, so we can consider this an early dinner. Anyway, as I was saying, where I'm taking you to eat is the other half of my surprise."

A short while later, we arrived at the Restaurant Seegrube, which had a rustic, Austrian charm and could pass for a very large house. Its exterior was all wood and resembled a chateau, complete with window boxes and shutters. Picnic-style tables surrounded the front and sides of the property. With a view this gorgeous, I couldn't see how anyone would choose to dine indoors — well, at least in the warmer months.

No one was seated at any of the tables.

"I guess it's too cold to eat outdoors," I said to Mark.

"Well, yes and no. You get a few brave people, mostly the locals, who don't mind eating in the cold. But the reason you don't see anyone dining out here today is that I rented the restaurant for a few hours. This way we have it all to ourselves." Mark said this nonchalantly, as if it were every day that someone rented an entire restaurant at the top of the Alps.

"You didn't!" But of course I knew he had. Just like when he reserved the Kingscote for our first date in Newport. Somehow he always managed to surpass his previous surprises.

"I would do anything for you, Bianca. Anything."

Our eyes locked. I had never loved anyone the way I loved him. And just when I thought of how my feelings for him couldn't possibly grow any stronger, they did.

I walked over to him and stood on my tiptoes so that our faces touched. Placing my hands on his shoulders, I whispered, "I love you so much, Mark."

"I love you more."

This was a game we often played. I usually replied with, "No, I love *you* more." But I was too overcome with emotion at that moment to play along. Tears filled my eyes. I kissed him. We hugged each other and stared at the Alps.

"Excuse me? We're ready for you now, if you'd follow me."

A woman dressed in a traditional Austrian folk costume led us to a table.

"While you can't go wrong with any of the tables at the Restaurant Seegrube, this table does have what we believe is the best view of the Alps," the hostess said proudly.

"Your waiter will be with you shortly."

Mark sat alongside me on the bench. I wondered why he wasn't sitting opposite me. He saw my questioning glance and said, "This way I can watch the view with you."

"You're too adorable, Mr. Vitale!" I playfully nudged his side with my elbow. He nudged me back.

We drank steins of beer and ate our first course, goulash accompanied with the most delicious rolls. Then our entrees of Wiener schnitzel came out. The veal was so tender.

After dinner, Mark patted his stomach. "If I die today, I will have died a satisfied and happy man. Now, if you'll excuse me, Bianca, nature calls. Feel free to order dessert for both of us. Surprise me."

"Oh, so I finally get to surprise *you.*"

"Hey! I like receiving them as much as I like giving them." Mark winked before he left in search of the restroom.

I couldn't stop looking at the view but knew I should decide what I wanted for dessert. It wasn't hard to choose once I perused the menu options. Naturally, I wanted the traditional Austrian dessert of *Apfelstrudel.* I wanted to keep this trip as authentically Austrian as possible.

Once Mark returned from the restroom, we decided to head inside to eat our dessert. The sun had now fully set and it was getting quite cold, especially at this summit.

The interior was dimly lit, adding to the restaurant's romantic ambience. Soft jazz was coming from a live quartet.

"I know you're sore from skiing this morning, but think you can bear to dance with me for a song or two?"

I smiled, and that was the only confirmation Mark needed to know that I would dance with him. Ever since our first date, dancing had become one of our favorite things to do together. Mark had introduced me to jazz, and we'd been to jazz clubs both in Newport and Boston. He'd promised to take me to a few of the more famous ones in New York City. I loved dancing with him, feeling his body pressed up close against mine as we swayed to the music.

As promised, Mark took me back to the Hungerburg station after we left Seegrube. We did a little shopping and then rested up in one of the cafés before heading to the funicular to return to Innsbruck. Mark was right about the lighting and the dramatic nighttime view of the station and the bridge that spanned the Inn River. The funiculars were also lit up. In the distance, we saw quick flashes of light coming off them as they sped through.

Once we stepped off the funicular in Innsbruck, we made our way over to where we had parked our car.

"This afternoon and night have been magical, Mark. I'll never forget them."

"Neither will I, Bianca. Now let's get back to our hotel before I just collapse here and fall asleep."

"That makes two of us!" I laughed.

Driving along the winding, dark roads that led to our hotel, we sang Christmas carols. Though we were exhausted, we still made the most of our time together. Mark's appreciation for life and his never wasting a moment to be happy were the qualities I loved most about him.

Chapter 4

Mark and I strolled through the streets of Innsbruck's Old Town, which was also known as Altstadt von Innsbruck. It was a charming, picturesque village where no cars were allowed. Historical and modern buildings were equally breathtaking in their architecture. And, of course, the mountains' backdrop further added to the town's allure. Winding side streets housed a few museums as well as restaurants and cafés.

We approached a crowd standing in front of a building. From the distance, it was difficult for me to see the building except for the gold top gleaming in the sunlight.

"The Golden Roof, Altstadt von Innsbruck's most famous landmark," Mark said.

After a few tourists left, I was finally able to get a better view of the Golden Roof. Several sculpted reliefs and painted murals adorned the house's façade.

"It's gorgeous. Do you know how far back

it dates?" I asked Mark.

"Fifteen hundred. There's also an interesting piece of history attached to it. The roof was decorated with over two thousand fire-gilded copper tiles to commemorate the wedding of Emperor Maximilian I to Bianca Maria Sforza." Mark smiled as he said this.

"His wife's name was Bianca?"

"Yes. I swear, I didn't make this up. It's just a coincidence. Anyway, the emperor and his wife would use the house's balcony to view tournaments and any other events that were conducted here in the square."

"Would you like a photo?" A middle-aged American tourist and his wife gestured to my cell phone camera.

"Oh, yes! That would be great." I handed my cell phone to the man and showed him where to click to take the photo. "Just be sure to get the gold roof. I know with all these tourists around, you won't have a chance to get the entire building."

The man nodded. "One, two, three!"

"Thank you." I took my cell phone back and viewed the photo.

"How is it? Do you need me to take another?" the tourist asked.

"No, thank you. It's perfect."

Mark shielded his eyes from the sun as he looked at the photo. "Not bad. We'll have to blow it up when we get back home. I think that's the best picture of us yet."

"Mark, let me get one of you alone in front of the building."

He posed for me, making a silly face.

After we were done taking photos, Mark took my hand and led me toward the shops. "Let's do some shopping."

I was immediately drawn to a hand-knit sweater boutique. I always had a weakness for beautiful wool sweaters.

"Let's go in here, Mark."

"Why don't you go ahead? I just want to browse in a men's shoe store I saw. This way you can take your time trying on sweaters. I'll come get you. I'm sure you'll take longer than me." Mark grinned.

"Not all women take forever shopping." I shook my head as I entered the store.

It actually didn't take me long to pick out four sweaters I fell in love with. Two were for me and the other two were for my mother. Before paying for my sweaters, I lingered for a few more minutes. Once I was satisfied that I'd seen all of the merchandise and didn't want anything else, I headed over to the cashier. Mark stepped into the boutique after I finished paying.

"Too late!" Mark snapped his fingers. "I wanted to get that for you."

"You've already paid for so much. I know I'm only a vet tech, but I'm not completely poor!"

"Okay. I thought you were."

I swatted Mark's arm playfully. "You're being a bad boy today."

"Guilty as charged." He held up his hands in resignation.

After leaving the sweater shop, we browsed in a few other stores.

"Can we take a break at one of the cafés? These boots I'm wearing today aren't the most comfortable."

"Sure. I have a favorite café from the last time I was here. Follow me."

We turned onto a side street that was, much to my astonishment, devoid of tourists. I suddenly stopped.

"What's the matter?"

"You have to take a picture of me on this street. Just look at the perspective with the narrowness of the street and the buildings that seem to slope inward, not to mention the mountain in the backdrop. I know this will make a great shot."

I pulled my phone out of my purse and handed it to Mark. Then I struck a pose, placing my hands on either side of my hips and bending my knees to my left. Turning my face to the side, I puckered up my lips.

Mark couldn't stop laughing.

"Sexy! Okay, now let's do a serious one too."

I stood this time with my hands behind my back and smiled.

After taking the photo, Mark examined it and said, "*Bella* Bianca."

Mark linked his arm with mine and led me to a tiny café. As we approached the door, I could smell the espresso, and pastries that had probably just come out of the oven. The café was practically empty, with just one other couple seated. We took a table at the back.

"Nice and cozy," I said.

"Just how I like it."

We ordered café lattes and two popular Austrian sweets. Mark ordered a slice of Sacher torte, a chocolate layer cake with an apricot preserve filling and a chocolate ganache frosting. I ordered a *marillenstrudel,* or apricot strudel.

As we waited for our coffee and desserts, I took my compact out of my purse, inspecting my hair and makeup. When I lowered my compact, I saw a small gift-wrapped box sitting in my dessert plate. Mark was sitting with his elbows on the table and his chin resting in his hands, waiting for me to notice the gift.

At this point, I knew it was no use scolding him anymore. He'd made up his mind that he was going to surprise me every day of our stay here. I just shook my head and smiled. And I had to admit, I was enjoying receiving his surprises so much that I had begun to wonder what my next one would be.

I was about to untie the bow on the box when Mark interrupted me. "It's not completely covered in gift wrap. You can just lift the cover."

I did as he instructed, and the first thing I saw was a flash of gold that glinted brightly under the lights from the chandelier overhead.

"Oh! How cute! It's a small replica of the Golden Roof house we visited!" Carefully lifting the ceramic piece out of the box, I admired its details, which were exactly like the adornments on the Golden Roof.

"I love it! Thank you, Mark! I'll think about our trip every time I look at it." I leaned over the table and kissed him on the lips.

The waitress came over with our orders. Once she left, Mark took my hand in his. "Bianca, this gift symbolizes more than just our trip to Innsbruck. You know how crazy I am about you. I think about you almost constantly when we're not together. I was even daydreaming the other day during a meeting at work. I know I can't be with you twenty-four/seven, but I'd like to be with you as much as I can. I want you to move in with me."

I was taken aback. Of course, things had been going so well with us, so this would be the next logical step. But I still wasn't expecting it.

"If you need to think about it, please take some time. I know I'm springing this on you since we haven't discussed living together before."

"No," I said. Mark's face looked crestfallen before I added, "What I mean is, I don't need to think about it. I'd love to move in with you. I also think about you every moment we're not together." I squeezed Mark's hand. He squeezed mine back before releasing it to stroke my cheek with the back of his hand.

"Someday I'm going to build your own gold house."

"Oh, I don't know about that. It'll be tacky. I'd settle for a modern design, much like the homes I've seen you design for your clients." I giggled.

"I guess my sarcasm is rubbing off on you. Rest assured, your house will be my best design because you'll be my muse."

After we had our pastries, we ordered more coffee and lingered in the café, enjoying its cozy, intimate surroundings and each other's company. As I sipped my café latte, I glanced out of the window I was seated next to and noticed a child staring at us. I wondered how we must have looked to her. Could she tell we were madly in love? And was she able to detect the glow in our faces that came from planning our dreams for the future together?

Later, whenever I reflected on that afternoon in the café, I couldn't help but think how foolish we were, for all we talked about was how happy we would be, never anticipating the trials that would surely come.

CHAPTER 5

Mark and I returned to Innsbruck's Old Town on Christmas Eve. We walked through the Christmas Market that was held there every year. Innsbruck actually had four different Christmas Markets in different parts of the city. Lights shaped as snowflakes and icicles dangled from the overhead cables, and a lit Christmas tree completed the magical scenery. The Alps looked more dramatic at night as their snow-capped peaks loomed over the village.

We decided to have a quiet Christmas Eve. Earlier, Mark had arranged for our hotel to bring a late dinner to our room. I couldn't help but be a little surprised — and disappointed — since he'd had something grand planned for me almost every day of our trip. In addition to it being Christmas Eve, it was also my birthday. It seemed odd that he wasn't going to mark either occasion in a more memorable way.

Then again, we were quite exhausted after the long day we'd had yesterday, when Mark had surprised me by driving to Salzburg, where we took the original *Sound of Music* tour.

We visited all the famous sites where the movie had been filmed: the Mirabell Gardens, where Julie Andrews's character, Maria, sang "Do-Re-Mi"; the Leopoldskron Palace, where the famous boat scene was filmed; the gazebo at Hellbrunn Palace — my favorite — where Maria and Baron von Trapp kissed; Nonnberg Abbey, which is still a convent today; the gorgeous Salzburg Lake District; Mondsee, where Maria and von Trapp's wedding was filmed for the movie. And, of course, throughout the bus tour, the original soundtrack from the movie played. I was in *Sound of Music* heaven, to say the least!

As we strolled through the Christmas Market, I linked my arm through Mark's.

"I love Christmas Eve more than Christmas Day."

"I think I do too. For me, it's the waiting for the birth of Christ at midnight. I love the suspense of it all."

I laughed. "Suspense? It's not like we don't know what happens!"

"You know what I mean. There's a certain

excitement building up."

"True. I think I love Christmas Eve so much because it's more of a big deal in my family. We have our big Feast of the Seven Fishes, and we open our gifts at midnight, although some years we went to midnight mass and waited to open our gifts after we returned home from church."

"I'm sure it has something to do with it being your birthday as well." Mark winked.

"Well, believe it or not, I almost forget it's my birthday, but not when I was a kid. I made sure my parents remembered that I was due double my share of gifts since it fell on Christmas Eve. Now, as an adult, I'm more focused on Christmas like everyone else is." I pouted, pretending I was upset that the attention was deflected from my birthday.

"Well, we'll have to rectify that. You will *never* forget it's also your birthday on Christmas Eve as long as you're with me." Mark kissed me lightly on the lips.

We walked over to the lit Christmas tree in the square. Mark took a few photos with his cell phone camera. Then we stood with our arms wrapped around each other and stared at the lights on the tree.

Mark turned to me, his expression becoming somber.

"I was going to wait until midnight to give you this next gift, but I can't. And the moment feels right."

"Well, I'm going to wait until midnight to give you my gifts."

Mark ignored my comment. I wondered if he had even heard me. Suddenly, he looked very pale.

"Are you feeling all right, Mark?"

"Oh, my boot is unlaced."

He bent down and began tying his boot. I shrugged my shoulders and returned my attention to the star on top of the Christmas tree. I used to love to make wishes as I looked at the star that adorned my family's tree when I was a child. My thoughts were interrupted by Mark, who was tugging my hand. I looked down and saw he was now on one knee, holding an open black velvet box. Inside, the most beautiful princess-cut diamond shimmered brilliantly.

"Bianca, you've already made me the happiest I've ever been. I can't imagine spending the rest of my days without you as my wife. I want to share every moment with you. Your love has made me a better person, and I know together our lives will be rich ones. Will you do me the honor of marrying me?"

Mark's voice cracked a little. In the year

that we'd dated, I had never seen him nervous. Tears fell down my face.

"Yes, yes, yes! I'll marry you."

Mark slipped the ring onto my finger and then stood up, lifting me high in the air as he spun me around.

"Oh, and happy birthday, by the way!" Mark shouted as he continued twirling me around.

Tears continued to stream down my face as I laughed. My gaze landed on the star atop the village Christmas tree, and I thought about how all of my dreams were coming true.

CHAPTER 6

"Wake up! Wake up! Santa's here!"

Mark's voice roused me out of a deep slumber.

"I'm not ready to wake up. Santa can wait."

"No, he can't. It's Christmas. You don't want the day to be over in a flash because you were too lazy to get out of bed, Bianca!" Mark pulled the blanket off me.

"All right. All right. I'm getting up. What time is it anyway?"

"Seven A.M. My favorite time of the day!"

"Seven? Mark, we went to bed at close to two! You could've at least let me get in another couple of hours of sleep."

"If you want, you can take a nap in the afternoon. I just couldn't wait to open gifts." Mark was grinning from ear to ear, like a schoolboy. I couldn't resist smiling.

"You're too much!"

"I've lit the fireplace to make it feel even

cozier in here. And I ran out to the bakery to buy a few Danish. Room service should be here any moment with a fresh pot of coffee."

"The bakery was open already?"

"Of course! Bakers rise early to get all of their baking done."

"Sounds like it should've been your calling." I threw my pillow at Mark.

"I'm going to ignore that because it's Christmas, or else I would be pummeling you right now in a pillow fight!"

I got out of bed and went to the bathroom. After I brushed my teeth, I splashed cold water on my face, hoping it would wake me up. Suddenly, I remembered what had happened last night. Mark had proposed to me! Glancing down at my left ring finger, I admired my gorgeous diamond. It really had happened. I hadn't been dreaming. I remembered falling asleep staring at all of the diamond's sparkling facets. Guilt stabbed me for a moment as I thought about how I had greeted Mark this morning.

I stepped out of the bathroom. Mark was at the door. Room service had arrived with our coffee. Quickly walking over to the Christmas tree in our room, I picked up one of Mark's gifts before he returned and had time to notice. I placed it under two

Danish on his plate. Fortunately, the Danish were huge and the gift was fully concealed.

Mark carried the tray containing the coffee to the blanket he had set up on the floor in front of the fireplace.

"I didn't know you were getting fruit and cheese in addition to the coffee."

"I didn't. This is the hotel's complimentary Christmas gift to us. They brought it up while you were brushing your teeth."

I got down on my knees next to Mark, who was sitting cross-legged while he poured coffee into our cups. I kissed him on the cheek and whispered, "Thank you for making last night so special. I can't wait to be your wife."

Mark put the coffee carafe down before hugging me. We kissed for a long time. Soon, we got lost in the moment and made love, forgetting about our breakfast.

When we finally got around to eating, Mark didn't notice the gift I'd hidden under the Danish even after he devoured one.

"I can never get enough Austrian pastries! Maybe we should move here and open our own bakery."

"We don't have to open our own bakery. We can just come here every year."

"True." Mark picked up his second Danish. "Hey! What's this?" He took the gift I'd left for him on his plate, holding it out to me questioningly.

"My special Christmas gift for you. I can't believe you didn't notice it after picking up the first Danish."

"How could I? These Danish are humongous! Thank you." Mark leaned over and kissed me.

"Well, don't thank me yet. Open it first and see if you like it."

"Something tells me I'll love it!" Mark smiled as he tore off the wrapping paper from his gift.

"Wow! A platinum watch! This is gorgeous, Bianca, but it must've cost you a fortune. You shouldn't have."

"Shhh! You deserve it. And who says you're the only one who's allowed to splurge on me? Turn it over."

Mark turned the watch over and read aloud the engraving I'd had the jeweler etch into the back.

" 'May every moment of your life be filled with happiness.' Bianca! That's beautiful. Thank you!" Mark hugged me for what felt like a long time. We sat silently, enjoying the moment.

"It's going to be hard returning home and back to work. When I'm with you, all I want to do is have fun." Mark began massaging the back of my neck. It felt so good that I was tempted to make love to him again.

"I know. But just think: we'll be moving in together. I'm so excited thinking about that!"

"And don't forget, you'll also be planning a wedding."

"I'm kind of surprised you asked me to move in with you, Mark, considering you knew you were going to pop the question. Why didn't you wait to ask me to move in with you until after you proposed?"

"I figured asking you to move in with me before I asked you to marry me would throw you off. Usually, when couples move in together, some time passes before the question about getting married comes up. I wanted the proposal to be a complete surprise. And from your reaction, I can tell it was."

"I don't think I've ever been that surprised in my life."

"If you'd rather wait until after we get married to live together, I understand, Bianca."

"Are you kidding me? I don't believe in wasting one second."

Mark laughed. "Good. I just wanted to make sure. Okay, now it's your turn." Mark got up and strode over to the Christmas tree. He returned to my side with a large box.

"Here's your first gift, but it's my favorite one — well, my favorite after the engagement ring. And that was your birthday gift. This is the first of your Christmas gifts."

"No, it's not. What about this trip and all the other wonderful surprises you've given me this week?"

"Ah! Those were just 'I love you' gifts."

I kissed Mark on the tip of his nose. "You're too adorable."

"I know, but I never tire of hearing your compliments. So keep them coming!"

I opened the large box only to find it contained another slightly smaller wrapped box. I raised a questioning eyebrow in Mark's direction, but he merely gestured for me to keep on going. But after I unwrapped the second box, another smaller one lay inside that one.

"Okay, this is a joke. Where's the real gift?"

"Keep unwrapping."

Sighing, I opened the next box and the next one, until I finally got to a very small box.

"Well, I know this has to be it since you can't place another box inside this one."

Mark remained silent, but I detected a smirk.

I removed the gift wrap from the small box and opened it, gasping when I saw what was inside — a white gold necklace with a stunning rainbow pendant made up of multicolored crystals.

"It's absolutely breathtaking, Mark!"

"I bought it here in Innsbruck. Remember the day I left you alone to shop for your sweaters? I ran over to a crystal shop I had seen. They're Austrian crystals, not Swarovski, though. The shop is owned by a local crystal artisan. All of his jewelry is one of a kind. I wanted you to have a custom-made piece that no one else would have."

"I love it! Thank you so much." I threw my arms around Mark's shoulders and kissed him.

"Whenever you're going through a tough time and are feeling sad or hopeless, I want you to look at this rainbow and think of my love for you. I want you to remember that no matter what obstacles might lie in our future, we can overcome them because we have each other. Promise me you'll always remember that, Bianca?"

I nodded my head. "I promise." We kissed again.

"Now I'm the one not looking forward to

leaving Austria." I exhaled deeply as I leaned back into Mark. He stroked my hair.

"Well, I have a confession to make."

I pulled away from Mark, looking him in the eye.

"While you were sleeping last night, I went online and reserved a hotel for us in . . ." Mark's voice trailed off.

"In where?" The suspense was killing me, and Mark knew it.

"Oh, in . . ."

"Mark!"

"In Lake Como!"

"You didn't! I've always wanted to go there!" I covered my mouth with my hands. "But don't you have to get back to work? I'll be fine since I took two weeks off to take care of some things at home."

"You forget, I own my business. I can do whatever I want."

"We're going to Lake Como!" I giggled like a school-girl who had just met Santa.

"We'll take a bus to Lake Como. But don't worry, it's not one of those stuffy, crowded buses. It's a luxury coach that only reserves smaller groups. We'll be going over the Brenner Pass. Have you ever heard of it?"

I shook my head.

"It's a highway that connects Austria and Italy. The views are astounding. That's why

347

I decided to reserve the bus tickets. This way I won't have to worry about keeping my eyes on the road while driving. I can enjoy the sights with you. We'll rent a car in Lake Como for the week."

"You know you're only making it that much harder for when we have to finally leave Austria?"

"I know. But who cares? After you said yes to my proposal, I felt we should celebrate and be together alone for another week. Is that so bad?"

"No, it's not. I love you, Mark Vitale. And I'll love you forever."

"That's a promise I'm going to hold you to."

While Mark helped me put on my necklace, I silently asked myself if it was really possible to be this happy.

"Is it all right, Bianca, if I jump into the shower before you? We need to hurry if we don't want to be late for church."

"Go right ahead."

I walked over to the bed and sat down on the edge. I couldn't stop staring at the sparkling crystals on my rainbow pendant. And then the oddest thing happened. Although I was the happiest I had ever been in my life, a brief flash of sadness washed over me. Maybe it was because as I stared at my necklace, Mark's words about facing obstacles came back to me. But I had promised him if I ever felt sad, I would look at my rainbow charm and remember his love for me. And that's what I did in that moment. The sadness lifted, yet I still felt a bit unsettled.

CHAPTER 7

Two days after Christmas, Mark and I were on the luxury bus en route to Lake Como. The bus hugged the curves of the cliffs like two lovers locked in a tight embrace, winding its way around the breathtaking Brenner Pass. The highway cut through the Alps along the Italian and Austrian border. Dramatic mountain peaks, waterfalls, and monastery upon monastery dotted the striking landscape. Frequent but brief showers were the norm at this elevation and were a welcome occurrence because of the rainbows that appeared once the rain ended.

I didn't tell Mark this for fear of sounding corny, but it was ironic that he'd chosen a necklace with a rainbow pendant because I had always adored rainbows. And there were so many of them today as our bus traveled over the Brenner Pass. My mother used to tell me when I was a child that rainbows were proof of God's existence, for only God could create such a magical phenomenon. She also told me that God was trying to show us that while there might be storms in our lives, there was always hope, much like what Mark wanted me to remember whenever I had to go through a difficult time.

Applause from the bus's passengers startled me, taking me out of my thoughts. Whenever our driver snaked his way around a difficult, extra-narrow curve, the passengers stopped talking and remained quiet until we successfully cleared the bend. Then, once we did, cheers and applause filled the air. It had now become a game for the passengers.

A group of college students from Ireland were especially enthusiastic, yelling repeatedly, "Bravo! Bravo, maestro!" Our bus driver, Domenico, was from Italy. The students settled down only when Domenico gave a victorious wave.

"So, have you given any thought at all to our wedding?" Mark asked me.

"We've only been engaged for four days, Mark!"

"I know, but I also know how special weddings are for women. I'm sure you've had some idea of what you would like."

I smiled shyly. Mark elbowed me. "Come on! Out with it."

"Well, you're going to think I'm a bit of a narcissist, but I always envisioned myself getting married in the thick of winter, and if it's snowing, all the better."

"I can't say I'm surprised, since your name is Bianca and you were born during a blizzard on Christmas Eve. Why not come full circle and get married in the winter too?"

"When you put it that way, it makes me feel even more ridiculous!"

"It's not ridiculous. I think it's beautiful — and fitting for you. My only reservation is that I'll have to wait a year for you to become my wife."

"I need time to plan the wedding — unless you'd like to elope?"

"Oh, no! Your parents would kill me for depriving them of seeing their only daughter get married. Your brothers would have my head too."

"You got that right!" I laughed.

"So a winter wedding. Now we just have to pick a date."

"Definitely not Christmas. I don't want our anniversary to compete with the holiday and my birthday. I want it to be its own special day."

"I wholeheartedly agree. So that leaves us with any week besides Christmas week in

December or the months of January and February. If you hope that it snows, your better bet would be January or February. Then again, in Rhode Island we can be assured of getting snow in December as well."

"Definitely not December. Again, it's too reminiscent of Christmas. How about the first week in February? And February is the month of love because Valentine's Day is celebrated then. It would hold some symbolic significance too."

"Then why not get married on Valentine's Day?"

"Too cliché. And again, I want to keep our anniversary separate from any other occasion."

"Okay. The first week in February it is, then."

Mark took my hand and kissed it, holding it against his chest. I could feel his heart beat. Whenever we lay in bed together, I fell asleep with my arm draped against his chest. The sound of his heart beating always comforted me.

The sky clouded over once again, and soon rain began falling in steady rivulets. We had another hour to go until we reached Italy. I prayed it would just be a passing shower since a heavier downpour would inevitably delay our trip. No sooner had this thought entered my mind than the rain suddenly came lashing down like arrows showered on a battlefield.

"*Merda!*" the bus driver whispered.

Since Mark and I were sitting in the front, we could hear Domenico cursing as he slowed his speed.

The Irish teens seemed oblivious to the rain and our need to go slower. Earlier, their laughter had subsided whenever Domenico had maneuvered around a tight curve. But now they trusted Domenico's driving skills and continued chatting even after the last few twists in the road. For the next twenty minutes, the rain pelted down. Lightning flashed through the sky.

"Whoa! Would you bloody look at that?"

One of the Irish teens pointed at the bolt of lightning that had just struck. At this elevation in the Alps, the lightning storm was a spectacular show as several other flashes of light streaked the sky. Many of the tourists on the bus quickly snapped photos. A clap of thunder reverberated from the ground beneath the bus, causing a few of the young girls to shriek. The boys wasted no time in making fun of them.

"*Basta!* Calm down back there," Domenico shouted at the kids.

"We're just having a little fun!"

"Be nice to the girls, okay?" Domenico glanced in his rearview mirror.

I had turned my head to look at the kids behind us when, without warning, I felt the bus lurch forward a few feet before it came to a stop. When I looked out of the windshield, I saw Domenico had narrowly missed rear-ending the car in front of us. The driver blasted his horn at Domenico.

"What the bloody hell are you doing?" one of the Irish teens shouted.

"Silenzio!" Domenico yelled back. The jolt the passengers had received a moment before made them heed Domenico's order. He resumed driving. The storm had finally passed and the traffic was easing up.

"Are you all right?" Mark asked me.

"Yeah. I just got a little startled, like everyone else."

"That definitely woke me up. I hadn't been able to fully wake up yet." Mark yawned.

"We should nap a bit before we get to Italy."

"Sounds good to me," Mark said as he rested his head on top of mine, which was propped against his chest.

I hadn't realized how tired I was, but within minutes I felt myself falling asleep.

■ ■ ■ ■

"Oh my God!"

I didn't know how much time had elapsed before I was awakened by several passengers screaming. Before I could register what was happening, the bus swerved from side to side. I almost fell out of my seat, but Mark grabbed my arm, steadying me.

The rosary that hung from Domenico's rearview mirror swung back and forth frantically, slamming against the windshield.

Mark braced my chest with one arm and with his free hand held the rail on the seat back in front of us. Our eyes locked for a moment before Domenico lost control of the bus.

CHAPTER 8

I wake up suddenly in a cold sweat. My heart is racing. It starts to slow down when I see Mark sitting at the foot of my bed.

"Are you having that nightmare again?" he asks me, concern written all over his features.

I nod my head. Lately, whenever I wake up, I feel extra foggy, more disoriented than usual. Today, a headache accompanies the fogginess. It must be the sleeping pills my doctor prescribed for my recent bout of insomnia.

Mark says, "Five years, Bianca."

"I know."

"Can you believe it?"

I shake my head. "No, I can't believe it will be five years since we got engaged. It feels like only yesterday."

"It's time, Bianca."

"Time for what?"

"You need to let me go."

357

"How can I let you go if you're already gone, Mark? You left me, remember?" My voice rises sharply.

"It wasn't my choice. You know that."

"The hell it wasn't! If you hadn't been so concerned about bracing me, you might've been saved."

"You would've been killed too."

"And I would've been with you . . . forever." My eyes fill with tears as I turn away from Mark, not wanting him to see my pain, though I'm sure he must hear it in my voice.

"You are with me and will be with me forever."

"I want you here with me in *this* life." I turn back toward Mark, but he's gone. And as always after he's visited me, the despair deepens.

"Damn you!" I grab the glass of water on my night table and fling it in the direction in which Mark had been sitting. The glass crashes against my bed's foot post. My rage soon turns to tears as I collapse on my bed and cry. Moments later, the phone rings sharply. I hesitate a moment before answering it.

"Hello."

"Excuse me, miss. It's the kitchen. We noticed you hadn't placed a room service order for breakfast this morning. We just want to confirm you won't be needing breakfast delivered today."

I had forgotten. But I feel silly telling them that, so I merely say, "No, thank you. I won't be having breakfast in my room this morning."

I hang up and sigh deeply. I guess I'll have to venture out earlier today so I can get a bite to eat. Not that it matters. My appetite has dwindled dramatically since the accident, and my mother never fails to remind me of all the weight I've lost.

Slowly getting out of bed, I walk over to the window and stare at the cascade of mountains that make up the Austrian Alps. Closing my eyes, I remember skiing down one of those slopes with Mark. I loved racing him in anything — running, swimming, skiing. When we skied that slope, I had caught up to him, but then, without any warning, he'd tumbled forward. He'd lain motionless in the snow until I reached him. I was terrified. But when I kneeled at his side to check his vitals, he lifted his head and stuck his tongue out at me. Before I could yell at him, he pulled me toward him and kissed me. We lay in the snow, oblivious to the cold, and kissed for what felt like hours.

Wiping away tears, I shake my head. This was a bad idea. I can't believe I let Dr. Pierpont persuade me to take this trip. What was she thinking? What was *I* thinking? Dr. Pierpont was convinced it would help me to heal and finally move forward with my life if I came to Innsbruck and confronted my demons. Besides the psychic mediums I had consulted, Dr. Pierpont had been the only person in whom I'd confided about seeing Mark's ghost everywhere. My family and friends were already worried about me. There's no way I could — or would — ever tell them.

It wasn't until about four months after the accident that Mark began visiting me. I'd been in a horrible state those four months until he came to me. At first, I thought I was dreaming. Then I thought I was losing my mind. I researched paranormal activity — in particular, ghost sightings — and was startled to learn of the many people who had seen the ghosts of loved ones who had departed. After getting over my initial shock and fear, I welcomed Mark's visits. I felt happy again whenever I saw him. But the euphoria would always come crashing to a severe halt after he left. And his sudden exit would remind me he no longer belonged to my world. Every visit sent me into a deeper spiral of depression until I was reunited with him the next time. And while I was happy when Mark was with me, I also ached — for I couldn't touch him. I couldn't kiss him or make love to him again.

Lately, anger had begun to set in, and I would lash out at Mark the way I had this morning. I was beginning to feel like he was taunting me by consoling me when I cried, reminding me of our love and the wonderful memories we'd shared. But then he would vanish almost as quickly as he had appeared.

And now I can't help feeling troubled by what he'd said earlier. The last few visits, he'd kept bringing up that it was time for me to let him go. He was starting to sound like Dr. Pierpont. Lately, I'd even been considering ending my therapy sessions. While it had helped to confide in my shrink about Mark, and even to talk about my overwhelming grief, I didn't like the direction my therapy was heading. Dr. Pierpont kept talking about how I needed to start going forward with my life and gain closure over Mark's tragic death. Intellectually, I knew I couldn't keep continuing like this. But in my heart, I wasn't ready to say goodbye to Mark.

This was now my third day in Austria, and instead of feeling better, I felt worse. Of course, Dr. Pierpont told me it would be difficult — extremely difficult. But she was convinced taking this trip would be the tipping point in my recovery. But the worst is yet to come. I still don't know if I'll be able to follow through on Dr. Pierpont's last exercise for me while I'm here in Austria.

The past few days, I'd visited all the places I'd gone to with Mark when we were here five years ago — the Hungerburg Funicular, the restaurant at the top of the mountain in the village of Seegrube, the Old Town. I even took a horse-drawn carriage ride. Though I felt a little odd taking the ride by myself, I quickly forgot any awkwardness once the carriage went through Innsbruck and memories of Mark beside me returned.

I had even wanted the same hotel room from our last visit, but it was already booked. This room, however, is almost identical to the one Mark and I had shared, with a few changes to the decor. Though I'm sure even the suite we stayed in has undergone a few changes in the five years that have passed. I know I'm torturing myself by having chosen the same hotel where we stayed, but I feel less guilty because Dr. Pierpont was the one to suggest this trip as part of my therapy.

Before I came back to Austria, I wondered if I would see Mark's ghost here. He didn't disappoint me and had shown up a few times as I revisited the places we'd been to together when I first came to Innsbruck.

I rub my left hand with my right, and my heart stops for a moment when I realize my ring finger is bare. But then I remember I left my engagement ring back home in Newport, and relief washes over me that I haven't lost it. Dr. Pierpont's first exercise for me before taking the trip to Austria had been to leave my ring behind. Before leaving for the airport, I had begun to walk out of my apartment when I realized I was still wearing it. I had almost left it on and figured Dr. Pierpont would never know. But for some reason, I decided to take it off and leave it in the key dish in my foyer.

I still called Mark my boyfriend. We had only been engaged for a few days before he was killed. I'd barely had enough time to get used to the idea of having a fiancé, and then he was taken from me. Back home, everyone wasted no time in referring to Mark as my fiancé, even though he was gone. Part of me almost wished he had never proposed. It just made the possibility of what future we could have had and its loss all the more painful.

Sighing, I shake my head. My stomach grumbles, reminding me that I still haven't had breakfast. I head into the bathroom to take a shower and force myself to go back into the world of the living.

CHAPTER 9

I'm eating breakfast at a local café, pretending to read a German newspaper. Ridiculous, I know, since I have no clue what it says. Instead of reading the news headlines, I'm contemplating leaving Innsbruck and abandoning Dr. Pierpont's crazy experiment of having me come here to get closure. God, I hate that word. As if anyone who's lost a loved one could ever fully get closure. Anyway, this has become a daily routine of mine — debating whether I should just get on the next plane. It would be easy. Staying here and reliving my memories of my first trip with Mark is what's been difficult.

"Good morning. How are you?"

I look up. There's something familiar about this man, but I can't place where I've seen him before.

"Good morning. I'm well, thank you." I give a shy smile and then glance down at my paper, hoping he'll get the hint that I don't want to be disturbed.

"It's Bianca, isn't it?"

I look up, surprise registering on my face.

"Yes. I'm sorry. Have we met before?"

He extends his hand. "Jack Gruner. I'm the manager at the Innsbruck Chalet. I checked you in when you arrived."

So that's where I had seen him.

"I'm sorry. Now I remember."

"Have you been enjoying yourself?"

"It's been fine." I avert my gaze and play with my teaspoon.

"I take it you're in Austria to spend the Christmas holidays here?"

"Partly."

Jack is about to ask me another question, but I interrupt him before he can do so.

"I'm sorry." I glance at my watch. "I need to get going. I'm meeting my boyfriend in Old Town."

For some reason Jack frowns, but then nods and says, "Of course. It was nice to meet you — well, again, at least." He laughs.

"It was nice to meet you too. I'm sorry I didn't remember you right away."

Jack holds up his hand. "No worries. I'm sure I'll see you at the hotel. Have a nice day."

"Thank you. You too."

Jack walks over to the bar, where he takes

a seat and gives his order to a waitress.

Without bothering to ask my own waitress for the check, I take a bunch of euros out of my wallet, more than what my breakfast probably cost, and leave them on the table. As I quickly make my way out of the café, Jack turns and waves to me. I wave back but don't meet his gaze.

Once outside, I can feel my pulse racing, and it takes some time until it returns to normal. Walking slowly back to the hotel, I deeply inhale the fresh mountain air. The temperature is the highest today that it's been since I first arrived in Austria. I'm still dressed in all my layers, yet the crisp air is making me feel lighter somehow. I let my mind empty of all thoughts except for the pristine natural beauty before me. Austria truly is gorgeous and one of my favorite places in the world — even if it reminds me of Mark.

My thoughts return to Jack Gruner. For some reason, meeting him rattled me. I could tell he was going to ask if he could join me if I didn't quickly make up my excuse of meeting my boyfriend. And then I couldn't get out of the café soon enough. What really bothered me was how he frowned when I mentioned my boyfriend. Perhaps he was disappointed to learn I'm not single? Or maybe he could tell I was lying? Suddenly, I remember that he checked me in when I first arrived, so he knows I'm staying at the hotel alone. My face burns at the possibility that Jack realized I'd lied. But just because I didn't check in with my boyfriend doesn't mean I don't have one. I could be having a long-distance relationship with someone who lives here in Austria. Yes, that's it! But again, I remember Jack's frown and know he must've been thinking that no one else checked into the hotel with me. The likelihood that he thinks I have a boyfriend living here in Austria is slim. I feel like such an idiot.

Now I regret not bringing my engagement ring. If I was wearing it, I wouldn't have to make up these silly lies about my imaginary boyfriend to Jack or any other men who might express an interest in talking to me. Shrugging my shoulders, I tell myself it doesn't matter what Jack thinks of me. I'll never see him again after this trip. Besides, I didn't come here to have fun and socialize. I just want to keep to myself on this trip, alone with my memories of Mark — or with his ghost, when he decides to pay me a visit.

CHAPTER 10

I decided to wake up earlier today and go for a hike through one of the trails that are near my hotel. Hiking has always calmed me. Back home, when I can't get to a hiking trail, I go for very long walks, especially when I'm feeling stressed.

I'm about a quarter of a mile on the trail when, seemingly out of nowhere, a strong gust of wind kicks up. Though I'm dressed warmly, a chill runs down my body that I can't seem to shake.

"Hey! Think you can beat me this time?"

I turn around. Mark's ghost is standing a few feet behind me, holding up a snowball to me in challenge.

I shake my head and continue walking up the mountain. But Mark appears in front of me, blocking my path.

"What's the matter? Think you won't be able to beat me again?"

Part of me doesn't want to deal with Mark

right now. But just like when he was alive, I can't resist his devilish smile.

"What makes you so sure you beat me the last time we had a snowball fight here?" I cross my arms in front of my chest, a smirk on my face.

Instead of responding, Mark throws the snowball he's holding at me.

"Hey! No fair! We didn't call start yet!" I yell at Mark, but he's disappeared.

Thinking he's vanished, I see a flash of his gray jacket, the same jacket he'd been wearing the day he was killed, darting behind one of the trees. Every time Mark's ghost appears to me, he's wearing the same clothes he wore the day he died.

Looking around to see if anyone else is coming up the mountain, I take off at a run, yelling, "I'm coming!"

Mark dodges in and out of the trees so fast. I can't help thinking he has the advantage since he must just float through the air. Isn't that, after all, what ghosts do? But he appears to be very much alive, as handsome as he ever was and full of life and energy, just the way I remember him.

"Gotcha!" I squeal excitedly after hitting him with my third snowball.

"It's not over yet!" Mark yells.

I hide behind a tree, waiting to get a

glimpse of him before I strike with my next snowball. But suddenly, I feel myself fall forward. When I look up, Mark is on top of me, pelting my coat with snowball after snowball. I laugh. I can't help but note that I can't feel his weight on me. If only I could touch him. Though I've tried the other times he's visited me and know it's not possible, I can't resist trying to wrap my arms around him in a hug this time. He notices and smiles but doesn't say anything. We then lie side by side in the snow, staring into each other's eyes.

"You know you'll always have me, Bianca."

"Stop, Mark. Please."

"It's true, though. No one can ever take away from you what we had. I'll always have been a part of your life and a part of you. You can still be happy without me."

"I'm happy when you visit me, Mark."

"Not always. You were pretty mad at me this morning."

"I'm sorry. I was just hurt when you told me I had to let you go."

"I know."

"Can we just have a good time for now? No more heavy talk?"

"Okay."

I get up and start running. "Chase me if you can!"

As I run higher up the trail and through the maze of trees, I realize this is why I haven't gotten on the next flight back home. While it's been painful reliving the memories I had with Mark when I first came to Austria, it's also felt like time has stood still, especially when his ghost appears to me here. And now having this snowball fight and chase reminds me of our first day in Innsbruck together. It's too intoxicating to give up.

I stop, just in time to duck a snowball Mark has thrown in my direction.

"Hey! I thought we were just going to chase each other. No more snowball fights!"

I'm laughing and out of breath, but I still take off after him, throwing as many snowballs as I can. But none of them manage to hit Mark. He disappears behind a row of trees to my left.

But before I can find him, he shows up again behind me and says, "You've got company."

He nods in the direction of two teenage boys who are staring at me. Their faces say it all. Of course they think I'm crazy, having a snowball fight with myself. Naturally, Mark is gone, and I can't help feeling angry with the teens for cutting my time with him short. Doing my best to ignore the boys' stares, I make my way back down the mountain. Soon, my thoughts drift to my family back home in Newport.

My mother phoned this morning. Amazingly, it's only the second time we've spoken while I've been in Innsbruck. My father has probably stopped her from calling me more often, telling her not to worry about me and to give me space. I had called Mom after I landed to let her know I'd arrived safely. Of course, she'd been concerned about my coming here alone, but Dad and my brothers had convinced her I'd be fine. I think they realized how important it was for me to take this trip.

My family had been devastated when Mark died. In the year we'd been dating, my parents had grown very fond of him. And, of course, my brothers had been such good friends with him. While they had loved him, they also wanted me to move on. Though it's been five years since the accident, my brothers and parents know better than to broach the subject with me anymore. The few times they tried in the past always ended with me yelling at them.

Dr. Pierpont told me it's natural for my family to want me to be happy and move forward, but she also told me I needed to do it on my own terms and when I'm ready.

At least she makes me feel normal — or as normal as someone who's been mourning her fiancé for five years and seeing his ghost can feel.

I'm about halfway down the mountain when I hear a soft whimpering to my right. Then I notice a trail of paw prints in the snow that end by a tree. Walking over to the tree, the whimpering gets louder. A beagle sits on the other side of the tree, licking frantically at its paw.

"Hey, little guy. What happened to you?"

The dog looks excited to see me and stands up, limping toward me. His left hind foot is bleeding. I glance around, hoping to see the beagle's owner, but no one is in sight.

I carefully try to lift his foot to inspect it closer, but he yelps and pulls it back. Accustomed to the animals at the vet clinic reacting the same way, I know I need to distract him with a treat to get nearer to that foot to make sure he's not seriously injured.

I take off my scarf and tie it around the beagle's foot; not too tightly, because I don't want to cause him any more pain than he's already in. And if something is embedded in his foot, I don't want to risk pushing it deeper. If there is a foreign object in his foot, once I get it out, I can apply more pressure to stop the bleeding. Picking the dog up, I make my way back to the hotel. I'm sure they'll have a first aid kit I can use.

Before going into the hotel lobby, I go to the lodge and buy some beef jerky. Back outside, I give the beagle a piece of the jerky. While he's happily chewing on it, I remove the scarf from his foot and take another look at it. This time he doesn't pull back when I lift it up. I see what the cause of the bleeding is. A nail is wedged into his foot. I'm going to have to get it out before it gets infected.

Wrapping the scarf back around the beagle's foot, I give him another piece of jerky before scooping him up once more into my arms and heading toward the hotel lobby. A pretty strawberry blonde greets me.

"Hello, Miss Simone. How are you today?"

"I'm fine, thank you."

Though the desk attendant remembers my name and I've seen her several times during my stay here, I have no idea what her name is. I glance at her name badge.

"Beatrice, I found this dog on one of the trails. It looks like he stepped on a nail and hurt his foot. Is it possible you've seen this dog before and know who his owner is?"

Beatrice takes a closer look and says, "I thought that was Chauncey, but I couldn't fathom why he would be with you. I thought it was another dog that happened to look like him. Chauncey, what trouble have you gotten yourself into now? And where's your collar?" Beatrice leans over and scratches Chauncey on the head.

Relieved, I say, "So you do recognize him?"

"Of course. That's Jack's dog."

"Jack? The hotel manager?"

"Yes. That's the only Jack we have working here."

"Is he at work today?"

"He's off, but I'll phone him and let him know you have his dog."

"Thank you. That would be great. I'm so glad we know who the dog belongs to. I take it from what you said that Chauncey is known for getting into scrapes."

"Yes. Chauncey is quite feisty. But we still love him, don't we?" Beatrice plants a kiss on Chauncey's nose. "Now, if you'll excuse me, Miss Simone, I'll place that call to Jack."

I wait for Beatrice to make the call. I hope Jack is home; I'd rather wait to get permission from him before I treat Chauncey's foot.

Beatrice hangs up. "He said he'll be right over. He didn't even notice that Chauncey was missing. But after I told him you'd found him, he noticed the back door of his house was open. If you'd like, you can leave Chauncey here with me and I'll hand him over to Jack once he arrives."

"Thank you, but I want to treat Chauncey's injury. I'm a vet tech and could do it. I'd feel better knowing he's going to be all right, so I'll just wait for Jack."

"Chauncey's gotten a hold of your heartstrings already, I see." Beatrice smiles.

I walk over to the couch in the lobby and take a seat.

About twenty minutes later, I'm standing behind one of the floor-to-ceiling windows in the hotel lobby, looking for any sign of Jack. Chauncey seems to be getting restless too, so I'm hoping the view outside might distract him a bit. Suddenly, Jack's outline comes into view. But I can't be seeing right. It looks like he's dragging a sled.

But then, as Jack gets closer to the hotel, I see the sled isn't empty. A boy of about nine or ten is in it. Jack stops pulling the sled and squats down beside the boy, saying something to him before running back toward the parking lot. The boy's face is etched with worry lines. But he remains seated in the sled. Jack comes back into view, running and pushing a wheelchair. Once he reaches the boy in the sled, he lifts him and places him in the wheelchair. He pushes the wheelchair through the hotel entrance doors. Is the boy Jack's son? Was I so arrogant and self-absorbed to think that Jack had an interest in me when he's probably married?

Suddenly, I feel embarrassed as I remember how I had abruptly parted from Jack in the café that morning, and how I had lied about meeting my boyfriend. Just like those boys on the mountain who witnessed me laughing to myself and throwing snowballs at no one, Jack must think I'm absolutely crazy.

I quickly sit down on the couch before Jack can see I was staring at him through the window. Once he spots me, he points me out to the boy, who then takes control of pushing his own chair as he quickly makes his way over to my side.

"Chauncey! How could you go out without me?"

Chauncey lowers his eyes, barely meeting the boy's gaze.

"Bianca. Thank God you found him. I can't believe I didn't notice he was gone." Jack gestures to the boy, "Bianca, this is my son, Christopher." Turning to his son, he says, "Christopher, Bianca is a guest at the hotel. We're very lucky she found Chauncey."

Christopher shakes my hand and says, "Thank you so much for finding my dog."

I'm touched by the boy's good manners.

"You're welcome, Christopher."

"Come here, Chauncey." Christopher leans over in his chair, reaching for Chauncey. I hand him over to Christopher, who plops him onto his lap and wheels the dog around the lobby as he continues to lecture him. But Chauncey is now looking directly into Christopher's face, as if he's saying he's sorry. The sight is at once amusing and endearing.

"I apologize if Chauncey disrupted your plans, Bianca. Thank you again for finding him. You saved my life. Christopher would've murdered me if anything happened to that dog." Jack says to me in a low voice.

"No worries, Jack. I'm just glad I found him. As for his injured foot, I'm actually a vet tech. With your permission, I'd like to treat Chauncey's foot. Fortunately, the nail he stepped on isn't embedded too deeply, so I can probably pry it out with a pair of tweezers. If you'd rather take him to an animal clinic I understand, but it would be quicker if I did it. Besides, I don't think his injury is severe enough to warrant a trip to the vet. If his bleeding doesn't stop shortly after I remove the nail, you can take him to the vet clinic."

"That would be great, Bianca. Thank you. But are you sure it's not too much trouble? I wouldn't want to put you out any more than I already have today."

"It would be my pleasure. I just need a first aid kit. Oh, and a towel."

"No problem. I'll be right back." Jack disappears behind the reception desk and goes through two swinging doors. He soon returns with the first aid kit and a couple of towels.

"Is there an empty room where I can treat Chauncey?"

"We'll go to the conference room."

Stepping back out into the lobby, Jack motions for Christopher to follow us.

"Christopher, Bianca works in a veterinarian's office back home. She's kindly offered to take out the nail that got stuck in Chauncey's foot. I'm going to need you to hold Chauncey down and talk soothingly to him so he doesn't jump while she's trying to pull out the nail. Can you do that for me, big guy?"

"I'm your man, Dad. And if there's anyone Chauncey will listen to, it's me."

Jack looks at me and smiles.

We lay out one of the towels on the conference room table and place Chauncey on top of it. I position the beagle on his back so that his injured foot is raised in the air.

"He looks funny lying down like that." Christopher laughs.

"It's important we keep his foot raised to help slow down the bleeding. Can you hold him with your hands on either side so that he doesn't roll over?"

Christopher nods his head and places his hands firmly on either side of Chauncey's stomach. Chauncey looks nervous, as if he knows what's going to happen next.

"Is this going to hurt him a lot, Bianca?"

"A little. But it'll be over almost as soon as I pull the nail out. He'll have some tenderness in his foot, of course, but he won't be in excruciating pain. Also, he shouldn't walk a lot for the next day or two. Just take him out to relieve himself, but no extended walks for let's say two days, to be on the safe side. And make sure he won't be able to run out of that back door in your house again."

I look at Jack when I make my last request,

giving him a stern glance. He looks away sheepishly for a moment. When he returns his glance my way, I smile, letting him know I was just kidding. He holds my gaze a moment longer, and now it's my turn to look away. I feel my pulse quicken. Mentally shaking my head, I focus on the task ahead.

First, I clean Chauncey's wound with some Betadine antiseptic soap. Then I disinfect the tweezers with rubbing alcohol. Fortunately, I always carry a pair of tweezers in my purse because I often don't have the time to get my brows waxed when I'm busy with my hectic work schedule. I talk to Chauncey in a gentle voice, and Christopher is also giving him words of encouragement. I do this with all of the patients at the vet clinic where I work. I've always found it makes a difference in helping to keep the animals calmer.

Chauncey lets out a yelp, followed by a soft bark, after I extract the nail. I then press a sterile gauze pad over Chauncey's wound for a few minutes before checking to see if the blood is letting up, which it seems to be.

"Good. He's not bleeding a lot, so we won't need to take him to the vet. I'll just wrap his foot now and he'll be ready to go home."

I squeeze a generous amount of ointment onto a clean gauze pad and place it over Chauncey's wound before fastening it with an adhesive bandage, making sure not to wrap it too tightly so I won't cut off circulation to his foot. When I'm done, I see Jack staring at me intensely.

"Wow! You're a pro. You did that so quickly."

"Years of experience." I shrug my shoulders, letting him know it's no big deal. "I also have two dogs who get into scrapes from time to time."

"What are their names?" Christopher asks me.

"Frenchie and Sheila. Frenchie is a French bulldog and Sheila is an Australian shepherd."

"How clever!" Jack says.

"Oh, the names aren't that clever. I think they're pretty obvious, but I didn't care. Also, naming Sheila was a bit inaccurate."

"Why is that? Australians call girls sheilas. It's perfect for an Australian shepherd."

"They're actually an American breed. I'm not sure why they're called Australian shepherds. Now Chauncey, that's a great name for a dog."

Jack laughs. "Yeah, I know."

"I chose the name!" Christopher proudly

holds his hand in the air.

"Yes, that's true. When I asked him why Chauncey, he said he'd heard it on TV a few days before we adopted him. And then, when he met Chauncey, the name came back to him and he thought it fit. I have to agree. I can't think what else we would've called him. He's a Chauncey through and through." Jack gives Chauncey a playful tug behind his ears.

"By the way, where is Chauncey's collar?"

"He's always snaking his neck out of it, no matter how snugly I fasten it. Our vet embedded him with a chip, so hopefully if he gets away again, someone will think to take him to the local vet to identify him by that."

"He's not getting away again. I'm making sure of that!" Christopher chimes in.

"I'm sure you will. Well, we should let Bianca get back to her day."

"Make sure Chauncey gets some rest for today. And when he needs to relieve himself, be sure to tie a plastic bag, like a grocery bag, over his foot to protect the dressing before taking him out. I'll change his dressing in a couple of days and check his foot to make sure it's healing properly."

"Will do, Doc." Jack salutes me.

"I'm not a doc, but thank you."

"Have you ever thought of taking your career all the way and becoming a veterinarian? After witnessing you treat Chauncey, it's obvious you're a natural."

"Thank you. That's nice of you to say. I was never a great science student, unfortunately, so vet school is out of the question. Even the courses I took to become a vet tech were challenging, to say the least. But that's all right. I'm happy with what I do."

"But you've learned so much at the clinic where you work. I'm sure veterinarian schools appreciate the practical experience as much as the book experience."

"They do, but I'd still need the test grades."

"Have you ever thought about getting a tutor and really applying yourself to it?"

"I don't know. The idea has run through my mind a few times, but there's been a lot going on in my personal life the past few years, so I haven't been able to consider it more."

Jack nods his head thoughtfully and purses his lips before saying, "Well, only you can know when the time is right."

I'm taken aback for a moment by his words since I had been thinking only this morning about my family having pressured me to move forward. Though I know Jack is talking about my career and not Mark, his words still send a shiver down my spine.

Suddenly, Chauncey is sitting up on the conference room table and looking to the corner over my shoulder. His back is slightly hunched and he's whimpering.

"What's the matter, Chauncey?" Jack rubs his back, but Chauncey steadfastly looks in the same spot.

"Come on, Chauncey. You need your rest." Christopher leans over in his wheelchair and picks up Chauncey. Jack follows them out as I roll up the towels and put the supplies I used back into the first aid kit.

"Coming, Bianca?" Jack glances over his shoulder before leaving the conference room.

"Yes, I'll be right there. Let me just finish packing this stuff up."

As soon as Jack leaves, I feel goose bumps run down my arms even though I'm wearing a HEATTECH T-shirt and a thick wool sweater.

"Bianca."

I look toward the conference room door expecting to see Jack, but then I hear from behind me, "Right here."

Mark. Now I realize what Chauncey was looking at earlier. He'd seen Mark. But of course, Mark waited until I was alone before he made his presence known to me. Not that it mattered. No one else saw him. Besides me, only animals could see Mark's ghost. A few times Mark had shown up at the vet clinic where I work. The pets I treated always saw him. And my own dogs, Frenchie and Sheila, had seen him too. They always whined mournfully when they saw him. Mark used to spoil them rotten when he was alive.

"Must you always sneak up on me, Mark? Isn't there a way to let me know you're here without scaring me?"

"I wish there were, but I have little control in that area." Mark grins.

"I can't talk to you long, Mark. They're waiting for me." I say this in a sad voice, not wanting to hurt his feelings. That is, if ghosts have feelings . . .

"I just wanted to say Jack has been through a lot too."

"And how would you know that?"

Mark gives me an exasperated look, as if to say, *Come on!*

"Never mind. That man's problems aren't any of my concern. And what are you trying to prove? That I'm not the only one who's in pain? Is this your way of telling me to stop feeling sorry for myself?" I can't hide the bitterness in my tone.

Mark looks at me with the saddest expression. Whenever he does this, I can't hold his gaze for long, and I glance down, busying myself by putting away the first aid kit supplies.

"I just miss the Bianca I used to know — the vibrant woman who never wasted a moment and who loved to laugh. I can't remember the last time I heard you laugh — that is, when I'm not visiting you."

"I can. It was that morning on the bus to Lake Como. A day never passed that you didn't make me laugh when you were alive. I miss you so much, Mark."

"I miss you too, Bianca, and you know I'll always love you. Don't be upset with me. I just want the best for you. That was all I ever wanted."

Tears fill my eyes. I look up to tell Mark that I'm not upset with him, but he's gone. And my anguish is soon replaced by anger. But instead of giving in to it, I compose myself before going out to the hotel lobby.

As I approach the lobby, I see Jack standing outside the entrance. He carefully lifts Christopher, who's holding Chauncey, and places him onto the sled. Jack quickly pulls the sled through the snow to their car, leaving the wheelchair behind. My heart goes out to Christopher.

Beatrice interrupts my thoughts.

"Miss Simone, Jack asked me to tell you to wait. He'll just be a moment. He wanted to get Christopher settled into his car."

"Thank you, Beatrice."

I think about what Mark said about Jack having been through a lot. Of course, he must've been referring to Christopher being paralyzed. I can't help wondering what happened to him.

"Earth to Bianca."

I jump when I see Jack is tilting his head so that our eyes meet.

"Oh! I'm sorry. I was just thinking."

"I can see that." Jack smiles. "Christopher asked me to apologize for not saying good-bye to you in person. He's getting over the flu and was starting to feel pretty tired, especially with all the excitement over Chauncey. I asked one of the workers to take him home for me since I have some business I need to tend to here. But he wanted me to tell you again how grateful he was for your finding Chauncey and treating his foot. He said he's going to think of a special way to thank you. By the way, if you prefer, we can bring Chauncey here for his follow-up, so that you don't have to find a way of getting to our house. That would probably be easier for you."

"Oh, it was my pleasure taking care of Chauncey. And Christopher doesn't need to go out of his way to show me his appreciation. The look on his face was enough thanks for me. I hadn't thought about how I'd get to your house to check on Chauncey's foot. I almost forgot for a moment that I'm not back home in Newport, with access to my car. So yes, if you don't mind, that would be great if you and Christopher could bring Chauncey here in a couple of days for me to see how his foot is healing."

"Will do. Newport? Are you from Rhode Island?"

"Yes, I am."

"Ah! A fellow New Englander, though I know Rhode Island has more of a cosmopolitan feel to it than ultra-rural Vermont, where I'm from." Jack winks.

I laugh. "Oh, I don't know about that. So, you're not originally from Austria. I had noticed you have an American accent. How long have you lived in Innsbruck?"

"About a decade now. I was born in Vermont, but my parents are actually from Austria. We visited almost every year when I was a child. I always felt more Austrian than American and knew someday I would probably make it my permanent home. Seven years ago, I finally decided to take the plunge and move out here. It was pretty easy for me to find work because I worked in hotels back home. I even lived in New York City briefly, while I worked at the Helmsley Park Lane Hotel."

"And your wife likes living in Austria?"

Jack's expression darkens. "She passed away some time ago."

"Oh, I'm so sorry."

"Thank you. It's just me, Christopher, and Chauncey."

I want to ask Jack how she died but don't want to intrude on his privacy. An awkward silence ensues before Jack says, "Well, I'll finally get out of your hair, but before I leave, can I recommend a few sites you might not have visited yet?"

"Thank you, Jack, but I'm feeling tired, so I might just take it easy today, stay in my room and read."

"You can do that at home. You shouldn't waste any of your days here. When do you leave Innsbruck?"

"I haven't decided yet. The vet clinic where I work is closed for the last half of December and the first half of January. I just bought a one-way ticket and figured when I felt ready to leave, I would."

Jack raises his eyebrows in surprise. "So you like to live in the moment. Not plan

391

anything in advance."

"Sort of. Well, I've been that way more the past few years."

Jack looks at me with concern but merely nods his head. "Nothing wrong with that. We can get too bogged down in thinking about the future and forget to live in the present."

I smile. He returns my smile and holds my gaze for a moment before I glance away.

"Anyway, if you and your boyfriend are free tomorrow night, you should go into Altstadt. There will be a choir of boys singing Christmas carols, including my son."

My cheeks flame hot as I remember how I had lied to him the day before at the café.

"I'm sorry, Jack. The truth is, I'm actually here by myself. I don't have a boyfriend. Since I'm traveling alone, I like to err on the side of caution."

Of course, that's not exactly true, but I need to save face somehow in this awkward moment.

"No worries. I understand. Well, if you can make it tomorrow night, I know Christopher would be thrilled. But no pressure. I take it you've already been to Altstadt and know how to get there?"

My mind quickly flashes back to the day Mark proposed to me in Altstadt. A jolt of pain shoots through me.

"Are you all right, Bianca?"

"Yes, I'm fine. I'll try to make it. Thank you for the invitation." I offer a small smile in hopes of reassuring him that I really am okay.

Jack returns my smile. "Enjoy the rest of your day. And again, thank you so much for everything you did for Chauncey."

"It was my pleasure. Enjoy the rest of your day as well." I make my way toward the elevator. I can feel Jack's gaze on me, but I don't dare turn around.

CHAPTER 11

The next evening I'm dressed to go out but feel frozen in place. I can't make up my mind if I'll go to see the choir in Altstadt. Spending all this time alone with my thoughts is beginning to take its toll on me. It would be good to be around people, to distract myself a bit by talking to Jack. Sighing, I put on my coat before I change my mind again.

As I approach the square, I see the boys from the choir are taking their places. A large crowd has gathered. I try to find Jack. It doesn't take me long to spot him because I assume he must be in the front, along with the other proud parents watching their boys perform. Jack is holding Chauncey, who's wearing a thick wool sweater. As I had instructed Jack, a plastic bag is tied around Chauncey's foot. Chauncey's gaze remains fixed on Christopher.

Sadness fills me when I see Christopher

in his little wheelchair. But he doesn't seem to notice or care that he's the only boy who isn't standing. He's smiling and waving to his father and Chauncey.

I walk over to Jack and touch him lightly on his shoulder.

"Bianca! You made it!"

"Yes." I reach up and pet Chauncey, who leans over and tries to lick my face. Jack tries to pull him away, but I say, "That's okay." I stretch my neck closer to Chauncey and let him give my cheek a couple of swipes with his tongue.

Jack laughs. "You do have a way with animals!"

"I see you followed my orders about keeping Chauncey's foot wrapped. If you'd like, I can take a quick look at his foot after the show. That way you wouldn't have to bring him to the hotel tomorrow."

"It's no trouble bringing him in tomorrow. Besides, my babysitter won't be able to stay with Christopher tomorrow afternoon, so he and Chauncey will be coming to work with me. But if you have plans tomorrow afternoon, then by all means, you can look at Chauncey's foot after the show tonight."

"No, tomorrow afternoon is fine."

The choir begins to sing "O Tannenbaum." Jack and I turn our attention to the boys. They're very good. I'm glad I came. I'm enjoying watching and listening to the choir and not thinking about myself and Mark for a change.

Halfway through the performance, Christopher rolls his chair to the front and center of the choir. Except for a few boys who sing backup, Christopher is the only one singing as he belts out the tune to "Little Drummer Boy." His voice is beautiful. I look at Jack, who is absolutely beaming.

Christopher's song wraps up the performance and the boys bow to a round of cheers and applause. Jack and I make our way over to Christopher.

"That was fantastic!" Jack high-fives his son and then gives him a quick hug. Chauncey leaps out of Jack's embrace and onto Christopher's lap as he offers his own congratulations in the form of a few licks across his face.

"Christopher, you have a beautiful voice. 'Little Drummer Boy' is my favorite Christmas carol."

"Thank you, Bianca. It's my favorite too. And thank you for coming to see me. I'm sorry I didn't get to say good-bye to you yesterday."

"That's all right. I hope you're feeling better. Your father mentioned you were getting over the flu."

Christopher nods his head. "Yeah. I think I'm all cured now. I'm just glad I got sick now and not for Christmas. That would've been the pits!"

I laugh. "It definitely would have!"

"Bianca, will you be coming with us for hot chocolate and dessert?"

"Oh. I —"

"I was going to invite you, Bianca. Please join us." Jack looks at me expectantly.

"All right. Thank you."

We head over to a nearby café. Jack pushes his son's chair even though Christopher tells him he can do it himself.

"Pretend you're in a limo and someone else is doing the driving. This is your night, big guy."

Christopher shakes his head, but he's grinning, loving the attention his father is showering on him.

I offer to walk Chauncey on his leash, but after a few feet the plastic bag wrapped around his foot is distracting him so much that he's begun to tear at it with his teeth. I scoop him up in my arms before he can completely tear the bag off.

When we're seated in the café and our orders of hot chocolate and desserts have arrived, Christopher begins asking me questions about what it's like to be a vet tech. I regale him with unusual stories from the vet clinic and make a few jokes. I love seeing him smile. His sandy blond hair is the same shade as Jack's, and he has the same kind eyes. At one point while Christopher is talking to me, I notice out of the corner of my eye that Jack is staring at me. I can feel my cheeks flush.

After I'm done discussing the world of a vet tech, Christopher says, "Cool! I think I want to be a vet tech when I grow up, Dad."

Jack and I laugh.

An hour later, Jack announces it's almost time for Christopher to get to bed.

"I thought this was my night! I should get to stay up as late as I want." Christopher pouts.

"When you're eighteen, you can do that. But until then, you still have a bedtime."

On the way back to the hotel, Jack lets Christopher wheel himself. Christopher is quite strong for his age and is wheeling at a good pace ahead of us. When we reach a street that is a bit steep, my face fills with worry as I watch Christopher wheeling downhill at a rapid pace. Jack notices my anxiety.

"He'll be fine. He's a pro at steering now."

I nod my head, hoping he's right.

"Jack, may I ask how —"

"Car accident. The same one that took his mother's life."

I stop walking for a moment, taken aback by the news that Jack also lost someone he loved in a car crash. When Jack looks at me questioningly, I merely mutter, "A cramp in my leg."

"Do you need to sit down? There's a bench just a couple of feet away, if you can hop to it. Of course I can carry you, if you'd like." Jack is smirking.

I force myself to laugh and say, "That's okay."

Bending over, I pretend to massage my leg for a moment before resuming walking.

"How long ago was the accident?"

"Seven years ago. Christopher was only three. I was at work when it happened. Jennifer was driving. She hit a patch of ice and her car swerved out of control and hit a tree. She died later at the hospital. It was a close call for Christopher, but he pulled through."

I try to remember when Jack told me he moved here. "Was this here in Austria?"

"No, in Vermont. A few months after the accident, I decided to move here."

He doesn't have to explain to me why he decided to move here. Although he had told me the other day he always wanted to live in Austria, I'm sure the timing of his move had to do with wanting to escape the memories he'd had with his wife back home.

As if reading my thoughts, Jack says, "I guess I needed a fresh start."

"I can understand that."

We continue to walk the rest of the way to the hotel in silence. Mark's words come back to me: *"He's been through a lot."*

I think about telling Jack that I know exactly what he's been through and is feeling, but the words remain choked in my throat. It's crazy, but I feel that once I share the pain of my loss with someone other than my shrink, it'll somehow be less my own. And I'm not sure I'm ready yet to give that up.

CHAPTER 12

The next evening, I'm sitting across from Jack at a restaurant in Old Town. Before we parted ways last night, Jack told me he wanted to treat me to dinner to thank me for finding Chauncey and treating his foot. I wanted to tell him that wasn't necessary, but instead I accepted. I don't know why I did, but after I accepted, I knew I couldn't take it back. Now, I'm fidgeting in my seat, nervous at what Jack's expectations for tonight might be and feeling guilty that I'm on what feels like a date even though I keep telling myself it isn't.

Thankfully, Jack is doing most of the talking. I'm surprised at how long he can keep small talk going when it suddenly occurs to me that he's as nervous as I am, but in his case he tries to cover it up by chattering away.

Deciding to take a chance, I interrupt Jack in midsentence, and before I can change my mind, I blurt out, "You're nervous, aren't you?"

Jack pauses, looking surprised, then mildly embarrassed. I give him a tender smile, letting him know it's okay. He laughs softly. "It's that obvious, huh?"

"Only because I'm nervous, too, although I'm the opposite. I'm very quiet when I'm feeling anxious. So I'm glad you've been doing all the gabbing because the silence between us would've been absolutely unbearable!" I laugh.

"Well, thank God that's over. I give you credit for just throwing it out there." Jack takes a sip of his wine. "Ah! I don't know what's gotten into me. I'm usually not the nervous type."

"No apologies necessary. It's nice to see you're human." I raise my wineglass and make a toast. "To being human — and letting it all hang out!"

Jack taps my glass with his. "Yes. To letting it all hang out." His eyes meet mine and we laugh.

"You don't need to feel nervous with me, Jack. I'm probably the most unpretentious person you'll ever meet."

"I can tell that, Bianca. Likewise, you don't need to feel anxious around me. But now it's my turn to be bold and ask why you're feeling nervous."

"It's been awhile since I've been on any-thing remotely resembling a date — not that this is a date, but you know what I mean."

I can't believe I've just said that. Jack looks disappointed. Seeing his disappointment makes me regret my choice of words.

"I'm sorry, Jack. I just don't want to presume anything."

"No worries. I understand. Besides, I did tell you I wanted to treat you to repay you for taking care of Chauncey's foot. Lord knows you saved me a hefty vet's bill." Jack smiles, and I feel relaxed in his presence once again.

"So, it's my turn to ask why you're ner-vous."

"Oh, look. The waiter is approaching our table, just in time to save me." Jack drums his fingers on the table and looks up in the air, whistling softly.

I shake my head at him but decide to let him off the hook.

But after the waiter takes our order, Jack returns to the subject and says, "I'm nervous because I've enjoyed your company the few times I've been with you, and I guess I want to make a good impression. There. I've let it all hang out."

"Impressive." I take a sip of my wine, and

part of me is startled at how coy my tone sounds. I haven't heard myself use that flirting tone since . . . since Mark.

I decide to steer the conversation toward safer ground and ask Jack questions about his work. He takes my lead and in turn asks me questions about my job, as well as my family.

Before I know it, the end of the night has come and Jack is walking me back to the hotel.

"I take it your house isn't too far from here since I found Chauncey in the hiking trails near the hotel."

"Yes. I live only ten minutes away, but I had to wait for Christopher to finish getting ready. That's why it took us a bit longer to get to the hotel after you'd found Chauncey. I rent the house, so it's not quite mine."

"Really? I would've thought since you've been here for several years now you would have purchased it."

"I know. I guess after Jennifer died, it's been hard for me to make any permanent decisions."

"You came to Austria, though."

"I had no choice. I was a wreck after she passed away. If I wanted to pull myself together so that I could be there fully for Christopher, I had to go somewhere fresh. I guess I haven't wanted to buy a house here just in case we decide to move back to the States."

"But I thought you had always seen yourself living in Austria. When you told me that, it sounded like it would be a permanent move."

"I know, but I keep wondering if it might be better for Christopher to live in Vermont. My parents are still there, as well as Jennifer's family. I feel guilty sometimes that I pulled Christopher out of their lives, although they understood."

"Have you been back to visit?"

"Twice. And Jennifer's parents have come to visit a few times. They're good people. I made it clear to them that they would always be in our lives."

"I can see how it would get lonely here, just you and Christopher, without your relatives."

"You forgot Chauncey."

"Ah! How could I forget Chauncey? How long have you had him?"

"I adopted him when Christopher and I came to Austria. I thought it would be a good way to occupy him. After Jennifer died, he was constantly asking where Mommy was. I had hoped since he was so young — three at the time — that he would . . ."

"Forget?" I place my hand gently on Jack's arm. His eyes fill with tears.

"Isn't that horrible? Hoping my son would forget his mother? Of course, I didn't want him to forget her, but I also couldn't bear the thought of how much he was suffering without her. I think that was part of what made dealing with Jennifer's death so hard. I just couldn't accept that my son would no longer have his mother."

"Don't be so hard on yourself, Jack. From what I've seen of Christopher, he's a fine boy. He seems happy. I'm not saying he doesn't miss his mother or having one, but he also seems like a very strong boy. You've done a wonderful job with him."

Jack puts his hand on mine and gives it a light squeeze. "Thank you." He sighs. "As a parent, you're always wondering whether you're doing right by your child. You're always second-guessing your choices. I try to follow my gut, but I know I can't get it right all the time."

"Well, you seem to have gotten most of it right. So stop worrying."

Jack stops, and before I can react, he's kissing me. I'm stunned. I give in to his kiss, but then I realize what I'm doing and step back.

"I'm sorry, Bianca. I don't know what came over me."

"It's just . . ." I place my hands on my temples, unable to give him an explanation. Feeling overwhelmed, I merely say, "It's late. I'll be all right walking the rest of the way back by myself. Thank you for dinner, Jack."

I hurry away, but Jack runs after me.

"Bianca! Wait. I can still walk you back."

I wait for him to catch up, knowing it's no use trying to outrun him.

"You really don't need to escort me. I'll be fine."

"I know, but I want to."

We continue walking in silence. Once we reach the hotel, Jack says, "Look, Bianca, I lied back there when I said I don't know what came over me. We toasted to letting it all hang out, so I'm going to risk making you run again, but I don't care. I want to be nothing but honest with you. I like you, Bianca. A lot. I kissed you because I wanted to. And taking you out tonight wasn't just about repaying you for treating Chauncey. I just used that as an excuse. I wanted to get to know you better and spend some time alone with you."

"So you're not going to repay me for taking care of your dog?"

Jack looks at me, surprised. My comment has left him speechless.

Instead of waiting for him to come up with a response, I merely say, "Good night, Jack," and walk away. I can feel his eyes on me as I let myself into the hotel.

When I reach my room, my pulse is absolutely racing. I don't know what to think about tonight. Although Jack caught me off guard with that kiss, I didn't push him away immediately. I even gave in and kissed him back for a moment. And his confession that he likes me made me feel . . . dare I say it? Happy. Then why was I so cruel, taunting him about not repaying me for taking care of Chauncey's foot? He must think I'm sadistic to make a comment like that after he revealed his feelings for me.

Shaking my head, I fling my handbag across the room. I'm disgusted by how I treated Jack. I'm disgusted that I'm having feelings for another man, and here in Innsbruck of all places. I didn't come here to fall in love. Austria was my special place with Mark. This was where Mark proposed to me. This was where I lost him. Throwing myself onto my bed, I sob uncontrollably.

CHAPTER 13

Christmas Eve has arrived. It's been a couple of days since my date with Jack. He called me the next day to see how I was. The conversation felt strained, but we were polite with each other. I couldn't help feeling that he was trying to keep me at a distance now. That should've made me feel relieved, but it only saddened me.

I'm brushing my hair, getting ready to go out for breakfast, when I hear a soft knock at my door, followed by "Room service."

Frowning, I answer the door.

"Room service, mademoiselle." The bellhop has a French accent.

"I'm sorry. There must be a mistake. I didn't order room service."

"Room twelve oh five. You are Mademoiselle Simone, correct?"

"Yes, but I didn't place an order for room service."

"It says here it's complimentary — a gift

from the hotel for your birthday."

"How do they know it's my birthday?"

The bellhop shrugs his shoulders. "Is it on some form they ask guests to fill out, perhaps?"

I remember that when I reserved the room online, I did have to fill in my birth date.

"Please, hold on." I walk over to my purse and take out a few euros to tip him. He's pacing back and forth, no doubt anxious to return to work. He doesn't even offer to push the food cart into my room.

"*Merci.* You can leave the cart outside your door when you are finished." With a nod of his head, he hurries away.

"Merci." I push the cart into my room. There is a small vase with white roses on the cart. An envelope with my name on it lies beside the utensils. I open it.

Dear Bianca,

Needless to say, you left me quite speechless the other night when you asked me if I wasn't going to repay you for so kindly treating Chauncey. I suppose I deserved that, after taking such liberties by kissing you. Please accept my sincerest apologies. I promise I won't bring up that awkward episode anymore!

A little Christmas ghost told me that

today is your birthday, which didn't surprise me. A person as special as you had to have been born on a special day like Christmas Eve. I'd like to repay you for taking such good care of Chauncey by taking you to the Alpenzoo. My noble son Christopher mentioned to me again that he wanted to show you his appreciation for rescuing Chauncey and making him better. He suggested inviting you to the zoo. I hope you will join us. If you can't come, I understand. I'll be downstairs working the desk this morning because Beatrice has the flu. You can stop by — or call the front desk — and let me know.

Jack

P.S. I hope you like the roses. They're a small birthday gift from me.

I can't help but smile at Jack's note. And how sweet of Christopher to remember he wanted to do something nice for me. I will go. It would be rude of me not to, especially since Christopher wants to show me his gratitude for taking care of Chauncey.

I look at the roses. Jack could've picked any color. Well, not red; everyone knows red roses are meant for love and romance. I'm sure after his faux pas of kissing me the

411

other night, he wants to play it as safe as possible. Maybe that's why he chose white. White is pretty neutral. After our first date, when Mark had given me white roses, he'd told me it was fitting not only because my name means white but also because white roses signify new beginnings. Does Jack know what white roses convey? And if so, is he trying to tell me he wants a new start after his misstep the other night? Or am I reading too much into this? He probably just bought white roses to choose any color besides red. Still, I can't help but find it a strange coincidence that he had given me the same color roses that my deceased fiancé always gave me.

Pushing the thought out of my head, I eat breakfast and then head downstairs to tell Jack I will join him and Christopher on their outing to Alpenzoo.

To make it as fun as possible for Christopher, we decide to take the lift from the Hungerburg cable car to reach Alpenzoo, even though we could've just walked for half an hour from the city center or taken the bus. Alpenzoo claims to be Europe's highest zoo. When we reach the zoo, I'm dazzled by the spectacular views. Christopher, who's no doubt accustomed to Austria's panorama after living here for seven years, doesn't even give it a second glance. His focus is on the animals, in particular the bears and wolves.

Most of Alpenzoo's exhibits feature species found in the Alps. Christopher holds my hand as his father pushes his wheelchair. My heart tugs a bit at Christopher's gesture. I can see he wants to feel as if he's leading me while he tells me about the animals.

"I take it you come here often?" I ask Christopher.

"We used to come every month. Now I think it's every other month or so."

"Oh." I look at Jack and smile. He returns my smile.

"I think someone is trying to impress you with his own animal expertise."

The comment flies over Christopher's head as he goes on to tell me about the next exhibit, which features reptiles.

Having Christopher with us has taken away some of the awkwardness Jack and I have been feeling after our date. I actually feel relaxed and am enjoying myself. And Jack doesn't seem to be anxious.

A few hours later, we're back at the hotel. I'm about to thank Jack and Christopher for inviting me and take my leave when Jack says, "So, I know it's Christmas Eve and

413

your birthday, Bianca. Do you have anything planned to celebrate tonight?"

I don't have anything major planned; I'll have to see how my spirits are holding up. Often, it's at night that I feel the most down and am thinking about Mark. While I'm tempted to be vague with Jack, I don't have the heart. He's a good man, and he's been very candid with me.

"I don't have any set plans. I was going to have some dinner and then maybe take a walk to Old Town. If I'm not too tired, I might even venture out again to go to midnight mass at the Cathedral of St. James."

"Oh, you have to go, Bianca! I'll be singing in the choir. Please say you'll come!" Christopher pleads.

"Christopher, it's not nice to put pressure on Bianca. You can invite her, but don't beg her or make her feel like she has to attend."

Christopher looks down into his lap. His cheeks are turning crimson.

I kneel beside him and tilt his chin up with my hand. "I wouldn't miss hearing you sing again for the world. I'll be there!"

Christopher's eyes light up.

Jack looks at me when I stand back up and mouths the words *thank you*. I can't help but wonder if he's also thanking me for not letting him down, in addition to Christopher.

When we get back to the hotel, Christopher shakes my hand and says, "I had a great time today. I'll see you later in church."

I bend down and kiss Christopher on the cheek. The action surprises him, but he looks pleased. "I had a great time, too. Thank you so much for inviting me. And yes, I'll see you at midnight mass tonight."

"Christopher, I'm just going to walk Bianca to the elevator."

My stomach knots up a bit as Jack escorts me inside and to the elevator bank.

"Thank you, Bianca. If you haven't noticed already, my son is absolutely crazy about you. I'm sorry he put you on the spot like that about midnight mass."

"Please, Jack. I'm crazy about him too! He's a wonderful boy. I loved hearing him and the choir sing the other night. And thank you for inviting me to the zoo. You know, you really didn't have to repay me for treating Chauncey. I was just saying that to trip you up the other night. I'm sorry."

"I know, and you did a great job of it. I couldn't think of a good comeback. You're turning me into a pathetic blob of jelly. Thank you for the apology, but I suppose I deserved your crack after overstepping my boundaries and kissing you."

At the mention of our kiss, our eyes meet for a moment before I clear my throat and look away. I reach for a cough drop in my purse to distract myself further from Jack's gaze.

"Oh, I almost forgot. Thank you for the roses."

"You're welcome. I have to admit, they weren't just a birthday gift but also an I'm-sorry-for-acting-like-a-wild-boar gift."

"I suspected as much. But you didn't act like a wild boar. I'm sorry too for reacting the way I did."

"Please, Bianca. There's no need for you to apologize."

"Thank you." I look down at my feet, suddenly feeling shy.

"Is there any way I can get a do-over? If no one is joining you tonight, will you have dinner with me again? I promise I'll be on my best behavior." Jack crosses his heart with his hands. I can't help but laugh.

"That would be nice. I enjoyed talking to you the other night."

"You did?"

"Yes, very much."

Jack's face is absolutely beaming. "I had a great time too. So, how about I pick you up around seven? I'll have to swing back to the house to drive Christopher to church around eleven. You could hang around with me until then, since you're going to the service."

"Sounds good."

"Great. Oh, and I'd like to take you to a more formal restaurant than the one we went to last time. You don't have to wear a dress — I wouldn't do that to you in these freezing temps — but I wouldn't want you to dress too casually and feel uncomfortable."

"Thanks for the warning. I think I can find something in my luggage."

"Great. Speaking of freezing, Christopher is probably halfway there. I'd better run."

I wave as Jack hurries out.

Panic begins to set in as I realize I actually might not have anything dressier to wear to dinner tonight. Glancing at my watch, I see I have a good two hours before I have to start getting ready for dinner. Instead of going up to my room, I walk over to the city center to do some shopping. I know there's no lying to myself now. This is definitely a real date.

CHAPTER 14

Jack and I are seated side by side in the Cathedral of St. James. Mark and I never visited this cathedral, which helps to lessen my guilt at being out with Jack. We're both quiet as we take in the astounding baroque architecture. My thoughts drift to our dinner earlier.

It was uneventful in the sense that Jack did abide by his promise of not doing anything to make me feel uncomfortable. We talked about growing up in New England and how much we loved the winters there even though they can be especially grueling. Jack made me laugh with a few stories from his childhood and the antics he pulled both at home and in school. Likewise, I made him laugh with stories of my brothers and how they would delight in playing pranks on me because I was the youngest and the only girl in our family. I also told him about Nonna and how close

I'd been to her. I didn't look up until I was done talking about her, and I noticed Jack was staring at me with a hint of a smile. Something about the way he was looking at me made my heart stop for a moment.

He surprised me with a birthday cake he had bought at one of the local pastry shops. Thankfully, he didn't have the staff sing "Happy Birthday" to me in German — although that would've been memorable! We each couldn't resist having two slices. I asked the kitchen to cut a generous portion of the cake so Jack could take it home for Christopher. I took the remainder.

Jack breaks in on my thoughts. "Though we come here on Sundays for Mass, I'm still awed every time I step into this cathedral."

"Yes. It's quite breathtaking."

The choir begins walking out onto the stage. Christopher soon follows in his wheelchair. My heart tugs at the sight of this brave boy. He's had misfortune in his life and has managed to move on. Then again, he was so young when his accident happened. He's been in a wheelchair most of his life. Still, there must be times when he wishes he can run like the other children. There must be times when he wonders why this happened to him, and why his mother was taken away. If he can be so happy and confident, what's my excuse? Suddenly, shame fills me as I think about how selfish I've been the past few years, shutting myself off from my family and friends. True, I needed time to grieve, but I let myself fall ever deeper into a well of self-pity.

The choir begins a rendition of "Hark! The Herald Angels Sing." The choir's performance is flawless. I glance around at the audience; everyone is rapt by the singing. Jack's expression is full of pride. He must feel me watching him, for he turns in my direction and winks. My face reddens, but I can't help but smile.

I'm enjoying myself. In fact, these past few days I've spent with Jack and Christopher have been a welcome distraction. My thoughts, for once, haven't been completely consumed by Mark. Suddenly, I realize I haven't seen his ghost since that day in the hotel's conference room, after I treated Chauncey's foot. Is he perhaps angry that I've been spending so much time with Jack?

Unconsciously, my hand is playing with the rainbow charm Mark had given me for Christmas.

"Is that a rainbow?" Jack asks.

I was so lost in thought that I hadn't even noticed the choir had stopped singing and it was time for intermission.

"Yes. Playing with it is a nervous habit of mine. I don't even realize when I'm doing it." I stop playing with the charm.

"Are you nervous?" Jack's voice drops to a husky whisper. The sound of it sends a tingle straight to the pit of my belly.

"No. My mind just drifted and I was daydreaming a bit. That's all."

Thankfully, Jack lets me off the hook and doesn't ask me what I was daydreaming about.

"It's a beautiful necklace. Was it a gift?"

I nod my head. "A Christmas gift." I open up my purse and busy myself by pulling out my compact and applying powder to my face. Jack picks up on my hint and doesn't press me for further details on my necklace.

But just when relief washes over me, Jack says, "You never did mention what brought you to spend the holidays alone here in Innsbruck. You've talked about your family and how close you all are. I can't imagine why you're apart from them during Christmas."

I pause before responding. "It was important I take this trip alone. My family understood."

Jack's face looks pensive. He begins to say something but stops. I'm hoping this will be the end of it. But then he blurts out,

"Bianca, I don't mean to pry. I'm sorry. I just wanted to let you know that I'm here if you need someone to listen. I've always been told I'm a great listener."

I'm touched by his concern. He's been nothing but open with me about his own loss. I place my hand on Jack's arm. "Thank you. I can tell you're a great listener. I'm sorry for being so evasive. It's just . . . well, it's just this has been a difficult trip for me, Jack. I've been reliving some painful memories. I was here five years ago with someone very special. He was my fiancé, actually. And he was . . . he was killed in a bus crash."

There. I've said it. I haven't been able to utter those words to anyone. When Mark was killed, the police had offered to contact our families, so I didn't have to actually break the news to them. And whenever I met someone new at work, I never shared with them that I was engaged before. I didn't wear my engagement ring to work because I was constantly washing my hands at the vet clinic.

It's almost as if I tried to act like none of it ever happened. I never met Mark or had a yearlong relationship with him. We never came to Austria. Mark was never killed because he never met me. And without warning, I realize in this moment why I haven't allowed myself to move forward with my life. Deep down, I blame myself for Mark's death. Somehow, I've been feeling all along that if he'd never met me, he wouldn't have been in Innsbruck that Christmas or taken that bus over the Brenner Pass. He wouldn't have been preoccupied with bracing me before the crash to save *my* life.

Tears fill my eyes and I can't stop them from falling. Jack places his hand over mine, which I've forgotten is still on his arm. He doesn't say anything. He doesn't have to. He knows exactly the pain I'm feeling. He knows what it's like to lose the love of your life in an instant.

He pulls a silk handkerchief from his coat pocket and hands it to me.

"Oh, thank you, but I'll ruin it."

"Like I care."

And before I can protest again, Jack is patting my tears dry. The action moves me. When he's done, I take the handkerchief.

"Thank you. I'm sorry I fell apart."

"We all need to do that from time to time. Lord knows I have. It's really the only way you get through it. For some reason, we often tend to do our best to be stoic when we go through something painful, but that only delays our grieving."

"How long did it take you to fully mourn Jennifer's loss?"

"Years. I think the first two were the worst. Then, after that, it got better little by little. But trust me, there are times I still cry over her, especially when I see what a special boy Christopher is turning out to be. I wish she could be here to witness it all. I wish he could have his mother back."

"She is witnessing it all, Jack. She might not be here, but I'm confident she is watching over both of you."

I wish I could tell Jack about my seeing Mark's ghost, but I don't want him thinking I'm a total nutcase. Of course, that's why I can be so certain that Jennifer knows what a wonderful son she has. I wonder if she's watching us now.

"Bianca, I have a confession to make. And before you get upset with me, please hear me out."

"What is it?"

"I actually knew about Mark already."

"What? How?"

"The bus crash made the news. Remember, I was already living here in Innsbruck at that time. I had read about it in the papers, and there was even a photo of the two of you together. I almost didn't recognize you when you checked into the hotel.

You've lost quite a bit of weight since that photo was taken, and your hair was much shorter back then."

I had let my hair grow after Mark's death. It was easier than getting the frequent haircuts a short hairstyle demanded. It was just another excuse for me not to go out as much. Except for work and grocery shopping, I rarely went out. My family often forced me to go on outings with them, but there were times I faked being sick so they'd leave me alone. I'm sure they knew I was lying.

"Anyway, your name sounded familiar, and then I thought I had seen you somewhere before. So I Googled you and saw again the news reports about the bus crash and Mark being killed. I'm sorry I didn't say anything sooner, Bianca. But I wanted you to tell me when you were ready. I know how hard it is to open up to someone you've just met about such an incredible loss."

I feel a momentary flash of anger that Jack hadn't told me he knew about Mark, but then again, if the roles were reversed, I probably wouldn't have brought it up either. How do you bring up such an awkward subject with someone you've just met? Naturally, he realized how painful the subject would be for me because he went through a similar loss. I decide to let my anger fade.

"Well, I guess I should thank you for not pressuring me to talk about Mark. But you had no problems opening up to me about Jennifer even though you barely knew me."

"That's because I've fully dealt with her loss. It's not so difficult for me to talk about her anymore."

"So you knew who I was all along." Embarrassment washes over me. "No wonder you frowned when I told you the other day at the café that I was meeting my boyfriend." I shake my head. "I'm such an idiot. I'm sorry again for lying to you."

"It's understandable. Don't be so hard on yourself, Bianca. I didn't take it personally. Besides, you didn't owe me anything. I was just a stranger. I thought maybe you had met someone else and were here with him. But I have to admit, I did find it kind of odd you would return to the place where your fiancé was killed with someone else."

"And didn't you find it odd that I would return here at all? I'm sure you must think I'm some sadistic person who loves to suffer." I offer a halfhearted laugh.

Jack takes my chin in his hand and forces me to look at him. "Hey! I never thought any such thing."

We remain silent for a few minutes.

"Are you mad that I didn't tell you right away that I knew who you were?"

"I was mad at first. But then I understood you didn't want to force me to talk about anything I might not be ready to. Only someone who's lost a loved one could understand that."

"That's true."

"But I'm warning you, I'm not always this generous with my forgiveness. So watch out from now on!" I wave my index finger at Jack. He laughs.

"I'm glad I finally told you. It was weighing on me."

"So, you were wondering why I chose to spend Christmas apart from my family."

"I have my suspicions as to why. You've come here to finally deal with Mark's loss. You haven't fully healed yet."

"Perceptive in addition to a great listener." I laugh softly.

I'm surprised I can joke, though I know Jack can see through my weak attempt at humor as a way to mask my enormous pain.

"Yes, you're right, Jack. But it wasn't my idea. I have my shrink to thank for sending me here. It's been sheer torture revisiting all the places I'd been with Mark."

"But surely there was also some joy at

remembering how happy you were and the love you shared for each other even if those memories inevitably also brought pain."

"There was."

"So, do you feel coming here has helped at all?"

I shrug my shoulders. "Yes and no. I haven't taken my shrink's most important test yet."

"Test?"

"She gave me a few exercises, tests — whatever you want to call them — to complete. The first one was leaving my engagement ring at home. I was still wearing it these past five years. I managed to pass that test. The second was actually getting on the plane and coming here. The third was to visit a few places I'd been to with Mark. But the final and most important test, which I'm still not sure I can go through with, is . . ." My voice trails off.

Jack puts his arms around my shoulders and whispers, "It's okay. You don't have to tell me if you don't want to."

"It's just hard for me to even say the words." Sighing deeply, I continue. "She wants me to take the bus that goes over the Brenner Pass en route to Italy. It's the same route that Mark and I took when he was killed. My psychiatrist thinks that's the only way I'll get closure — to relive those moments before the crash. It's crazy, isn't it?"

I'm desperately hoping Jack will agree with me.

"It seems crazy when you first hear it. After all, who would want to relive that horror? But eventually, when you're stronger, you'd be surprised at how much it can help, Bianca. I visited the site of Jennifer's crash. And while I wasn't in the car with her and Christopher, just seeing where it happened brought some closure for me. But I know your situation was different since you were in the bus during the accident. You saw Mark die in front of you."

I begin crying again. "I didn't actually see him die. I was unconscious after the crash and didn't wake up until I was at the hospital. The doctors had tried to save Mark, but he was pronounced dead about an hour after he was brought to the emergency room. The intellectual side of me knows I need to do this, but my heart is screaming no. I don't think I can take feeling that pain again."

"It will be hard, Bianca. I'm not going to gloss over that. But I think you're a lot stronger than you give yourself credit for. Ultimately, the decision is up to you. If you do decide to go through with it, I can come with you, if you'd like."

"You'd do that?"

"Of course. It always helps having someone by your side when you need to do something this difficult."

"Did you have someone with you when you visited Jennifer's crash site?"

"Jennifer's parents. Christopher and I were visiting them in Vermont, about two years after the accident. They hadn't seen where she'd died and wanted to place a small cross at the site. They were planning to go on their own, but then I decided I needed to go as well. I'm glad we were together. It helped tremendously."

The intermission is over and the choir takes the stage once again.

Jack leans over and whispers into my ear, "Think about my offer. I'm here for you, Bianca."

We turn our attention to the choir. Christopher is now center stage and singing "Silent Night," which happens to have been Mark's favorite Christmas carol. I feel a breeze blow through my hair, and I turn around in all directions, trying to see if Mark's ghost is somewhere near; I've come to recognize the signs that precede his visits. But he's nowhere in sight. Closing my eyes, I let the lyrics of "Silent Night" soothe me.

For the first time, I feel some of my burden has been lifted in telling Jack about Mark. Is he right? Am I strong enough to take the bus ride through the Brenner Pass?

CHAPTER 15

I wake up late on Christmas morning. Looking at my watch, I see it's twenty past eleven — too late to have breakfast delivered to my room. I'll just ask for coffee to be brought up, and as soon as I'm ready, I'll venture out to see what restaurants are open for lunch. I'm sure the pickings will be slim because of the holiday.

Once room service arrives with my coffee, I plop back down in bed and take my time sipping it. I'm feeling absolutely lazy, and since I have no plans for the day, I can lounge around. Christmas Eve was nice. I shake my head, thinking about all that Jack did for me to make my birthday special, from inviting me to the Alpenzoo to taking me to dinner at one of the fanciest restaurants in Innsbruck, and then watching Christopher perform during midnight mass. After the service was over, Jack and Christopher escorted me home. Jack gave me a kiss on the cheek and told me he would call me today, even though I told him I would understand if he didn't; it was Christmas, after all, and he'd be busy celebrating with Christopher. But he just smiled and walked away.

There's a soft knock on my door. I yell, "Coming," as I hurry out of bed. Grabbing my silk robe from the closet, I slip into it before opening the door.

"Merry Christmas!"

"Jack! What are you doing here? Shouldn't you be with Christopher?"

"Actually, we had our Christmas celebration this morning. Of course he got me up at the crack of dawn so he could see what Santa brought him. Then I cooked brunch. Every year, we have Christmas dinner with the parents of Christopher's best friend. They've become like a second family to us here. I decided to bow out this year, but I wouldn't dream of letting Christopher miss it. So he'll be there the rest of the day and night. He's sleeping over. Anyway, I figured no one should be alone on Christmas, so if you're not sick of me yet, how about hanging out with me?"

Jack gives me a sheepish grin, his eyes holding an expectant look. I'd noticed before he's a handsome man, but suddenly,

433

I'm realizing just how good-looking he is, especially when he gets nervous and smiles the way he's smiling now.

I laugh. "Sure, why not? I'd love to hang out with you. But I'll need some time to get ready. As you can see, I woke up late."

Jack glances at my robe, and then his eyes grow heavy as they travel lazily down my body. I suddenly regret drawing attention to my bed attire. His eyes have now rested on my chest. Glancing down, I see that in my haste to answer the door, I forgot to tie my robe. My chemise's plunging neckline is giving Jack an ample view of my cleavage. But I can't wrap my robe around myself now because Jack will know I've seen him checking me out.

Instead, I turn my back to him and nonchalantly say, "You can make yourself comfortable while I get ready, or if you'd rather wait in the lobby. I promise I'll be no more than fifteen minutes."

"Fifteen? I've never known a woman to get ready that fast."

"I've always hated taking long showers, and with the early hours I put in at the vet clinic, I value my sleep more than my beauty." I glance over my shoulder at Jack, who's stepped into my room but is still staring at me. This time his gaze is fixated on my legs.

"On second thought, I think I will wait in the lobby. I just remembered I need to go over some things with the manager who's on call today. You can take longer than fifteen minutes. Don't rush on my account." And with that, Jack hurries out of the room.

The tingling warmth I felt as Jack looked at my body is still with me. I don't know what I was thinking, inviting him to wait for me in my room. But that's just it: I wasn't thinking. Could it be that subconsciously I was hoping Jack would kiss me again?

Shaking these thoughts from my head, I jump into the shower. I haven't felt this longing since Mark. I miss having someone to confide in, to hold me, to love me.

I decide to take an extra ten minutes and apply some eye shadow, as well as put my hair up into a slightly tousled chignon. And in keeping with the holiday, I wear black velvet jeans with a gorgeous deep red, off-shoulder sweater I couldn't resist buying in town yesterday when I bought the outfit I wore to dinner last night. I had opted for a body-hugging knit dress in emerald green, which contrasted nicely against my dark hair. Although Jack had told me he didn't expect me to wear a dress in this cold weather, I'd bought a pair of wool tights to keep me warm. Jack had taken in my appearance appreciatively when he picked me up for our date but was able to muster more control than he had earlier. This morning, I felt as if he were completely undressing me with his eyes.

Taking one last look in the mirror before I leave, I head downstairs to meet Jack, wondering what he has in store for us.

We're in Jack's car, heading ever higher up a mountain. The roads leading here were mostly deserted. Everyone has probably already arrived wherever they're celebrating their Christmas. I soon drift off to sleep.

I'm awakened by a gentle nudge.

"Bianca. We're here."

Rubbing my eyes, I look outside my car window and see a beautiful Swiss chalet cabin. Then I notice there are other similar-styled cabins spread out along the top of the mountain.

"Where are we?"

"The hotel also rents out these cabins. I thought it would be fun to have our Christmas dinner here rather than at a restaurant."

My pulse races. I'm a bit nervous to be spending all this time alone with Jack. But I can see he's gone to so much trouble. He's unloading the trunk of the car. Of course, he's come prepared. I make my way to the back of the car and help him unload all the groceries he's bought.

"Wow! Look at all these groceries. How long do you plan on keeping me up here?" I keep my tone light, making jokes to conceal my anxiety.

"Well, it *is* Christmas. I have to cook you a grand feast."

"Oh, Jack, you shouldn't be going to all this trouble, especially since you cooked brunch for Christopher earlier. Do you really want to do all this cooking on Christmas? It's a holiday. You should be relaxing."

"Cooking is how I relax. I love it, so stop worrying."

"Well, let me help you at least. Cooking is one of my passions too, although I haven't been keeping up with it lately."

My love of cooking was another pastime I had let fall by the wayside after Mark died. I was also an avid reader, but I can't remember when I last picked up a book.

"Really? We'll have to see who's the better cook!"

"Are you challenging me, Mr. Gruner?"

"We can have our own *Iron Chefs* competition."

We carry the groceries over to the chalet. Jack plops his down on the ground and fishes a key out of his jeans pocket.

"Whew! For a second, I was afraid I'd forgotten the key. Can you imagine making that trek all the way back down the mountain?"

"I would've told you to forget about coming back up here." I laugh.

"And miss this?" Jack holds open the door and gestures at the interior.

I step through the threshold and am taken aback by how beautiful the furnishings are. Instead of featuring a more cozy, quaint Austrian-style decor, the chalet is decorated in an ultramodern, luxurious style. White plush couches adorn the living area. A beautiful fireplace decorated with holly and a wreath featuring white roses hangs from the mantelpiece. To the fireplace's left, an eight-foot Christmas tree stands. It's also adorned with white roses and silver ribbons.

"Step into the kitchen." Jack motions with his head in its direction.

"It's huge!" My eyes practically pop out of my head as I take in the very spacious kitchen, which looks like a professional chef's.

"How much does the hotel charge to stay here?"

"A lot."

"And they had no problem with you using

it today?"

"It's one of the perks of my job. We're allowed to stay in any of the hotel's properties, free of charge, as long as they're available."

"Nice!"

"I'm glad you like it. I paid one of the teenagers who works at the hotel to decorate it for us. I'm sure you noticed the white roses?"

"I did. I thought that was a coincidence."

"Well, after the bouquet of white roses I gave you yesterday morning, I thought it's a safe color, and I figured you must like the color white since your name is Bianca. But I must admit I also had ulterior motives for choosing white. It's a more neutral-colored rose to give."

"So you do know about the meanings of different-colored roses?" I laugh. "I thought most guys were oblivious to that sort of thing."

"Not me. I'm a sucker for sentimentality. And trust me, after my faux pas on our first date, I wasn't going to commit another one." Jack's face suddenly registers that he's just referred to the first time we had dinner together as a date. "Ugh . . . I mean, the first time we had dinner."

I walk over to Jack and take his hands in

mine. "It's okay, Jack. It *was* a date. You knew it. I knew it. That's probably why you went with the moment and kissed me."

I meet Jack's gaze head-on. And before I can change my mind, I lean in and kiss him softly on the lips. Jack kisses me back, and it's much different from that urgent kiss he gave me on our first date. This one is very gentle. His hands release mine as they wrap around either side of my face. We continue kissing for another minute. Our kissing gradually becomes more intense. I'm about to step back before things get too heated, but Jack beats me to it. He stops kissing me but pulls me into his arms and holds me. We stand there hugging each other, not saying a word.

Finally, Jack pulls away. "I'd better get in the kitchen if we hope to eat today." He grins. Before he leaves, he kisses me on the head.

I walk over to the Christmas tree and look at the angel perched on top. What am I thinking? I'm due to return home in a few days. Jack lives in Austria. He has a son and a life here. Is this just a Christmas fling? No. It doesn't feel that way, and Jack doesn't seem like the kind of guy to just have a meaningless fling. Then what exactly are we doing?

I hear voices outside. Going over to the window, I see a couple laughing as their sled comes to an abrupt stop. Stepping out of the sled, they make their way to one of the cabins in the distance. The man has his arm draped around the woman's back. I miss feeling that connection to someone else. I miss feeling happy. These past few days with Jack have changed something for me. Dare I say it? I finally have felt joy — an emotion I thought would always be dead to me in the wake of Mark's death.

I go into the kitchen to help Jack with dinner. I might not know where this is headed, but for today, I don't care. It's Christmas, and I just want to enjoy being in Jack's company.

CHAPTER 16

The majestic panorama from the Brenner Pass seems more vivid to me now than when I first saw it five years ago. I didn't realize how much I blocked of that day, but now as I see the beautiful landscape before me, I begin to remember how awed Mark and I were at the scenery. I remember now the monasteries upon monasteries situated at the edge of cliffs . . . the numerous waterfalls cascading down from the mountains . . . the hawks gliding in the sky.

After spending Christmas with Jack, I decided later that night that I would go through with Dr. Pierpont's final test and take the bus over the Brenner Pass. I asked Jack to accompany me. We had to wait until the end of the week, when he had time off from work. Of course, my anxiety just grew until the day finally arrived.

Jack hasn't let go of my hand since we boarded the bus. Neither of us has said much. Just every so often, he whispers, "You can do this. I'm here."

I nod, and soon another voice fills my head. It's Mark's. Snippets of our conversation that day on the bus come back to me, when we discussed what our wedding would be like. I remember the Irish college students. They were having the time of their lives. A few of them were killed too, as was Domenico, our bus driver.

I scold myself as I talk to Mark in my thoughts. *We should have gotten married on Christmas Day, right here in Innsbruck, Mark. You were right when you didn't want to wait a whole year. But no, I had to have my fairy-tale winter wedding. My parents would've understood, and we could've had a celebration once we were home. I'm sorry.*

For some reason, since Mark's death I've often given myself a guilt trip over not getting married as soon as possible, in Austria. That way, he would've been my husband when he died.

I see the highway pass indicating we're only a mile away from Trento, Italy. A chill sets into my bones. We crashed not far from here.

I let go of Jack's hand and place my feet up on the edge of my seat, hugging my knees toward me. I can feel Jack's gaze, but as always, he senses when to leave me alone.

And then those moments before the crash come flooding back: my waking up suddenly to bloodcurdling screams from the passengers . . . the bus listing wildly to the left and right . . . Domenico's rosary beads frantically hitting the windshield. I can even feel the nauseous feeling that had formed in my stomach. And then, of course, Mark's arm braced so tightly across my chest that it hurt. I shut my eyes tightly, not wanting to think of the last thing I'll ever remember from that horrific crash. But then I remember that's the whole point of this test. I need to remember everything, see everything just as I saw it that day. I stop fighting. I let myself see Mark's eyes as we looked at each other, possibly knowing it would be the last time we ever saw each other again. Tears fall silently down my face as I feel a sharp stab of pain piercing my heart. It hurts as much as it did when I first learned upon awakening in the hospital that Mark had died.

Jack pulls me into him as he holds me. I rest my head in his lap, and soon the tears become sobs as I let myself cry uncontrollably. Jack strokes my hair and whispers, "It's okay. It's okay."

Once my crying has subsided, I sit up.

"Are you all right?" Jack's face looks so sad. No doubt he must've also remembered how much it hurt him to visit Jennifer's crash site. He must've remembered the pain he felt as he watched me in anguish.

"I'm better now. Thank you."

Jack holds my hand tightly. I look out my window. Just as on that day five years ago, a few showers have passed. The sun begins to come out. I see my reflection cast in the window. My eyeliner is smeared and my eyes are puffy. I glance at Jack, but he's looking straight ahead, absorbed in his own thoughts. Returning my attention back to the window, I almost gasp when I see Mark's image. He's staring at me and smiling. It's the most beautiful smile I've ever seen. Mark holds up his hand. I press my own against the glass. I hear him whisper, "I'll always love you, Bianca. Be happy."

I mouth the words *I'll always love you too.* Mark's image slowly fades, and in its wake the most magnificent rainbow appears. I remember when he gave me my necklace and made me promise to look at the rainbow charm whenever I felt sad or hopeless. Tears fall down my cheeks as I realize Mark won't be visiting me anymore. But it's all right because for the first time since he died, I'm finally ready to let him go.

EPILOGUE

Lake Garda, Italy, one year later

I stare at the image of the bride decked out in a wedding dress that pays homage to Princess Grace with a modern twist. The A-line gown is silk except for a Chantilly lace overlay that adorns the top half of the bodice. The sleeves are also covered in lace and are short, reaching almost to the bride's forearms. Peeking beneath the lace bodice is a modest, straight-edged neckline. A veil with a delicate lace trim is pinned to the back of a loose bun that hangs low. Two small white rose buds are tucked into the side of the veil. Pearl teardrop earrings are the only jewelry the bride wears.

It's still hard for me to see myself as a bride, even though the image of one is staring back at me in my dresser mirror. My mother, who will also be my matron of honor, has given me some time alone before I make my walk down the aisle.

For the first six months after I met Jack, we had a long-distance relationship. It was difficult, to say the least. But then Jack landed a job as a senior manager at The Vanderbilt Grace, a historic boutique hotel in Newport. I was worried about Christopher and how he would adjust to making such a big move, but that kid never ceases to amaze me. Though he was a little "bummed," as he put it, to leave his friends in Innsbruck behind, he told me he was happy that he'd be closer to his grandparents, and to me as well.

A month after Jack moved to Newport, he proposed to me, and I didn't hesitate in accepting. The best was when Christopher told me he couldn't wait to call me Mom.

I told him he didn't need to wait until the wedding and could start calling me Mom right away. Naturally, Christopher will be Jack's best man. I can't wait for the three of us to be a family.

So here I am in Lake Garda, Italy, one week before Christmas, about to have the winter wedding I'd always dreamed of. After the wedding, Jack and I will spend our honeymoon in nearby Verona. Jack thought it would be romantic to start our marriage in the city of *Romeo and Juliet.* Jack had asked me if I was certain about getting mar-

447

ried during the Christmas season since I had lost Mark then. I told Jack that though I had suffered loss during Christmas, that was also when I found love and hope again.

Looking out of my hotel window at the turquoise waters of Lake Garda and the serene mountains standing guard over it, I think back to my trip to Innsbruck last year. Revisiting the places I had been with Mark and remembering the feelings we shared had reminded me how special love could be when it's with the right person. I also now see the signs he was giving me to show me that it was okay to love again and that Jack was the one: finding Chauncey on the hiking trail . . . Christopher singing "Silent Night," Mark's favorite Christmas carol . . . Jack giving me white roses. . . . There's no doubt in my mind that Jack was Mark's final Christmas gift to me. Closing my eyes, I send out a thank-you to Mark, wherever he is.

I turn away from the window and check the clock. It's time. Taking my bouquet, I glance in the mirror once more before heading out to begin my new life with Jack and Christopher.

Dear Reader,

I've had a lifelong fascination with the paranormal, so when my editor approached me about writing a Christmas-themed novella, naturally I thought of doing a story about a woman who loses a great love but is later visited by his ghost.

Why the fascination with ghosts? It all began when I was five years old. A friend of my sister's, who was nine years old at the time, had lost her father a few months earlier. One summer evening, my sister, her friend, and I were playing in the backyard of my home. The backyard faced a long driveway, and the street could be seen from the yard. We were standing, talking to one another and deciding what we would do next to occupy ourselves. I was facing the driveway, looking out toward the street, when suddenly I saw a man come into my line of vision. He was walking very, very slowly as he crossed the street. I could only see the back of him, but I remember thinking that he looked a lot like my friend's father, who had passed away. He had the same hairstyle, the same clothes, the same gait. And then I noticed he was carrying in one hand a cake box from a bakery. I remember thinking how that very day was my friend's birthday. And then the man held up his free hand, as if he were waving to us. I whipped my head toward my friend, who had also turned her head toward me. Both of our eyes were wide open, and she said, "You saw him too!" I nodded my head. My friend told my sister that we had seen her father. But my sister hadn't been facing the driveway, so she had to take our word that we'd seen him when she hadn't. My sister gave our friend a sympathetic look, obviously not believing her. We ran down the driveway to the street to see if there was any trace of her father's ghost, but there wasn't.

Later that evening, over dinner, my sister recounted what had happened to my family. She told them how I had also seen my friend's father. My mother asked me if that was true. I nodded my head emphatically. But none of them would believe a five-year-old really knew what she was seeing and was probably just agreeing with her friend.

I remember feeling so sad for my friend and that no one would believe her if she told anyone else what we saw.

As the years went by, I forgot about that incident until after my own father died when I was sixteen. When someone you love dies, you're left with a lot of questions and struggle with your beliefs. And when I did remember seeing my friend's father's ghost, I tried to hold on to it, to believe that there was an afterlife and I would see my father again. Sometimes I wonder if that's why I had seen my friend's father — to remind me there is life after death.

But as we get older, we inevitably become more rooted in reality and become more skeptical. So again, I forgot about what I'd seen all those years ago until I had another brush with the paranormal three years ago. Through the job I had at the time, I was able to receive comp tickets to hear an author speak about her book, which was about communicating with spirits. A medium who supposedly could communicate with spirits would also be speaking at the event and trying to reach the spirits of audience members' loved ones. My husband and I decided to attend. We both kept our expectations low, and my husband told me that when the medium spoke to me, I should offer as few clues as possible about my father. After the author spoke, there was a break, and I introduced myself to the author and the medium. I'd forgotten about what my husband had said and mentioned I had lost my father, and that some of what the author said I could relate to. When we stepped outside to stretch our legs during the break, my husband of course was annoyed with me that I'd offered the details I had.

The time for the medium to contact the spirits of loved ones came. For a few people, she was able to reach the spirit of the person they asked her to contact. For others, she was not able to do so. I wavered between skepticism and being surprised at some of the specific details she was able to give a few of the audience members. She reached me last, and by that time it was late, and most of the other audience members had left. She asked me who I wanted her to reach and the death date of the deceased. So the clues I had given her earlier didn't end up mattering. Instead of speaking to me first, my father wanted the medium to relay a message to my husband. Both of us must've gone as white as a sheet when we heard what the message was — for it was something that only my husband and I knew. Tears quickly ran down my face. I was moved that my father seemed to be looking out for me in death as he had looked out for me in life. My father had a lot to say to both of us. In fact, of all the readings the medium gave that day, she had the most information for me. I felt bad for the other audience members who had only received some information, and for the people whose loved ones she couldn't reach, especially since they had paid for their tickets. Here I was with complimentary tickets to this event, and she had the longest message for me from my loved one.

My husband became a believer from that night forward, but I still remained skeptical. I desperately wanted to believe that my father had been communicating through the medium, but I couldn't help but wonder if the medium was just psychic, and that's how she knew all the details she was giving us. The next morning, my husband asked me if I had turned around his office swivel chair before we went to sleep the previous night. I told him I never touch that chair. He told me the chair was turned all the way around and was facing the table where we had our meals. (Our apartment features an open layout in which we have our living room, office, and dining area combined.)

He remembered the author and medium saying that after a spirit has communicated with their loved ones, they often give a sign to let us know it really was them communicating with us. We never found the office chair facing out like that again.

I'll never know if that really was my father communicating with us through the medium. But I still have no doubt that my friend and I did see her father's ghost that day all those years ago. I know what I saw, and the fact that my friend had seen exactly what I'd seen only convinces me more.

I also know for certain that anything is possible, and if we choose to believe in ghosts, guardian angels, Santa, or whatever else to help us know that we are loved and someone is looking out for us, then what's the harm in that?

I hope that my novella, *Seven Days of Christmas,* has helped you to believe in the power of miracles — no matter what form they might come in.

My third stand-alone novel, *Stella Mia,* will be released in January 2015. And like *Seven Days of Christmas,* it too tells the story of a great love set against the backdrop of beautiful Sicily and the Aeolian Islands. And if you haven't read my first two novels, *Bella Fortuna* and *Carissima,* they are currently available.

I love hearing from readers. You can contact me by visiting my website: www.rosannachiofalo.com.

Happy Reading!
Rosanna Chiofalo

■ ■ ■ ■

A Smoky
Mountain Gift

LIN STEPP

■ ■ ■ ■

CHAPTER 1

Veda dug in her purse looking for her key as she made her way across the front porch of the O'Neill farmhouse. She grinned as a loose board by the door creaked. That board had creaked in the same spot for as long as she could remember. As a young girl, she'd learned to step artfully around it when sneaking in late.

She dropped her suitcase and duffel to the porch to dig deeper for the house key. Shivering in the December cold, Veda turned to look out across the green lawn and winding drive leading up to the house. The narrow road curled through the valley to the old farmhouse before continuing up the mountain, each side of the roadway lined with the beautifully shaped cedar trees the O'Neill Farm was famous for.

The wind whispered around the corner of the farmhouse as Veda paused, rustling her hair and giving her an odd chill.

"The wind's kicking up on a still day." Aunt Rita Jean's words drifted across her consciousness. "There's a touch of change in the air; someone's coming."

"Well, that someone is me today." Veda whispered the words with a sigh as she twisted her key in the old lock and pushed open the front door.

Familiar emotions swamped her as she stepped inside the old house — a soft eagerness to be here tinged with resentment and regret. Veda's mother, Skyler, had dumped her at the O'Neill Farm every summer as a small child, flying off to one glamorous photo shoot after another, always too busy to deal with her. Then, after her tragic death in a car crash, whizzing down some European roadway, Veda had come here to stay. She'd had nowhere else to go and no one else who wanted her. But now, except for flying in briefly this summer for Rita Jean's funeral, she hadn't been back in eight years.

Veda carried her bags inside the door, dumped them, and headed to the car for more. After two trips unloading, she walked out on the porch to look around for her dog.

"Lucy," she hollered with a whistle. "Where are you?"

A stubby, gold-and-white corgi ran around the house in answer to Veda's call and began working her way up the porch steps on short, stubby legs — her tags jingling, her eyes bright with the excitement of exploring a new place. At the top of the steps, the corgi looked from Veda to the yellow Volkswagen parked in the driveway with a question.

"No, we're finished with traveling." Veda reached down to pet the corgi affectionately. "It was a long trip for you all the way from St. Augustine, Florida, eleven hours and almost six hundred miles, to be exact."

Lucy barked as if to affirm Veda's words.

Laughing, Veda headed across the porch to push open the door. "Come on in, Luce. You can explore our new digs since we're staying here for a while."

The words brought a fresh sweep of regret to Veda. She shrugged. Oh, well, it wasn't as though she had much choice in the matter. As Aunt Rita Jean used to say, the wind had changed, and *not* in Veda's favor.

Remembering her Uncle Sutton's note, Veda carried her bags back to Rita Jean's old room at the back of the house. She'd have preferred staying in her old girlhood room upstairs. However, Sutton had taken over much of the second floor after his and Rita Jean's father died, moving from his own smaller house on the upper property, not wanting Rita Jean to live alone in the big house. Veda also knew there was only one bath on the second floor. Sutton wanted her to be comfortable while she was here, and since he'd cleaned and prepared Rita Jean's room for her, she'd comply.

A rush of memories assailed her as she walked into the back bedroom. Nothing had changed, and Veda's heart wanted to weep at the loss of the aunt she'd loved so much, who'd mothered her for so many young years. She wandered around the room, running her fingers over the flower garden quilt on the bed, touching the floral-painted base of the old bedside lamp, pausing to look at photos on the chest of drawers, and then gazing up at the painting over the double bed of a field of mountain flowers blowing in the spring wind, the Smoky Mountains in the background. Framed on the dresser sat a picture of Rita Jean dressed in her old-time storyteller's garb — long dress, apron, and mobcap.

Beside the bed lay one of Rita Jean's many black journals in which she wrote her thoughts and quotes, things that might later be woven into her mountain stories. Veda picked up the book and leafed to a back page.

" 'The wind has its reasons,' " she read.

" 'We just don't notice it as we go about our lives. But then at some point we are made to notice. The wind envelopes you with a certain purpose in mind.' " She stopped, noting the author of the words was the Japanese writer Haruki Murakami. Unusual. More often Rita Jean's quotes and stories came from old Cherokee legends and writings, since her grandmother, Unole Watie O'Neill, had been full-blooded Cherokee.

"Unole is a funny name," she'd said to her aunt once.

Rita Jean had smiled. "It means Wind. And every first daughter in the bloodline is said to carry the gift of hearing the wind sing if she will listen."

Funny Veda remembering that conversation now. Her aunt Rita Jean was a firm, practical, hardworking woman who'd raised both her two young brothers and her baby sister after their mother died. Then, later, she'd raised Veda. Pragmatic and sensible, with a firm jaw, plain looks, and no-nonsense ways, it seemed odd whenever Veda glimpsed this other side of her aunt — this almost fanciful side.

"Are you a first daughter?" she'd asked that day.

Aunt Rita Jean patted her head. "I am,

and so are you, Veda Regina Trent."

Veda wrinkled her nose. "I never hear the wind sing and I never hear it say anything either."

"You will when the time is right," Rita Jean said. "Now you get out the silverware and set the table while I finish dinner." And that was the end of that conversation.

Hearing someone clear his throat, Veda turned to see Sutton standing in the doorway. She ran across the room to throw herself into his arms. She knew it embarrassed him — but pleased him, too.

He held her out at arm's length and studied her. He made a sign about her being too thin. Veda glanced toward the mirror. Perhaps he was right. She did look thinner. Stress always stole her appetite.

Her eyes slid over him with fondness. Sutton looked good for a man in his sixties, his face ruddy and healthy from the outdoors, his physique strong from his work with the trees on the farm, his hair almost white like Rita Jean's had been, and his eyes dark, merry, and astute. The O'Neills were ordinarily of hardy stock and long-lived. A bout of bronchitis, even with complications, shouldn't have taken Rita Jean's life, but the infection went systemic, her aunt's immune system turning on her and aiding it.

And she'd slipped away from them.

As if sensing her thoughts, Sutton patted his heart and looked around the room with a touch of sorrow.

"You miss her," she filled in for him. "I do, too."

He made a few signs to let her know he wanted her keys in order to move her car around to the shed. Veda found herself easily following Sutton's old system of signing and messaging. He was mute and had been since birth, but Sutton had developed his own unique methods of communicating with others — easier for him since he could hear and see well. He'd learned simple ways to write notes and utilize signs and gestures to communicate with his family, teachers, and school friends. Here in the country there had been little special education help or Individualized Education Programs in those days. But Sutton experienced few problems or teasing for his infirmity as he grew up. Townsend, Tennessee, was a little town at the base of the Great Smoky Mountains National Park, where everybody knew everybody else, and where the O'Neill family was loved and well-known.

It didn't surprise Veda to see that Lucy took to Sutton immediately, not even barking at him as he let himself into the house.

Sutton had always possessed a way with creatures and been intuitive about animals and people. Little got by him, and although Veda might fool Rita Jean in some matters, Sutton had always picked up on the truth, giving her a look or a raised eyebrow until she confessed all.

Veda wandered into the kitchen to wait for him to return, following the scent of something warm and fragrant on the air. Sutton let himself into the kitchen door a few minutes later, handing her back her car keys. He went to the whiteboard hanging on the wall by the landline phone and picked up a pen to write her a note: *I've started a pot of beef stew for our supper later,* he wrote. *And brought back one of Mary Connor's pies from The Last Deli.*

He opened the refrigerator to gesture toward some containers of pimento cheese and chicken salad. Pointing to her, he made an eating motion, asking if she'd had lunch.

"I ate up the road," she told him. "But I would like some of that lemonade."

He smiled and got down two ancient, colorful aluminum glasses from the shelf, dropped ice into them, and poured out lemonade. From the top of the refrigerator, he brought down a tin with a faded covered bridge scene on the top and popped it open to reveal homemade cookies.

Veda sat down in a white kitchen chair at his direction to drink lemonade and munch cookies, as she'd done so often with Sutton as a girl. It felt comforting to sit with him again in the old kitchen. Guessing her thoughts, he patted his heart, crossed his hands to touch both shoulders, and signed the words *I love you,* almost bringing tears to Veda's eyes.

He pulled out the little notebook and pen he always carried in his shirt pocket, tucked into one of those old-time, vinyl pocket protectors, and scribbled her another note. *Did you get the store closed out and everything taken care of?*

"Yes." She shook her head sadly. "And it broke my heart to sell out my stock and then let the auction company come and carry everything else away. I loved my little store, Sutton. I wish I hadn't been forced to close it."

Sutton patted her hand.

"I put everything I'd saved after college into that store, plus the inheritance I got from Mother. I felt so sure a vintage collectibles store would go well in downtown St. Augustine. After all, I'd lived there, worked part-time in stores much like that all during college at Flagler, and then worked for the Hargreaves in their store after graduation. I did well for the Hargreaves and got promoted. I really felt it was my time to strike out on my own when I saw that old shop come up for sale." She sighed. "It even had a little apartment in the back so I could keep my expenses down. But every year I seemed to slide further into the red and finally had no choice but to shut down."

Sutton's kind eyes watched her. *Everything will work out,* he wrote on his notepad.

"I hope so." The tears threatened at the backs of her eyes again. "I'm sorry I had to come back here and be a burden."

He looked annoyed at those words, shaking his head and even making a fist at her. *Didn't Reese tell you we needed you?* He wrote the words in agitation.

"Yes." She tried to smile at him, seeing she'd upset him. "He called me and said you had no one to manage the Co-op since Aunt Rita Jean died; he explained the store was having trouble and dissension with only the volunteer workers trying to keep it going."

You know I can't run it, Sutton scribbled, touching his mouth. *But you have good skills and a good education in business management. You can run it well. I know you can.*

And you worked in it as a girl.

"Thanks for your confidence in me. I appreciate that right now."

Catching her eyes with his, he pointed his index finger first to his chin and then toward her, signing, *I missed you, Veda.*

Veda reached across the table to take his hand. "I missed you, too."

Not wanting him to get the wrong idea, she added, "I'll stay for a while, until I figure out what I'm supposed to do next. Okay? I don't think I'm meant to stay here always." She hesitated, wanting to be honest. "As I told Reese, I can stay until things are stable and until the right person can be found to manage the Co-op. I want to help, Uncle Sutton. You and Rita Jean were always so good to me."

He nodded, seeming content with her words. *Thank you,* he wrote. *You know it's always busy here at Christmas.*

"How could it not be?" She smiled at him. "The O'Neill Farm is a Christmas tree farm."

As if that reminded him of something, Sutton glanced at his watch. In annoyance, he swept his hand across his forehead with the I-forgot sign and then wrote a quick note: *I need to make a tree delivery in Maryville before supper. Can you watch the stew on the stove and make some corn bread later?*

"Oh course. Don't worry." Veda smiled at him.

He grabbed his jacket off the coatrack and then, before heading out the door, he stopped again to write on the whiteboard beside the phone: *Be careful and keep the doors locked. We've had some thieves sneaking around, stealing our trees.*

"Stealing Christmas trees?" Her mouth dropped open in surprise.

He nodded, making a few signs to remind her that Christmas trees sold for a high price in today's market, once grown and cut.

"Well, I guess it's quick, easy money at Christmas for someone who is dishonest."

He added to his note. *If you ever have any trouble when I'm not here, or if you ever see anyone sneaking around, call Sheriff Swofford.* He pointed to a phone number on a list hanging by the phone.

"All right. I will." She gave him a kiss on his cheek. "Go deliver your trees. I'll be fine here, and I'll unpack while you're gone, watch the stew, and make some corn bread." She glanced down at the little corgi on the floor at her feet. "And don't worry. Lucy will bark if anyone comes around."

He raised an eyebrow.

Veda laughed. "Well, you're the exception, Uncle Sutton, and I can tell Lucy is crazy about you already. She even slept on your shoes while you drank your lemonade."

He reached down to scratch the little dog's head, muttering a soft, guttural noise at her, and then turned to let himself out the door. She heard him whistling as he made his way to his truck. It always seemed odd to Veda that Sutton could whistle so well when he couldn't speak, but whistling didn't involve the vocal cords, only the lips.

Veda unpacked, took the dog out for another walk, puttered in the kitchen, and then settled down in the front parlor to drink a second glass of lemonade and flip through the local newspapers she'd found on the kitchen table. Time to catch up on the news.

The long drive from St. Augustine and the warmth from the fire Sutton had built earlier in the big fireplace soon almost lulled her to sleep. But a sound from outside and a low growl from Lucy woke her, rousing her to alertness. She put a calming hand on the little dog beside her and then cocked an ear to listen in the quiet. Glancing out the window, she could see it was nearly dark now. Darkness fell early in the mountains this time of year.

She heard another noise, then a rustling sound. It made Veda mad to think anyone would drive up the quiet back roads into the O'Neill Farm to pilfer the cedar trees Sutton worked so hard to plant, tend, and grow all year long for his Christmas sales. She decided to slip around to the back of the house, not turning on any lights, to see if she could see anyone outside. It might only be a possum or a deer snooping around the garbage area.

Getting up from her chair, she gave a warning command to Lucy not to bark, and then, on impulse, picked up the big shovel leaning against the side of the fireplace as a potential weapon. "Sutton told us to be careful," she whispered to the dog, as if in explanation.

Veda slipped out the back door onto the screened porch and crept across it toward the noise she still heard coming from outside. As her eyes grew accustomed to the dark, she could see a truck parked by the cantilever barn a short distance behind the house. A man emerged from under the side of the barn, carrying a tree. She watched him stow it in the back of his pickup and then return for another. He was apparently working alone, loading up the freshly cut cedars that Sutton probably planned to deliver to some of his client locations in the morning.

How evil. Her anger flared and she crept through the dark, keeping behind the shrubs and outbuildings until she could get closer to the barn. Dang thief! She clutched the shovel tighter, slipping behind a bush by the open-sided barn. She'd teach him to sneak up on O'Neill property and try to steal their trees!

As he leaned over to get the next tree, Veda stepped out from behind the shrub and whacked him on the back of the head. He fell to the ground with a groan, and Veda hurried over to the barn shelf to grab a loop of rope to tie him up before she called the sheriff.

Rolling him over as she dropped into a squat beside him, she looked straight into Reese McNally's face.

"Reese!" The words wheezed out of her. "Oh my gosh, Reese." She tried patting his cheek, but he seemed unconscious.

"Oh, man, surely I haven't killed Reese." She felt his wrist, finding a pulse, and then leaned over his face to see if she could feel his breath. Veda rubbed his hands and patted his cheeks, trying to wake him up.

Then her temper flared. "What in the

devil are you doing over here in the dark at our place, skulking around and stealing Christmas trees?" She kept patting his hand as she fussed. "That isn't like you at all, Reese. You used to be such a big chicken I had to fight your fights for you growing up. And you were never a match for me when we got into it over anything, either. I could always get you down on your face and make you holler 'Uncle.' "

Standing, she kicked at him with her foot. "You need to wake up. You know you're too big for me to get you into the house." She studied him on the ground, her voice dropping. "And look how you've grown — filled out that skinny frame you used to have. Filled it out rather well, in fact." Her voice softened as her eyes roved over him, noting the muscles under his T-shirt and lined flannel jacket, the strong, firm legs.

She crossed her arms, trying to steady her emotions. "I see you still have those black geeky glasses. Hope I didn't break those again when I whacked you." It had happened before. Veda leaned down to feel for the glasses, adjusting them on Reese's face, letting her fingers linger over his cheek.

"You know I hate you, Reese McNally." Her words dropped to a whisper now. "You're the main reason I never wanted to come back here, you cheating snake."

She kicked at him again for good measure, and then, resigned, went into the barn to get the old wheelbarrow. Coming back, she hauled Reese up and into it, before trundling the wheelbarrow down the hillside toward the house.

At the door to the kitchen, she propped it open and pushed the barrow right through the door, around the corner, through the broad hallway, and back into the parlor, where she unceremoniously dumped him on the sofa.

Sure that he was settled, she took the barrow back outside and leaned it against the side of the house. Then she stopped in the kitchen, shed her coat, and got out the first aid kit from under the sink. She wet a dish towel, filled a saucepan with warm water, and headed back into the living room to tend to the knot on Reese's head and the scratches on his face and hands from the fall.

Veda sat down beside him on the couch. "There's no way I'm calling the sheriff and admitting to him that I hit my own neighbor over the head with a fireplace shovel. At least not until I get you awake enough to tell me what in the heck you were doing skulking around our barn in the dark."

CHAPTER 2

Reese woke, his head throbbing and his
mind dizzy, to hear Veda Trent's voice fuss-
ing at him. He'd have smiled at her words
except he didn't want her to know he was
awake yet. He loved the feel of her hands
moving over his face — feeling for scratches,
he supposed — and then cleaning areas on
his cheeks, forehead, and hands. He inhaled
softly as she leaned over him. She still
smelled like cinnamon and vanilla. Years
ago, she'd told him the name of her per-
fume, something her mother bought for her
that she liked and kept using, but Reese
couldn't remember the name. He always
forgot girl stuff like that.

While she leaned over to re-wet her cloth,
he let his eyes slit open to catch a glimpse
of her. Of course, he'd seen her again at the
funeral this summer, dressed in a slim black
sheath with a jacket over it, her hair pinned
up primly. But other than cordially shaking

his hand at one point, she'd kept her distance from him, stayed close to Sutton, talked to old friends and neighbors, greeted the hordes of relatives and valley friends of Rita Jean's who came to pay their respects. It had come as such a shock to everyone that a vibrant, strong woman like Rita Jean O'Neill could contract a sickness and not recover from it, develop complications, and actually die. No one was prepared for the grief and pain of losing her. She held a place in the Townsend community and in the hearts of its people no one else could fill.

Reese had always felt angry at Veda that she'd traveled so far away to college and left Rita Jean after she'd been like a mother to her all through the years, loved and raised her. Didn't she owe her better? And him? And then to hardly ever come back to see anyone, either.

He groaned as Veda hit a tender spot with her ministrations and sucked in his breath. She leaned down toward his face. "Reese McNally, are you awake?"

"What do you think?" he asked in reply, pulling her down on top of him before he thought and kissing her full on the mouth.

She all but bit his lip pulling away, the little cat, but he got a taste of her again — one he hadn't had since the night of that awful fight they'd had when they were only seventeen.

"I hate you, Reese McNally." She hissed the words, rubbing her mouth as if to rub his taste away. "And what were you doing skulking around our barn tonight, stealing trees? I ought to call the sheriff and have you arrested."

A guttural sound of surprise from the doorway alerted Reese and Veda to Sutton's presence. He held the fireplace shovel, with blood on it, in his hands, his face white as a sheet.

"Oh, we're both fine, Uncle Sutton. Don't panic." Veda glared at Reese. "I just caught Reese skulking around our barn out back, stealing trees. I thought he was one of those thieves you warned me about and knocked him over the head." She said it all in a rush.

Sutton frowned and came over to examine Reese, making angry motions with his hands. He pointed at Veda and made a telephone sign.

"I know, I know." She rolled her eyes. "You told me to call the sheriff if I saw anyone, but I wasn't sure until I went out back if it was a person or just a possum or a deer or something. Then, when I saw it was only one man loading up our trees . . . well, I got mad."

Sutton made some signs about her temper, pointing to her hair, and shook his finger at her.

Veda Trent had fiery red hair — a lot like her temperament sometimes. She liked to call it russet or copper, but it had never been a subtle tone. You could see that red hair in a crowd a mile away. Reese smiled at the thought. With Indian ancestry in her bloodline, Veda missed out on the pale skin and freckles common to most pure red-heads, her skin tone more olive. But her eyes echoed the dark, rich brown characteristic of the Cherokee and the O'Neills. They all had dark hair and dark eyes, except for Veda and her mother, Skyler, who'd pulled a recessive blond gene from the family DNA pool — and a rare beauty as well.

Veda always hated being teased about her mother's stunning looks. *Too bad you didn't get your mother's beauty, Veda.* It made her fighting mad, set her off with a smart retort — but hurt her, too. Still, Reese knew Veda possessed more beauty, character, and depth than he'd ever glimpsed in Skyler Trent. He'd always felt glad Veda took more after the O'Neills in her looks and ways, even if she did get her daddy, Bobby Trent's red hair.

Sutton patted Reese to gain his attention,

signing to ask him if he was okay, encouraging him to sit so he could examine the back of his head where Veda had whacked him from behind. Sutton's probing fingers hurt like the dickens, but his grunts and signs soon assured Reese no real harm had been done.

Pulling out his little notepad, Sutton wrote, *You'll be okay. You'll have a knot, but I don't think there's real damage.* He stopped to sign, asking Reese if he wanted him to call his dad to come get him, or if he wanted Sutton to take him to Maryville to the hospital.

"Nah, I'll be okay." Reese reached around with one hand to feel the back of his head. "If you'll let me rest a little until my head quits swimming, I'll drive on back down the hill and over to our farm."

Veda, encountering another of Sutton's disapproving scowls, fluffed Reese's sofa cushion so he could lie back on it. She crossed her arms after she did so. "I still want to know why you were sneaking around our barn and loading up trees."

Reese rolled his eyes. "*Two* trees, Veda. I bought two Christmas trees from Sutton — one for the house and one for my law office — and Sutton told me I could come pick them up any time tonight or tomorrow."

Sutton made a guttural sound, putting a hand to his forehead to sign *I forgot* and pointing to Veda.

"You forgot to tell her." Reese grinned. "Well, that explains a lot, I guess. But apparently you did remember to tell her to watch out for those thieves who have been sneaking onto your property to steal trees."

He nodded.

Reese turned to Veda. "I didn't think you were coming until tomorrow, Veda, so I didn't think to come up to the house first when I saw Sutton's truck gone. He'd told me he had deliveries to do this afternoon and if he wasn't here to just drive up to the barn and pick out my trees."

"Fine, so now we know the whole story. Isn't that nice?" She smiled sweetly at him.

Sutton, overlooking her sarcasm, looked toward the kitchen and asked about the stew. He turned to make a sign inviting Reese to dinner, and Veda, happy or not about the invitation, headed off to the kitchen to heat up the corn bread and dish out their meal.

Reese smiled to himself while Sutton bathed the back of his head again. He rather liked the way this situation had turned out. He'd wondered how he might get into Veda's presence again. She'd avoided him for eight years, after all, with not even a call or a letter exchanged. But he could hardly blame her for not keeping in touch. After all, he'd married her old nemesis, Dee Dee Palmer. And hadn't that turned out to be the worst mistake he ever made?

Oh, well. Maybe he could get things straightened out with Veda while she stayed here to help with the Co-op, and maybe not. He'd have to wait and see.

At the dinner table in the big country kitchen, Veda made an effort at conversation, knowing Sutton expected it.

"How is your father?" she asked.

"Good," he answered. "As ornery as ever, still working the old Texaco station and memorabilia store every day."

The McNally family owned an old-time Texaco station on the Townsend highway, which also contained a pick-up store for small groceries and a memorabilia section filled with Texaco collectibles tourists and locals loved to browse through.

"I always loved your dad's Texaco museum, and he always let us get a free cold drink from the cooler." She smiled at the memory. "Does he still sell those Nehi grape sodas? Do they even make those anymore?"

"They do." Reese buttered another corn bread stick. "Dad still makes an effort to get the old Nehi grape and orange sodas and a line of old-time drinks and candies other stores don't usually sell. Goes along with the ambience of his place. A lot of people stop in for that reason alone."

Reese appreciated the effort it cost Veda to make polite small talk to please her uncle. "I built a log cabin where our farm fronts the highway and opened my law office there two years ago," he said, helping her out. "My cousin Eleanor — you may remember her, several years younger than us — runs the office for me. You'll have to drop over to see her one day. The law office is adjacent to the Co-op. You can't miss it."

"How nice." Veda paused, spoon in hand. "And how does Dee Dee like you being back in Townsend? I always thought she saw you as her ticket out of this small hick town. Seems like I remember her saying that."

Sutton frowned at her, but Reese chose to answer despite her tone. "Dee Dee and I have been divorced for six years. Perhaps you forgot that, Veda. I came back from the apartment at the University of Tennessee after she left and commuted to finish my education. Dad helped me take care of our daughter, Pamela, since Dee Dee walked out, leaving both of us behind with little thought." He caught her eyes with his. "She married the man she ran off with later on. They live in Las Vegas, where I believe he owns or manages one of the big casinos. We seldom hear from or see her, and I can count the times she's come home to see Pamela on one hand." He held up three fingers. "She gave up custody and decided she could do better than to hang around with either of us."

"She always was flighty and self-serving." Veda glared at him, refusing to show sympathy. "I'd think you might have known that, as many times as she teased and made fun of you when we were younger."

"People make mistakes." He met her eyes. "And they pay for them. All of us."

Her face flushed. "Are you talking about my store?" Anger tinged her voice, along with hurt.

"No." He backed off. "I was talking about *my* life, Veda."

Sutton looked back and forth between them, a warning in his eyes.

Both resumed eating, letting the quarrel go.

Sutton initiated some conversation then, catching Veda up on aspects of the farm, getting Reese to fill in the details around his notes and signs. He wanted Veda to remember the Christmas Tree Shop was now open in the small, tin-roofed cabin at the beginning of Cedar Hill Lane, behind the Co-op parking lot. The Townsend Crafts Co-op and the shop sat on O'Neill land, which stretched uphill toward the mountains past the family farmhouse, only a few blocks off the highway, and then up the hillside through the Christmas tree farm, passing Sutton's small house and another barn.

Sutton scribbled a note to Veda, reminding her that Walker Tenney and his grandson, Bovee, a mentally challenged teen, were living in his old house rent-free in exchange for work on the farm right now.

"Bovee's a nice kid," Reese told her. "And a hard worker. I pay him and his grandfather to do things at our farm, too."

Veda cut pie for the three of them, put the plates on the table, and then picked out a few pieces of stew beef to spoon into a dish for the corgi.

"I probably need to tell you more about the Co-op so you'll be prepared for what you may find there," Reese said as they dug into one of Mary's homemade pies, all of them legend around the area.

Veda sat back down to cut into her own piece of pie. "With Thanksgiving just past and the Christmas season heading in, the store will probably be busy."

"Yes, it will. The Co-op always gets a lot of holiday traffic. The homemade crafts items sell well for Christmas gifts, and people like the holiday wreaths, painted tree ornaments, and decorations."

Finishing his pie, Sutton let them know he needed to drive up the road to load some more trees on the upper farm to bring down to the barn.

"Do you want me to help?" Reese asked.

Sutton signed *No,* pointing to Reese's head as he did. He pulled out his notepad and wrote a note to Veda. *I'll drive Reese home in his truck when I get back, and you can follow me in your car and bring me home. I don't think Reese should drive tonight.*

Seeing the note, Reese argued. "Listen, Sutton, that's not necessary. I'll be fine." But Sutton pocketed Reese's car keys, as though he was still a kid, and gave him a warning shake of his finger before heading out the door.

Reese sighed, his eyes moving to Veda's. "Guess you're stuck with me a little longer."

"Yeah, lucky me." She got up to begin cleaning the table and putting the food away.

Trying to overlook her innuendos again, Reese took a breath. "Perhaps I should update you about the Co-op while we wait."

"All right," she conceded. "Want some coffee?"

He nodded and she poured them both a cup, putting sugar and creamer on the table before sitting back down.

"As you know, the Co-op sits on O'Neill land and essentially belongs to the O'Neill family, but Rita Jean set it up as a type of legal cooperative for the artisans who sell their work there." He briefly sketched out for her how the legalities of that worked. "I am one of the members of the Co-op's board and its legal adviser. I also began to help Rita Jean with the accounting and the books after I moved back to Townsend."

"How many people are selling products and working in the Co-op now?" she asked.

"About twenty people sell handcrafted items and goods in the Co-op and eight volunteer to help run the store. Those who volunteer in the store make more profit on their items than those who don't. That's the way Rita Jean set it up."

"I remember," Veda said. "It's a good incentive to keep the store manned without having to pay for outside help."

"As you may also remember, Rita Jean took a small salary as manager for the Co-op, which is the salary I felt the Co-op could continue to pay you."

She looked across the table at him. "Why did you ask me to do this, Reese? I was stunned when you called out of the blue and asked me if I would fill in."

He considered her question. "Sutton told us in a board meeting that your shop had failed and that you were selling out. He also mentioned you didn't have another job lined up yet. We all thought it might be a sensible solution to see if you'd be interested in managing the Co-op since you had a good background in store management and had worked in the Co-op as a girl." He hesitated. "And because you're an O'Neill."

"Why didn't someone on the board or one of the volunteers step up to take the management role?"

"None of them wanted it. The board members all carry other jobs, and the volunteers are also artisans and crafters. They want to continue to create their art — quilts, pottery, ceramics, whatever. And most have other life commitments as well."

"Nice to know I was chosen by default."

He set down his cup after finishing the last of the coffee. "I think we were lucky to get you, Veda. I'm sorry about your business. I really am. I know it must have hurt a lot to lose it. I can imagine how I'd feel to be forced to close up Dad's Texaco station

488

or my legal practice. You put your heart into these things. It's not just a business." He paused. "But the closing gave us a chance to get your expertise and help with the Co-op after a rough transitional time. I thought, in a way, you might like helping to get your aunt's business back on its feet. I don't want to see it close, too, Veda. It meant a lot to her and it means a lot to the people in this rural area to have a place to sell what they make."

She gave him a tentative smile. "You can actually be nice sometimes, Reese McNally."

He watched her for a moment before he spoke again. "Look, Veda, I know there are hard feelings between us from the past, but a lot of years have passed now. We need to find a way to get along better while you're here. I work with the business, my office is next door to the Co-op, and our families are neighbors. The property lines of the McNally and O'Neill farms join. We used to be good friends, and . . ."

"You can stop right there, Reese." She sent him a steely glance. "*Used to be* is the right term. We used to be a lot of things, but those times are past. Now we are two people who have to work together congenially for a time. I want you to remember, as I told Sutton tonight, that this is a temporary work position for me. I'll be looking for another store to manage again, like the Hargreaves' store I ran in St. Augustine before I opened my own place. I don't want to stay here. Too many painful memories stir in the air. I find it hard to breathe here sometimes. I don't plan to settle in."

Before Reese could pose a response, Sutton came in the back door, letting in a cold blast of December air — highlighting Veda's words and sending a chill to Reese's heart. His earlier optimism that he might bring Veda around while she was here took a decided nosedive.

CHAPTER 3

Two weeks later, Veda sat on a stool by the downstairs register in the Townsend Crafts Co-op, finalizing the work schedule of her employees for the coming week. The volunteers generally worked the same days and times each week, but doctors' appointments, illnesses, and other complications usually necessitated some rearrangements in the schedule.

Veda was surprised at how quickly she'd settled into her work at the Co-op. The people around the community and the shop's artisans and volunteers seemed pleased and relieved to have her managing the store.

Loreen McFee, one of the locals visiting the store the day before, offered a typical comment. "It jest seems right somehow having you here at the Co-op, Veda Trent, you being Rita Jean's girl and all."

Mrs. Marsden, shopping the same day,

chimed in. "You know, Loreen, I taught Veda's daddy, Bobby Trent, in the fifth grade — hair as red as Veda's. He was takin' pictures with a little camera of his own even back then, a real artistic boy, and enterprising, too. I can see why he went far."

Loreen laughed. "He went *far* from here, that's for sure, and carried Skyler O'Neill away with him. It about broke Rita Jean's and their daddy's heart for Skyler to leave the way she did, and her only eighteen. Henry O'Neill sure was sweet on that youngest girl of his, and he grieved over her runnin' off to the big city and marrying Bobby Trent at some courthouse on the way. Not even havin' a proper church wedding. It happened right after Skyler's oldest brother Ruben got killed in the military, too."

She turned to Veda, as if remembering her, and shifted the subject. "We all felt real sorry to learn about your mother gettin' killed in that tragic way, Veda, and over in some foreign country, too." She sighed. "Skyler sure turned out a beautiful woman, though. I collected pictures of her modeling in those big-city magazines for a long time. I might still have some in a box if you'd like them for keepsakes, Veda. I guess it makes you real proud to remember how famous your mother got to be. Your daddy's right well-known for all those photographs of models he takes, too. I'm sorry your parents split up, but it seems like those celebrity types have trouble keeping their marriages together."

Veda saw Mrs. Marsden lean over to Loreen to add, "I can tell you someone *else* besides Rita Jean O'Neill whose heart was pure broken up when Veda went off to college." She glanced toward the Co-op's side window to the view of Reese's law office next door.

"Isn't that the truth?" Loreen dropped her voice, as if Veda couldn't hear both of them easily in the small store. "And that Dee Dee Palmer he married wasn't worth the paper a dollar bill is printed on — ran off and left Reese with a little two-year-old while he was trying to finish his college schooling. I remember he had to move back to Townsend and commute to school so his daddy could help him with the child and all. It was a shame. Poor little mite."

This was the kind of talk Veda heard her whole first two weeks back in Townsend. You'd think she hadn't been gone eight years at all. She'd caught up on every gossip scandal in the valley in barely more than a week and, in most cases, learned more than she cared to about others' business, including her own and what people knew about it.

Beth Robbins came out of the back room, carrying her coat and searching for her car keys in her purse. It had been a treat for Veda to find Beth working as one of the crafters and volunteers at the Co-op. She'd been one of Veda's few friends in school, except for Reese. Beth had married a Maryville boy, Matt Robbins, whose family owned an auction company on the highway between Maryville and Townsend. Now they lived in a house on the Little River, close to the old swinging bridge Veda had loved so much as a girl.

"Do you know, Matt Robbins got me out on that thing and started swinging it about the first day we moved in our house," she told Veda, laughing. "It nearly scared me to death, but of course he thought it real funny, and so did Laurie." Laurie was Beth's eight-year-old daughter, and the couple also had a young son who'd just turned two.

"I'm so glad to be able to work here at the Co-op a couple of days a week," Beth confided. "It gets me out of the house, lets me talk with people who like crafts, and gives me a better idea of which of my things people like the best." Beth, a skilled seamstress, created one-of-a-kind purses, wall hangings, aprons, children's clothing items, dolls, and an assortment of charming small crafts, that were piled in baskets and on shelves around the store.

She walked closer to the register where Veda sat. "Is it all right if I go home a little early?" she asked. "I need to pick up Laurie at her Brownie meeting. Mother has Jacob, but I didn't want to ask her to get him out in the car just to drive over to get Laurie at the church when it's right on my way."

Veda smiled at her. "You go on, Beth. I'll finish the schedule and post it on the bulletin board and then close up."

Beth glanced over at the Christmas tree in the corner, its lights twinkling and blinking. "We did a real pretty job decorating that cedar tree you brought in from the O'Neill Farm. But it seems like every day we need to put more ornaments on it, since everyone keeps buying the ornaments off the tree instead of looking for duplicates in the baskets underneath."

"I know." Veda could see several bare spots on the limbs now. "I'll add a few ornaments to the tree before I go home, too.

Beth leaned on the counter. "Plans are coming along really well for the special Christmas Eve service at the church. I'm glad you're going to be here for that this year."

The O'Neills had always gone to the Creekside Independent Presbyterian Church in Townsend, their family being one of the original church founders. Veda had started going with Sutton since coming back, because at the O'Neills, if it was Sunday, you always went to church and that was that.

Beth started pulling on her coat to head outdoors. "You know, Reverend Westbrooke wanted me to ask you if you'd consider reading one of Rita Jean's stories in her memory at the service. She told a story on Christmas Eve every year. This will be the first year since she died. . . ." Her voice drifted off.

"It's a nice idea, but I'm not a storyteller like Rita Jean," Veda said.

"But you've heard all the stories since you were only a girl — many of them over and over again. You said once you practically had them memorized." Beth smiled. "Surely you could tell or read one of her stories for the service. It would be a nice tribute. Reverend Westbrooke already talked to Sutton about it. I know he'd like it if you'd fill in for Rita Jean this year." She paused. "It's tradition, Veda. It won't be the same

Christmas Eve service without one of Rita Jean's stories."

A group of tourists coming in the shop saved Veda from more argument and, noting the time slipping away, Beth waved and headed out the door.

Veda greeted the new customers and let her eyes follow them around the shop. They oohed and aahed, especially over all the Christmas decorations, and Veda felt pleased to watch them stopping to notice all the holiday crafts and decor she and the volunteers had worked so hard to arrange.

The Townsend Crafts Co-op made its home in a red-roofed log cabin on the highway. A shady porch and rockers greeted visitors in the front, with Christmas lights twinkling among cedar greenery on the porch railings. On the door hung a large wreath decorated with pinecones, chestnut balls, berries, and a big red bow. Veda and the staff had created similar wreaths for sale in the store and all the crafters had made Christmas gift items to sell during the holiday season. On the rustic shelves around the store were handmade Christmas socks, bowls and baskets of handmade tree ornaments, spicy bags of holiday potpourri, pumpkin- and evergreen-scented candles, and handmade nativity scenes. The rest of the store held the usual array of crafts on consignment — quilts by Estelle Ogle, wooden canes and hand-carved birdhouses from Emmett Springer, Arthur Chance's old-time brooms and baskets, Carol Ann Poston's colorful ceramics, Farley Wheaton's tinkling wind chimes and whimsical garden stakes, and the Seagrens' rich glazed pottery. There were other crafts, of course, but Veda knew these the best because they'd been fashioned by her store volunteers.

A small girl came in and began to wander around after Veda checked out the visitors at the register.

"My dad's next door," she explained, pointing toward Reese's law office, as if in answer to a question Veda hadn't asked. The child moved to the display rack of candles and began to pick them up, unscrewing each jar to sniff.

"Ummm," she said after a minute. "This is my favorite."

Veda walked closer to her. "What flavor is it?"

"Christmas cookies!" She grinned. "I love Christmas cookies."

"Me, too."

The girl studied her. "I know who you are," she said. "You're Veda, Rita Jean's niece. She used to talk about you all the time."

Veda lifted an eyebrow. "Well, I don't think I know you yet."

She shrugged. "Oh, I'm Pamela Renee McNally. My daddy is Reese McNally and that's his office next door. My granddaddy is Harold McNally and he works across the street at his Texaco. We live on the McNally Farm, up Chestnut Springs Road, the next road right beside Daddy's office." She studied Veda again. "You should know that. You played there when you were little because you and my daddy were friends."

Veda realized, looking at Pamela, that she should have guessed this was Reese's child — same dark brown, wavy hair and chocolate brown eyes, her face much like old pictures of Reese's mother.

"You don't look like Dee Dee," Veda said without thinking.

"Good." Pamela made a face. "Because I don't like her, and no one around here has anything good to say about her either."

"I'm sure she has her good traits." Veda made an effort to be polite.

Pamela looked at Veda pointedly. "I don't know why you'd say that. You didn't like her. I know you used to fight her. My granddaddy told me. I also heard she stole my daddy away from you when you were sweet-hearts."

"You hear a lot of things around here. It's a small town." She picked up a candle to sniff the crisp evergreen fragrance. "But your daddy and I broke up before he started dating your mother."

"Maybe." She wandered across the store. "You don't have your tree up yet at your house," she said, changing the subject and walking over to the decorated cedar in the store. "Why not?"

"I haven't been here long. I guess I haven't had time." Veda realized she hadn't even thought about the fact that a tree hadn't been put up at the farm.

"Rita Jean always put the tree in the front window where you could see the lights from the road. She always made her own wreath, too, like yours on the big door." She gestured toward the front of the store. "And she always made Christmas cookies. I helped her. Sutton liked them. He'll be sad if you don't put up a tree and make cookies."

A niggle of guilt pulled at Veda's conscience for not picking up Rita Jean's role of making Christmas at the house. "Maybe I'll do that tomorrow. I don't have to work then."

Wide eyes turned to hers. "Can I come help? I don't have school then. Rita Jean always let me help ice the sugar cookies and shake sprinkles on them, and she let me put the cinnamon dots on the gingerbread men."

Before Veda could answer, the door opened to let Reese in.

Veda felt a catch in her stomach at the sight of him. He didn't have movie-star looks, but he was tall and nice-looking in his own way, dark-haired, olive-complected, with warm brown eyes behind his glasses, and a lock of hair that never stayed in place because of a cowlick. He'd always been a smart, serious, geeky kid, but he could be fun, too, with a quirky sense of humor and an impulsiveness that could surprise you. When he smiled, like he did now, it lit up his whole face and always softened a spot in Veda's heart.

"Pamela, we need to go home," he said. "And Veda needs to close the store."

"Veda is letting me come up to Rita Jean's to help her decorate her tree tomorrow and make Christmas cookies," she announced. "She hasn't even put her tree up yet or made her cookies, and you know I always helped Rita Jean. It wouldn't be fun for Veda to have to do it all by herself now, with Rita

Jean gone. It would be sad. And you know Sutton won't help. It's his tree time and he has to open the Christmas tree store all day on Saturday for people to buy his trees."

Reese sent Veda a questioning look.

"We were talking about decorating the tree and making cookies tomorrow," Veda said, not sure what else she wanted to reveal.

His eyes followed Pamela as she crossed the room to pick up one of the rag dolls Beth Robbins had made. "You may not know it, but Pamela spent a lot of time with Rita Jean. Your aunt took care of Pamela a lot for me." He ran a hand through his hair, looking for words. "At our place it's just Dad and me, so Pamela loved being with Rita Jean. It gave her a woman to spend time with, and it's only a short way between the properties on the path through the fields between our house and yours."

"I know." Veda could remember she and Reese practically wearing down that old path running back and forth between each other's houses growing up. Halfway between the properties, they'd even carved their initials in the trunk of an old oak tree by the property fence.

Reese pulled at his ear in the distracted way that always meant he was thinking. "If you don't mind Pamela coming, it would mean a lot to her, Veda. Dad and I are not very good at cookie making and girl talk. Pamela has really missed Rita Jean." He lowered his voice. "We've had some pretty bad crying times since her death."

Veda's eyes drifted to the child, remembering her own loneliness at having a mother who had no time for her, and little interest in her either. She remembered, too, how Rita Jean had filled that void for her, made her feel loved, important, and valued for who she was.

"I miss Rita Jean, too." She let her eyes meet Reese's. "Bring Pamela over in the morning, after I've had a chance to eat breakfast with Sutton and drag the decorations down from the attic. I'll pick up some cookie-making supplies on my way home."

Veda watched him study her face, trying to see into her thoughts like he'd always done. He nodded at last. "How about if I bring lunch after your morning of cookie making with Pamela, sample what you girls create, and then help decorate the tree? It's always good to have a guy to string the lights. Sutton might be too busy to do it."

Veda dropped her eyes from his, considering the offer. She busied herself straightening the candles on the display rack while she did. She'd carefully avoided Reese these last weeks, dodging him whenever possible. But with Pamela with them, it should be all right.

"I guess that would be okay," she said at last.

He started to reach a hand toward her but then pulled it back. "Thank you," he said. "We'll see you tomorrow. I'm sure this is all Pamela will talk about tonight." He glanced over at the child, noticing her still playing with the handmade doll.

Reese leaned toward Veda. "Put that doll back for me after we leave," he whispered. "She seems to like it, and I could use a few more Christmas presents to wrap up."

Veda smiled. "It's a nice one. Beth made it. There are clothes to go with it, too. Want me to pick out a few outfits to box up with it?"

"Yeah." He sent her one of those smiles again that always tugged at her heart. "She'd like that. Especially if Beth made them. She and Beth's daughter Laurie are best friends, getting into that spend-the-night stuff, giggling and talking on the phone now."

"I did that some with Beth, too. I remember." She laughed.

Pamela bounced back their way, her eyes bright. "What time should I come to your house tomorrow, Veda?"

"Your daddy and I decided about ten would be good."

"I'll be *really* nice and polite." She turned to her father. "You don't have to give me the talk."

He pushed her toward the door, grinning. "I probably will give you the talk anyway, you minx. Come on, let's go. Dad will be wanting us home for supper."

They headed outdoors, and Veda followed to lock the front door behind them and hang the CLOSED sign in the window. Returning to the counter, she finalized the work schedule, tacked it on the bulletin board, hung a few more ornaments on the Christmas tree, and then started counting out the register.

Before going back to get her coat, she picked up the doll Pamela had taken such a fancy to. Brown-eyed with brunette hair, it resembled Pamela. The child looked nothing like her mother. Veda could still see Dee Dee in her mind, blond, pretty, shapely — always one of the prettiest girls in school, like her own mother had been, a queen bee with a court of dedicated followers. Spoiled, too, and used to getting her way in everything — and to getting everything she wanted. But Dee Dee wasn't kind, and she

505

enjoyed teasing and hurting others.

Aunt Rita Jean had said, "Don't worry over that girl and what she thinks. She's the type who would pull the wings off a butterfly with no regret if it brought her special attention."

Still, it had been hard to ignore Dee Dee Palmer. She'd made life hard for Veda from the first day they met at school. Probably because Veda wouldn't bend to her, wouldn't kowtow to her. Dee Dee had made Veda pay for that for years. Especially after Veda fought her on the playground and bloodied her nose because she teased and taunted Reese. That day had bonded Veda and Reese, and put them both permanently on Dee Dee's hit list. That is, until senior year, when Dee Dee started flirting with Reese and showing him decided attention.

Veda had stopped Dee Dee on the school stairwell one day, blocking her path. "Why are you flirting with Reese McNally? You've never liked him or me. What kind of game are you playing? If you're trying to set Reese up for one of your little schemes, you'd better stop it right now. I'm on to you."

Dee Dee had tossed her head. "I simply figured out that Reese McNally is about the *only* boy in our class who's going somewhere after we graduate. He's going to law school. Lawyers make good money. I like money and I want to get out of this hick mountain town. I'm interested in *anybody* who might help me accomplish that — even Reese McNally."

She'd trilled a laugh. "I know Reese *thinks* he likes you, but do you really believe he'll pick you over me after he gives it a little thought? Look in the mirror, Veda Trent. You didn't get your mother's looks, and you got your father's red hair and weird ways. Everyone always called him odd — like they call you odd." She'd looked Veda up and down. "What's so special about you? Think about it. Are you a cheerleader? Did you win any senior awards? How many people stood in line to get you to write in their yearbook?"

Dee Dee had given Veda a nasty smile. "Reese has been shaping up the last year or two, getting better-looking, pitching for the baseball team. He even got a letter jacket and got admitted to the honor society. I hear he might be valedictorian. And what have you been doing? Nothing. Just playing around on that tree farm, working part-time in your aunt's little Co-op. Still a loser. You certainly didn't take after your parents, did you? Your mother was a famous model and your daddy is still a well-known photographer. Travels everywhere, I hear. What are your plans after graduation? Simply going to hang around poky little Townsend and keep living off your aunt and uncle?"

Looking back, Veda knew Dee Dee had hit all her tender spots that day. She hadn't made any special plans for after high school, and she already knew Reese seemed more focused and confident than she, more sure of who he was and where he was going. Although Veda knew Reese disliked Dee Dee and laughed at her efforts to attract him, Dee Dee had seeded doubts in Veda's heart about their relationship, along with hurt. She'd stirred a restless discontent in Veda, too, a yearning to find who she was in her own right, a need to prove herself, get out on her own and be someone special.

Veda hugged the rag doll to herself. "Dee Dee was right, you know. She did get Reese in the end — exactly like she said she would."

Sighing, Veda picked out some outfits for the doll and found a box to put the doll and clothes in. She tucked the box on a shelf in the back storage room before cutting the lights and gathering up her coat and hat to head outdoors.

She checked her watch. Still plenty of time to run to the market and pick up the groceries to make cookies. Sutton didn't close the tree shop until late on Friday nights, now that the holiday season had settled in. He'd told her earlier that morning that he'd be home late, and for her to make dinner for herself and not wait for him. Perhaps she'd pick up something at the store for dinner while she was there, and maybe get a movie from the Redbox.

She'd also start looking for jobs on the Internet. Staying here only seemed to bring back painful memories every time she turned around. With regret, Veda wished she'd found some excuse not to entertain Reese's daughter — or Reese — the next day.

CHAPTER 4

On Saturday at around noon, Reese let himself in the front door of the O'Neill farmhouse to the sounds of girlish laughter coming from the kitchen and the scents of sweet, holiday sugar cookies and spicy gingerbread drifting on the air. He stopped to drop two extra boxes of multicolored chaser lights beside the freshly cut cedar tree in the front window of the living room and then headed for the kitchen.

"Daddy!" Pamela held up a gingerbread man she'd just finished decorating. "Look what I made!"

"Very distinguished." He walked over to examine the gingerbread man with its green icing bow tie, white outlining, happy smile and eyes, and red cinnamon dots for shirt buttons.

"I've named him Mr. Ginger." Pamela studied him with childish satisfaction. Over her jeans and T-shirt, she wore an apron heavily spattered with cookie dough, candy sprinkles, and flour. Veda looked equally festive in a bib apron dusted with more cookie bakings, her red hair pulled up in a ponytail in back and her eyes twinkling like the lights on a Christmas tree. Reese's heart jolted. Ever since he'd been a scrawny kid, Veda had made his heart pump.

"As you can see, we've been having a good time." Veda gestured around at the plates and cookie sheets full of lavishly iced sugar cookies and honey-brown gingerbread girls and boys.

Reese let his eyes wander over the familiar cookie shapes of trees, stars, ornaments, Santas, snowmen, and reindeer, all painted with multicolored sugar icing and embellished with sprinkles, cinnamon dots, silver balls, and creative outlining. "You girls really did some beautiful work here."

Pamela beamed. "I helped Veda cut out the cookie shapes and got to put on the sprinkles, dots, and balls after she squirted around the outlining." She frowned. "I tried to do that part, too, but I kept messing up. It's like squiggling out skinny toothpaste, and you need to be real careful."

"Outlining is hard." Reese laughed at her description. "But you've made wonderful cookies."

He reached over to wipe a dollop of icing off Veda's cheek and felt the old connection kick in at the touch. He watched her pull away with a frown, turning to dump some dishes in the sink.

"What did you bring for lunch?" she asked, avoiding his eyes.

"By request from Pamela this morning, I picked up cheeseburgers and fries from The Last Deli."

"And big dill pickles?" Pamela chimed in.

"And big dill pickles right out of Mary's mason jar on the counter." Reese dropped his take-out bags on a cleared spot on the table.

"Move some of those cookie plates over to the sideboard and to the kitchen counter," Veda directed. "I'll set out silver and get the plates down. I see you brought drinks."

They chitchatted over lunch, Pamela dominating the conversational topics with talk of cookie making, Christmas gifts, and the ongoing holiday activities at school and in the community.

"I'm going to be an angel in the Christmas Eve nativity pageant at church," she told them. "So is Laurie, and Mrs. Beth is making our costumes. We get wings and everything."

"That's nice of Beth." Veda dipped a French fry in a dollop of ketchup.

"Beth said you were going to tell one of Rita Jean's stories since she can't do it anymore." Finishing her lunch, Pamela got up to pick out a decorated reindeer cookie for dessert, nibbling off the head first with a grin.

Reese raised an eyebrow at Veda. "I didn't know you were planning to do that."

Veda crossed her arms with annoyance. "I'm not. I'm not a storyteller like Rita Jean."

Pamela wrinkled her nose. "Anybody can tell stories if they want to, and you've heard all Rita Jean's stories and even have her old storytelling clothes. Sutton said you could do it."

Veda gave a disgusted snort. "There's an art and a gift to good storytelling."

Pamela considered that. "Rita Jean told me you needed to listen to the wind sing and then the right story to tell, and the way to tell it would come to you."

"That's what I mean." Veda got up to begin cleaning off the table. "Aunt Rita Jean had a gift for storytelling. I don't have that."

"Are you sure?" Pamela asked with child-like innocence. "Maybe you're not listening hard enough."

"Yeah, maybe you're not." Reese grinned. "You are a first daughter, after all."

"Those old legends are fanciful and not always true." Veda sent him a warning glance.

"Well, I think you should tell a story at the service to be nice," Pamela said. "Everyone wants you to because you're Rita Jean's niece. It's like a tribune."

Reese laughed. "I think you mean *tribute,* an act to show gratitude and respect."

Pamela smiled. "Yeah — a tribute for Rita Jean."

Seeing Veda still scowling, Reese remembered how she'd always felt alternately fascinated and disdainful of Rita Jean's Indian legends and beliefs, ridiculing the concept that she might carry some special gift through her Indian bloodlines. "Veda, I think you could manage a short story for Rita Jean's memory. It doesn't mean people expect you to become a mountain story-teller. They just want you to do this in remembrance of your aunt this first Christmas without her."

"I'll think about it," she said. "And you'd better get in there and get those lights on the tree. I want that tree fully decorated before Sutton comes home tonight."

The afternoon drifted along, bittersweet.

They decorated the tree with all the old handmade ornaments and collector Christmas balls used on the O'Neill trees for as many years as Reese could remember. He felt swamped with memories the whole afternoon, of making up stories about the tree ornaments with Veda, writing out lists for Santa, sitting and poring over the Sears toy catalog that came in the mail, and making surprise gifts for their family to wrap and put under the tree. On the mantel in the parlor, he could see a photo of the two of them sitting on the fence rail by the barn at only ten, both in jeans and straw hats, laughing and happy. When had things gone wrong between them? Had it started with Dee Dee or before?

By the time they completed the tree, Pamela was wearing thin after a long day of excitement. Reese helped her pack up half the decorated cookies into empty tins and took her home. He felt sure Veda was ready for a rest, too. An eight-year-old could stretch your nerves, even when you lived with her every day.

Shortly after dinner, Reese realized with annoyance that he'd left his cell phone at the O'Neills'. Pamela and his dad sat piled up on the couch watching TV, so he leaned into the den to let them know he was running over to the O'Neills' to pick up his cell. Dusk hadn't fallen yet, and the air felt crisp and clear with a full moon beginning in the sky, so Reese decided to walk over. He threw on his coat and a scarf at the back door and headed across the familiar path behind the McNally Farm. It wound through the fields, over the fence by the old oak, and along a wooded pathway lined with cedar trees and now-bare hardwoods to the side yard of the O'Neills' place.

Sutton let him in the front door, pointing with pleasure to the decorated tree lighting up the front window. On a tray by the couch lay a pile of cookies, which Sutton had been nibbling on while reading the newspaper.

"Where's Veda?" Reese asked.

Sutton walked two fingers across his open hand in answer and took out his notepad. *She went walking,* he wrote. *Seemed to be feeling moody.*

"Where'd she go?"

Probably to the rock, he scribbled, making a sign for the cemetery in further explanation. *Losing Rita Jean and the store has been hard for her.* He paused and added, *She's looking for herself, I think.*

"Well, tell her I dropped by to get my phone," he said.

Sutton walked him to the door and then

gestured toward the hill behind the house. He made a climbing sign with his fingers, raising his eyebrows at Reese in a question.

"Maybe I will," he said, starting down the porch steps. "But she might not be glad to see me."

After Sutton closed the door, Reese, following his suggestion, walked around to the back of the house, followed the dirt road by the barn, and then began to make his way up a well-worn path to the O'Neill family cemetery on the top of the ridge.

A short time later, he moved out of the woods into the cemetery clearing. He walked through the family plot of old grave sites, past the ruins of a rock chimney and a settler's cabin, and then uphill on a winding path to the top of the ridge. Veda sat on a huge, flat limestone rock, looking out at the darkening sky and the view across the overlapping mountain ranges. It had always been her favorite place to come to think.

She turned, hearing his footfall. "What are you doing here?"

"Nice night to be out. Clear, not too cold, with a full moon. Thought I'd take a walk."

"Did you get your phone?" she asked, not easily fooled.

"Yep." He edged out on the rock to sit

down beside her, draping his feet over the edge.

"Sutton told you I'd be here, didn't he?"

"He mentioned you might have walked up here."

She sighed. "He's always read me too easily."

Reese waited, looking out over the mountains, feeling the peace of the place and the quiet of the natural scene steal into his senses. Far in the distance, he could see some of the lights of the town beginning to wink on in the valley. It seemed like only yesterday that he and Veda had sat here as kids, each quiet, dreaming their own private dreams.

"What happened to us?" he asked at last.

"You married Dee Dee Palmer." She glared at him.

"Why do you think I did that?" he asked.

She snorted. "I have no idea."

"My first date with Dee Dee was for the prom — just to spite you — after we fought and you told me you wouldn't go with me, like we planned. I was angry, Veda. You were going with someone else; I didn't want to sit home alone. Dee Dee invited me to go after she and Josh Wheeley broke up, and I said yes."

"So? That doesn't explain why you married her." She pulled her knees up to wrap her arms around them.

Reese waited, needing to know her thoughts.

A small silence fell before she spoke again. "I still remember the night Aunt Rita Jean called and told me you'd gotten married. I was staying with Daddy that summer after senior year, trying to figure out what I wanted to do after high school, where I wanted to go to college, what I wanted to study. I'd pretty much decided to come back to Townsend, go to Maryville College nearby, where I'd already registered, study business so I could learn how to open my own store someday. I liked working at the Co-op and thought I might like to own a little store of my own one day. The one nice thing Daddy did for me was say he'd pay for me to go to college."

She paused and sighed. "I knew we'd been angry at each other, but I thought we could probably work it out after I got back. Then Rita Jean called. She said she didn't want me to learn about you getting married from someone else, or to come back to Townsend not knowing." Veda turned anguished eyes to Reese. "I cried all night afterward."

He crossed his arms, dropping his eyes from hers. "Didn't you figure it out, Veda? I heard Pamela telling you her birthday today — February twenty-first. She's eight years old. I got married in early August. Think about it, Veda, and do the math."

Reese could almost hear her mind ticking. "August to February is only six months."

"So it is."

A little silence ensued. "Oh my gosh. She did exactly what she said she would."

"*Who* did what she said?" He tried to follow her words.

"Dee Dee." Veda turned wide, shocked eyes toward him. "She bragged to me at school that she was taking you to the prom. I said, 'It's only one date, Dee Dee,' but she laughed and said 'One date is all I need, Veda Trent. I told you I'd get Reese if I wanted him, and there are all kinds of ways to ensure you get exactly what you want with a nice guy like Reese.' "

Reese felt stunned at her words but then shook his head. "Well, Dee Dee was accurate about that, I guess."

Veda punched him. "Nobody forced you to sleep with her, Reese McNally."

"I was a geeky kid, Veda. You know that. Didn't drink, didn't run around. An all-around nice guy who didn't know much about what alcohol does to morals and inhibitions." He kicked a rock over the edge of the ridge. "I don't even remember that night. Isn't that pitiful?"

She rolled her eyes but waited for him to finish.

"I married Dee Dee because it was the right thing to do. I changed my dormitory arrangements from living with Lewis Connor in the guys' dorm to living with my new wife in married student housing. Dee Dee took a few classes that fall, and we managed all right for a time, discovering college life for the first time together, but then her pregnancy kicked in, the baby came, and she grew unhappy. She said she wasn't having any fun anymore."

"Did she cheat on you?" Veda asked.

"Yeah, until it became a joke and everybody felt sorry for me."

"But you stayed with her and kept trying for Pamela," Veda put in, knowing Reese well enough to realize that's what he'd do.

"She became the old Dee Dee we knew pretty quickly, taunting and ridiculing, making me feel like nothing. You know how she was."

"Yes," she said quietly.

"One day I came back to the apartment to find her packing her bags. She'd met someone at one of the bars she frequented in the evenings, while I studied at the apartment and watched Pamela." He picked up a stick to turn it in his hands. "She said she was tired of being married to me and was leaving with some man she met to go out West to Las Vegas. 'That's a happening place,' she told me."

He snapped the stick in two, remembering. " 'What about Pamela?' I asked her. 'You can have her,' she said and shrugged, like she was simply giving me an old dress she no longer wanted."

Veda slipped a hand into his. "I'm sorry, Reese."

"Yeah." He pulled his hand away, embarrassed.

"So you got full custody."

"No legal challenge to that," he replied, knowing his voice sounded sarcastic.

"Why didn't you tell me?"

He turned his eyes to hers. "You never asked, Veda, just went off to school and on with your own life somewhere else. And what point would there have been?" Reese threw the stick over the mountainside.

Veda hesitated before she spoke again. "Dee Dee always told me if you ever thought about it much, you'd pick her over me — that I wasn't as pretty as her or as popular, that you were already more focused and growing away from me."

He turned to her in shock. "And you believed that crap?"

"She had a way," Veda said in reply, looking off into the distance over the ridge.

"Yeah, she did," he admitted. "She made our young lives a misery and then found a way to ruin my adult life as an extra perk." He could hear the bitterness in his own voice.

They sat quietly for a time. A hoot owl's sound echoed nearby, and the smell of cedars drifted to them on the winter breeze from the forest nearby.

"You did get Pamela from it all," she said at last, turning to look at him. "She's wonderful, nothing like Dee Dee, Reese."

"Thank God," he replied. "Dad says she's all McNally through and through."

Her eyes slid away from his. "I never came back because I couldn't stand to see you and Dee Dee and your child as a family. I felt awful when Rita Jean died this year, knowing how often I'd stayed away. Knowing I wouldn't ever have time with her again."

"Did you visit her grave tonight?"

"Yeah." Her voice grew soft. "I told her all the things I'd done today to try to take her place and told her I'd even tell a Christmas story in her memory at the church, like everyone wants me to."

"Have you ever tried storytelling?"

"No, not ever. It was Rita Jean's gift. Rita Jean's legacy. Never mine."

"You've never heard the wind sing?" He teased her a little with the words, glad to move the focus off himself.

"No. I got Rita Jean's practical side, but not her fanciful one."

"You'll do fine with whatever you do."

She got to her feet. "I'd better start back. It's getting dark and Sutton will worry."

Reese pulled himself up.

Veda bit her lip, obviously considering whether to tell him something else that was on her mind. "Pamela said her mother told her she wasn't pretty when she visited her the last time."

Reese sucked in a breath. "Dang woman."

Veda giggled. "Pamela also said she kicked her for it, and told her it was mean. She must have inherited some of her mother's gumption to do that."

"Ouch." Reese hunched his shoulders.

Veda smiled a Cheshire cat grin. "Pamela said she didn't get in trouble with her grandfather when she told him about it. He said it was exactly the sort of thing Veda Trent would have done."

Reese laughed at that and then let his eyes

lock onto Veda's. "God, I've missed you so much, Veda." And before he could think, he pulled her into his arms and pressed his mouth to hers, trying to draw out all the sweetness he remembered from their early years together.

Veda stiffened at first, tried to pull away, then yielded, wrapping her arms around his neck and opening her mouth to his. It was heaven, and Reese took full advantage of the moment, letting his hands rove under her wool jacket and over her body, the memories of shared times rolling back through his mind and emotions.

"Quit that." She swatted at his hands as they tried to slide under her shirt. "I haven't been married like you, remember? You know things I don't know yet."

He checked himself, happy with her words. "Are we okay, Veda?" he asked.

She met his eyes with an honest gaze. "We're better, Reese. But we're both different now. And we can't go back."

"But we can go forward," he suggested.

"Yes, but I'm still not sure yet if that *forward* for me is meant to be here or somewhere else, Reese. So don't read too much into this moment." She stepped away, straightening her jacket and wrapping her wool scarf around her neck.

Then she started back down the path. "I'm taking one day at a time, Reese. I've made mistakes, too, and I want to be sure about the next step and direction for my life. I still don't know if Townsend is the place for me. In some ways, I've never belonged here, like everyone else. It's always seemed like I was just passing through."

Chapter 5

Veda settled back into life in Townsend over the next week. She and Sutton seemed to fall into an easy routine of sharing the cooking and cleaning at the farmhouse. Occasionally, Veda helped out at the Christmas Tree Store, although Sutton and Walker or Bovee usually handled the hours that the small store was open. With December here, Sutton opened the store all day Friday, Saturday, and Sunday, and took trees to the vendors he sold to annually the other days of the week.

At breakfast, Sutton reminded Veda that they were expected for Christmas brunch with the McNallys. It had been a tradition for years for the two families to get together Christmas morning at one farm or the other.

Sutton pulled out his notepad. *Can you buy some gifts for us to take?* he wrote. *I'm not very good at gift buying.*

Veda nodded, not excited at the prospect

of an intimate family day with the McNallys but not wanting to let Sutton know how she felt and spoil his pleasure. He signed a few ideas of what she might consider looking for in gifts. *We'll need to take food, too,* he scribbled. *But we can decide about that closer to the time.*

Realizing she had the day free, Veda decided to head over to Maryville to the mall to look for gifts. She'd stop in Townsend for others on her way back.

Later that afternoon, as she drove back down Highway 321 into Townsend, she made a stop at the Apple Valley Country Store for a cute stuffed animal for Pamela, and then at the woodcraft store to look for a carved bird for Reese. He'd collected them ever since he was a kid and had also tried whittling a few of his own. Veda grinned, remembering some of the comical results.

Noticing the MIMOSA INN sign as she drove down the highway, Veda decided to stop in and thank Grace Teague for hosting the Co-op party at the bed-and-breakfast. Jack Teague sat on the Co-op board, of course, but it was still a generous gesture. She turned into the long drive and parked.

Grace answered the door herself.

"I'm Veda Trent," Veda introduced herself,

putting out a hand. "I wanted to stop by to thank you for hosting the Co-op party. It's really nice of you to do that. I know this must be a busy season for you."

"It's a joy to do it. Jack and I are so proud to be a part of the Co-op in even a small way." She held open the door. "Come in. I have hot spice tea back in the kitchen and some pumpkin bread."

"I'd love some." Veda smiled and followed the gracious blond woman toward the kitchen. She wore tailored slacks and a pullover sweater of teal blue to match — still a beautiful woman at midlife, and beautifully put together. Yet even with her beauty, Veda sensed a kindness about her, too. Veda had learned with her mother and with Dee Dee Palmer that beauty and kindness didn't always go hand in hand.

The Mimosa Inn, a charming Victorian bed-and-breakfast, sat on a lush green lot along the banks of the Little River in Townsend, next door to the church Veda attended, and down the River Road from the gleaming black shay engine beside the Little River Railroad and Lumber Company Museum, the rustic Heartland Wedding Chapel, and Miss Lily's Cafe.

Veda's eyes wandered around as she walked back toward the kitchen. "You've done a beautiful job fixing up Carl and Mavis Oakley's old inn."

Christmas decorations nestled in nearly every corner: garlands looped up the stairwell and lavishly decorated trees graced several of the downstairs rooms. Veda spotted a ceramic nativity scene on a sideboard, arrangements of holiday candles and fresh greenery on the dining room tables, and a collection of Christmas nutcrackers marching across a fireplace mantel. "Your Christmas decorations are wonderful, too."

"Thank you." Grace smiled, gesturing to a chair at the kitchen table. "It was fun decorating for the holidays, and the girls enjoyed helping."

Veda remembered then that Jack had two daughters by a previous marriage. She searched her memory for the girls' names. "I'm trying to remember their names," she admitted at last.

"Meredith and Morgan." Grace set two mugs of steaming, fragrant spiced tea on the table and then brought over a loaf of pumpkin bread from the counter before sitting down herself.

Veda put her hands around a warm mug. "The girls were only toddlers the last time I saw them, about eight years ago. It wasn't easy for Jack, raising them by himself."

"No." She cut a slice of pumpkin bread and passed it to Veda. "And I think the experience of being left with children to raise is one of the ties that bonded Jack and Reese McNally. He has the law office next to the Co-op. I think Jack mentioned your families are close."

Veda laughed. "In a small town like this, I'm sure you've heard more than that, Mrs. Teague."

"Please call me Grace. And, yes, I've heard that you and Reese were once a couple. I'm sure you also know Jack once had quite a reputation as a ladies' man around here."

Veda dropped her eyes.

Grace's lips twitched. "The nice thing about life is that it is full of surprises, and people change. I've enjoyed learning that. And I've come to terms with the fact that you can hardly sneeze in this small town without someone saying 'bless you' right afterward. There are few secrets here."

Veda took a bite of the pumpkin bread. "Ummm, this is great! It makes me think of my aunt Rita Jean's sweet breads. She made the best pumpkin and banana breads for the holidays."

"I'm glad I moved to Townsend in time to meet your aunt, and to hear her tell several of her wonderful stories." She sipped her tea. "It's nice that you're willing to share one of those at the church service."

Veda looked up. "I'd forgotten we go to the same church. I've only been back for a few weeks and have only attended two of the services with Sutton. It's a busy time with the trees."

"Yes, I'm sure it is, and it's dreadful that thieves have been stealing Sutton's Christmas trees." She pursed her lips. "There's something especially dreadful about learning someone would steal Christmas trees, isn't there?"

"Yes, there is, and it makes me really mad just to think about it."

"Have you finished your shopping?" Grace asked, changing the subject.

"I drove to Maryville and hit the mall today while I had the day off. I think I've finished the short list I have to cover." She caught Grace's eye then. "Is there anything I can buy for the Co-op party, or anything at all I can do to help with it?"

Grace waved a hand. "Nothing. I have more help than I need already, and all of us are just so grateful you were willing to come to manage the Co-op, if only through the winter, while we put out feelers for another manager."

Curious, Veda asked, "What made you decide to move to Townsend and buy the Mimosa Inn? Sutton said you come from a big city and have family there."

She laughed. "I wasn't escaping, simply looking for a way to be useful after being widowed for several years. I'd always loved bed-and-breakfasts and found myself attracted to this one." She paused, a small smile touching her lips. "It's a long story, how I came to discover the inn and decided to stay. Perhaps I'll tell it to you one day, but right now I think I see the girls coming back with the dogs. They've had them out for a walk."

The kitchen door opened to let in a sweep of cold air, along with two young girls and two small corgi dogs.

"Oh, they look like my Lucy." Veda crouched down to let the dogs sniff her hand. "I have a corgi, too."

"Remember your manners, Sadie and Dooley." Grace spoke to the dogs in a warm, firm voice.

Both dogs sat and extended a paw to Veda.

"They want you to shake hands," explained one of the twins, shrugging off her jacket and tossing it across a chair. The other girl removed her jacket and hat, too, revealing to Veda that the two were identical in looks — both about eleven or twelve and with the same brown hair and merry eyes.

Veda shook hands with the dogs, who then padded across the kitchen to find their food and water bowls.

"This is Veda Trent." Grace made the introductions. "And Veda, these are my daughters, Meredith and Morgan Teague."

Veda shook the girls' hands, feeling they were old enough for the formalities now. "I remember both of you only as babies in the church," she said. "I've been away from Townsend for eight years now."

"You're Rita Jean's niece who's come to run the Co-op," Morgan said, sliding into a kitchen chair. "It's a cute shop."

"Yum. Can I have some of this pumpkin loaf?" Meredith leaned over to sniff the fragrant bread still on the table.

"Me, too?" Morgan asked, taking another empty chair.

"Yes to both of you, and I'll pour you cups of spice tea, as well. It's really cold outside today."

Veda took that opportunity to stand. "I need to go on home, Grace. I have a carload of gifts to unload and supper to make for Sutton and myself."

Grace stood. "Let me walk you to the door."

They walked down the hallway together.

"I'm so glad you came by to meet me, and I look forward to seeing you again at the party this Friday evening." Grace reached into a holiday bowl by the door, snagged a candy cane, and tucked it into Veda's pocket. "Come back any time."

As Veda drove home, the scene of Grace and her daughters played through her mind. She'd seen so much love and warmth among them. Would it be that way with she and Pamela if Reese and she got together? Despite her desire to be strong and independent, Veda also yearned to be loved — to be part of a family where she belonged. Coming back to Townsend had dropped her into an uncomfortable dilemma, with a desire to stay and a desire to go. She felt really torn with the situation, and there were no clear answers. Reese wanted to go forward with their relationship, but could they? She was afraid there were too many painful memories of the past to move beyond.

CHAPTER 6

Reese, sitting at his desk in the law office, glanced at his calendar. Less than two weeks until Christmas. His eyes skimmed over the other events marked throughout the month. He looked at the calendar a lot these days, worrying that Veda might decide to move on in the New Year. He'd seen a printout of employment opportunities on her desk only this morning when he dropped by with some papers for her to sign.

"What's this?" he'd asked, picking it up.

She flushed. "A few job openings one of my friends, Stacy Parsons in St. Augustine, sent me. We were roommates in Ponce de Leon Hall at Flagler College." She pointed to a small photo on her desk of herself and a smiling, dark-headed girl with their arms linked. "She's my best friend there."

"And she misses you," he put in, dropping the printout back onto her desk.

"Yeah." She leaned back in her worn desk

chair in the upstairs Co-op office. "I was lucky that I met up with Stacy when I went to Flagler. She and I hit it off right from the start." She smiled. "Stacy is the assistant director of tourism in St. Augustine now, and helps plan programs, projects, events, tours, does marketing, and helps with the St. Augustine website. She's trying to find me a job so I'll come back."

"I see." He pointed to another photo of a cute, aqua-blue building with crisp white trim. "Is that your shop in St. Augustine?"

"That *was* my shop: Vintage Collectibles, right on Orange Street, a charming little avenue in the downtown historic district. St. Augustine is such a wonderful old city, Reese, with Spanish architecture everywhere, moss-draped oaks mixed with palm trees, colorful cottages, horse-drawn carriages trotting down the street, and a touch of sea breeze floating in on the air sometimes from the ocean nearby."

"You liked it there." He sat down in the chair beside her desk.

"I did." Her eyes wandered to the shop picture. "One of the few happy memories I have of spending time with my mother and father together was in St. Augustine. Mother went down there for a photo shoot and Daddy shot the pictures. They had separated by that time, but they still maintained an amicable relationship. We all stayed in a downtown bed-and-breakfast and enjoyed happy times together around the city and at the beach. A lot of the photos for the shoot were taken on the Flagler campus. It has incredible historic Spanish buildings, fountains, and gardens. The school stayed in my memory, so when I realized I couldn't come back to Townsend for college, it was one of the first places I thought of."

"You decided this after you heard I married Dee Dee, didn't you?"

She gave him an annoyed look. "I told you that before, Reese. Stop trying to make me feel guilty for not wanting to come back to a place where my boyfriend just married someone else." She flipped back her hair. "I only halfway belonged here anyway. I never felt I truly was part of this town, like everyone else."

"Why? You had family here, roots, people who loved you."

"I guess it looked that way, but I always seemed to be waiting for some sense of connection that never came."

"And you found that in St. Augustine?"

She shrugged. "Yes, sort of. I wasn't always living something down or living in someone else's shadow. I was simply Veda

Trent there — not Rita Jean's niece, Skyler Trent's daughter, or the odd girl who got dumped by her family and never really fit in. I got a fresh start there."

"Do you want to go back?"

Veda blew out a long breath. "I wish I knew what I wanted, Reese. I seem to be waiting for something. I feel pending, like the legal term."

"Awaiting decision or settlement; awaiting conclusion."

"Yeah, pending." She shifted in her chair and then got up to walk across the office to look out the dormer window. "It's spitting snow," she said.

"Yeah." He waited for her to go on.

"You know, I've been reading Rita Jean's journals and old stories, trying to decide on a special one to read or tell at the Christmas Eve service." She picked up her thoughts again. "Rita Jean wrote out many of her favorite stories in her journals, and she wrote down thoughts her grandmother, Unole Watie O'Neill, shared."

"The Cherokee grandmother?"

"Yes." She watched the snowflakes falling outside. "In one story Unole told, she was trying to decide, as a young girl, whether to stay with her people or to marry my great-grandfather, Brannon O'Neill."

"I guess it was hard to think of leaving her people," he said. "Transportation was more limited, people less connected in the early 1900s, and I'm sure Unole knew she'd experience prejudice."

"She did." Veda came back over to sit down, leaning toward Reese. "Unole went to the Wise One in their village for help. The Wise One told her, 'The way will be shown to you and you will know. The wind will speak to you — and in the place where the wind speaks to you that is where you belong.' "

Reese knew enough from Veda's seriousness not to laugh. "Do you think maybe your way will be shown to you? Is that what you're waiting for?"

She made a face. "It's a silly thought, I guess."

"Perhaps your heart will tell you what to do, Veda."

"Hearts are unreliable." She slanted him a sharp glance.

Deciding not to answer, he glanced at his watch. "I have a client coming. I need to go." Reese stood. "I'll pick you up for the Co-op party this Friday night. It's dressy versus casual — suits for the men, holiday dresses for the women. Jack Teague said he and his wife have decorated the inn lavishly for the holidays and this event. Jack's on the Co-op board."

"I know. I went to meet Grace Teague at the inn earlier this week. Lovely woman." She grinned at him. "She has two corgis just like Lucy."

Reese turned to go, wishing he had the right words to say before he did.

And now he sat in his office, mulling over that earlier meeting with Veda, wishing he could convince her that his heart wasn't as unreliable as she thought. He wished he could erase the past years, start again.

Eleanor leaned into the office. "I'm back from lunch," she said. "You can run over to the Deli now and eat with Lewis Connor. I think you told me earlier you planned to have lunch with him today."

"I did." He looked up at his younger cousin, so much a McNally in looks, with her dark hair, brown eyes, tall build, and olive complexion. "Have you ever been in love, Eleanor?"

She smiled at him and leaned against the door frame. "At least ten times." She laughed. "Usually unrequited love."

"Do you think we McNallys are doomed to that, to unrequited love?"

"I hope not." She glanced out the window to where the snow had built to a light layer on the ground. "I want a home, family, someone to spend my life with. I hope to meet a guy who will love me, too." She straightened her glasses. "I'm not a beauty, but I'm hoping someone will see my good points someday, and love those things about me."

Reese felt surprised at her words. Awkward himself when younger, he hadn't realized his cousin felt somewhat uncomfortable in her own skin, too.

"He's out there, Eleanor, and you're more beautiful than you realize — outside as well as inside."

She blushed. "Thanks."

"How's school coming?" he asked, knowing Eleanor was still taking paralegal classes.

"Straight As." She grinned at him. "We McNallys are smart, if a little geeky."

Reese put his computer to sleep and handed Eleanor a stack of papers. "Here are the notes for the will that needs to be drawn up for Mr. and Mrs. Norton, who I met with earlier."

"I'll get to work on it while you're at lunch."

A swirl of December cold air hit Reese as soon as he stepped out the front door. The temperature was dropping. If it kept snowing, chances were good it would stick. The fields already showed about an inch of snow, and white had begun to decorate the roof-tops.

Cutting across the highway, he walked the short block to The Last Deli, which the Connor family had owned for as long as he could remember. Cecil and Mary Connor lived across the highway on a side road, and their son, Lewis, had been Reese's friend since childhood. Lewis, now married, worked in the Deli, helping his parents run the small restaurant, gift shop, and pick-up grocery store. He and his wife, Leanne, had built a newer home on the property near Lewis's parents' house.

Reese opened the door to the sound of Christmas music blasting out on the radio, and Mary in the kitchen, singing along to a favorite song. Lewis crossed the floor from the register to brush the snow off Reese's jacket and toss it on a peg by the door.

"Good timing. The place is quiet after the lunch rush, and with the snow, I doubt we'll have much traffic the rest of the day." He pulled out a ladder-back chair at a table by the window and sat down. A red-checked oilcloth covered the table, and the black-and-tan squares on the linoleum floor showed wet spots where snowy boots had recently tracked in and out.

"Dang, it's really coming down, ain't it?" Lewis looked out the plate-glass window. "Wish this had waited until Christmas. I'd like a white Christmas this year."

Reese settled into a chair across from Lewis, his eyes moving fondly over his friend's full-figured frame, his wiry reddish-brown hair, and the bit of chin beard he'd added to his appearance in the last year. He wore the white shirt, khaki pants, and Deli apron that marked the standard everyday uniform of the Connors.

"Mom's making us a couple of Reuben sandwiches with Swiss and adding home-made slaw and potato salad on the side. Sauerkraut on my Reuben, but none for you, since you don't like it." He leaned back in the old chair, glad to get off his feet for a while. "She's made pecan pie for dessert."

"Mary!" Reese called to her over the music. "If you weren't married, I'd marry you myself for your cooking."

She waved a hand at him in dismissal, obviously pleased.

"So, what's going on?" Reese asked his friend.

Lewis, always talkative, began to entertain Reese with customer stories, giving him a needed laugh. "Lordy day, people are funny." He grinned. "But I love working

544

with the public, don't you?"

Reese, remembering the odd little couple who'd come to his office earlier to draw up their will, agreed. Mrs. Norton had a quirky habit of repeating every single point her husband made — "Like Clyde said . . ." — and it had been hard to keep a straight face.

"You and Leanne going to the Co-op party at the Mimosa this Friday?" Reese asked, knowing that Lewis, as well as his mother, served on the Co-op's board.

"Shoot fire, the Connor women wouldn't miss it, Reese." He laughed. "Gives them a chance to get gussied up in fancy holiday dresses. I had to go get a new suit for the dang thing."

"Lewis picked up too much weight this year around his middle and couldn't button the old one," his mother announced, coming over with two loaded plates for their lunch.

Her eyes moved to Reese's. "You bringing Veda Trent to this shindig on Friday to meet all of us on the board and to get to know all the artisans she don't know already?"

He nodded.

"Well, that's good." Mary hesitated. "You think there's any chance you might get back with her?" She threw out the question in the candid way only she could get away with. "You know I'm right direct."

"Gosh, Maw, that's kind of personal and in your face, don't you think?" Lewis winced.

"Well, Reese knows I've watched him grow up since he was rat high, and I know well enough how he loved Veda Trent all his life before getting hooked up with that Palmer girl." She patted Reese on the shoulder. "I'd like to see the two of you get back together. So would your daddy. Might clear the way some for he and Martha Seymour."

Reese raised an eyebrow.

"Geeze, Maw." Lewis rolled his eyes.

"What about Martha Seymour?" Reese asked, remembering the personable blond widow who worked at the Heritage Center. He knew his dad had taken her to a few events, and gone out to dinner with her a few times.

"They're gettin' right sweet on each other." She smiled and pushed a strand of short reddish hair off her face. "I watch things like that with people comin' here all the time to eat. You see a lot, workin' in a restaurant, hear a lot of stuff, too, and mostly folks don't pay you no never mind while they're here."

Reese, surprised, considered Mary's

words. She did know his father well. "You think Dad's getting serious about Martha Seymour?"

"Would you mind if he did?" Mary asked, propping a hand on one hip. "He ain't dead yet, you know, just widowed all these years — first needin' to raise you and then helpin' with Pamela after all that happened."

"I'd never mind Dad finding his own happiness," Reese answered with honesty. "But he hasn't said anything to me about getting serious about anyone."

"Well, he wouldn't." Mary glanced out the window. "Looks like it's lettin' up. I'm glad. The town needs the Christmas business and traffic of the holidays. We don't need no big snow knocking out the tourist trade."

She turned and headed back to the kitchen. "Lewis, you come get them two pieces of pie I cut for you boys when you're ready for them. I'm going to sit down in the back for a bit and put up my feet while it's quiet in here."

"Listen, Reese." Lewis leaned forward. "Don't pay too much mind to Maw. You know how she is about speaking out."

Reese followed Mary Connor's back with his eyes. "She's probably right, you know. She doesn't miss much around here. I'll have to probe Dad a little to see if he's serious about Martha. It wouldn't bother me, Lewis. She's a good woman, from what I've seen — friendly, conscientious, well-thought of at the Heritage Center. I hear she gardens, has a lot of friends. I don't have anything against my dad seeing her. I even handled Martha's legal affairs a few years ago, when her husband died. He left her in good shape."

"Yeah, they retired down here from up north in Michigan somewhere and bought one of them big places in Kinzel Springs in that gated community. Posh place they bought; pretty gardens and grounds." Lewis scratched his head. "I took some catering over there for them before Mr. Seymour passed."

Reese finished off his sandwich.

"You know, I seen Veda Trent when she came over here to eat one day." Lewis pushed back his own plate. "She looked real pretty, still had that thick red hair hanging down her back. Seemed more confident and sophisticated somehow. More growed up."

He walked over to the counter and brought back the two pieces of pie Mary had cut and left plated there. "You think you and she might get back together?" he asked.

"I don't know." Reese pulled a piece of

pie toward himself and cut into it, not saying more.

Letting the subject go, Lewis asked, "Who do you think is sneaking up to the O'Neills' to steal off their trees? I hate that happening to Sutton. He works hard all year with the farm and he don't deserve someone coming in and pilfering his trees."

"It's a mystery. The sheriff can't discover who's done it." Reese walked over to the counter to pour himself a cup of coffee. "It's only happened a few times, but the thieves seem to know the farm well: where Sutton keeps the trees, when he's cut fresh ones, when he, Walker, or Bovee aren't on the place keeping watch."

"Well, I don't like the idea of folks sneaking around here breaking the law." Lewis scratched his head. "Makes me think of when that guy everyone called Crazy Man was stalking people, leaving notes and stuff. Glad he got caught."

Reese glanced at his watch. "I need to get back."

The door opened, letting in a group of people. "Yeah, and it looks like I need to get back into the kitchen."

They said their good-byes, and Reese walked back to the office. As he crossed the highway, he glanced toward the window in

Veda's office at the Co-op. Looking toward the heavens as he did, Reese didn't mind offering up a little prayer that Veda would decide to stay.

"Lord, forgive me for the mistakes I made with Veda before, and help me get a second chance with her. Help me find a way to let her know how much I love her, have always loved her." He felt a catch in his throat. "Lord, please don't let her leave me again. You know there's never been anybody but Veda Trent in my heart. I know it's my fault she left before and didn't come back, but it's going to kill me if she leaves again."

CHAPTER 7

Veda studied herself in the mirror in her aunt's bedroom. She'd tried on four of Rita Jean's old storyteller costumes, but none seemed to suit. Her aunt had been dark-haired, her hair streaked with gray in her later years. Bright, rich colors and calicos had suited her, but they looked garish on Veda. After an hour, Veda finally put together an outfit that seemed to suit her — a simple shirtwaist dress in a deep leaf gold, with a russet shawl and a long white apron that tied around the waist, helping to cinch in the dress to fit her better. Rita Jean's high-topped black boots ran a half size too large, but with the laces drawn tight, they worked good enough for an evening's event.

The small corgi sat on the floor, watching Veda with interest.

"I think this will do, Lucy." She smiled at the little dog. "These colors don't clash with my red hair and are simple and more my style."

Veda tried on yet another of the mobcaps and wrinkled her nose. "Yuk, these are not me at all. They suited Aunt Rita Jean, but I look ridiculous in them, and in those old-timey sunbonnets I tried on, too."

She climbed up on a stool to dig around on the top shelf in the closet for more hat possibilities. A broad straw garden hat she tried on looked too casual, and a lavish floral hat absurd, but at the back of the closet she found a small, old-fashioned chip bonnet with a ribbon tie for under the chin. Pulling her long hair back, she slipped the bonnet on and examined the effect. It was simple and much more her style, framing her face and sitting toward the back of her head. She tied the ribbon to one side and decided this look would have to do.

She turned to find Sutton in the doorway, grinning. "What do you think?" She turned around slowly so he could get the full effect.

He made a sign with two thumbs up for *you look good.*

Veda untied the chip bonnet, laying it on the bed. "I admit I'm nervous about doing this, Uncle Sutton. With school and the business, I learned to speak to groups when

I needed to, but this is different. I think a person either is born with a storytelling talent or she's not."

Sutton shook his head, pulling out his notepad to write, *You used to tell stories to your dolls and to the animals around the farm.* He grinned. *I sometimes hung around and listened. I thought you did real good.*

She laughed. "That was a long time ago, Uncle Sutton, and it's hardly the same. But I said I'd do this in Rita Jean's memory, and I will."

Veda sat down on the corner of the bed. "I think I know two or three of her stories well enough by heart that I can tell them without taking notes to refer to. It will be better if I can simply talk them as I remember them." She wrinkled her nose. "The ones I know best are Indian legends, rather than Christmas-themed stories. Do you think that will be all right? Rita Jean told a lot of those old legends, even at Christmas sometimes."

Before he could answer, Reese walked into the room. "I've called the sheriff, Sutton. He's on his way."

"What's happened?" Veda stood up, shocked at his words.

"Those thieves sneaked onto the upper farm again to raid some more trees." He propped a foot on the stool Veda had been standing on. "Bovee heard them and came out. They didn't hurt him much, but they locked him in the tack room in the barn. Dropped the bar over the door so he couldn't get out. He's a little simpleminded, you know; it scared him a lot."

Seeing Veda's face blanch, Sutton signed, *he's okay.*

"When did this happen?" she asked.

"About three hours ago, as best we know," Reese answered. "When Walker got back from helping Sutton at the Christmas Tree Store, he found Bovee gone, saw truck tracks near the barn, and then heard Bovee hollering for help. Walker called the sheriff, who called me to go over to tell Sutton at the store, since my office is next door. I drove up with Sutton in his truck."

"Has Sheriff Swofford caught these people, now that Bovee saw them?"

Sutton made a mask gesture across his face.

"I see. They wore masks." Veda paced around the room. "I can't believe I was right here in the house when they drove up the hill to do this. It makes me so mad! I didn't even hear a car or truck go by!"

"Sutton got worried when Walker called. He knew you were here at the house alone."

Veda gave Sutton a hug. "I'm fine. Like I said, I never even heard them. They're just stinking, dirty thieves, interested in stealing to get money."

"Maybe," Reese put in, "but they roughed Bovee up when he fought."

"Is Bovee really all right?" Veda bit her lip.

"Yes. He has a black eye and a bruised arm, but he's okay. With two of them, he didn't stand much of a chance."

Hearing a knock at the front door, Sutton gestured that he'd walk to the door to let the sheriff in. Veda started to follow and then glanced down at her long dress.

Reese gave her a slow smile. "Nice costume."

"I suppose." She lifted her chin. "But I need to change."

He turned. "You change and I'll go help Sutton communicate with the sheriff, see if he's found out anything."

A little later, Veda and Reese stood in the front yard, saying good-bye to the sheriff. Sutton had already driven back to the Christmas Tree Store and Reese had decided to walk home through the field.

"Come walk me halfway," Reese said, when the sheriff left.

Veda felt flooded with memories at the words. She'd heard them a million times

555

growing up.

"Ah, come on," Reese added as she hesitated. "It's not that cold today, and the snow has melted off."

She nodded and buttoned her coat as they started down the drive to the path between the farms. "I was glad when the sheriff said the thieves didn't take many trees this time. Finding Bovee probably spooked them. Made them leave quicker."

"Still, the losses are eating into Sutton's profit base. It isn't right."

"I know."

Reese changed the subject. "Do you have a nice dress figured out for the Co-op party tomorrow night?"

Veda smiled. "Yeah, one of my vintage finds I brought from the store. It was too pretty to sell, so I kept it."

"I'll look forward to seeing it." Reese gave her a hand to help her over a tree limb in the path.

She stopped to look at him. "Reese, I don't want you thinking of this as a date or anything. I only thought it would be nice if I went with you, so you could introduce me to everyone."

His dark eyes studied hers. "All right, Veda."

He didn't say more, and they walked on

down the pathway, through the short woods and to the fence line of the two properties.

Veda's eyes ran up the limbs of the giant oak tree that grew beside the fence. "I remember climbing high into those branches many times."

"Me, too." Reese gave her a boyish grin. "That old tree served as pirate ship, cowboy hideout, and official headquarters of the Cougars Club."

"I'd forgotten that club." She giggled. "We made up a secret code and used paw prints to sign our club messages."

"We had some good times growing up." Reese's eyes slid over her.

Veda felt her heartbeat quicken. The feelings between her and Reese, no matter what had happened in the years between, still ran strong.

As if sensing her thoughts, Reese stepped closer. "I used to come and sit in this tree and think about you when you didn't come back."

"Before or after you married Dee Dee?" She knew her voice sounded nasty, but she couldn't help it.

"Before and after." He kept his voice level and patient.

It had always been hard to provoke Reese. He smiled. "I used to think about that old

Tony Orlando song when I sat up in the tree, 'Tie a Yellow Ribbon Round the Old Oak Tree.' "

Veda laughed despite herself. "Good grief, Reese, that was an old 1970s song, not even our era." She pushed at him. "And it was a dumb song, too."

He crossed his arms, refusing to be baited. "It wasn't dumb to me. It was about a man who'd been a prisoner, coming back home and wondering if his sweetheart still loved him. If she did, there would be a yellow ribbon around the tree. If not, he'd stay on the bus and move on."

"And you related to that song in what way?" She shook her head.

His voice dropped. "I'd been a prisoner, trapped in a marriage with Dee Dee, and then finally got freed and was able to come back home." He moved closer. "I always wished I might come to the oak one day and find you here, waiting for me."

"And find a yellow ribbon tied around the old oak tree?" She knew she was using sarcasm to protect herself.

He stepped closer and put his hands on her arms. "I've always regretted what happened, Veda. I always dreamed somehow you'd come back to me."

"I came home to work in the Co-op for

Rita Jean and Sutton, Reese." She kicked at a pinecone at her feet as she spoke, keeping her eyes focused on the ground. "Don't read a yellow-ribbon story into why I came back."

He ignored her. "I love you, Veda. I've always loved you. I think, deep in your heart, you still have feelings for me. Don't block me out. Give me a chance to show you I care."

She looked up at him then, and into those deep brown eyes of his. A big mistake, as he pulled her into his arms and kissed her before she could think of another smart answer. And then she was swamped with feelings.

Reese traced his tongue across her lips and then deepened the kiss, drawing her tight against him, warming her in the cold December air until she forgot it was winter. Forgot for a moment all the hurt, all the years in between.

Giving up her resistance at last, she kissed him back. It seemed so sweet to do so here under the old oak, where they'd kissed good night and said good-bye so many times in the past. Where Reese had first whispered the words "I love you" to her. Such precious memories.

His hands slid under her hair, his lips slid

down to her neck, behind her ear, and then back to her mouth again. Passion flamed now, their emotions heightening. Veda had forgotten passion and how good it felt, how it engulfed and surged through the blood. There had been kisses since those young years, of course, heightened senses occasionally, but nothing like this. Only with Reese McNally had she ever felt like this, God help her.

"Enough." She pulled away, knowing she was panting, excited, thrilled, but afraid to go further. Afraid of more.

He put his lips against her forehead, tender now. "I have never loved anyone like I love you, Veda Trent. I have never felt with anyone what I feel with you. Please stay, and let's see if our love can grow, if we can build a future together. I want to sleep with you every night; I want to have a child with you. I want to spend every day with you and grow old with you."

Veda closed her eyes. "You're confusing me, Reese. I want to stay for the right reasons."

He drew back to look down at her. "Isn't love reason enough, Veda?"

"It should be." She gave him an honest answer. "But it isn't. I keep wanting something more."

He snorted. "Some sign?"

"No." She tried to answer from her heart. "Some knowing. It's hard to explain."

He backed away, giving her a cross look. "You said it's like a pending time for you, that you seem to be waiting for something."

"I am."

Veda watched a flash of exasperation cross his face. "You think it's dumb."

His eyes met hers. "You seem to think it's dumb that I believe love is enough to keep two people together."

Veda's anger flashed. "Not necessarily. But life is also about the well-being of individuals, of each person feeling they are walking in the direction they should walk, finding the meaning they are meant to find." She shrugged. "You don't understand that. You've always known you belong right here, felt your roots and meaning are here. I'm not sure that's true for me."

He studied her. "You're hard for me to understand sometimes, Veda. You make life so complicated, when I think it's much simpler."

She felt provoked. "Reese, you see things as you-man, me-woman, tie a yellow ribbon around the old oak tree and live happily ever after."

He grabbed her arm. "Don't make that

sound trite, Veda."

Seeing the pain cross his face, she backed down. "I'm sorry, Reese. I didn't mean to be catty. Happily ever after isn't such a bad thing. I know that."

He rubbed his neck. "I don't mean to rush you, Veda. I know you have to follow your own heart."

She tried to think what else to say.

Reese stepped into the silence. "I imagine it would be hard for you to decide to be Pamela's mother, too, knowing she's Dee Dee's daughter."

Veda felt shocked. "You think I'd hold that against that precious child after all she's been through? As though it was her fault Dee Dee is the way she is?" She hugged herself in the cold. "My heart goes out to Pamela more for how she's been used, rejected, and mistreated through all this. It would make me love her more, not less, Reese."

She put a hand to Reese's face. "Whatever I decide, it won't be because of Pamela. It would be all too easy to love Pamela, Reese."

Veda saw the relief sweep across his face.

"You've always worried too much." She leaned up to plant a kiss on his lips, now cold from standing outside so long. "Rita Jean always said things have a way of working out; not always as we want, but they work out."

He ran a tender hand over her hair. "I love to look at you, Veda, to be with you, to talk with you — even to argue with you."

She sighed. "Yes, and we'll both freeze to death out here under this old oak if we don't head inside." She patted his cheek. "I'll see you tomorrow night, Reese. Six o'clock. Don't be late."

"I'll be there, Veda." He surprised her, grabbing her to kiss her passionately again. "See you tomorrow." He turned to walk down the path toward the McNally Farm.

Veda looked after him. *Grown a little assertive, haven't you, Reese?*

Smiling at the thought, she headed back toward the house.

CHAPTER 8

The next evening, Reese walked into the cozy kitchen of the big McNally farmhouse dressed in a dark suit, a crisp white shirt, and a Christmas red tie. His father and Pamela sat at the table finishing up dessert from dinner.

"Oh, you look pretty, Daddy." Pamela sighed. "I wish I could go to the party."

"You would be bored." He leaned over to kiss her forehead. "It's one of those adult parties where people stand around and talk."

Harold McNally gave him a thumbs-up sign. "You do look good, son."

"Are you sure you don't want to go, Dad?" He leaned against the kitchen counter. "I could still get a sitter."

"No." His father smiled. "Pamela and I have a big evening planned here, with two Christmas movies from the Redbox."

"Ms. Martha is coming over to watch

movies with us, too, and bringing snacks." Pamela's eyes brightened. "She makes good snack mix, with nuts and pretzels and cereals and stuff. Even with M&M's in it."

Reese raised an eyebrow at his father.

He fiddled with a napkin. "Martha wasn't busy tonight, so I thought she might like to join us. The Christmas season is hard when you're by yourself."

Pamela slid out of her chair. "I'm going to go call Laurie," she said. "Have a good time, Daddy."

Reese waited until she left the room. "Are things getting serious with you and Martha?" he asked. "I know you've been seeing her for some time."

Harold pushed up his glasses and ran a hand through his now-white hair. "She's a fine woman," he answered.

Reese nodded. "I like Martha Seymour."

His father looked relieved. "You don't really expect love to creep up on you when you're nearly an old man."

Reese grinned. "You're fifty years old, Dad, hardly an old man."

"I guess." He smiled then. "She does make me feel young and sparky in many ways. I hadn't thought that would come my way again."

Reese laughed and clapped his dad on the

back. "Take joy where you can find it, Dad. Life is short. You know Pamela and I only want your happiness."

He studied Reese. "Would you two be all right if I decided to hitch up with Martha and move in with her down the road in Kinzel Springs?"

"You could live here. This is your home."

He waved a hand. "Nah. She likes her place, and I'm getting real comfortable visiting in it. Pretty mountain home." He glanced up at Reese. "I'd like to think maybe you'd stay on here at the old home place, marry again, and raise some more McNallys."

At Reese's flush, he stood to put a hand on his son's shoulder. "I've been praying you and Veda would get back together. I know you've never stopped loving her, and I saw the way you both looked at each other when she came by to drop off Pamela last week. The old feelings are still there."

Reese dropped down into a kitchen chair. "I still love her, Dad, but she's not sure if she's ready to commit to me and stay here. You can't really blame her after all that happened."

"Veda's no fool; she knows what Dee Dee was like." He sat back down across from

Reese. "You've explained things, haven't you?"

Reese scraped a hand through his hair. "Yes, but I'm not sure she forgives me. Betrayal is hard to get over. Maybe I don't deserve to get Veda back, Dad. I acted like a fool."

"Everyone makes mistakes, son. But we don't have to pay for them the rest of our lives." He reached across to pat Reese's arm. "Give her time."

"Speaking of time, I'd better head to the O'Neill place to pick her up."

"Well, you have a good time. I'll clean up a little here in the kitchen and then go check on Pamela."

A short time later, Reese and Veda mingled among the fifty or more guests at the Mimosa Inn. As Reese introduced Veda around, his gaze kept drifting over her bare shoulders above the dark green velvet dress she wore. The dress was the perfect color and style for her, setting off her hair and coloring, the sleeves dropping off the shoulders, with a knotted velvet rose tucked in the V above her breasts. A drop necklace with a glittering gold Christmas ball hung around her neck.

"You really look beautiful tonight," he whispered to her as the couple they'd been talking to moved away to the refreshment table.

"You've said that." She grinned at him. "You look handsome, too."

Her eyes moved across the room, then, to where Jack and Grace were welcoming late guests. "I remember when Jack Teague was quite the ladies' man around Townsend. Grace seems to have brought a big difference to his life."

"Yes, and everyone is glad for the change, and for all Grace has brought with her — reopening the Mimosa, becoming active in the community, and taking on Jack's girls with such love." He paused. "I've always felt a connection with Jack: both of us used by somewhat disreputable women and left with children to raise."

"I'd almost forgotten his story until Grace mentioned it the other day."

Reese saw Lewis and Leanne Connor heading their way. "Remind me someday and I'll tell you Jack and Grace's story, Veda. It's a good one."

The evening moved along pleasurably. The gracious old Victorian inn was decorated gloriously for the season, with a huge Christmas tree, draped in gold and burgundy ornaments, strings of period bubble lights, and curling, shiny gold ribbon, setting the scene in the main room. The mantels over the inn's fireplaces echoed the gold and burgundy color scheme, with rich fruits, pinecones, and nuts mixed among the greenery. All the tables glittered with candles, and a lavish spread of Christmas hors d'oeuvres, tiny festive sandwiches, colorful fruit and vegetable platters, and a tempting array of holiday sweets covered the sideboards and buffet. Even the air was enticing, filled with the spicy aromas of Christmas greenery, holiday candles, potpourri, and baked goods.

Veda networked with Reese and on her own, among the members of the board and with the Co-op crafters and artisans, at ease and laughing. It did Reese good to see how loving and welcoming everyone acted to Veda. She could hardly feel like she didn't belong here.

"I think you've been the center of attention all evening," he told her at one point. Noticing her face seemed flushed, he asked, "Do you want to walk outside for a moment? Grace and Jack decorated the back porch, the old gazebo, and strung lights all over the trees. It's a pretty sight at night."

Reese steered Veda down the hallway and out the back door of the Mimosa Inn. They moved through the screened porch, stuffed with wicker furniture, and outside to the patio. The night was clear, with stars twinkling in the skies to accompany the display of white lights around the property.

Veda hugged herself against the chill, looking around in wonder. "This is beautiful, Reese. It must have taken days to put up all these lights."

He pointed toward the river behind the inn. "Jack even strung lights along the swinging bridge."

An odd gust of wind whistled around the corner of the building, blowing Veda's skirt tail. She straightened her dress, a strange look passing over her face. She shivered, looking around.

"It's cold. I guess we'd better go back in," he said.

Another gust of wind blew up from the river, stirring the leaves on the shrub beside them, swishing across them.

Reese felt Veda tense, and then she gripped his arm. "We have to go home, Reese. Something's wrong."

"What do you mean, something's wrong?" He frowned at her. "We can't simply leave all of a sudden. It would be rude."

"Well, then, make something up." She stayed tense beside him, as if listening for something he couldn't hear.

"Look, Veda . . ."

She shushed him. "Sutton is in trouble. I can feel it." She glanced at him in wonder. "I can hear it."

"What do you mean, you can hear it?" He felt annoyed. "This isn't a time to get weird, Veda."

She looked toward the river. "I'm leaving with or without you, Reese McNally. And we have to go now." Veda turned and headed back into the house. "Will you take me, or do I need to ask someone else?"

"I'll take you," he grumbled. "Go in the back bedroom and get our coats, and I'll make some sort of excuse."

Veda said nothing as they sped down the highway toward the O'Neill Farm except, "Hurry." As they neared the turn off the highway, she tensed again and leaned forward, looking out the window. She turned around in her seat, mumbling a set of numbers, while Reese made the turn.

"Call the sheriff and give him this license number." She repeated the numbers again to him. "It's the thieves. I saw their truck pulling out of the road to the farm as we pulled in."

"How do you know it was the thieves?" He glanced in the rearview mirror as he pulled out his phone.

"You just tell the sheriff I saw a truck leaving our private drive with the back loaded with trees. That's enough to tell him."

"You're acting odd, Veda. What's going on?"

She kept her eyes on the road ahead, hugging herself in the cold. "Just hurry, Reese. Sutton is in trouble."

The next hour went by in a whirl. Reese and Veda found Sutton in a heap on the floor of the cantilever barn behind the O'Neill farmhouse, unconscious, with his head bloodied.

"I'm sorry I didn't believe you," Reese said to Veda at one point, while they sat with Sutton, waiting for the ambulance.

"It's okay. I almost didn't listen myself." She patted his cheek. "Thanks for bringing me home. I'm sorry we couldn't stay at the party longer."

"It doesn't matter." He stood as he heard the ambulance's siren.

The emergency personnel soon had Sutton loaded, assuring Veda and Reese that they didn't see any serious damage but cautioning them that only tests would reveal his condition accurately. Veda insisted on riding in the ambulance with Sutton, Reese following in his car.

It proved to be a long night in the emer-

gency room before they were assured Sutton
was all right and could come home.

CHAPTER 9

The next week moved swiftly for Veda, as Christmas closed in. Sutton returned to work at the Christmas Tree Shop after a day of rest, the thieves — a trio of local brothers — were found up the highway after the theft and all arrested, and the Co-op grew more crowded with last-minute shoppers every day.

Veda baked the night before the Christmas Eve service at the church, making several dishes to take to the potluck dinner afterward. She stood now in her storyteller's outfit, adjusting the chip bonnet at the mirror.

Sutton leaned into the bedroom, letting her know it was time to go. He smiled at her, gesturing to Rita Jean's picture on the dresser. *She'd be proud,* he signed.

"I hope so, and I hope I'll do credit to her."

He nodded, winking, and then tapped his

watch, reminding her it was time to leave.

When they arrived, the little white church by the river was packed for the service. Many in the valley who didn't attend the church regularly came to enjoy the holiday service and to share in the big dinner afterward, held next door at the Mimosa Inn.

Sutton and Veda stopped to greet Reese, his father, and Martha Seymour as they walked in the front door.

"Sit with us," Reese said, taking Veda's arm. "I already delivered Pamela to the back to get ready for the nativity pageant."

Inside, a hush eventually fell over the church as the lights grew dim and the service began. Reverend Westbrooke led the congregation through the Bible readings of the Christmas story, while the children entered the sanctuary, acting out the parts of the familiar account of Jesus's birth. Between each part of the story, the choir led the congregation in singing the beloved hymns of Christmas, so familiar to all.

Veda's heart lifted at the words of the old songs, "O Little Town of Bethlehem," "It Came Upon the Midnight Clear," "Angels We Have Heard on High" — with a special wave from Pamela — plus "Away in a Manger" and "We Three Kings." At the end of the pageant, everyone stood to sing "Joy to the World" as the children filed to their seats.

A short message followed from the pastor, and then it was time for Veda's story. Saying a little prayer to herself, Veda walked up to the stage to look out at all the people of the Townsend community.

"Aunt Rita Jean loved you all," she said. "And she loved sharing a special story with you every Christmas Eve. I hope you will enjoy this story I've chosen to share with you tonight."

She moved closer to the edge of the stage, holding the hand mike so her voice would carry to all. "In ages past," she began, "the old ones were the storytellers. It was the way things were passed on to the next generations. The Cherokee revered the Great Spirit, who created and presided over all the earth and provided for His children. The Cherokee believed spirits presided over everything, although only the Great Spirit was worshipped."

Veda paused as a wisp of a breeze whispered through the church, making the flames of the candles flicker. She suddenly knew the story she'd planned was not the one she'd tell tonight.

She felt new words rise up inside her, and

her voice grew bolder. "The Spirit of the Wind was called Oonawieh Unggi in Cherokee. Native Americans believed one could hear the Great Spirit in the wind and see Him in the clouds. In the Cherokee tribe that my great-grandmother, Unole, was raised in, it was believed that the first daughters in the Watie family were given a special gift and could hear the wind sing. My great-grandmother was a first daughter, my aunt, Rita Jean, was a first daughter, and I'm a first daughter. The story a first daughter is to tell travels on the wind, and the story I am to tell you tonight is a story about Oonawieh Unggi, the Wind God of the Cherokee."

Looking out to see her audience, rapt and eager, Veda continued, the words coming to her as she told the tale. She remembered, as Rita Jean had taught her so many years ago, just where to pause, where to drop her voice or let it rise, and where to repeat ongoing phrases to knit the story together. In her heart, she heard the whispered words *very good, daughter,* as the story moved along, and she knew of a certainty, then, that the age-old gift of storytelling had been passed down to her. She could feel the story in her bones as she told it, and the words came easy and free.

There was a moment of pure silence when Veda ended her tale, and then the applause began, people standing to their feet, several wiping away tears. Vincent Westbrooke came to hug her impulsively, telling her that she'd given sweet tribute to her aunt in the service and made the memory of her rise lovingly before them all.

As Veda slipped back into her seat, Sutton leaned over to give her a kiss on the cheek, rubbing a hand over his heart to let her know he was touched and pleased. On her other side, Reese slipped a hand into hers to squeeze it.

The service closed with the singing of "Silent Night," as the congregation passed the flames of lit candles throughout the church, followed by a lively rendition of "We Wish You a Merry Christmas," as Santa came in with ho-ho-hos and a sack of presents for the children.

The rest of the evening and the dinner at the Mimosa passed in a happy blur for Veda. So many people came to hug her and tell her how Rita Jean's memory had been blessed by her story and how it seemed as though Rita Jean was present with them, telling the story herself and keeping them mesmerized with the telling.

Pamela received a glittering angel ornament for the tree from Santa, to remember being in the pageant, and she came to show it to Veda.

"You were very good as an angel," Veda told her, examining the pretty ornament Pamela laid in her lap. "I think this ornament even looks like you." She held it up. "Look, it has dark hair."

Pamela grinned, taking the ornament back. "You did good, too, Veda. I told you that you could tell a nice story like Rita Jean."

"So you did." Veda grinned back.

"Daddy says you and Sutton are coming over to our house for Christmas brunch." The child's eyes brightened. "You can see what Santa brought me for Christmas when you come."

"I'd like that," she said. "And I'm bringing blueberry muffins with cream cheese glaze because you said you like them."

"And Rita Jean's breakfast casserole?" Pamela straightened her skirt.

"Yes, and Rita Jean's casserole. And pumpkin bread and sausage balls for your daddy."

She nodded. "Those are his favorites."

"I know," Veda said, remembering Christmas brunches the two families had shared for years and years.

Pamela leaned over conspiratorially. "My daddy has a Christmas gift for you, but he won't tell me what it is."

"He's very secretive." Veda grinned at her.

Laurie skipped over to join them, with Beth following, and the subject changed. The rest of the evening moved on as if in slow motion, filled with joy and ease.

The next morning, Veda picked up the phone to call Reese on his cell. "Merry Christmas," she said. "I guess with a child in the house, you've been up since dawn."

She heard him groan.

"Listen," she told him, "Sutton and I have loaded the truck and he's driving over with the food and stuff." She hesitated. "But I want you to meet me at the oak."

"It's spitting snow," he grumbled. "Have you looked out the window?"

She clamped down on her impatience. "I know that, Reese. But could you do just this one little Christmas favor for me? Humor me, all right?"

"Well, sure," he said, realizing he'd annoyed her. "How soon?"

"Oh, give me ten minutes, I guess."

"Okay." He paused. "What's this about, Veda?" His voice sounded worried.

"I'll tell you when I see you." She hung up before he could ask more.

Veda hurried to get to the oak ahead of Reese and then waited where she'd planned, so she could see him coming down the path.

As he rounded the corner, he stopped abruptly and simply stared. Then he moved slowly toward the tree, looking around for her.

"Do you think you could catch me if I jump?" she called, startling him.

He looked up into the branches of the giant oak to see her perched on one of the limbs over his head.

"I think I could manage it." A faint smile played on his lips.

Taking him at his word, Veda pushed herself off the limb and fell into his arms. "Merry Christmas, Reese McNally."

He leaned over and caught a quick kiss, but Veda saw the tears in his eyes before he did.

"Awww, don't cry, Reese," she said, scrambling out of his arms to stand on her feet. "Remember what I told you about being a crybaby when we were little?"

Ignoring her, he turned his eyes to the tree once more. "When did you do this, Veda? When did you come out here and tie yellow ribbons around the tree?"

"I came out earlier, before I even called you." She moved closer to wrap her arms loosely around his waist, smiling up at him. "Do you like it?"

"What does this mean, Veda?" He looked down at her, his brown eyes serious now. "This isn't one of your jokes or something, is it?"

"No." She punched at him. "And you're spoiling my surprise with all your worries. Don't you get it, Reese? It's my way of telling you I'm staying."

"You're staying?" He seemed to have trouble processing the words.

"S. T. A. Y. I. N. G." She spelled out the letters slowly.

"I know how to spell," he said. He put his hand under her chin to turn her face up to his. "What changed your mind?"

She crossed her arms in irritation, "I never changed my mind, Reese. I just hadn't made up my mind before."

"Oh, yeah, I remember. You said your decision was pending."

"Well, it's not pending anymore." She put a hand up to his face again, letting her fingers caress his cheek.

"What's changed?" He searched her face as he asked the question.

"I heard the wind sing." Her voice dropped with the words.

He looked puzzled.

"Like Unole said. Remember?" She gave him a tentative smile. "Please say you understand. It's important to me."

He considered her words. "You connected with your heritage. You got the knowing you've been seeking in some way."

"Yes." She smiled at him.

"How did it happen?" He pulled her to sit down beside him on the log by the fence they always climbed over.

She paused to find the right words. "First at the Mimosa. Remember when we were outside and that touch of chill wind blew around the house and then came again?"

"Yes."

"I could hear in the wind that there was a problem with Sutton. I got this urgency that I should go home right away." She hesitated. "With the second wind it grew clearer. It was as though I could hear the words singing on the wind: *Go home right now. Go home right now.*"

He looked at her. "That's kind of spooky, Veda."

"It was," she agreed. "But I'm glad I listened. And on the way home, I got a check to notice that truck passing by us, to get the license number. I knew it was the thieves."

"Well, anyone might have expected that

with a truck coming out of the farm road loaded with Christmas trees."

She pushed at him. "You didn't notice the truck, smarty. And I might not have noticed it either without that little feeling."

"Okay." He pulled his scarf closer around his neck against the chill.

Veda looked into his eyes, wanting him to understand. "Then, at the church, when I got up to tell my story, it happened again. Didn't you notice the air swirling in the church, the candles flickering?"

He touched her face. "I was too busy watching you, waiting for your story. So proud you were going to share for Rita Jean's memory."

"Something stirred in me then, too, Reese. I had a story all planned, but something welled up inside and gave me another story to tell."

He considered that. "It was a good story you told."

She punched his arm. "You are so pragmatic sometimes, Reese McNally. Don't you see? I *knew* what story to tell. I heard the wind sing. It came to me what story to tell, and the gift to tell it welled up inside me, too."

He reached over to brush snow from her hair and to touch her cheek. "I'm glad,

Veda. Unole spoke to you."

"Yes." She sighed, seeing that he understood at last.

"So what does this mean?" he asked.

"It means I know this is where I'm meant
to stay, that this is where I belong."

"And that's why you put the yellow ribbons on the tree?"

She smiled at him. "So you'd know I
meant to stay — just like you used to
dream. I know it's hurt you that I took such
a long time making up my mind."

He fell silent for a minute, and while he
paused, some church bells in the valley
began to peal. The sound of them carried
on the air, filling Veda with a sense of peace
it seemed she'd been seeking all her life.

"Would you have left me if these things
hadn't happened, Veda?" Reese's face
looked anxious.

She leaned nearer to kiss him gently. "I
don't think I could have left you, Reese,
even if these things hadn't happened. Every
day I knew more and more how much I still
loved you." She paused. "But don't you see
how much this means to me? I feel so right
in myself for the first time. I feel like I not
only belong with you but that I belong here.
I know the store is my legacy, the people
here are my legacy, and you — you're my

legacy. I know of a surety I'm meant to be here. And I am the new storyteller. The gift has been passed to me."

He smiled then. "I see."

His eyes moved to the tree again, swathed in yellow ribbons growing wet from the falling snow. "It's a great Christmas gift, Veda. Thank you." He shivered and leaned over to kiss her again. "Does this mean you'll marry me and that we'll do the happily ever after thing?"

"Probably," she replied saucily, pulling away to stand and dust the snow off her pants and coat. "But I want the whole courting and dating thing first. I want time for us to get to know each other in a whole new way." She hesitated. "And I want time for Pamela to get used to me, and to feel like I belong to her, too."

"I don't think you'll have any problems there." He stood also and took her into his arms. "We'll do the courting thing, Veda, but it might be hard to wait too long to do the marrying thing." His mouth dropped to hers in a fiery, passionate kiss, taking her breath away in the cold winter air. "I love you more than life, you know."

Veda relished the warmth of his arms and the solid sense of knowing she was exactly where she needed to be at last.

"We'd better head back before everyone comes looking for us," Reese said with reluctance, taking her hand to start walking down the path toward the McNally Farm. "I'm sure Pamela is champing at the bit to get into the Christmas brunch and all the fixings. And I know she can't wait to show you all her Christmas gifts."

"She told me you bought something for me," Veda teased. "But she said you wouldn't tell her what it was."

"If I'd known what would happen today, I'd have bought an engagement ring."

She smiled at him. "There's time enough for that later."

He leaned over to catch another kiss. "Hmmm . . . if I recall correctly, you have a birthday next month."

"That might be a little too soon." She wrinkled her nose. "We might not have enough courting and dating and all that behind us yet."

They walked on in the thickening snow of Christmas morning toward the lights of the McNally farmhouse.

Reese tucked her hand into his arm, pulling her closer. "I wish Rita Jean was here to see this happy ending," he said, his voice softening.

"Oh, I think she is," Veda answered, as a

twist of wind slipped through the trees and lingered around them.

Dear Reader,

If you'd like to read the story of how Grace and Jack Teague met and how the Mimosa Inn came to be, look for Lin Stepp's Smoky Mountain novel, *Down by the River,* published by Kensington in June 2014. And for more Smokies pleasure, watch for the next heartwarming story, coming soon in January 2015, *Makin' Miracles,* set in the charm of downtown Gatlinburg.

Lin Stepp

ABOUT THE AUTHORS

Fern Michaels is the *USA Today* and *New York Times* bestselling author of the Sisterhood and Godmothers series, and dozens of other novels and novellas. There are over seventy-five million copies of her books in print. Fern Michaels has built and funded several large day-care centers in her hometown, and is a passionate animal lover who has outfitted police dogs across the country with special bulletproof vests. She shares her home in South Carolina with her four dogs and a resident ghost named Mary Margaret. Visit her website at www .fernmichaels.com.

Nancy Bush is the *New York Times* and *USA Today* bestselling author of *Nowhere Safe, Nowhere to Hide, Nowhere to Run, Hush, Blind Spot,* and *Unseen,* and *Something Wicked, Wicked Game,* and *Wicked Lies* in the Colony series cowritten with her sister, bestselling author Lisa Jackson. She is also the coauthor of *Sinister,* written with Lisa Jackson and *New York Times* bestselling author Rosalind Noonan. Nancy lives with her family and pug dog, The Binkster, in the Pacific Northwest. Readers can visit her website at www.nancybush.net and check out her blog at www.nancybush .blogspot.com.

Rosanna Chiofalo is also the author of *Bella Fortuna* and *Carissima.* An avid traveler, she enjoys setting her novels in the countries she's visited. A first-generation Italian American, her novels also draw on her rich cultural background. When she isn't traveling or daydreaming about her characters, Rosanna keeps busy testing out new recipes in her kitchen. She lives in New York City with her husband. Readers can visit her website at www.rosannachiofalo.com.

Dr. Lin Stepp is a native Tennessean, a businesswoman, and an educator. She is on faculty at Tusculum College, where she teaches psychology and writing. Her business background includes over twenty years in marketing, sales, production art, and regional publishing. But closest to her heart is her beloved series of contemporary novels set in the Smoky Mountains of East Tennessee. Visit her on the web at www.linstepp.com.

The employees of Thorndike Press hope you have enjoyed this Large Print book. All our Thorndike, Wheeler, and Kennebec Large Print titles are designed for easy reading, and all our books are made to last. Other Thorndike Press Large Print books are available at your library, through selected bookstores, or directly from us.

For information about titles, please call:
(800) 223-1244

or visit our Web site at:
http://gale.cengage.com/thorndike

To share your comments, please write:
Publisher
Thorndike Press
10 Water St., Suite 310
Waterville, ME 04901